THE CURIOUS AFFAIR OF
THE
MISSING MUMMIES

Lisa Tuttle was born and raised in Texas but moved to Britain in the 1980s. She now lives with her writer husband and their daughter on the side of a Scottish loch. She has written more than a dozen fantasy, science fiction and horror novels. You can find her on Facebook at www.facebook.com/lisatuttlewriter.

Praise for Lisa Tuttle

'Tuttle does a lovely job of putting us back in the foggy streets of Victorian London in this lively, entertaining blend of murder mystery and supernatural adventure. Arthur Conan Doyle would have approved'
George R. R. Martin, bestselling author of A Song of Ice and Fire on _The Somnambulist and the Psychic Thief_

'Lisa Tuttle has quietly been writing remarkable, chilling short stories and powerful, haunting novels for many years now, and doing it so easily and so well that one almost takes it, and her, for granted. This would be as big a mistake as not reading Lisa Tuttle'
Neil Gaiman, author of The Sandman series

'Excellent!'
Juliet E. Mckenna, author of _The Thief's Gamble_, on _The Witch at Wayside Cross_

'This John W. Campbell Award-winning author remains one of fantasy's best'
Publishers Weekly

'A wonderful mystical journey . . . beautifully written and researched. I absolutely loved it'
Alison Littlewood, author of _The Hidden People_, on _The Witch at Wayside Cross_

THE CURIOUS AFFAIR OF
THE
MISSING MUMMIES

Jesperson and Lane Book III

LISA TUTTLE

Jo Fletcher
BOOKS

First published in Great Britain in 2023 by

Jo Fletcher
BOOKS

Jo Fletcher Books
an imprint of Quercus Editions Ltd
Carmelite House
50 Victoria Embankment
London EC4Y 0DZ

An Hachette UK Company

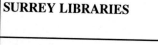
TPB ISBN 978 1 52942 274 0
Ebook ISBN 978 1 52942 276 4

10 9 8 7 6 5 4 3 2 1

Typeset by CC Book Production
Printed and bound in Great Britain by Clays Ltd, Elcograf S.p.A.

MIX
Paper from
responsible sources
FSC® C104740

Papers used by Jo Fletcher Books are from well-managed forests and other responsible sources.

This one is for Judith Clute and Sofía Rhei

CONTENTS

CHAPTER ONE

An Evening in Gower Street

Jasper Jesperson had been in a restless, dissatisfied mood all week.

True, we had little to do at present, but our last case, which had concluded more than a month ago, had been especially taxing, both physically and mentally, and the prospect of a rest had appealed to us both. I had gone to Paris for a fortnight with my sister, leaving my partner to his own devices, and on my return found him absorbed in his studies – some practical, others esoteric. He was interested in so many things that he was rarely at a loss for how to fill his time. He regularly met with fellow devotees to practise various martial arts, attended public lectures and walked for hours through the varied neighbourhoods of London.

As for me, I had read, gone to the theatre and written up my notes on our last case, careful to change names and other details that might allow readers to identify the innocent people involved. Now, on a warm evening near the beginning of June, I sat in the drawing room, which we had appropriated for our office, on my side of the large desk, trying not to be irritated by the restless pacing up and down of the man behind me. If he wanted exercise, the weather was good, and there was nothing to keep him indoors.

'What do you think of "The Curious Affair of the Artificial Ape and the Deadly Diamonds"?' I asked, looking at the as-yet untitled manuscript in front of me.

'I never think of it, since it was concluded.'

'I meant as a title. Unless you wish I should not have written about it – at least, not for publication?'

'That is your decision entirely.'

His flat declaration did not invite discussion, yet I persisted. 'That is not true. Surely you have not forgotten that it was your idea, when you first advertised for an assistant, that part of my role should be to chronicle our adventures?'

'I have not forgotten,' he said, stopping his restless movement to stand in the middle of the room. 'Have *you* forgotten you are not my assistant – and never were – because we agreed from the beginning to be equal partners?'

The memory of that first meeting, in this very room, made me smile. 'Jesperson and Lane, private investigators,' I said fondly. 'Do you realise, at the end of this month, we shall have been in business for one year?'

'If we are still in business. Are we, even now?'

My happiness shrivelled beneath his dark look. 'I think so. Unless you mean to give it up.'

'Not by choice.' He sighed. 'But look at us. How have the

past six weeks been spent? Without work. For you, travel or writing, but mere idleness for me.'

I rebuked him gently. 'You have not been idle.'

'It is not in my nature to do nothing. But in terms of *business*—'

I interrupted, reminding him that we had solved our last case in April and it was now only the first week of June. 'We might begin a new investigation at any moment – there is clearly a demand for our services.' I gestured at the letters and unanswered telegrams piled on his side of the desk. 'Is there really nothing there to interest you? I admit, some appear to be concerned with rather small matters, but, as we know, even the smallest mystery sometimes unfolds into a greater one. And even if it does not, at least there may be something on which you may exercise your talents, if you are so determined to work.'

In two long strides he was beside the desk, where he snatched up a sheaf of paper. Glancing at the one on top, he said, 'A man believes his wife is entertaining gentlemen behind his back.' He tossed it aside and looked at another. 'A woman wishes us to confirm her fears that husband has taken a mistress.' Another (in a whining voice), 'My servants are stealing from me.' Another. 'Ah, this may suit *you*, Miss Lane. The woman fears her husband will kill her unless she agrees to a divorce. Would you care to write her a friendly letter advising her to agree to the divorce?'

'They are not all like that.'

'No.' He flipped through several pages. 'Here. A diamond and emerald bracelet has been stolen, along with several valuable rings.'

'That does not interest you?'

He shook his head. 'It is a matter for the police, who have, indeed, been informed. If *they* ask for our help, I should be happy to comply. But I suspect there will be clues enough for them to follow unaided.' He dropped the pile onto the desk and turned to look out of the window. I saw by the change in his posture that something in the street outside had caught his attention.

'What is it?'

'Unless I am very much mistaken, someone is coming to us for help.'

My heart lifted at the prospect of a new client, and I smiled to myself, but murmured, 'I hope his problem concerns neither his wife or the servants.'

'Certainly not. He is too young and poor to keep a servant – and while neither youth nor poverty will stop a determined young man from an unwise marriage, he does not look like a married man.'

Too poor to marry, but evidently not too poor to wish to hire a private investigator, I thought, as the sound of knocking proved his first deduction, at least, was correct.

The thin, bespectacled young man in a shabby brown suit introduced himself as Edward Sand. 'I have come to you in confidence,' he began at once. 'It is a matter – well, you may say it is a matter for the police, but there are good reasons for—'

'Please, take a seat, Mr Sand,' Jesperson said. 'I perceive you are a scholar, and that you have come to us directly from your work at the British Museum.'

Grey eyes widened behind the convex lenses. 'Yes.'

'What do you do there?'

'I have the honour to be Assistant to the Keeper of Egyptian and Assyrian Antiquities,' he said, sounding both proud and anxious.

'A recent appointment, I think?'

'Indeed. I have held the position for just over a month.'

'The crime you have come to us about is in connection with your work.'

Dropping his gaze, he agreed.

'A matter for the police, you said—'

'No!' He looked up in alarm. 'I said it is *not* a matter for the police, no matter what you might think—'

'If something has been stolen from the British Museum, it certainly is,' Jesperson said, rather sternly.

'I did not say *stolen* . . . that is to say, a few things from my work-room are missing, but there may be some other explanation. In any case, they are not valuable. I think the police would laugh at me. And you must understand how it would look, if word got out – what it could do to the reputation of the Museum. It might attract more ambitious thieves and – oh, how much worse that would be.' He stopped and, turning to me for the first time, gave me a beseeching look.

I assured him he could count on our discretion.

'You had better tell us your story and let Miss Lane and me judge how best to proceed,' Jesperson said, sounding unusually stern. 'Begin at the beginning, whatever you perceive that to be.'

LISA TUTTLE

'Thank you.' The young man adjusted his spectacles. 'It was when I arrived this morning – as soon as I went to my work-table I saw at once it was not as I had left it. Some things had been moved around; chiefly, some scrolls of papyrus that I had hoped to categorise today. But the first thing I realised was missing was my *tyet* – that's a small amulet, in shape rather similar to the *ankh*. It is also called the Knot of Isis—'

I tore a sheet from my notebook just as Jesperson rolled a pencil across the desk to him.

He quickly sketched the simple figure as he went on, 'They are commonly found in burials, always placed upon the throat. Protective amulets, you know. About three inches long. Normally made of some red stone or glass, or sycamore wood. Mine was uncommon in that it is made of iron. Mr Budge said he'd never encountered one like it and was far from certain what period it should be assigned to. Without a secure attribution, he had no intention of putting it on display, so he gave it to me.'

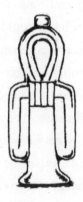

6

'Gave it to you – to catalogue?'

A faint pink flush rose in his cheeks. 'Gave it to me as a gift. A sort of welcome present . . . Mr Budge has a habit of such gestures – he can be very generous.'

'And the papyrus scrolls?' Jesperson prompted.

'It was when I tidied them up that I noticed one was missing.'

'Can you describe it?'

Looking even more unhappy, Mr Sand shook his head. 'No, I had not had a chance to examine them. They looked similar, all from one large shipment that arrived this past winter. The papyri were found in the same tomb as the sarcophagus with the mummy we call "Mummy X" – perhaps you have read about it?'

'The Mystery Mummy,' Jesperson said, a gleam of interest in his eyes.

'That is the one. It has not yet gone on display, although the carved and painted sarcophagus is a very fine piece of work. It will soon have a place of honour in one of the galleries, but for now, it remains in the Keeper's office, where it has had a number of notable visitors.' He laughed. 'And some not so notable – Mr Budge is happy to show it to anyone who asks, and to entertain his visitors with the story of its discovery and the theories about its identity.' He paused, frowning. 'If the missing papyrus is like the others, it is probably a prayer or an invocation to one of the gods. But of course, since I had not examined it, I cannot be certain even of that.' He subsided into a gloomy silence.

Jesperson gave him a moment before asking, 'And that is all?

The only things missing are an amulet that belonged to you, and one papyrus scroll?'

Mr Sand blinked and emerged from his thoughts. 'No, there were other things, stranger still – although I cannot be certain they were taken at the same time. Indeed, I might not have noticed they were gone if I had not made such a thorough search of the room. But there is no doubt about it: two or possibly even three mummies are missing.'

Mummies? Valuable or not, it was astonishing to me that he had not spoken of them immediately.

'Two or three?'

Mr Sand grimaced. 'I regret I am unable to be more precise. There are a great many of them stored on shelves at the back of the room. It was when I started my search that I saw they had been moved about somewhat. At first I was worried in case mice – or even a rat – had got in. Vermin are a problem where mummies are concerned; they will chew on the wrappings, you know. But a closer inspection revealed empty spaces. At least two are no longer there.'

I wondered at the *sangfroid* of a man who shared his work-place with dead bodies as well as rats and mice, yet had not immediately noticed when 'two or three' of the dead company had vanished.

'These mummies,' said Jesperson, interrupting my train of thought, 'were they part of the latest shipment?'

'Oh, heavens, no. They have been there an age, and you may imagine the dust they've collected. The Museum is always being given donations of that sort, and I suppose it is difficult to refuse the generosity of the public. But there is simply no room to put more than a small fraction of the holdings on permanent display. And even were there five times as many galleries, it would be a waste of space to display more than a few, even of the more interesting or unusual animals.'

'Animals?'

He nodded. 'It's different if they are well presented, with painted coverings or sarcophagi, but apart from the odd well-preserved crocodile or ibis, which were considered sacred, of course, well . . .' He shrugged. 'If you've seen one mummified cat . . . I cannot imagine what would drive anyone to steal one – let alone two or three.'

I found it just as inexplicable as he did, but not Jasper Jesperson.

'Really? You cannot imagine why someone did this?'

Mr Sand looked at him, perplexed. 'No, I cannot. Can you?'

'Consider what was taken.' He itemised them, holding up his fingers. 'One, a personal item, of value only to you. Two, a papyrus, which might be of interest to a scholar, or snatched merely because it came most easily to hand. And finally, several small and absolutely worthless animal mummies.'

Mr Sand nodded. 'It is as I said: nothing worth stealing – and yet *someone* took those things.'

'Someone you know.'

He stared. 'Who?'

'Mr Sand, the person who took those things did it to get your attention, or to get you in to trouble. You must have some idea.'

9

He shook his head in bewilderment. 'I am not the sort of person who makes enemies. And if I have one, unbeknownst to me, I cannot see what he hopes to achieve – and by such roundabout means! He has stolen from me *and* from the Museum – but such insignificant things that few would even notice their absence. How could that get me in to trouble?'

'Why have you come to us today? Why did you not simply tell Mr Budge and let him handle it?'

The faint pink flush rose again in the young man's cheeks. 'The Keeper is a busy man. I had rather not trouble him with such a trivial matter.'

'Theft is never a trivial matter. But if it was not theft, then it is perhaps something which Mr Budge might have cleared up at once, if you had but asked. What if *he* took those things? If not, he should be informed. The man is not an ogre – indeed, you have commented upon his generosity. He gave you a job, and he gave you a gift, yet you fear telling him that his gift has gone missing –and a papyrus, at the same time. If he had made that discovery himself, you might have fallen under suspicion, but if you were the one to report the loss, he could not possibly accuse you of being the thief.'

'He might – no, he could, and he would, because he has done so before,' Edward Sand blurted.

Jesperson's expressive eyebrows rose. 'Something like this has happened before?'

'Not to me – to my predecessor.'

Clearly relieved to have it out in the open, Mr Sand told us that his predecessor, one Alistair Campbell, had been forced to leave his position as Assistant after several papyri went missing.

'Campbell went straight to the Keeper and asked where they were. He thought Mr Budge must have them.'

But Mr Budge did not, and when his search revealed nothing, suspecting a thief, he went to a certain small shop in Museum Street. Amongst the papyri and other exotic items were two or three he thought he recognised, although the scrolls bore no identifying marks. The dealer was reluctant to discuss their provenance, but Mr Budge was persuasive and he did at last admit them to be recent acquisitions.

'Although he claimed not to remember where they came from, he did think they might have been purchased from an impoverished student – along with for instance, a rather pretty little scarab carved from malachite.' Mr Sand looked at me as he ended, 'The dealer suggested to Mr Budge that if he put it in a gold or silver setting, it would make a lovely brooch for a lady.'

He heaved a great sigh. 'Poor Campbell! That scarab had been a gift to him from Mr Budge, and he had sold it to the dealer in Museum Street when he couldn't pay his rent, because his usual pawnshop wouldn't give tuppence for an ugly stone bug. Of course he was no thief – he'd never steal anything from the Museum, no matter how broke he was – and it is no crime to sell something of your own, but there was no arguing with Mr Budge about it. He can be kind and generous, but when he makes his mind up about something, he is a fury. Campbell was allowed to resign – he was lucky not to be reported to his college or charged with theft. Still, word gets out, you know, though everyone acquainted with Campbell knows he is a thoroughly decent chap as well as a d— I beg your pardon, Miss, I mean to say, a very sound scholar.'

'Interesting,' Jesperson murmured. 'What time did you leave the Museum yesterday?'

'Shortly before five o'clock. Most days I stay later, but I have a regular engagement on Wednesday evenings.'

'I believe the Museum closes at six o'clock, and reopens from eight until ten in the evening?'

'Yes, that's right.'

'And what time did you arrive at work this morning?'

'At nine. I always try to get there an hour or so before it opens to the public.'

'During regular hours, how difficult would it be for a visitor to the Museum to enter your work-room?'

He made a dismissive gesture. 'I always lock the door when I leave.'

'Who else has a key?'

'Mr Budge, of course. And I suppose some other members of staff – attendants, the night-watchman.'

'You saw no signs of a break-in? Or heard of anything suspicious elsewhere about the premises?'

'No. And there are guards – our night-watchmen. It would be more difficult to break in after hours than to slip past one of the guides when the museum is crowded. I understand that for someone who knows what he is doing, picking a lock is not so very difficult.'

I repressed a smile as I thought of Mr Jesperson's skill in that field.

'Was Mr Budge still there yesterday when you left?'

'I believe he was. He rarely leaves until gone six o'clock.'

'Do you know if he had any visitors late in the day?'

'He frequently has visitors.'

'It would be useful to know if he was alone after you left.'

Edward Sand leaned forward and, nostrils flaring slightly, said in a low, intent voice, 'I beg you, not a word to Mr Budge. I have put my trust in you.'

'We will not betray that trust. Unless at your direction, we will say nothing to him that could possibly rouse his suspicions.' Jesperson went on briskly, 'I am reluctant to abandon my idea that the thief is someone with a grudge against you. Perhaps this person also bears an animus against Mr Campbell, for a similar reason. Could it be someone who had hoped to be appointed to your position?'

Mr Sand looked at him with a pained smile. 'My position? Pleased as I am to have it, it is a lowly one. We Egyptologists are not ballerinas vying for the leading role, you know. And for anyone to steal something from the very institution one hopes to be employed by would be to take an incredibly foolish risk. He would have to be mad. And while it is true that the study of ancient Egypt has attracted many with extreme and unusual views, only a serious scholar could hope for such an appointment, and, frankly, I cannot think of anyone like that. There must be some other explanation.'

Mr Jesperson looked thoughtful. 'You are probably right. But one must start somewhere. You are a friend of Mr Campbell's?'

'I have that honour.'

'Would you object if we spoke to him? It would mean sharing what you have told us.'

'I do not mind Campbell knowing. If you think he could help, I would be happy to introduce you. What's the time? He will be at home, I dare say, and his rooms are only a few streets away.' He jumped up from his seat. 'Why, it never occurred to me that the same person might be behind both incidents – yet it makes a sort of sense. And if you manage to find the culprit, you will not only help me, but clear his name as well.'

CHAPTER TWO

Egyptology

Mr Sand's friend lived in a small, dingy street off the Charing Cross Road, in a single room at the top of a small, dingy house. Mr Campbell turned out to be a powerfully built Scot in his early twenties who stood nearly as high as my own excessively tall friend. The narrow, low-ceilinged room must have been an uncomfortably cramped lodging, but, although surprised to find such a delegation outside his door, he did not hesitate to welcome us in, and did his best to make us all comfortable.

After listening in mounting surprise to Mr Sand's concise explanation for our visit, he exclaimed, 'Another theft? Man, you must warn Budgie to keep a closer guard on his visitors – some of them have very light fingers.'

Mr Sand looked at him seriously. 'I have not told him, and you know why, Ali.'

'Aye, but the man is nae fool. He must see this cannae be coincidence.'

'No, but he might suspect *you* – what if he imagines you are taking your revenge? Mr Jesperson thought the thief must be someone who wished me ill.'

Mr Campbell scoffed at that. 'The very idea is absurd. My friend hasnae enemies.'

'And you – do you have enemies?' Jesperson fired the question back.

'Och, aye, a few,' he said with a chuckle. 'But they are the kind who would attack me openly, not sneak around behind my back, stealing trifles to make me fret – that isnae their style.'

'Any idea whose style that might be?'

He looked thoughtful. 'I doubt it was done with any thought to harm Eddy – or Budgie. There must be some other reason. Sure, this was no ordinary mercenary thief.'

'My thought exactly,' said Jesperson warmly. 'It could be about the papyri – both times. They might have been taken by a collector, or a scholar—'

'A scholar of sorts,' Mr Campbell interjected. 'Self-taught and suspicious, likely a crank with a bee in his bonnet, seeking proof in old texts. Like as not, he didnae intend to steal, but meant only tae borrow them, thinking tae return them after he'd copied down whatever information he was after.'

'Then why sell them to the dealer in Museum Street?'

Mr Campbell shook his head. 'He never did. Budgie claimed he had found them, and I suppose he convinced himself of it, but he didn't know them as I did. But he was too angry to let me confirm it.' He sighed. 'But if I'd said he was wrong he'd have called me a liar, and it was bad enough to be called a thief.

The plain truth is, he was sore affronted that I'd sold his wee giftie that he wanted to think the worst of me. He might have had more sympathy – his own beginnings were lowly enough. A man must eat and pay his rent, no matter the sacrifice. He had nae right to call it theft – it's no a gift if it comes w' strings attached. The scarab was mine, to keep or to sell.'

Jesperson looked sympathetic. 'I do understand. Do you know what the papyrus contained? More prayers and invocations to the gods?'

Mr Campbell looked at Mr Sand, who shrugged. 'My best guess, based on the others.'

'Mine were different,' said Mr Campbell. 'Quite technical, you might say, about mummies, and the procedures for the preparation of the corpse.'

'And yet that does not explain the theft of the amulet,' I said.

'Some folk have light fingers. Maybe it was just too easy to slip into his pocket,' said Mr Campbell. But he frowned, dissatisfied with his own explanation, and turned to Jesperson. 'I must say, for someone to take Budgie's gift to his new assistant seems a bit too much for chance. If it was a person who knew how I lost my job, and wanted to get rid of Eddy, too . . .'

'You just said your friend has no enemies.'

'*He* doesn't, but Budgie has plenty.'

'Are you quite certain nothing except those few papyri were taken when you were there?'

'I didnae go and count all the mummies, if that's what you're asking.' He suddenly grinned at his friend. 'Hi, Eddy, are you certain sure those wee beasties were all present and correct when you left the building yesterday?'

This sally called forth a reluctant smile from the solemn Mr Sand. 'I never took any sort of inventory before today. I can't tell you how many mummies there were to a shelf, or what sorts they were. But I know they were still there yesterday.'

'How do you know that?'

'Because from my seat at the work-table, whenever I look up, those shelves with the mummies on are directly in my line of sight. And this morning, I noticed there was something a bit different in my usual view. *That* was really why I went over there – there was no reason to think I'd find either the *tyet* or the missing papyrus so far from the table, but . . . I could see there was something not quite right over there. When I got closer, I noticed the gap, and that's when I saw they were all dusty, as usual – but there was no dust at all on the bare shelf where there should have been two small animals.' He looked at me and added, 'I think most likely it was two.'

Mr Jesperson clapped his hands softly. 'Bravo. Well observed, Mr Sand. So let us begin with the idea that we are in search of one thief who took several papyri listing the technical details of mummification, and then, on a second visit, something which may have been an appropriate prayer, a protective amulet always interred with the deceased, and two or three small mummies.' He looked at the present and former Assistants. 'What does that suggest?'

Mr Sand looked blank, but Mr Campbell's thoughts were

evidently running along similar lines to those of my partner, for he said dryly, 'A fellow determined to mummify his beloved poodle?'

'I think a cat would make a more likely pet for one of those solitary, cranky and impoverished aficionados of the ancients who wished to improve his understanding by the closest possible examination of some actual mummies.'

Mr Campbell said, 'It wouldnae be the maddest thing I've ever heard. Egyptian culture continues to draw believers. You may know there are men and women in London today who practice what they claim to be authentic rituals handed down from the priests of Egypt, the original practitioners of the "dark art" – so called not because it adheres to evil, of course, but because it was believed to have originated in that country, whose ancient name meant "black" or "dark", in reference to its rich, black soil.'

'Do you know any of these modern dark magicians?'

'We do not mix in the same social circles.' He smiled. 'But it is impossible to spend much time at the British Museum without encountering a few of them. Mr Budge welcomes all comers. He is always willing tae answer questions, and will grant reasonable requests, but there are some things he will never agree to. He will have no one camping out overnight, no séances, no "borrowing" of items – "We are not a lending library," he often said when sending me off to deal with some over-zealous seeker of truth.' He looked at Mr Sand. 'Do you find him the same?'

'I have not been there very long,' said Mr Sand, 'but it is

true: his visitors do take up a great deal of his time, although he never seems to mind.'

'When the deadline for his next publication draws near, you may see his patience start to fray. He may ask *you* to take over; perhaps even allow you to give them the tour of the storerooms. It is a special treat to be allowed "behind the scenes" where they can handle the ancient relics instead of only looking at them through glass.'

'Could these things have been taken during such a tour? If Mr Budge was still in his office when you left, might he have shown something in your work-room to a visitor?'

'Yes, but . . . he'd never leave anyone there alone.' Mr Sand looked worried. Guessing the reason why, I said quickly, 'You have our word: we will say nothing about your problem to Mr Budge, or anyone else.'

'So do not be alarmed if you happen to see us in the Museum tomorrow,' Jesperson added.

'Do you expect to find a clue in the Egyptian galleries?' Mr Campbell asked us with a sly smile.

Jesperson responded at once. 'You did say that anyone who spends much time there cannot help but encounter modern would-be inheritors of the ancient Egyptians' wisdom.'

'True enough.'

'Might you be so kind as to suggest a few names?'

Mr Campbell abruptly walked across the room to stand beside the window. He gazed out at the darkening street for a moment before turning to stare at Mr Jesperson. 'What do you mean?'

'You have followed my reasoning, I think. Whoever took those things from the storeroom is no common thief. At first I thought it must be some form of petty revenge, but Mr Sand has no enemies – and Mr Budge has far too many! The things that were stolen are all connected with ancient Egyptian ideas about death. Yet my best guess at motivation has brought us no closer to identifying a single suspect.

'Modern London is rife with secret organisations, cults and religious sects new and old. No idea is too illogical, esoteric or extreme to attract a devoted following, and of all the dead religions of the world, that of Egypt holds a special and perennial fascination. But who amongst these Anglo-Egyptian magicians might be driven to steal such apparently insignificant items? I am asking for your help – if you know the name of someone who belongs to such a cult?'

'They are very secretive, naturally,' said Mr Campbell uncomfortably. 'I am not even aware of the existence of any such organisation – only rumours.'

'And yet you mentioned the people anyone might encounter at the museum . . . ?'

He flushed slightly. 'I only meant there are certain individuals – cranks, we might call them – like the shabby gentleman who spends his days divining mysteries from a close study of hieroglyphic texts, and the lady who spends hours meditating in the Egyptian galleries, believing she may receive telepathic messages from beyond, and there are always those who distinctly recall having once been a slave or a prince in Thebes.' He sighed.

'They may be mad more than in touch with a deeper truth, but they are harmless.'

Jesperson gave him a hard look. 'And yet one of those harmless individuals may have done something – in their mind, perhaps quite justified – that caused you to lose your job, and has now put Mr Sand's position in jeopardy.'

Mr Campbell cast a reproachful glance at Mr Sand. 'Eddy, I really think you ought to tell Budgie about it.'

'The mystery will not be resolved simply by telling Mr Budge,' Jesperson said shortly, echoing my own frustration. 'Why will you not help us?'

'I will help however I can, do whatever it takes to recover the missing objects – to help my friend and clear my name,' was his robust reply. 'But you are asking me to name a suspect – and how can I? The thief might be anyone – a collector who bribed an attendant, or someone who feels some hostility towards me or Budgie, or, who knows, the Egyptian Exploration Fund. It might even be a school-boy prank.

'I will no' bear false witness, nor point the finger of suspicion at people for their beliefs. You have nae right to ask me to prove some wild theory by blackening another man's name.'

'I never said—'

'You are the detectives. It is your job to uncover the truth, and you willnae find that in a list of mystics or amateur Egyptologists. I will do nothing that might lead to someone else being falsely charged with a crime as I was.'

His hands curled into fists at his sides, and we understood that the interview was ended.

We walked home by a winding, indirect route, for, as I did not need to be told, time for reflection was needed, and my partner was always an active thinker, more likely to make some hidden connection or get a new idea when in motion.

The street lamps had been lit, but it was not yet fully dark; the summer twilight still prevailed, and it was pleasant to be out in the warm, dry air, especially as there was enough of a breeze to disperse the fog that forever lurks in corners of this great, filthy city.

As we passed a building with a grand entrance flanked by two large, seated figures wearing Pharaonic regalia, Jesperson wondered aloud, 'What is it about that ancient culture? It strikes a chord with so many, both mystifying and attractive – I feel it myself; do you?'

I had to admit that I did. The Egyptian galleries in the British Museum had long been a favourite haunt, a visit there a special treat since childhood.

'You and your mother actually went to Egypt,' I said, 'yet you rarely speak of it. Was the reality a disappointment?'

His answer came slowly. 'No. Certainly modern Egypt and its people are very different from what one might expect. The great monuments and treasures of their ancestors lie all around, but the people are Arabs now, and feel no more direct connection to that vanished culture than you or I with the Druids and the builders of Stonehenge. If I have not said much about our time in Egypt, it was not for lack of interest but because our time there was so short. My best stories and strongest memories are of places where we lingered longer.'

I stopped as we passed a wall heavily plastered with advertisements, my eye caught by more ancient Egyptian imagery: used for a brand of cigarettes, a recently published novel, and an *eau de toilette*, as well as a now-closed theatrical production. I was struck by the thought that there might be just as many different reasons for someone to steal authentic fragments of this history that was being used to sell so many disparate products. How would we ever find the culprit?

But I uttered no word of discouragement or doubt, for Mr Jesperson was happy, alert and absorbed, his restless curiosity gripped once more. That it seemed to me a very minor affair was no matter; we were back in business.

CHAPTER THREE

At the British Museum

Next morning, we went to the British Museum. Since taking up residence with the Jespersons on Gower Street, I was near enough to visit whenever I liked, so I was as well-acquainted with the public building as any other regular visitor, though the offices and storage rooms were terra incognita.

Jasper Jesperson, perhaps unsurprisingly, knew all about them. He had, he told me while we were walking down Gower Street, called on Mr Budge before our partnership commenced, when the Keeper of Egyptian and Assyrian Antiquities had been the Assistant Keeper in Charge.

'Money being a problem, I thought to sell a few of the souvenirs we had picked up on our travels, and wished to have some idea of their possible worth, so as the Museum is practically on our doorstep . . .'

'Did you have so many things from Egypt?'

'Only a few. But I knew the name of A.E. Wallis Budge from his useful little primer on hieroglyphics. I was keen to make the acquaintance of such a well-known scholar and express my admiration. If he proved amenable, I planned to show him the few amulets and a papyrus or two that we'd picked up while we were there. If I was lucky, perhaps he would offer to buy them.'

'What is our excuse for calling on him today?' I asked as we came in sight of the familiar edifice.

'He was kind enough to take an interest and invited me to come back and let him know how Mother and I were getting on. So I shall have to grovel a bit first, and make my apologies for leaving it so long.' He pulled a rueful face. 'Of course, he may not even remember me.'

I had to laugh, knowing what a strong and lasting impression Mr Jesperson generally makes on everyone he meets. There is his striking appearance, for he is extremely tall and slender, with a head of red-gold curls and piercing blue eyes set in a long, mobile face. Then there is his indefinable charm of personality, combining as he does a sharp intelligence with flights of fancy, and the quick, keen interest he takes in other people. Unless he is disguised or playing a part, as he has sometimes been obliged to do in pursuit of the truth, Jasper Jesperson is not an easy man to overlook, or to forget.

'Mr Budge encounters a great many people,' Jesperson said, a bit defensively. 'And it has been almost two years since our only meeting.'

'All the same, I shall be most surprised if he does not remember you.'

We walked through the gates into a courtyard filled with

26

people coming and going, and up the steps into the entrance hall, where Jesperson spoke to one of the attendants, a bored-looking young fellow with a wispy moustache, asking, 'Might we call upon Mr A.E. Wallis Budge this morning?'

'Mr Budge is not in just now.'

'When do you expect him?'

'I really could not say, sir. If you care to leave your card, I shall have it conveyed to him.' He covered his mouth, barely hiding a yawn.

'Never mind; we'll try later.'

'Just as you like, sir.' Then, looking past us at a pair of elderly ladies who had timidly approached, 'Yes? May I help you?'

As long as we were there, I thought we might pass the time enjoying the exhibits, and with one accord, we turned to the left and entered the sculpture galleries. These rooms, filled with Roman antiquities and Greco-Roman statuary, always evoked in me a melancholy mood, for they brought back memories of my late father, who had loved to bring my sister and me here, hoping to imbue in us his passion for the classical period. As I had no desire to be deflected from thoughts of the investigation that had brought us to the Museum today, I walked through the long galleries at a brisk pace, not even pausing to pay homage to my old favourites, the colossal winged lions with human heads. I slowed only upon entering the first of the Egyptian galleries.

Here, it felt appropriate to pause and linger, taking time to appreciate stone sarcophagi, obelisks and broken sculptures of long-vanished rulers of that ancient land. Of course, it was the black basalt tablet inscribed in three different languages, the famous Stone of Rosetta that had provided the key to understanding the meaning of hieroglyphics, which proved to be the single most fascinating object for Mr Jesperson. He was still standing in rapt contemplation when I passed on into the central of the three galleries, and he had still not caught up to me when I wearied of the armless torsos and colossal heads in the third. I did not bother to wait for him, but took the stairs up to the next level.

The first room was filled with mummies and their painted coffins, displayed in highly polished wooden and glass cases, but it had also attracted considerably more visitors than there were in all the long galleries downstairs; there were even a great many children, accompanied by nannies or governesses. Rather than join the crush, I decided instead to pass through to a further room, where I knew some animal mummies would be on display.

I side-stepped to avoid a lady in a red dress, but she had the same thought, and as we both moved to the same side, we came face-to-face. I recognised her, but could not immediately think why she might be familiar to me. I guessed her to be in her mid-thirties, with eyes of a peculiarly light brown that shone almost golden in her soft, gentle face. The effect had been emphasised and made more exotic by the use of dark kohl.

We both spoke at the same moment.

'I beg your pardon.'

'I do apologise—' and at the sound of her voice, I recalled her name. Our eyes met, and once again we spoke in unison:

'Miss Dawes?'

'Miss Lane, is that really you?'

A rush of nervous laughter, then:

'It has been an age! How are you?' I asked.

'Tolerably well. And you? You look in the bloom of health, I must say. Still keeping busy with the Society?'

Of course she meant the Society for Psychical Research, and I recalled that Miss Violet Dawes believed herself to be a psychic medium, with the spirit of an ancient Egyptian priestess as her 'control'.

'No,' I replied, 'not for the past year.'

Her eyebrows rose. 'No? And your friend – the lady with the eye-patch?'

'Miss Fox.'

'Indeed! I have not seen her for some time, and wondered what could have happened, for the two of you were such stalwart fixtures of the Society . . . is she still . . . ? No? I hope she is well?'

'I have not heard from Miss Fox for some months,' I said a bit stiffly.

'Oh dear. You seemed such devoted friends. I hope there was no quarrel.'

'No, nothing like that,' I said quickly. 'We remain on the friendliest of terms. Perhaps you did not realise that I was employed by Miss Fox, to assist in her investigations? My business with the Society was ever on her behalf. And since she ended her formal connection with the Society very nearly a year ago, I was obliged to seek other employment.'

'Oh, I had not realised! But about your friend—'

'Her friend is here. Have you been talking about me?'

Relieved by his arrival, I turned to Mr Jesperson and with mock severity, scolded him. 'Do you imagine you are my only friend? Miss Dawes, allow me to introduce you to Mr Jesperson. Mr Jesperson, Miss Dawes.'

As they exchanged the usual cordialities, I could not be unaware of the speculation in her eyes as Miss Dawes looked from Mr Jesperson to me. I suppose it would have been easy enough to satisfy her curiosity by explaining that we were business partners, but to declare ourselves investigators where others might hear, so near the scene of the crime, would perhaps have been unwise. I would have liked to have ended the unexpected encounter then, with a friendly but final farewell, but to my surprise, Mr Jesperson invited Miss Dawes to join us for a cup of tea.

'What a lovely idea.' She smiled at me. 'It would be a pity to part so soon. It has been such an age since we last saw one another.' She looped her arm through mine and pressed it as if we were old, dear friends – a pretence I found peculiar, if not downright sinister.

The refreshment room was downstairs, squeezed into a narrow space off the main Egyptian galleries and presided over by a grim-looking woman. Miss Dawes and I took our seats at one of the tables while Jesperson went to order the tea.

'Quickly, before your friend returns – for we all know men do not like women's gossip – tell me what has become of Miss Fox? For I cannot fathom why she should have vanished so suddenly. She is missed at meetings – indeed, both of you are sorely missed.'

'That is kind of you to say.' It was a relief to hear there had been no open scandal after Gabrielle's determination to find irrefutable evidence for psychic abilities had pushed her over the line into fakery – the true reason for our parting of ways.

I recalled that when I had observed Miss Dawes in a trance state, I had never found any reason to suspect her of trickery. She was an ardent believer who did not charge for her services, and provided comfort to many of those who attended her séances.

'Miss Fox is travelling at present, and has no immediate plans to return to London,' I said and, hoping to lay that subject to rest, I tendered a polite enquiry as to Miss Dawes' own career as a medium.

'I am no medium,' she solemnly replied. At my look, she smiled. 'You are surprised. As was I, at first. But the truth *would* make itself known. You remember Seshemetka?'

When I did not, she prompted, 'My spirit guide, or as they called it, my "control"?'

The light dawned. 'The Egyptian princess?'

'Priestess. But I was misled by the talk of controls and guides into believing she was a spirit quite separate from me, when, in truth, *I* was Seshemetka.'

Here was a surprise. Nearly every medium known to the

Society for Psychical Research had the help of a spirit who acted as a conduit to the spirit world, allowing other spirits to speak through them. The question of who or what these helpful entities might be was much discussed amongst psychic investigators. Were they more highly evolved souls who had once been living people, or were they something other, non-human, like angels, daemons or elementals? Another idea – admittedly, not a popular one with the psychically gifted – was that they had no separate existence but were unconsciously created secondary personalities that emerged in the trance state. It was, in my experience, unprecedented for a medium herself to embrace the theory that the guiding spirit she depended upon was a product of her own mind.

At that moment Mr Jesperson arrived bearing a tray with three thick white china cups filled with muddy-looking tea, and a plate with three small rock cakes.

'I'm sorry, but there was little choice,' he said, gesturing at the colour of the tea. 'I had to beg for a larger jug of milk and more sugar; I hope this will suffice. And these were the only cakes.'

'Never was something more aptly named,' said Miss Dawes with a rueful look at the rock cakes. 'I shall abstain. I cannot afford to break another tooth.' She took the cup he offered. 'Thank you, sir.'

'My pleasure.' He settled himself in the chair opposite. 'Do you come often to the museum, Miss Dawes?'

'Of late, it has become a second home to me – the Egyptian rooms, at least.'

'You are a scholar – an Egyptologist?'

'Oh, no, sir.' Turning to me, she asked, *sotto voce*, 'Dare I explain?'

'I wish you would,' I said, 'I am myself in the dark.'

She looked crestfallen. 'But I have told you: *I* am Seshemetka.'

'Yes, but what do you mean by that?'

'That I have lived before. I was born almost three and a half thousand years ago in Thebes, where I was a temple maiden and a priestess in the service of the goddess Bastet.'

To escape the hypnotic intensity of her gaze I lifted my cup and tried the tea. It tasted quite as unpleasant as it looked.

'Fascinating,' Mr Jesperson murmured.

She gave him a look that was challenging, yet still managed to be faintly flirtatious. 'Do you mean I am a fascinating case study? You imagine me to be deluded?'

'Not at all.' His look in return was utterly straightforward. 'I have spent time in Tibet and in India, where reincarnation is accepted as a fact of life. As a result, more people there remember experiences from previous lives – as might people here in England, if their memories were not denied or disparaged. Am I right in supposing you have known this fact since childhood?'

I could see his interest was making her warm to him. 'Oh, yes indeed. But it disturbed my parents so badly that I quickly learnt never to speak of such things, and as a result, I *did* forget . . . I thought those early memories to be no more than dreams.

'Later, I was induced by friends to try mediumship, and Seshemetka spoke to me when I was in a trance state. Everyone assumed she must be my spirit guide, and I naturally took their word for it. It was some time before I began to remember who I really was,' she concluded softly.

'Does seeing the things in the Egyptian galleries help you recover more memories?' I asked.

She stirred her tea thoughtfully. 'Not really,' she said after a moment, 'or not *specific* memories, at least. But when you consider how many millennia are represented by the collection – some of them from a thousand years before my birth in the eighteenth dynasty, and others many centuries after – how could most of those things mean anything personal to me? But when I am there, surrounded by so many relics of that culture, I cannot help but feel a sense of home-coming. Although, to be separated from everything by a sheet of glass, to be forbidden to touch things I long to handle, is frustrating.'

'If you ask him, the Keeper might permit you to handle some of them.' Mr Jesperson spoke casually, his attention on the rock cake he was immersing in his tea.

'Ah!' She gave a happy chuckle. 'I see that you know our Mr Budge. Always so generous and helpful! Just so, I *did* ask, and he allowed me to hold a pretty little comb, the sight of which had struck a chord deep within me. And there are things in his office or from the storerooms – amulets and other small items – that he is happy to let his visitors examine. As long as you are careful not to intrude too much on his time, of course.'

'As a matter of fact, we have come here today to call upon Mr Budge,' I said. 'I do look forward to meeting him.'

She put down her empty cup, firmly refusing Jesperson's offer to get her another. 'I am sure I have detained you for long enough. Do please give the dear man my very best regards.'

'We certainly will. How nice it has been to see you again, Miss Dawes.'

'I am very pleased to have made your acquaintance,' said Jesperson as we all stood up. 'And I hope we shall meet again soon. I should like to learn more about Seshemetka. Perhaps you will call on us? We are not far from the Museum – 203A Gower Street, next to the news-agent.'

I knew, even before her expression changed, how his words must sound to her, and I jumped in quickly, 'I lodge with Mr and Mrs Jesperson.'

But my words were, if anything, even more shocking to her. With a wary look at Mr Jesperson she said, 'Your wife must be a very unusual woman if she does not mind you squiring another lady – your *lodger* – around town while she is stuck at home.'

'Mrs Jesperson is my mother. And Miss Lane's position is far more than that of a mere lodger,' he said gently. 'If you do find yourself passing, we should be very happy if you should like to call on us. Good day, Miss Dawes.'

Taking my arm, he smoothly steered me out of the refreshment room, leaving her looking bemused.

'Why did you say that?' I demanded.

'Would you rather I let her go on thinking what she was thinking?'

'No. But now she imagines . . . she must surely suppose we are engaged to be married!'

We came to a halt in one of the Egyptian galleries, back amongst the stones, statues and sarcophagi of illustrious ancients. He looked down into my eyes with an expression I could not quite make out as he said, 'Would that be the most terrible thing for her to think?'

'I should rather she did not think of me at all,' I blurted uncomfortably.

He gave a short laugh. 'You may put her right when she calls – which she is sure to do very soon, when we shall have more chance to quiz her.'

At that moment a group of people entered the room, and we moved on. Lowering my voice, I asked, 'Do you suspect *her*?'

'She is one of the cranks mentioned by Mr Campbell – surely she must be the lady who communes with mummies? – and her desire to hold, perhaps even to possess, objects she recognises as having once been a part of her daily life might have encouraged her to steal a few unimportant items.'

'Surely not mummified animals?'

'Why not? The ancients revered them. Seshemetka, as a priest-ess, would be accustomed to handling them in their mummified state. Nearly all their divinities were represented as animals, in whole or in part – Bastet, for instance, was a woman with a cat's head. There are entire cemeteries filled with the carefully pre-served bodies of cats, respectfully interred there in her honour.'

I had to admit that it made as much sense as any other reason for stealing a mummified cat, and wondered what the other, smaller, stolen mummy had been. A mouse, perhaps, for the cat to hunt in the afterlife? Or a kitten? It was hard for me to imagine Miss Dawes committing such a theft, especially when the things she wanted could be easily purchased, but if, for some short period of time, she was under the control of an ancient Egyptian spirit who held to a different moral code, then perhaps she could have done so, untroubled by the scruples of her modern self, serene in the knowledge that this papyrus scroll or that mummified cat was hers by right.

'Come along,' my partner urged softly, drawing me from my brief reverie. 'Budge must surely be in his office by now.'

CHAPTER FOUR

Meeting Mr Budge

Jesperson remembered the location of the office from his earlier visit, and this time, rather than risk being turned away by an attendant, we did not ask, but went there directly.

The door was decorated with a gleaming brass name-plate identifying the office of the Keeper of Egyptian and Assyrian Antiquities, E.A. Wallis Budge, Litt.D., F.S.A.

'Come!' called a voice from within in response to Jesperson's knock, and in we went.

The office had a smell of antiquity – of dust and stone, old paper, and the very particular scent of ancient papyrus. It was cosy and cluttered, a cross between a library and a storehouse of ancient objects that included clay bricks, papyrus scrolls, fragments of incised stone and pottery, painted tiles, statues of animal-headed deities carved from stone, and, most strikingly, standing against one wall, a full-sized anthropoid coffin, a sarcophagus doubtless painted to resemble the individual it had been made for, although with a golden, mask-like face. It was such a beautiful piece that I wondered why it was not amongst those on display to the public.

'May I help you?'

The Keeper of Egyptian and Assyrian Antiquities rose from his chair behind a large, untidy desk with a challenging stare. He was a stocky, sturdy-looking man in his late thirties with a round, clean-shaven face beneath a thatch of thick rufus hair. Sharp, curious eyes observed us through the round lenses of his gold-framed spectacles.

Mr Jesperson adopted the pose and voice of a humble suppli-cant before the throne. 'It is surely too much to think that you will remember me, Dr Budge, for it has been at least eighteen months since I first took the liberty of calling upon you uninvited and unannounced, and you—'

'And I,' the other man interrupted, stepping around the side of his desk and staring hard at him, 'I helped you with advice and bought from you a small, somewhat commonplace steatite scarab in your possession – not for the Museum, for we already have hundreds of the things, but as an act of personal kindness. You were hard-up, but no beggar; there was something about you that impressed me. You had gumption. You believed in yourself and, by Jove, I believed in you. In a way, you reminded me of myself as a young man, and I was prepared to give you a chance. I bought that scarab – one of several small antiquities you'd picked up on your travels – and I invited you to come back in a few months and tell me how you were getting on. You said you would, but I waited in vain for that second visit, and I began to think my trust in you had been entirely misplaced and that, rather than rising, you had sunk further still, unable to earn an honest living—' His nostrils flared and his eyebrows rose. 'Jesperson! That's your name. Tell me, *Jasper Jesperson*, what brings you here today, after so long without a word – and will you kindly introduce your friend?'

Mr Budge's speculative eye raked me from head to foot before he turned his gaze once more upon Jesperson. 'Well, sir? Have you nothing to say for yourself?'

Jesperson had kept quiet, making no attempt at any response until Mr Budge fell silent. Now, his stance was almost a parody of abjection. His voice was soft and meek.

'Sir, I can only apologise. I was – still am – deeply grateful for your kindness to me, and never forgot it. I confess that I took your invitation to return as mere politeness, thinking you would soon forget me.

'I delayed in part through embarrassment . . . I should even say, a sense of shame, because of that scarab. I knew it was not worth the money you gave me for it – indeed, I recognised that you had neither need nor desire for it, and took it only out of pity. As a proud young man – perhaps excessively proud – I could not bear it; much as we needed the money, happy as I was to be able to give it to my mother, it was unpleasant to feel I was in your debt.' His voice cracked slightly and he fell silent, as if overcome by recollected emotion.

Mr Budge looked moved by this response. The rage which had surged up so quickly vanished even more suddenly. Relaxed and friendly, he was a different man.

'Now, now,' he said jovially, 'you were wrong to think I ever pitied you, but your feelings do you honour. I see I was not mistaken in my initial assessment of your character. You *are* the fine, upstanding young man I took you for, and if my small act of kindness was all the help you needed, I am glad. Let us say no more about it. I am happy to see you looking so well. You have settled on a career, I presume? And have had some success?'

Jesperson straightened out of his abject slump and gave his questioner a bashful grin. 'I hope you will think so when I tell you about it. Allow me to introduce you to my partner, Miss Lane.'

'How do you do?' he responded, turning to me with a questioning smile. 'Partner?'

With a flourish that made it appear as if plucked from the empty air, Jesperson presented him with our business card. 'Miss Lane and I are consulting detectives. We solve mysteries, great and small.'

'An unusual pursuit, but I am sure you . . . both of you . . . are very good at it,' he said, with another slow, speculative look at me. To avoid having to meet his gaze, I turned my own to the beautiful mummy case.

'That is the mystery I hope to solve myself,' said Mr Budge, moving closer to me.

'Is that the Mystery Mummy?' Jesperson asked.

'You have read about it, of course. Tell me, Miss Lane, do you suppose the occupant of this case to have been a man or a woman?'

41

I looked at the gold face. The eyes, with light flecks in the iris and a thick black outline, made me think of Miss Dawes. 'A woman, I would guess.'

'Good. I agree. The delicacy and beauty of the face is utterly feminine. And yet, and only a student of ancient Egypt could know this, the headdress is in the masculine style, and the name on the cartouche – just there, see? – is that of a man.

'But closer inspection shows that the cartouche has been painted over an earlier name, which is now impossible to read. The headdress, too, may be a later addition. Other clues, such as the gods and goddesses invoked, and references along the side to events in the past life of this individual, are mixed, although most of the pursuits and achievements strike me as declaring the occupant of this sarcophagus was a man.'

Jesperson suggested the coffin could have been designed for a woman, but the death of another family member, most likely her husband or brother, had made some alterations necessary.

'I have considered that possibility.'

'What about the tomb?' I asked. 'Was there nothing there to indicate the identity of this occupant?'

'I see you have not followed the newspaper stories as closely as your partner, Miss Lane – or perhaps the finer details have slipped your mind.' He smiled, as if to show he intended no criticism. 'If I may explain?'

'Please.'

'The tomb itself was constructed more than three and a half thousand years ago—'

'Eighteenth Dynasty,' said Jesperson.

Mr Budge shot a baleful look at him. 'Perhaps. It is difficult to be certain, for the tomb was thoroughly ransacked many centuries ago. Everything valuable was taken, and much else destroyed. It has been of interest chiefly for the wall-paintings, which, yes, Mr Jesperson, do contain references that indicate they were painted not long after the war against the Hyksos, when Egypt's independence was re-established – and likely during, or not long after, the reign of Amenhotep.'

I studied the gilded wooden coffin. The paint looked so fresh, it was hardly possible it could be thousands of years old. 'You said all the valuables were taken, but this was left untouched?'

'Ah. What the robbers did not find, and no one suspected for centuries, was the secret room. Only a year ago, an amateur Egyptologist with a bee in his bonnet about sacred geometry, measured the tomb inside and out and, finding the measurements did not match, realised there must be another chamber. The door to it had been sealed and painted over, but he managed to find it, and it was forced open.

'Inside, along with this coffin, were all the usual grave goods one might expect for a person of consequence. Unfortunately, the discovery was made by an unaffiliated amateur, and a careless one at that. If he even thought to hire guards, he did not pay them well enough to preclude them being bribed, or perhaps simply stealing whatever looked most valuable. One way or another, thieves made off with the more portable treasures.

Luckily, an agent of ours was able to acquire this for us, along with some writings on papyrus.'

'Did they offer any suggestion as to who was in the coffin?'

Mr Budge shook his head. 'I have not yet had a chance to read them all, but from my somewhat cursory examination, they are exactly the sort of thing one might find in any tomb: protective spells and rituals, chapters from the Book of the Dead and so on – I still hold out the hope that there might be a personal name and perhaps even a brief biography within those papyri. But the walls were unpainted, which, in conjunction with the contradictory symbols on the coffin, suggests a need for both haste and secrecy. The deceased may have been of royal blood; certainly burial in that place suggests a connection to the reigning Pharaoh. Perhaps the secrecy was due to some sort of power struggle, with one side determined to protect the body of the deceased – without it, the soul could never hope to achieve immortality. Their enemies could not be content with mere death, but would wish for utter *annihilation*, for as long as the mortal remains survived, there was always the chance that he – or she – might ultimately triumph. It is a puzzle. Perhaps one day, new discoveries may shine a light on that lost chapter of history, but until then, I hope to settle one issue, at least.' He looked at us with a teasing smile.

Humouring him, Jesperson said, 'Do not leave us in suspense, I beg you.'

Mr Budge chuckled. 'Oh, but I am in suspense, too, you know. Still, the twentieth of June is not so very long to wait now – I shall send your invitation to . . .' He held up the card Jesperson had handed him and looked at it closely. 'Ah, Gower Street! You are very near, only a short walk from the University.'

'Invitation?' I asked.

'To the unwrapping! It is to be the same place where I unrolled my last mummy. I expected at that time that it should be the last I should ever do, at least in public.'

I saw a flicker of something – could it be alarm? – cross Mr Jesperson's mobile features. 'A public unwrapping? I thought they had rather gone out of fashion.'

Mr Budge snorted. 'What do I care for fashion? Oh, some of these new archaeologists do not like them – they go on about the damage to the body, even destruction, but the risks are worth taking when there are important questions like this to be answered. Only by stripping away the outer wrappings can we ever know who this mummy was – at the very least, after I am done, we will know if it was male or female. And there are sure to be other things to find – a tyet, a heart scarab, and other amulets, some of them perhaps inscribed with the name that one bore in life. And there may well be a papyrus scroll, either held between the hands or laid beneath the feet, invoking the protection of the gods for his or her journey through the Underworld.'

'You might also find out those things by investigating in private, accompanied by your assistant and perhaps a few students,' Jesperson said carefully. 'Is there such an interest from the public that you choose to make a show of your research?'

He had spoken mildly, but Mr Budge's look darkened. 'There is always an interest in such things. I should know better than you about that. And my publishers will be happy for the chance to sell a few more copies of my new book, which is to be published this very month. The publicity garnered will be good for the Museum as well. I must keep all these things in mind.'

'And the damage to the mummy does not concern you?'

He scowled. 'I am a professional, Mr Jesperson. I know what I am doing. Whether it is done in private or in public, I shall proceed with the utmost caution. And even if the thing is, in the end, too damaged, perhaps too badly disintegrated to be displayed, that matters little, very little, compared to what we may learn in the process. The body of someone who died more than three thousand years ago should have returned to the earth in the usual course of events, so how peculiar it is – how *unnatural* – that anything of it remains. Do you seriously think that its loss should concern me? Or anyone with a rational mind?'

Jesperson smiled suddenly, showing his teeth. 'Of course not. I beg your pardon if I appeared rude by raising potential objections, but I have a penchant for playing Devil's advocate. I am entirely in sympathy with your desire to solve the mystery of the mummy's identity, and I am very much looking forward to observing the process.'

Gradually the high colour faded from Mr Budge's face and he gave a grudging laugh. 'I should have realised you are not one of those . . . Well, the trouble is, some people *do* object to what they consider to be "desecration of the body" – but I suppose we cannot hope for the great British public to adopt a rational, scientific attitude all at once! But admission is by invitation only, so we shall not have to contend with foolish thrill-seekers, only those with a genuine interest.' He turned an enquiring look upon me, and I mustered what enthusiasm I could about the prospect of seeing a mummy unwrapped.

'Excellent! You are clearly an intelligent and adventurous young woman, Miss Lane, and it has been a great pleasure to make your acquaintance. And I am happy to know you have not forgotten me, Jesperson. I have your card' – he patted it – 'and I shall be in touch very soon.'

It was a plain dismissal, and after I had passed along Miss Dawes' regards, we dutifully took our leave of him. Then Jesperson stopped at the door. 'I wonder—?'

'Yes? What is it?'

'Do you still have that that little green scarab you bought from me?'

Mr Budge gave him an odd look. 'Yes . . . yes. Strangely enough, it has come back to me very recently.'

'Come back? What do you mean? Did it go away?'

'I gave it away, to someone I thought I could trust. Sadly, he betrayed that trust by selling it – I know this, because I was able to buy it back from the dealer he'd taken it to.'

'Why so disapproving? If it was a gift, freely given, surely it was his right to give it away himself, or even sell it?' Jesperson protested. 'He must have had a good reason – perhaps he was strapped for cash?'

Mr Budge looked at him with suspicion. 'Why do you defend a man you do not even know?'

Jesperson shrugged. 'I suppose I am naturally argumentative. Like you.'

The other man's mouth dropped open, and then he laughed. 'A hit, a palpable hit! That must be why I like you, Jasper Jesperson! And that despite being so irritated by you – you remind me of myself!'

Still laughing, he went to his desk and shuffled through some things for a moment before turning back with a small stone scarab in his hand.

'For you, as my gift.'

'No, no – it is yours – you bought it from me,' Jesperson protested, backing away.

Mr Budge kept his hand extended, the small object lying on his open palm.

'A lady once told me that to sell a scarab – which is a powerful protective amulet, representing the life force – was to court bad luck. She said they may be *bought,* but not sold, only given away.' He paused thoughtfully. 'Did it bring you bad luck, when you sold it to me?'

'Certainly not.'

'Well, then, that could be because it was not the usual business transaction. You *gave* me the scarab, and rather than buying something I had need of, I gave you some money, out of kindness.'

Jesperson looked unconvinced. 'More likely it was because we are both rational beings, who do not believe in superstition.'

'I am not so sure that is true of me,' Mr Budge replied, 'because I hope that if I give it to you now, it will bring good luck to us both.'

Jesperson allowed him to put the scarab into his hand. 'Thank you.'

'Thank *you*,' he replied cheerily. 'And farewell until we meet again – on the twentieth, at University College.'

CHAPTER FIVE

Memories of Egypt

We walked home in silence, Jesperson so lost in thought that my attempts to initiate conversation went unheard. But I had known him long enough not to feel slighted, for I knew that whatever ideas he was turning over in his mind would be shared with me in due course.

And so it proved. Once we were home and settled in our accustomed places, one each side of the big old oak desk, with a pot of proper tea between us, Jesperson told me what had been occupying his mind.

'It gave me a queer sort of turn, when Budge spoke of unwrapping the mummy,' he began. 'My reaction was not inspired by any great interest in the ongoing arguments amongst Egyptologists regarding the proper treatment of such discoveries, even the bodies of the dead and other things that in the past were discarded as worthless dross.'

He frowned and raked a hand through his curls. 'My own immediate response was very nearly one of *distress* – which was as unexpected, and disturbing to me as to Mr Budge.' Another expression flickered across his face and he leaned forward, pursuing another idea. 'And why *did* my question annoy him so profoundly? Because someone – I wonder who? –has tried to talk him out of the unwrapping. Why? Perhaps it is the danger posed to the mummy's physical integrity, for it will most likely lead to its destruction – or is it to do with the public nature of the event?'

He shook his head dismissively as he leaned back in his chair again. 'But never mind. My own feelings had nothing to do with Budge's plan for his mystery mummy. It was clear to me it was connected to something that happened when I was a boy, when I myself witnessed the unwrapping of a mummy.'

I stared at him, surprised. 'You have never mentioned that before.'

'I have scarcely thought of it since.' With a distant look in his eyes he said, 'His words brought it all back to me – Cairo, the heat and dust, the smells, the shouts in the streets. It was so very different from London, which until then was the only city I had known. I was often in the Egyptian Museum – my mother still worried about me then, frightened I would come to harm in this foreign place, but she must have felt it safe for me to visit a museum on my own.

'There were often other English people there. I remember particularly a man called Henderson, a well-dressed gentleman of medium height, with sandy hair and a large moustache with the ends waxed into little curling horns. He seemed quite old to me; now I would say he was not yet forty. Mother told me he had come to Egypt for the sake of his wife's health, but I saw her only once or twice, on his arm, always shaded by a white parasol, going into or coming out of Shepheard's Hotel.

'One day I saw Mr Henderson in the street, accompanied by his usual dragoman, who was haggling with another local guide. I was filthy and dressed like a local, although the dragomans must have recognised me as a European, for they made no attempt to shoo me away – indeed, they rather ostentatiously ignored me, so I was able to learn the subject of their discussion was what they called an 'unrolling'. This was a popular tourist attraction in Cairo then, with visitors paying well to watch some ancient mummy being unwrapped. Photographs would be taken by an expert, and members of the audience could bid for anything of interest that was uncovered – an amulet, or jewellery, the guides told Mr Henderson, or a piece of papyrus, even parts of the mummy itself.

'But it appeared this particular Englishman was not going to content himself with a small souvenir or photograph of the unrolling: he wished to purchase the mummy itself. He wanted to have the mummy unrolled – and to keep it.' He grinned sarcastically.

'How did you get involved?' I asked. 'Did Mr Henderson invite you to come along?'

Jesperson laughed. 'Oh, no, he took no notice of a street urchin. But having heard where and when the unrolling was to take place, I made sure to be there, mingling with the small crowd who had gathered for the show, for a dozen tourists or so had bought tickets. It was clear Mr Henderson was not best pleased. He must have imagined – or perhaps the guide had led him to believe – that the unrolling would be a private show, for him alone. Although such a thing was possible, the guide told him, it would cost a great deal more, and it might take another week or more to arrange. He told Mr Henderson in no uncertain terms that he could ask for his money back and go, or make the best of it and stay.'

'He stayed – and so did I. It was assumed that as a European child, I must belong to one of the adults in the tent, although I did have to be careful, so as not to get thrown out. As I was so small, and hiding near the back, I did not have a very good view – and it was far more tedious than I had expected.' He grimaced.

'Of course, the wrappings of an ancient mummy could not be "unrolled" like thread from a spool. Some of the outer layers came off easily enough, but closer to the body, the flesh and cloth had merged. At one point, the adults all gasped with excitement and crowded in closer to get a better view, for some piece of gold jewellery had been found. And when the head was unwrapped, I heard some descriptive responses to the face that was revealed.'

His voice rose to a falsetto: '"Oh, how *hideous*! I thought they said it should be a princess – what about that lovely necklace?"'

After clearing his throat, he went on in his own voice, 'The face was in fact that of an old man, grim-looking, with shrunken cheeks, a wide grinning mouth, jutting chin and sharp nose: a most unpleasant-looking character. It may be unfair to judge a man's character by his appearance, especially when he has been dead for thousands of years, but that was my impression when I saw him for myself, and I must confess, it was so disturbing that the nameless man came back to haunt me in my dreams for some nights to come.'

He picked up the pot and refilled our cups before he spoke again. 'Just after the face was revealed, a woman screamed loudly, and then there was a babble of voices and Mr Henderson – who had managed to secure himself a choice position beside the head – keeled over.

'He was a big man – did I mention that? Not only tall, but portly. And he had been bending over the mummy when – well, when he fainted. He hit the table going down and somehow or other was caught by, or caught hold of, one of the mummy's arms and pulled it down with him.'

I shivered, feeling a *frisson* of horror. 'He pulled the mummy down on top of him?'

'Just one arm. The process of unwrapping must have loosened it at the shoulder joint and the weight of the living man pulled it right off.'

I could not decide if that was better or worse than fainting into the embrace of the whole mummy. 'What happened next?'

'Oh, there was general confusion. His dragoman tried to find a doctor or nurse amongst the party, but there appeared to be no one with any medical knowledge, or willingness to take on

54

the responsibility, in fact, so it was left to the dragoman to try to revive Mr Henderson.

'The woman who had screamed claimed she had seen a horrible sight – a sudden gout of blood had gushed out of the mummy's mouth – and that caused a general outcry, with most of the others eager to correct her, chiming in with their own very different experiences. I had not seen anything myself – I only got a good look at the mummy's face afterwards – but those who had seen were in agreement: *something* had come out of its mouth, but they disagreed about what it might have been. One man – he sounded German to me – said it had looked like a stream of smoke, and there was a perfectly logical explanation for that, for most probably it was an expulsion of dust particles released as the wrappings were pulled away. Others swore they had seen an insect – a large, shiny, black beetle, crawling over the lower lip and chin – but whatever it was, it had vanished without trace. It could not have been blood or any other liquid, for the corpse itself was desiccated and the wrappings were all dry. I wish I had been able to see for myself, but, as I had not, I was inclined to agree with the logical German gentleman. Yes, he said, he had been startled by the sight of something that appeared to emerge from the mummy's open mouth, but, on reflection, he thought a trick of light and shadow was to blame, transforming a swirl of dust into something quite inexplicable.

'But no one else agreed with him. Those who thought they had seen a black beetle crawl out of the mouth were adamant that it was an insect and nothing at all like a swirl of dust.

"Never mind that nothing living could have come out of a mouth so firmly shut for thousands of years," said a young Frenchman, "I know what I saw with my own eyes." He too had an explanation, that the air was full of such creatures and one might have landed on – or even in – the mummy's mouth for a moment before flying away. The German gentleman maintained that he had been much closer to the mummy's head and had been observing it fixedly, and there was, absolutely and indubitably, no beetle.

'The Frenchman took great exception to being told by a pompous German that he knew better, when the Frenchman knew what he had seen with his own eyes. I was at any moment expecting the two of them to challenge each other to a duel, which would have been much more exciting than a group of adults shouting at each other. But before the argument could grow any more heated the Englishman recovered consciousness. As soon as he was sitting up, being revived by a swig of brandy from a flask some foresighted man proffered, everyone spoke at once, demanding to know what he had seen, for surely it must have been something truly horrible, to make so strong a man faint.'

Jesperson paused to finish his tea, then continued, 'Henderson maintained he had seen nothing. He had been feeling a trifle unwell all day and had perhaps dined a bit too heartily; although he was not usually given to fainting, fits he had been overcome by the oppressive heat and nasty odour inside the tent. He had no opinion on the argument between those who had seen a swirl of dust or a gush of blood or a shiny black beetle – he had been better-placed than anyone for a view of the mummy's mouth, and he had seen it emit nothing at all.

'I could see that Mr Henderson was not enjoying himself. He declared he'd had more than enough of this whole mummy business; that he was returning to his hotel for a brandy and soda and that he'd be right as rain in the morning.'

'And was he?' I asked, wondering if this was going to be one of those curse-of-the-mummy tales that would end with the death of poor Mr Henderson.

Jesperson shrugged. 'The party broke up then; everyone seemed to have lost their appetite for any further unwrapping. I managed to hitch a ride on the back of someone's carriage and crept back into the house without anyone knowing I had been out. I felt quite pleased with myself. But I had terrible nightmares about the mummy coming to get me, and beetles flying out of its mouth . . .'

'And what of Mr Henderson?'

'What of him?'

'Well . . . did you see him again?'

'No, never.'

'And that did not worry you?' I asked, surprised by his casual response.

He was surprised by my surprise. 'Why would it? I am sure he never took any notice of *me*. We were never acquainted, you know. My mother did not know him, and we did not stay at Shepheard's Hotel.'

'But you used to see him at the Egyptian Museum, you said, or in the streets around the city – yet never since?'

'We left Egypt not very long after that incident. Why are you so interested in Henderson?'

'Why did you tell me the story about him?'

He gave me a puzzled smile. 'The story was about *me*. Earlier you wondered why I never spoke of my adventures in Egypt. The reason is simple: I was still a child, and we were there for only a very short time. Even this, my only adventure, is lacking as a story, for it has no real conclusion.'

'Do you know what happened to the mummy?'

'I imagine Mr Henderson took it back to England with him – well, assuming he survived. His fainting fit may have been a sign that he was already suffering from some disease that would kill him before he could return home.'

'The mummy's curse?'

'If you like.' He grinned. 'You are the writer – you decide what would make the most satisfactory end to my unsatisfactory little tale.'

I gave him a stern look. 'It would not be appropriate for me to invent something,,' I said. 'I am not a novelist.'

'Forgive me,' he said meekly. 'Of course, you must always stick to the facts.' He stood up. 'I'm going out for a walk. Tell Mother I expect to be back by dinner-time, but not to wait – I have a lot of thinking to do.'

I sat for a while after he had gone, turning the stolen objects over in my mind as if they were pieces of a puzzle, but although

I could see what they had in common, I struggled to understand how they were all worth stealing. I was inclined to think that Jesperson's initial idea was the most likely, that the thief was someone known to Mr Sand – and probably to Mr Campbell as well – who had taken the things almost at random, to prove a point or by way of petty revenge.

When I took the tea tray back to the kitchen, I found Edith putting a chicken into the oven to roast.

'Did I hear someone at the door?' she asked.

'No, only your son going out. He said he intends to be back for dinner, but if he's late, we should not wait for him.'

She pursed her lips. 'A thinking walk, is it, when he is so wrapped up in a puzzle as to forget the time? I am glad this new case is so interesting. When he is bored, everyone suffers.' She smiled at me.

'I am not sure it really is that interesting,' I said. 'It is quite a small matter – petty theft – but something about it has seized his imagination – maybe because of the Egyptian connection? I had quite forgotten that you'd been to Egypt. You often reminisce about your time in China, or Japan, or India, but it was only today that Mr Jesperson mentioned something that he saw in Cairo.'

She turned away from me to pick up the cups and saucers.

'Let me wash them,' I started, alert to the sudden change in her mood.

'I am sure you have much better things to do,' she said, placing the cups and saucers in the sink.

'I do not. If you will not let me wash up, then I shall dry,' I said, picking up a tea towel. She had been relaxed and happy to chat; now, at the mention of Egypt, she was not. It would have been polite to have taken the hint and changed the subject if I would not leave, but I was determined to discover why they were both haunted by what happened there.

'You were not there very long, I gather.'

'About two months. It was meant to be longer, but—'

She stopped, and I bit my lip, repressing the impulse to say it didn't matter. I let the silence build until, with a sigh, she gave in.

'It was not long after my husband died. We were left with almost nothing to live on, so it was a great relief when my cousin Caroline invited me out to Egypt. She was expecting her first child and I was to be company for her. I had never spent much time with Caroline – I had met her husband at their wedding – but this solved our immediate problem. Of course they would not pay me – I was a relative, not a hireling – but Jasper and I would have a home for a year, at least.'

She handed me a teacup to dry. 'Poor Caroline.'

'What happened?'

'The baby was early, poor wee thing, too early to survive. He died, and three days later, so did she.'

'I'm so sorry – that must have been difficult.'

She gave a short, bitter laugh. 'You have no idea. Mr Barraclough – Caroline's husband – went quite mad in his grief. At least, that is the kindest explanation. He blamed Jasper.'

'Blamed him – for what?'

'For the deaths of his wife and child. Yes, I know, it is hard to believe.'

I could only imagine the feelings of shock, indignation, grief and sheer disbelief Edith must have experienced all those years ago.

'It was mad, of course, but Mr Barraclough disliked my son from the first. He called him sly, insolent, too clever by half . . . when the simple truth of the matter was that Jasper was more intelligent, observant and well-read, even at his young age, than Mr Barraclough would ever be, and he never tried to hide it. In fact, Jasper liked to show off – well, you know what young boys are. And you know Jasper.'

It was somehow no surprise to learn that my partner's distinctive character had been formed at such an early age. 'But that does not explain how he – or anyone – could blame a child for such a thing. Unless . . .' I was struck by a worrying thought. 'I hope he did not pretend to have medical training?'

'Oh, no, of course not!' She almost laughed. 'And no one would have asked him. But there was nothing the doctor could do, in any case – her early confinement – the fact that the baby was so premature . . . But Mr Barraclough was fixated upon the idea that Jasper had caused the untimely birth.' She paused as she moved away from the sink and dried her hands.

'How could he possibly do that? Edith?'

I could see she was finding it difficult to reply, but at last she said, 'He – Mr Barraclough – claimed my Jasper had frightened her into giving birth before her time. Of course it was not intentional; even he did not say Jasper had *meant* to do it. But he would insist that the fright Jasper gave her led directly to . . . to the consequences, even though it was the night before she . . . But if it had really been caused by a convulsion of fear, surely it would have started at once, or at the very least, within a few hours? And Caroline was not the weak, shrinking little violet he would have had her be. She was not really frightened, only startled, and perhaps a bit disturbed, as anyone would be when awakened suddenly in the middle of the night. But I explained, and she understood, and she was quite calm when she went back to bed.'

'Did Jasper have a nightmare?' I asked, for I thought I had guessed how this all pieced together.

'Indeed,' Edith said sadly, 'he shouted out in his sleep, so loudly, he woke the entire household. But it was a while before I could wake *him*, and so he carried on raving about a terrible mummy coming after him with dark red beetles flying from its gaping mouth. And even when I did finally shake him into consciousness, he continued in the grip of the nightmare, insisting that the mummy was real, and it *would* happen; that the mummy must be destroyed before it killed someone.'

A chill ran down my spine. 'Do – do you know what inspired these night terrors?'

'He confessed the next day that he had seen a mummy unwrapped. It was strange that it should have affected him like that; he was never a nervous child, and he had already seen any number of mummies in various states of decay.' She shook her head slowly. 'But who knows where dreams come from? It may be easier to explain why Mr Barraclough decided to pin the blame on my son rather than the doctor who was unable to save his wife. The doctor – and do not think I mean to imply he was at fault; I doubt there was anything the cleverest man could have done – was a well-regarded member of the Barracloughs' social set, whereas Jasper was an interloper and an irritant, and I, his unlucky mother, had been of no help to Caroline at all. We were both, in his eyes, implicated in her death.'

She drew a deep breath. 'He made us leave the house the very next day – he barely gave us time to pack, not that we had much. His promise to pay our passage home was forgotten; he gave no thought to what poor Caroline would have wanted, nor to what we should do or how we should live. I was not entirely penniless, but I knew what little I had would not keep us for long, even in Egypt. But—' She forced a smile. 'Well, never mind. We survived.'

Jesperson came back from his walk in time for dinner and in a good mood.

'Have you solved the case already?' I asked, teasing.

'Not without more information. We must think of a way to learn more, not only from Sand, but from Budge too. But for now, considering the differences, I suspect the two thefts were by different people.'

The idea of two different thieves sounded unlikely to me, but Jesperson had made up his mind. 'You will soon see that I am right,' he said confidently. 'But how to find even one of them? We must have names. Campbell will not play and Sand does not know, but Budge may have the information we need. It is simply a matter of finding an excuse – the right approach – to acquire it from him.' He inhaled deeply, then rubbed his hands together. 'That smells like the chicken is ready, and just in time, for I am famished!'

It was about an hour after a most convivial dinner – the chicken was roasted to perfection; the potatoes crisp, and asparagus tender, followed by a bowl of strawberries and cream – that the telegram arrived.

Come at once to the Museum. Your services urgently required. A.E. Wallis Budge

CHAPTER SIX

The Mummy is Missing

The Museum was closed, but the guard at the front gate was expecting us.

We found Mr Budge in his office, flushed and highly agitated, repeatedly mopping his brow with a large white handkerchief as he spoke. 'Thank you for coming,' he said, shaking Jesperson by the hand. 'I never imagined I should have to call on your professional capacity – or not so soon! – but to go to the police would be to court most unwelcome publicity.'

'What has happened?' Jesperson asked, looking around the room. Although untidy, it looked much as before, a small treasure-house of dusty antiquities and learned books, a museum in miniature. Neither of us could see any signs of disturbance. 'Are you missing something? Stolen, you think?'

'Stolen,' came his emphatic, anguished reply. 'Someone has stolen my mummy.'

We turned to look at the carved and painted sarcophagus, the dark eyes and golden face as mysterious as ever. Mr Budge went to it and carefully lifted the lid aside to reveal it was empty.

'When did it happen?'

Mr Budge groaned. 'I wish I knew! It could have been days, weeks, perhaps even months ago. After the flurry of visitors shortly after its arrival, I had no reason to open the case again until – barely an hour ago.'

'Why now?'

He gave a deep sigh. 'To gratify Miss Dawes.'

I am sure I must have started at the name, but Jesperson said only, 'Please explain.'

Mr Budge glanced at me. 'Perhaps Miss Lane is aware . . . ? Well, then, she is a lady who believes herself to be the reincarnation of an ancient Egyptian priestess. She is no scholar, but she takes a deep interest in anything that might be contemporaneous with her supposed earlier life. Really, she is a dear, sweet soul, and it is hard for me to deny one of her requests. For some reason, she was very determined to look upon the face of – oh, I cannot recall the name she said, just that she thought it might be the mummy of one known to her earlier self. I had been on the point of leaving and I tried to put her off, but she had a bee in her bonnet about it, and insisted until I agreed to let her have her personal inspection, since only that could satisfy her. And then I removed the lid . . .'

He groaned and clutched his head. 'Oh, how lucky that I did! If not, I would be in ignorance still, and probably would not have known until the very evening of the unwrapping . . . Oh, the ignominy! Imagine, if I were standing before an audience of my peers . . . reporters, too . . . I should have been made a laughing-stock.' He shuddered, wiped his brow once more, then stuffed the handkerchief into his pocket. 'See here, you must get it back. If I must, I can postpone the unwrapping – I can find some excuse to put it off until later in the year – but I must have the mummy back. Will you help me?'

'You may count on it,' Jesperson said. 'Now you must tell us everything – not merely what you *know,* but any suspicions you may have. First: have you any idea *why* someone would take it?'

'Yes. There is only one possible reason: to embarrass me.'

'You have enemies?' I asked, making sure to sound scandalised.

A short, bitter laugh was the reply. 'I think perhaps you had better be seated. The recounting of the list of those opposed to my success may take some time.'

We seated ourselves as he started pacing nervously. 'For all my friends and supporters, there have always been those who have treated me with suspicion, envy and open disdain. My appointment to my present position as Keeper was delayed for years by their opposition, and they still wish to see me thwarted. It must be one of them who has taken the mummy – or arranged for it to be taken. It would not attract any ordinary thief, for in itself it is worthless. Without provenance, it has no value. So there can be no other reason for anyone to take it, except to hurt and inconvenience me. And if I had not discovered the absence until the night scheduled for the unwrapping . . .' He groaned again. 'Ah, the newspapers would have a field day!'

Beads of perspiration stood out on his brow, his eyes bulged slightly with anxiety and he groped again for his handkerchief. 'I have spoken of my enemies, but where to begin? Some of them are very highly placed – they would surely not risk being embroiled in a scandal, if it should come out that they had stooped so low as to steal from me. But *someone* has.'

Jesperson rubbed his chin thoughtfully. 'Perhaps we can narrow the possibilities by concentrating on when the mummy might have been stolen, and who might have had the opportunity. When was the last time you saw it?'

'That's not so easy to answer,' he said, going over to his desk and sinking into his chair with a sigh. 'As you know, it arrived before Christmas, when it received a good deal of attention in the press. Then, all through January, there was a parade of visitors keen to see our Mystery Mummy. Some were satisfied with an inspection of the exterior of the case, but most wished also to see the mummy within, still intact in all its wrappings and shrouded in mystery. It was this – the impossibility of knowing if the person whose remains were so carefully stored away had been a man or a woman, old or young, died naturally or by violence, and the curiosity expressed by so many, that made me decide to hold a public unwrapping.'

'When was that? When did you first speak of the possibility?'

'I am not sure. March or April, I suppose.'

'And after that announcement, did you happen to notice if the mummy was still there?'

Budge scowled. 'It was not an announcement. I spoke of it only to a few friends and colleagues at that point.'

'I am merely trying to fix a date,' Jesperson responded patiently. 'We know the latest the mummy could have been taken is yesterday, but when was the earliest moment?'

Mr Budge reached for the large leather-bound diary on the desk and pulled it towards him. 'I have not been in the habit of removing the lid unless there has been a special request. Appointments would be recorded, but not those who simply drop by – as you did earlier today. But it may jog my memory . . .' He turned the pages slowly, muttering to himself under his breath as he deciphered his notes from the past few months, until at last he slammed it shut and announced, 'It has not been opened since April – that is, not by me, and I should say not since the middle of that month.'

Jesperson and I both leaned forward, our eyes fixed intently on his face.

'What else happened in April?' Jesperson demanded, 'In or after the middle of the month?'

'What sort of thing do you mean?'

'I mean whatever it was that just came to your mind when you mentioned the middle of April.'

Mr Budge sat up straight in his chair. 'Perhaps I *do* know who did this. It is the sort of prank that a bored schoolboy might play, stealing something his master values, and not a small thing, either. It could not have been done on the whim of a moment, as with a smaller object that could be slipped inside a pocket or smuggled out in a hand-bag. The thief is probably someone who has been in my office more than once. He is aware of my schedule, my comings and goings, which means he is an insider – or has had help from a member of staff – one of the night-watchmen, most likely.' His expression combined anger at this treachery with pride in his own cleverness, and he rose to his feet, fists clenching in front of his chest as if he were imagining seizing hold of the thief.

Jesperson also stood up. 'Who is this schoolboy prankster?'

'Alistair Campbell – my *former* assistant, sacked on the eleventh of April.'

Jesperson gave no indication that he recognised the name, so Mr Budge added, 'He is the one I referred to when I mentioned the ungrateful recipient of my gift of your scarab.'

'You sacked him for his ingratitude?'

Mr Budge made a gesture of impatience. 'For something far worse – for dishonesty. In the shop where I found your scarab for sale I discovered some rolls of papyrus, missing from the same storeroom where Campbell worked. It was immediately obvious to me that he had taken them and along with the scarab, sold them to the shop-keeper.'

'What did the shop-keeper say?'

'Oh, he was useless – said he could not possibly remember where one or two papyri out of so many had come from; he thought most likely they were part of a large batch that arrived in December. He had agents in Egypt who provided most of his stock, but he did occasionally buy things from people who came into the shop. He recognised my description of Campbell at once – ah, yes, the student who barely a week before had brought him the little heart-scarab.'

'Along with the papyri?'

Avoiding Jesperson's steady gaze, Budge began moving things about on his desk and aligning them to no obvious purpose. 'Well, no, I told you he said he could not remember. But that was my fault, for by then he suspected I was looking for items that had been stolen, and of course he did not want to risk his reputation and perhaps be made liable for prosecution. None of his papyri had been marked as property of the Museum – I had no more proof they were stolen than he did. All I could do was buy them back, and I did.'

'What about Mr Campbell – did he admit to anything?'

'Only to selling the scarab. He denied being a thief and said he was hurt by my baseless suspicion. At first, he did not appear to take it seriously because—' He stopped, pressing his lips tightly together and shook his head, offering no further explanation, although it was not hard, given what we knew of the matter, to imagine what he had been about to say.

Jesperson tried to draw him out. 'Had you previously had any suspicions about him?'

'I would never have hired him as my assistant if I had the least doubts about his character. Everyone who knew him spoke very highly of him, and not only of his abilities as a scholar. I believed him to be poor, but honest.'

Abruptly giving up his futile efforts at tidying his desk, Budge turned to face us again. This time he did not look angry or proud, but humble. 'I was wrong, wasn't I?'

'About what?'

'Wrong to think he took those papyri. Yes, of course, poverty may drive even an honest man to steal. He might have told himself it was only temporary, that he would be able to buy – or even steal – them back again, and replace them before anyone knew they were gone.'

'That has been known to happen,' Jesperson said neutrally. 'Especially with gamblers. They will beg, borrow or steal, convincing themselves that their next win will be more than enough to cover all their debts. Is Campbell a gambler?'

'No. No . . . and he wasn't a thief.' He looked down. 'What I neglected to tell you is that it was Campbell himself who noticed the scrolls were missing and reported it to me.' His shoulders slumped and he looked up at me. 'What thief would draw attention to the fact that something had been stolen, Miss Lane?'

'Did that not occur to you at the time?' I asked gently.

'He did mention it in his own defence – but I was angry, and when someone engages me in argument, I become all the more determined to prove myself right, so I maintained that he had done so precisely to make himself look innocent. I insisted that I would have discovered the loss very soon myself – yes, I had given them to him to catalogue and translate, and I had no personal need of them, but they dealt with the subject of mummification, which – as he well knew – is of particular interest to one of my frequent visitors—'

'Pagan Brown?' Jesperson interrupted.

The name was unknown to me, and I looked at my partner for explanation.

I was not the only taken by surprise, for Mr Budge was staring at Jesperson.

'You know Pagan?' he asked.

'Only by sight, as a fellow ticket-holder to the Reading Room, and by reputation, from the many letters he writes to *The Times*, *The Saturday Review*, and various learned journals.'

'You are aware of his theories?'

'Only that they differ from those of most Egyptologists.'

'Yes, well, some of his theories are fantastical, but he's very sound when it comes to translations of hieroglyphics and hieratic texts. At present, mummies have captured his imagination so it was inevitable that he would at some point ask if he might have a look at any uncatalogued material on the subject. Campbell knew that as well as I – and Pagan is acquainted with Campbell; therefore, I argued, Campbell felt the need to establish his innocence by telling me some papyri were missing before I asked for them.'

'A convoluted argument,' Jesperson murmured.

Budge shook his head. 'There was never any evidence against Campbell. I was wrong to accuse him, entirely wrong to sack him – I admit it.'

'It would be a kindness to say that to Mr Campbell,' I suggested gently.

He gave a bitter laugh. 'Oh, yes, no doubt a grovelling apology and his job back is the ransom he wishes for the mummy.'

Taken aback, I stared at him in shock.

Jesperson said, 'Surely you do not suspect Campbell of taking the mummy?'

'As he was innocent of the first crime, he must be guilty of this greater one.'

Mr Jesperson's eyebrows arched so high they disappeared into his hair. 'I fail to appreciate your logic, Mr Budge.'

'How is this: I supplied the motive when I accused him of being a thief and sacked him without a reference. "Call me a thief," he says to himself, "very well, I'll show you thieving." It was an act of pure revenge. He don't want the mummy; it is no good to him. He only took it to hurt me. And therefore I can hope he has kept it safe.'

I could imagine the idea of revenge of that sort might well appeal to a certain juvenile nature, but Mr Campbell was surely too intelligent and honest for such a scheme. He had so much more to lose than Mr Budge.

'The one problem with your theory is that Campbell would have been inspired to steal the mummy only *after* he was sacked, by which time he no longer had easy access to your office,' Jesperson said carefully. 'If he had taken it while he was still working here, he might have found a way to smuggle it out without attracting suspicion. After he was sacked, it would be a very great risk to return, even after hours. He would be bound to attract suspicion.'

'Yes, of course, of course – he could not do it alone. Knowing I would suspect him, he would be careful to establish an alibi.

Therefore, someone had to do it for him. He was an affable man; he had made friends with many people here, including the night-watchmen.' Looking distracted, he went around to the other side of the desk and once again picked up his diary. He opened it, muttering to himself, 'Let me see . . . let me see . . .' before heaving a sigh and shaking his head as he closed it up again.

'No, of course I made no note of it; but I *do* remember that a night-watchman left us on the first or second of May.'

'Sacked?'

'No, no, Leary left of his own accord; he worked for the Museum for years, latterly as a night-watchman. I don't believe there were any complaints – no significant complaints, at least – about his service.

'Then why suspect him? Perhaps if he was looking for money . . . ?'

'There are reasons other than money why Leary might have wished to give aid to anyone who wished me harm.' With a significant slow nod of his head Mr Budge said, 'He was one of Renouf's men.'

I recognised the name, as anyone might who had followed the news for the past few years in London: Peter le Page Renouf had been the previous Keeper of Egyptian and Assyrian Antiquities. Forced by his age to retire, he had vociferously opposed the promotion of his former assistant. Although he was unable to win the appointment for his own favoured candidate, his unrelenting opposition was the reason Mr Budge had continued with the title of 'Assistant Keeper' for several years, with no increase in his salary, despite performing all the duties required of his predecessor, before he was at last awarded the title and wages that were the prerequisites of this job. He had not exaggerated when he said he had enemies.

'Not that it was any of Leary's business to play favourites,' Mr Budge went on, 'but for some reason, he practically worshipped old Renouf. Although I do not think Leary would have committed a crime against the Museum, if it were presented in the right light – as a harmless prank, a personal insult to *me* alone – he might have agreed. Or, who knows, perhaps he is one of those poor sillies who consider it a desecration to undress the dead, who think every ancient set of bones should be left to lie undisturbed where they were buried, however many thousands of years ago.' He sniffed. 'Yes, perhaps he took offence at the idea of the unwrapping and agreed to help move Mummy X to a place of safety.'

'Then we must speak to him – and perhaps to all the night-watchmen – but Mr Leary must be first.'

'I am certain of it,' said Mr Budge. His eyes flashed. 'Leary and Campbell are the guilty parties; together, they plotted their conspiracy against me.'

I saw that Jesperson was amused. 'Indeed? Well, if you have solved the case, you do not need us.'

'Oh, but I do, I do need you, indeed I do,' he said anxiously. 'I am counting on you to uncover all the evidence I might need to bring a case against them, and most importantly, of course, to bring my mummy back here safely and with a minimum of fuss, in the event that I decide not to prosecute.' He tapped the side of his nose with one forefinger. 'For now, I trust you will both keep my little problem a close secret.'

'You will find us the very model of discretion. Can you give us more details for this fellow Leary? Where he lives, for instance?'

'I have no idea where that man stays. Nor Campbell. But Smythe will be able to tell you—' He glanced at the ornate clock that rested on a corner of his cluttered desk and grimaced. 'Of course, he will have gone home long since – as should we all. I fear you will have to wait until the morning, but I'll write to him instructing him to answer all your questions.'

We waited while he scribbled a few lines on a card. 'There. Ask for Mr Arthur Smythe. He is a good man, he's been in charge of security for many years. He'll be able to tell you what you need to know.'

Jesperson tucked the card away in his pocket and shook Mr Budge by the hand, assuring him that we would be back in touch as soon as we had anything to report.

'I will walk you out,' he replied. 'I must get home. My wife will be wondering what on earth has become of me.'

At the gate, he introduced us to the guard, a large, rather gloomy-looking middle-aged man called Mr Bacon, and instructed him to help us in any way that might be required.

When we were once more alone together, I asked my partner if he expected an interview with Mr Leary would prove useful.

'Certainly it will,' he said in surprise. 'Leary is, if not our first suspect, at least the first possible witness. I think he may very well be able to tell us what happened to the mummy – if we can get it out of him.'

I recalled Mr Campbell's small, bare room at the top of that narrow house and wondered where he could possibly have a mummy hidden. I also recalled my impression of his character. 'But – you do not believe Mr Budge's theory?'

He snorted. 'Do you? Campbell is an honest fellow who has been badly treated. He is far too intelligent to get involved in such a prank, if prank it is. But Leary is an unknown and if Budge is right about him, he might well have been tempted to take part in such a scheme, especially if he was already planning to retire. Or perhaps he witnessed the crime and turned blackmailer to fund his retirement.

'Of course, these are only guesses, and they could well be as wide of the mark as Mr Budge's idea of conspiracy between Campbell and Leary. But there is no doubt that the man does have enemies, and the usual motives for theft do not apply to the abduction of an ancient mummified corpse. We shall just have to see what we can find out.'

He fell silent and did not speak again until we were outside our own front door. 'Do you not feel, as I do, Miss Lane, that we have finally grasped the end of a long spool of thread, one that, when unwound, will take us to the heart of this maze?'

CHAPTER SEVEN

The Search for Mr Leary

The next day, after a hearty breakfast (for, as Mr Jesperson said, with no way of knowing how long it would take us to track down Mr Leary, or what might transpire after that, we had better set ourselves up for a long day) we went to the British Museum to have a word with Mr Arthur Smythe, the head of security.

Mr Arthur N. Smythe was an elderly, alert, slim and nattily attired man who was able to supply us with Mr Leary's present address along with his Christian name – Patrick – and an explanation as to why he had left his job at the British Museum.

'His married daughter was wanting him to go and live with her, up Hampstead way, and then he got the offer of steady work from a gentleman in those parts and that made up his mind. He'd been promised fewer and more sociable hours for the same money he was making here working nights, and instead of paying for his lodgings, he'd have his meals and washing and all, and the company of his daughter, in a nice little house with a garden.'

'Entirely understandable,' said Jesperson with an encouraging smile. 'What sort of work, do you know?'

'He did not say, but I am sure he will tell you himself when you see him. Please give him my regards. Tell him Artie hopes he won't forget his old mates, and remind him I owe him a drink. But say that if he wants it, he'll have to call in here, because I ain't going all the way out to Hampstead to pay for his beer.' He chuckled as he bade us farewell.

'We can catch the number five tram at Holborn and get off at Parliament Hill; that will be best,' said Jesperson as we left the Museum.

It was a wonder to me that he always knew how to get to anywhere from anywhere in London, especially when so much of his life had been spent abroad. When first I met him, he had not been back in England for even a year, so it was unlikely that his encyclopaedic knowledge was gained through personal experience, yet I rarely saw him consult a map. I could only suppose that his quick, strongly retentive memory worked as well for routes and locations as it did for facts and figures.

It was a lovely, balmy Saturday morning and many of the people crowding onto the tram were in holiday mood, intent on heading to what I heard the conductor call "appy 'ampstead' for the day.

The address we had been given was in a row of workmen's cottages, small but of a neat, pleasant appearance. Jesperson rapped on the door and we waited. He rapped again, and this time I heard the sound of a window being pushed up close by.

When I turned to the right, I saw a woman leaning out of a window next door. She had her sleeves rolled up and a red scarf tied over her hair.

Seeing she had my attention, she called, 'Won't be long to wait; 'e's only gone down the station to meet 'is wife.'

'We're here to see Mr Leary,' Jesperson replied. 'Is this his daughter's house?'

'Oh, you mean the old man?'

'That's right. Do you know if he is in?'

She screwed up her round, pink-cheeked face in thought. 'Funny thing, that. He ain't one for sleeping the day away, but the only person I've seen come out today is Mr Balmer, and, like I said, he's gone to Paddington to meet 'is wife. She's been away all the week at 'er sister's.'

'Are you quite certain Mr Leary is at home? He's not answering the door. Could he have gone out early and you missed him?'

After a brief hesitation she admitted this might be so, although her expression remained doubtful.

'Do you know where he works? Perhaps we might better find him there?'

But we had exhausted her store of knowledge, or at least her willingness to help. 'That's nothing to do with me. You'd best wait and ask Mr Balmer.' She pulled her head back and shut the window, but she did not leave; evidently she had decided to keep an eye on us, in case we attempted to take advantage of the fact no one was home and break in to the house.

Jesperson knocked again, more loudly still, but without

81

conviction. There was nothing else to do but wait for Mr and Mrs Balmer to return and hope they would be willing to tell us where Mr Leary might be found. If not . . . My imagination baulked at the thought of keeping watch on the house until he returned, because I could not see anywhere on this little street where we might stand for long without attracting unwanted attention. Indeed, our presence was already attracting curious stares from at least one disapproving nurse-maid.

We decided to go for a walk, but when we returned, half an hour later, nothing looked any different. We were about to retrace our steps, to waste more time, when a hansom cab turned into the street and pulled up in front of the Balmers' house.

A short, strongly built man jumped out, setting down a case before helping the woman inside to alight.

'Please excuse the intrusion,' said Mr Jesperson, touching his hat as we approached. 'You are Mr and Mrs Balmer, I believe?'

With a suspicious look the man said, 'I do not think I know you, sir.'

'I do beg your pardon. My name is Jesperson. This is Miss Lane. We've come in search of Mr Patrick Leary – we were told he lives with you?'

'What do you want with my father?' the young woman asked.

'We were sent here from the British Museum.'

'He doesn't work there any longer.'

'Yes, so we have learnt from his old friend and colleague Mr Arthur Smythe,' Jesperson said with his most disarming smile. 'And we are very eager to speak with him. But there was no answer to our knock a short time ago, although your neighbour thought he was in. She was kind enough to tell us she thought you would be back soon, so we thought it best to wait, hoping you could tell us where he works. Perhaps he went out very early?'

Mrs Balmer exchanged a look with her husband, who said, 'He was still in his bed when I left this morning.'

'Surely he is not still asleep,' she exclaimed, sounding vexed. 'What time did he come in last night?'

'I never saw him, but it could not have been very late – unless he never came home at all.'

This last remark was clearly facetious, for the young woman rolled her eyes before saying to us, 'You had better come in, Miss Lane, Mr – Jesperson, is it? We'll all have a nice cup of tea while we wait for my father.'

We followed them to the front door, where Mr Balmer gave an exclamation at finding the door was not locked.

'He must be in, after all,' Mrs Balmer said, and then, to us, 'After working for so long as a guard he is very conscious of security; he would never go out without locking up.'

As she entered, behind her husband, she called out, 'Dad! I'm home!'

'I wonder why he didn't answer the door to you,' Mr Balmer said in a low voice, turning a measuring look on us. Did he imagine we might be bailiffs, or 'heavies', perhaps, come to collect a debt? If the thought had crossed his mind, it must have been our unsuitability for such a role that made him smile.

When there was no response from upstairs, Mrs Balmer touched her husband's arm and said, 'He must be out back.'

'Having a smoke, or skulking in the shed, maybe,' he replied, his slight smile broadening.

'Come in; I'll put the kettle on,' she said, leading the way into the kitchen. There was a window in the room that looked out onto a long, narrow garden, fenced on three sides, with a wooden shed at the far end. We all fixed our gazes upon that shed, anticipating that the door would open, but the only thing that moved in the garden was a fat brown thrush.

While Mrs Balmer filled the kettle and put it on the stove, Mr Balmer went out through the back door. Moments later, he returned and announced, 'Not there.'

A look of concern creased his wife's smooth face. 'But where—? He'd never go out and leave the door unlocked. Not Dad. Did *you* lock it?'

'No, because . . . well, I left the key, didn't I? And I called up to him, to say I was going . . .' He shook his head impatiently. 'He's gone back to sleep, that's all, and never heard us – you know what his hearing is like. I'll go up and see.'

We were not invited, but Jesperson was not one to let that stop him, and I followed. There were two doors at the top of the stairs, one either side of the landing; the one on the right was slightly ajar. Balmer knocked, then pushed it open. For a moment he stared, his mouth open for words that never came. As he rushed inside, we saw the cause of his shock.

There was a man lying face-down on the carpet: a tall man,

shirtless, wearing only his trousers, socks and shoes. One arm had been flung out to one side, the other hung down straight.

Mr Balmer crouched beside the fallen figure, between him and an unmade bed.

'Dad? Can you hear me? Oh, no—'

Jesperson went to him and offered his assistance. 'Here, help me lift him onto the bed.'

Together, the two men transferred the motionless man from the floor onto the bed, turning him so he lay on his back. Blue eyes stared sightlessly from a mottled, livid face, above a mouth opened in a silent cry.

'Is he dead?' Balmer asked in a whisper.

Jesperson pressed two fingers against Leary's neck, moved them to another spot, then lifted one of the man's arms and felt his wrist in search of a pulse. As he looked back down, his eyebrows shot up in surprise, but I did not understand what he had seen to cause such a reaction.

'Your glass, please, Miss Lane.'

I fumbled with my reticule, extracted the compact mirror and handed it to Jesperson, who held the glass over the open mouth for a few long seconds. After examining it, he shook his head. 'I am very sorry, Mr Balmer. Your father-in-law is dead. His death most likely occurred some little while ago – I take it you heard nothing, no cry, no sound of a fall during the night? No? The flexibility of his limbs suggests it was no earlier than yesterday afternoon, no later than early this morning. The *rigor mortis* has set in around the muscles of his eyes and mouth and in his neck, but it has not yet spread to the larger muscles.'

Balmer stared at him. 'Are you a doctor, then, Mr Jesperson?'

'No, but I do know something of physiology, and the effects death has on the body.'

'Why did he die? He was perfectly well when – we had breakfast together yesterday morning. Yesterday! What could have caused it? He is – he was a big, strong man, and never complained of any illness.'

Jesperson took a step back from the bed. 'As I told you, I am not a doctor. That judgement must be made by a qualified physician.'

'Yes of course.' Still shaking his head in disbelief, he smoothed his hair back from his face. 'A doctor. I must fetch a doctor. But first – oh, poor, dear Louise! Such a shock—'

Muttering to himself, Balmer backed out of the room and a moment later we heard his heavy tread on the stairs, slowing as, I imagined, he tried to think how to break the sad news to his wife.

Jesperson looked around the room with his quick, sharp gaze before turning his attention back to the body on the bed. 'Look here,' he said, lifting one of the arms and indicating the underside of the wrist.

'It is rather badly bruised, but I can't see how that could have anything—'

'Look more closely. Don't you see it?'

I forced myself to move closer to the dead man and to

concentrate. Almost hidden by the discolouration were two small red marks. I had seen spider bites that looked similar, and said so.

'That bite came from something much bigger than a spider. That is a snake bite.'

I knew that adders might be encountered in the wilder parts of Hampstead Heath, but surely this man could not have failed to notice if he had been bitten, and in any case, the bite of an adder was not invariably fatal, especially to a big, healthy adult. His response, if bitten by an adder, must have been to seek help at once, and if he couldn't get to a doctor immediately, he might have made a tourniquet to stop the poison spreading, not simply gone home and waited to die.

Jesperson looked perplexed by my logical argument. 'Who said anything about adders, or Hampstead Heath?'

'Adders are the only poisonous snakes native to Britain. Unless you mean to suggest that Mr Leary kept exotic reptiles . . . ?'

'Not *him* – but someone must. Look.' He went to the window, which was open about six inches, and rattled the sash to indicate that it was fixed. 'A thief could not enter, but the opening is large enough for a cobra.'

From below came a sound, a high, sad cry: Mrs Balmer, mourning the loss of her father, and I felt uncomfortable, an unwanted witness to grief and loss. Setting aside my bafflement about my partner's suggestion for the cause of this man's death, I said, with quiet urgency, 'We should go.'

He set his jaw. 'Not until I hear what the doctor has to say.'

'Do you expect him to agree with your diagnosis?'

'It is the only possible explanation. Death follows within thirty minutes to an hour after a bite from a cobra, and it is likely to be hastened by fear.'

'A *cobra*?' As always, his confidence was compelling, but I felt nonetheless there must be some other, more likely, explanation. Still, I saw no point in arguing at this point. 'We should go. They do not know us and they do not want us here at this unhappy time. There is nothing more we can do. Let us leave now, and—'

'Please don't go,' said Mr Balmer from the doorway. 'I must fetch a doctor, and I hate to leave Louise alone just now. Please, Miss Lane, might I ask you, as a favour, to go downstairs and sit with my wife – only until I return – I will not long detain you both.'

I was surprised that he should choose me, a stranger, over the woman next door – but perhaps she was no friend to them. 'Of course, I am very happy to stay, if she wishes me to.'

Mr Balmer left, promising to be as quick as he could, and I went into the kitchen, where Louise Balmer was sitting at the table with her head sunk into her hands. I could see she was shaking slightly, and the kettle was already boiling fiercely, so I set about preparing a pot of tea. By the time the tea was ready, Mrs Balmer's bout of tears had passed and she had dried her eyes.

'Your friend,' she started hesitantly.

'Mr Jesperson – he is upstairs. Shall I fetch him?'

'No – let him stay, please. If he doesn't mind. I meant to ask if he would stay with my father – only until the doctor arrives with my husband . . . only, I wouldn't want him to be . . .'

I assured her that her father would not be left alone, and thought how fortunate it was that her wishes should accord so neatly with Mr Jesperson's own desire.

'You are very kind – he is very kind. Oh, both of you are so kind to stay. This is such a shock. I cannot believe it. My father was never ill. He has always been strong and active, he's had hardly a day of illness in his life. He would have been sixty in August. Oh, I cannot believe he is gone!' She paused to draw a deep, shuddering breath, then turned to me with wide eyes, her mood abruptly altered.

'Do you think – could there have been some mistake? Perhaps, when the doctor comes, he will say it is not so, that my father is only sleeping or . . . or in a trance. I have heard of such things . . . There might be a way to bring him out of it – there might be something he can do, some medicine or procedure?' She looked at me so hopefully, I was almost tempted to encourage her dream, but no words came, and in my silence she heard the truth. She bit her lip, tears welling up again.

'Here, let me pour the tea,' I said, anxious to distract, and adding some milk, 'I will give you plenty of sugar – you have had a very great shock. Or perhaps some brandy—?'

'No, no I never touch spirits,' she said quickly, but like a good girl, she stirred the sugar I had prescribed into her tea, and after a few sips of the sweet, hot beverage, she rallied and began to tell me about her father. Despite her very real grief at his passing, it seemed she had not known him very well, for in his younger days, he had been a sailor, spending most of his time away at sea. She was grown up by the time he settled down in London and took a job at the British Museum.

'After my mother died, I wanted him to come live with us – we have plenty of room, not having been blessed with children – but Dad liked his job too much, and we thought he would stay there forever. It was a great surprise when he turned up to tell us he'd handed in his notice. He said he'd be working for a gentleman not far away, in Highgate – not nights but days, for better money.'

'What sort of work?'

'All sorts: odd jobs about the house, running errands, tending to the garden. The gentleman's wife was an invalid. When I heard that she had died, a few weeks ago, I thought he might say his services were no longer required, but Dad chuckled and told me not to worry. He said he had made himself indispensable. That's what he said, his exact words: "You may not think it, Ouisie, but he cannot do without me. I have made myself indispensable to his comfort."' She sighed, then gave a little start and covered her mouth with her hand. 'Oh dear!'

I leaned in towards her. 'What is it?'

'Mr Henderson.'

I felt a little shock along my nerves, for I could not help but connect Patrick Leary's Mr Henderson with the Englishman who had fainted at the unwrapping of a mummy in Egypt. Was it coincidence? Or could it possibly be the same man?

Mrs Balmer was still talking. '—will be expecting my father as usual, next week. Perhaps even today, although unless there is something special he had to do, usually he has Saturday as well as Sunday off. He will have to be told – but I do not know his address.'

'Perhaps it is amongst your father's papers,' I said, trying to be helpful, but she gave me an odd look.

'Papers? What do you mean? He could not write – he could sign his name, but nothing more. In any case, there was no need – he always had a good memory, did Dad. Only when he was away would he pay someone to write letters to my mother for him.'

I made an attempt to apologise for my thoughtless remark, but she was too much caught up in memories of her father to care. 'He always thought of us,' she said sadly. 'And now, look, I was not even here when he died. We do not know how it happened, but he was all alone. How terrible for him – if only I had been here! Why did I go away? I should never have gone. My sister could have come here, instead. I should have been here.'

'Mrs Balmer, you mustn't blame yourself. There is no way you could have known – you have told me he was in good health; there was no intimation of mortality. Even if you had been here, what could you have done?' Hearing my own words, I felt a pang of regret, for I did not wish to add to her pain. Perhaps she would rather feel guilty for going away than to accept how utterly helpless she, like all of us, really was in the face of death.

'I know you are right,' she said sadly, 'but I always imagined myself at his bedside, being with him as he died. And I thought that at the end we would say things to each other . . . important things . . . he might tell me something he was never able to say before . . .'

Dr Guelph, a local physician, was a stout, fashionably dressed young man whose most striking feature was a long, magnificently drooping sable-black moustache.

Mr Balmer led the way upstairs and I followed with Mrs Balmer, who was still clutching my hand.

We crowded together in the little room, watching the doctor conduct his post mortem examination, generally a fairly cursory affair, meant only to establish the fact of death. He took a stethoscope from his bag and listened to Mr Leary's unmoving chest, then turned to checking pulse points and holding a glass to the mouth as Jesperson had done. Finally, he peered into the corpse's wide, staring eyes before gently closing them.

Straightening up and turning to his waiting audience, the doctor confirmed that Mr Leary had been dead for several hours at least, and, given his state of semi-undress, suggested it was most likely he had died either just before retiring last night, or shortly after arising that morning. The cause of death, he said, was 'heart failure'.

We had heard that one before, when murder was not suspected, and as Mr Jesperson liked to say, everyone died of heart failure. The real question was: what had caused the heart to fail?

Mrs Balmer protested, 'My father did not have a weak heart – he never complained of any pains, or breathlessness – he was perfectly well when my husband saw him yesterday – was he not, my love?' She looked appealing at Mr Balmer, who nodded gravely in agreement.

'You may be grateful your father was such a strong and vigorous man, Mrs Balmer,' said the doctor. 'He was not enfeebled by age. But he was not young. And in a man of his age, very often the first heart attack is the one that kills. I understand how you feel. Your loss is unexpected, but I assure you, it was as natural and inevitable as the grief you now feel. I hope you may take some comfort in knowing that he did not suffer. Death came swiftly.'

He replaced his instruments and snapped his bag shut just as Jesperson asked, 'I wonder what you made of those marks on his wrist, Doctor?'

The doctor looked up in surprise, but instead of answering at once, he lifted one of Mr Leary's arms. 'I see nothing unusual.'

'On the other arm.'

Dr Guelph put down that arm and examined the other. He frowned. 'There is some bad bruising, certainly. Perhaps it came about when he fell – you said you found him face-down on the floor? – and then aggravated by post-mortem lividity. It is of no significance.'

'But – the bite-marks?'

Thinned lips showed his impatience, but the doctor returned his gaze to the veins at the wrist. 'I see what you mean. Yes, it could be a bite. A spider, perhaps. Or a cat scratched him, or he was caught by thorns. Mr Balmer, did you not tell me your father-in-law had recently been tending a garden? As there is no sign of infection, he will have received the wounds recently. But there is no reason to connect that incident, whatever it may have been, with his death. Mr Leary was felled by a heart attack, as any man of his age might be.'

Rather to my surprise, Mr Jesperson did not argue, but before we left the house, Jesperson asked Mr Balmer if he knew the address of his father-in-law's employer. 'I thought we might pay him a visit.'

'To inform him of the death? That would be kind of you,' Mr Balmer replied, but he was shaking his head. 'All I know of the gentleman is that he lives in a villa with a walled garden, near the cemetery.'

As we walked back to the tram-stop, I asked Jesperson if he had changed his mind about the cause of death.

He looked at me in surprise. 'How can you think so? *You* saw the marks as clearly as I. That was made by no spider or insect; it was unmistakeably the bite from a snake whose venom is fatal. Death would have happened within the hour.'

'But – *death by cobra*? In *London*? I can see how an *adder* might have attacked him, perhaps, but – no, it is too unlikely!'

He grinned at me. 'What is this fixation you have with adders?'

'What other snake would a man be likely to encounter in Hampstead?'

'The very worst kind – a human viper,' was his crisp reply. 'You appear to be clinging to the notion that Leary's death was natural or accidental, but I can assure you, it was neither. I am certain he was murdered, and the murder weapon was the deadliest of snakes. An unusual weapon, I will grant you, but not unlikely. For someone who had access to deadly snakes, it would be far easier to use one of his charges to do its deadly work while the human villain remains above suspicion, for I have no doubt he will be able to prove he was nowhere near the victim at the time of death.'

'But where would someone get such a deadly snake?'

'From one of Jamrach's menageries – or Wombwell's, or from Cross – surely you have seen the Exeter Exchange in the Strand? All of them – and there are many others – supply private customers as well as institutions.'

'I know there are cobras in the zoo in Regent's Park, but stealing one seems rather risky,' I said. 'But if you think the murderer may be a collector of serpents, or the owner of a small menagerie, we might look for someone like that who may have had some connection to the late Mr Leary. But why did you say nothing about this to Dr Guelph?' As usual, the length of his stride was forcing me to scurry to keep up.

'Because I did not wish to be sneered at and patronised. And imagine how poor Mrs Balmer would feel if I declared her father had been deliberately killed. I though it better to hold my tongue, at least until we have sufficient evidence to take to the police.'

CHAPTER EIGHT

The Return of Mr Henderson

There were letters to be written and some minor household matters to be attended to when we returned to Gower Street, so Mr Jesperson and I found no opportunity to discuss the death of Mr Leary until after dinner.

As we sat together in the front room in our usual seats at our big desk, I asked, 'Do you really think it was murder?' It was more as a way of beginning the conversation than because I had any real doubt.

'Unless you can make a convincing case for how Leary could have been *accidentally* bitten by a deadly snake in the normal course of things . . . and following that, how he came to die alone in his room . . . I am haunted by the suspicion that Leary himself stole a cobra, but why should he do such a thing?' He rested his chin in his hands and gazed moodily at nothing. 'Balmer described his father-in-law's job as a sort of general household help and handyman – you'd think if there were exotic snakes on the premises, Leary would have talked about it at home.'

Letting his hands fall, he sat up straighter. 'It is unfortunate that we don't have an address. How "near" is "near the cemetery", I wonder? Well, we shall just have to make the rounds, keeping a sharp eye out for walled gardens. It may not take long, if we are lucky.'

'But . . . won't it be listed in the Post Office directory?' I spoke tentatively, for it was so unlikely that this obvious course for finding Mr Henderson's address had not immediately presented itself to my partner.

He gave me a long-suffering look.

I stared back, boldly. 'Well?'

He sighed. 'That is not a useful suggestion.'

'You mean you have already tried?'

'I *mean*, there is no point.'

'You think Henderson would not be listed?'

His gaze sharpened. 'Henderson? What makes you think—?'

'Mrs Balmer said that was his name.'

His eyes blazed. 'And you never thought to tell me?'

'And you never thought to ask?' Indignant as I was that he should make this my fault, I felt guilty enough to try to justify my omission. 'After all, you had been speaking to Mr Balmer yourself – when I heard you ask for the address, but not the name, I quite naturally assumed you had already ascertained that fact.'

Jesperson gave a groan that turned into a laugh and he smote himself lightly on the forehead. 'And I knew you had been sitting with Mrs Balmer all the while I was having a jolly good look around the room upstairs. *Of course* while sympathising with her you would also be asking questions. Just because *Mr* Balmer knew so little, it does not follow that Leary's daughter would not know more about her father's new job.' He smiled at me in apology. 'It is too late to go charging off to Highgate tonight. Tomorrow morning we'll beard Henderson in his den.'

My heart beat a little faster. 'Do you think him the murderer?'

'I think we had best hang fire on that question. What else did Mrs Balmer say?'

'Not much. It was strange to hear that name so soon after you told me about the man you saw in Egypt. And . . . she did say he had hired her father because Mr Henderson spent most of his time caring for his sick wife, who died a few weeks ago, and I remember you said *your* Mr Henderson's wife was an invalid . . .'

'And yet Leary, for all he might have been an excellent night-watchman, had no experience of domestic service or gardening,' Jesperson added thoughtfully. 'Did she tell you how her father met his new employer?'

'No – but something she said did strike me. She had been worried when her father told her that Mrs Henderson was dead, that the gentleman would no longer require his services, but he'd laughed and told her, "I have made myself indispensable to his comfort."'

Our eyes met.

'You think he hired Leary to keep him quiet?' he murmured.

'And then found it was not enough? Now he'll be quiet forever,' I said, while thinking that blackmail and murder were too

98

extreme to make sense of a theft that was, on first sight at least, little more than a foolish prank. Could it be that the mummy was far more valuable than Mr Budge imagined? Perhaps there had been gold coins and precious jewels sewn into its dressings?

'There is something much deeper here than we know,' said Jesperson gravely, echoing my own thoughts. 'Our first clue led us to Leary, and he has led us to a man named Henderson, who may have a direct connection to an Egyptian mummy – but we are still very near the start of this maze, and somehow, I do not think that Mr Henderson will prove to be the monster lurking at its heart.'

The next morning, after consulting the Post Office Directory, we set off for Temple House, Swains Lane, Highgate.

Swains Lane took its name, so Mr Jesperson informed me, from its use in centuries past by swineherds driving their pigs from the countryside to the London markets. It was now the location of the main entrance to Highgate Cemetery. For much of its length it was like a steep, narrow alleyway, bordered on one and sometimes both sides by the high stone walls that enclosed the cemetery grounds. It looked less like a place where people lived and rather more a path for visiting the dead; however, there were in fact several fine houses on Swains Lane, just around the corner from the Highgate Literary and Scientific Institution, which was itself hidden from the casual view of passers-by by tall walls of red brick.

Mr Henderson's house was identified by a blue and white enamel plate on the gate.

'I wonder what temple he had in mind?' Jesperson mused as he pushed open the gate to a modest two-storey home of comfortable appearance made of the same red brick as the wall shielding it from the road. In front of the house was a slightly overgrown lawn dotted with dandelions and daisies, several young trees and a few flowering shrubs. There was nothing remotely threatening or sinister about the place, which did not appear to be an abode of serpents.

The man who answered the door was middle-aged, of medium height but rather heavyset, with a receding hairline above a long, clean-shaven, hollow-cheeked face. His sad dark eyes and a melancholy aspect were made more pronounced by the fact that he was dressed in full mourning.

'Mr Henderson?'

'May I help you?' His look was wary, and not welcoming.

'My name is Jesperson; this is my colleague, Miss Lane. We have been referred to you by our mutual friend, Wallis Budge. If it is convenient, I hoped we might speak with you, but if you had rather make it another time . . .'

Mr Henderson visibly relaxed. 'Budgie sent you? Then you are not some type of evangelicals?'

Jesperson laughed out loud at that. 'Whatever made you think so?'

Mr Henderson gave a dry little snort in return. 'Well, they do tend to come in pairs, and there has been a rash of them lately. I should have instantly realised that for all you are a pair, you do not fit the mould – I see no cases filled with tracts, and neither of you have that prim, self-congratulatory air of salvation about you.' He stepped back, opening the door wide. 'Please, do come in.'

We followed him from the little entrance hall into a long, shadowy room that put me in mind of a church. It was dimly lit by small flickering candles set about in various places and the curtains over the windows were draped so that daylight entered only in three narrow bars. The air was smoky, and filled with a strange spicy, cloying scent. I thought of the name Mr Henderson had given his home: Temple House.

'Oh, I beg your pardon – this must look very strange to you,' he said, and quickly crossed the room to part the draperies on the tall windows. 'But it is Sunday, you see. My wife was a pious church-goer; I am not, and it would be hypocritical of me to pretend, or to attend services only as a way of feeling closer to her. But I do pray, in my own way, and I find that candles and incense help create an atmosphere in which I can conjure her memory and remember her as she was in life.'

I followed his gaze to the wall above the fireplace, where there hung an almost life-sized portrait of a pretty, gently smiling woman. On the mantelpiece below it, votive candles flickered, flanking a row of half a dozen silver-framed photographs. I was standing too far away to make out the subjects, but it was easy enough to guess.

A feeling of pity for this bereft man welled up inside me, and I felt ashamed for having imagined him to be not merely a thief, but a heartless killer. 'I am so sorry,' I said impulsively. 'Please forgive us for intruding on you in your grief.'

Jesperson shot me a look of annoyance, but said in a soft, ingratiating voice, 'Please accept our condolences and deepest sympathy for your loss. Perhaps we have come at a bad time . . . ?'

'Not at all, not at all. It has been only two weeks since Mrs Henderson passed over, but her journey to death was a long, slow one. I shall never cease to mourn her loss, but do not think for a moment you are intruding,' he said, looking directly at me. 'I do not often have company, and I am grateful for the distraction. Please, won't you be seated?'

Illuminated by daylight, the room no longer had the look of a church, but rather resembled a museum. Two walls were lined with glass-fronted cases filled with Egyptian antiquities, too many to take in at a glance. The furniture was chiefly made of some dark, heavy wood. I saw a table with legs carved into the likeness of bird-headed men, and chairs so profusely decorated that they looked like ancient thrones. Instead of the cushioned seat I should have preferred, I sat upon a hard, high-backed wooden settle, the only concession to comfort being some rather primitive-looking woven rugs draped along the back.

Mr Jesperson continued to prowl around, examining the room's contents as if visiting a museum, peering first at a marble sphinx on the hearth, then at a set of canopic jars, before fetching up before the obvious *pièce de résistance*: a full-sized, brilliantly coloured and gilded mummy case that stood in a corner of the room.

'Wonderful,' he said, standing before it, his hands clasped behind his back. 'But not as old as the other pieces in your collection, I see – and of a very different provenance.'

'You have a good eye,' said Mr Henderson, looking surprised. 'What gave it away?'

'Her face.'

There *was* something about the face – it was less mask-like and more individual than many of the painted sarcophagi I had seen, but something else about it nagged at me, the certainty that I had seen it before.

As Jesperson asked, 'What did your devout, church-going wife think of it?' understanding burst upon me.

'It was not the first time she accused me of idolatry,' Mr Henderson replied, 'but she understood it was all part of my love for her and did not really mind. Her only stipulation was that the artist should not paint her as she was then. She wished, with pardonable vanity, to be remembered not as she had looked so near the end of her earthly life, but as she was in the early years of our marriage. The artist used that portrait upon the wall as his source.' He pointed at the symbols painted along the sides. 'And those rows of hieroglyphics tell the story of our life together.'

'It is a beautiful tribute,' said Jesperson quietly, backing away from the case.

'Thank you. Now, tell me, why have you come to visit this old hermit? Do you wish to see something in my collection? It is really not so special, not compared to others. What is your connection to Wallis Budge? Why did he send you here?'

'*Mrrrouw?*'

The unexpected high-pitched cry made us all turn as one towards the doorway, where a large tabby cat stood staring at us with wide yellow eyes, tail lashing from side to side. One front paw was lifted, as if it was hesitating, deciding whether to come in.

Mr Henderson, clearly familiar with the animal, spoke in a tone of gentle rebuke. 'Mewki! How did you get in here?'

'He is with me, Uncle. Did you know you had left your door open? You really must— Oh!' The speaker who had come into view behind the cat stopped suddenly, the smile on her face freezing at the sight of strangers. She was very beautiful, very much in the Pre-Raphaelite style, elegantly tall, with masses of long, curly golden hair, large dreaming eyes and full red lips. Despite her height and womanly figure, I could see that she was still a girl, barely sixteen, I would have guessed, if that.

'Open? Wide open? Or just ajar? I pushed it shut – perhaps it didn't catch.' Mr Henderson spoke rapidly, sounding a little fretful. 'There is something wrong with that door; I think the wood never dried out after all that rain last month. I told Leary to plane it down or find some other way to fix the problem, but he has done nothing as yet. I shall have to remind him again tomorrow – if he bothers to show up. He has become very lax of late. You saw him on Friday, did you not? He went away in the afternoon and never came back. I thought he must come yesterday to make up for those lost hours, but there has been no sign of him, and no explanation. Oh, why am I telling you all this? Forgive me – and do come in, my dear. The cat can stay.' When she didn't move, he repeated, 'Why don't you come in?'

'No, I won't,' she said softly, 'not when you have company. I came only to remind you dinner will be ready at two o'clock.'

'You are too kind, but I have imposed too often of late.'

The girl stamped one dainty little foot and I was abruptly put in mind of another artist, not a Pre-Raphaelite, but Sir John Tenniel, the famous cartoonist and illustrator whose depictions of Alice and her odd companions in Lewis Carroll's books had engraved themselves upon the public imagination. This girl could have been a more grown-up version of Alice herself, accompanied by an unsmiling Cheshire Cat.

I turned to my partner, hoping to catch his eye, but he did not notice, for his attention was fully transfixed by the scene framed by the doorway. On his face was an expression I had never seen before. I felt a sudden queer sensation, as if I had lost something.

'I am not being kind, and you never impose,' exclaimed the girl crossly. 'Grandmama insists. Cook always makes too much, especially on Sunday – she doesn't know how to prepare meals for two ladies with small appetites.' Her voice took on a wheedling tone as she added, 'We *need* you, Uncle. *Please.*'

His mournful face softened into a reluctant smile. 'Very well, Matilda. Tell your grandmother I shall be there at two o'clock.'

The girl scooped the cat into her arms and they were gone, leaving only the heavy sound of a door being firmly shut.

'It must be a comfort to you, having family living nearby,' I said, to break the silence.

'I have no family.'

'Was that not your niece?'

'Oh no.' A faint flush crept into the pallid face. 'I am "Uncle" only by courtesy. That young lady is a neighbour, an orphan who came to live with her grandmother a few years ago. We have no children of our own and a fond affection developed between my dear Emma and the girl, who often came to visit her, always with little gifts of fruit and flowers, and for ever reading to her. She always brought a ray of sunshine into the sick room. And as you have seen, she continues to take care of me – she says it is what Emma would have wanted.'

He looked down, frowning. 'But never mind that. Let us get on to whatever business it is that has brought you here.'

'You are a friend of Mr Budge,' said Jesperson.

'We have been acquainted for several years – what is that to you?'

'I mean, you are not one of those he would classify as an enemy.'

'Certainly not.'

'Unlike your man Leary.'

His eyes widened. 'What is this about? First you speak of Mr Budge, now it's Leary?'

'Patrick Leary used to work at the British Museum. Unlike you, he was no friend to Mr Budge. He remained ever-loyal to Peter le Page Renouf, who bitterly opposed Budge's promotion.'

'What has any of that to do with me?'

'You hired Leary, did you not?'

'Yes, to help me around the house and in the garden – not for his politics.'

'Why him? He was a Navy man, not someone with experience as a gardener.'

'I wish I had found such a man,' he retorted. 'As it turns out, Leary has not been entirely reliable. If it is he you want, you will not find him here. You had better seek him at his daughter's house. I can give you the address—' He was already moving towards the writing bureau, clearly wanting to draw this conversation to an end.

'You misunderstand, sir. We are not looking for Mr Leary. We know his whereabouts, and his fate. Mr Leary passed away quite suddenly on Friday evening.'

Mr Henderson started in surprise. His mouth sagged open. 'Friday! And I spoke ill of him for not coming back – he must have been taken ill – but he said nothing to me about feeling unwell – indeed, he was a man who generally enjoyed rude good health. Forgive me.' He sat down hard on one of the throne-like chairs and covered his face with his hands for a moment. Then, looking up at Jesperson he whispered, 'Was I too hard on him? Did I ask him to do too much? He never complained.'

If this man was a murderer, he was a most accomplished actor, I thought.

'His death was not caused by over-work,' Jesperson replied

coolly. 'It was heart failure, according to the physician. It was sudden and came without warning.'

'I see.' Then, in denial of his own words, he shook his head. 'But I do *not* see at all why you have come to me to ask about Leary – or anything else. Did Mr Budge really give you my name?'

'No,' said Jesperson, beginning to prowl about the room, 'not *your* name, specifically. Mr Budge hired us – Miss Lane and I are private investigators – he hired us to find out who was behind a prank – or something he *presumed* to be a prank, engineered by one of his enemies as a malevolent joke. But call it what he will, it is nonetheless theft.'

'He suspected Leary?'

'Yes. I need not tell you the reasons why. We went to his daughter's house, but he was already dead and thus beyond questioning, unable to tell us how to recover the thing he had taken. His daughter told us you had hired him.' As he spoke, Jesperson continued his restless perambulation around the room, sometimes nearer, sometimes further away from the man he addressed.

The pallor of Mr Henderson's face had increased, and tiny beads of perspiration stood out upon his brow. 'You say that as if – as if I employed him to play a prank on Mr Budge? No! I would never do such a thing – why would I? I wish him no harm – I am not his enemy, and whatever you may think of Leary, he was not the sort of man to steal from the great institution where he worked for so many years.'

'It does not matter which one of you took it, or why. What I care about now is getting it back.' As he spoke, Jesperson darted at the painted sarcophagus.

With a wordless cry, Mr Henderson tried to block him, but my friend was ahead of him. Seizing hold of the painted lid, he pulled it away. Despite its size and appearance, it was as light as a theatrical prop and came off easily in his hands, revealing the mummy nestled inside.

CHAPTER NINE

An Interesting Encounter

Jesperson smiled triumphantly as he posed like a showman exhibiting the main attraction. 'Will you explain *this* as the work of a clever local artisan? Is it not, in fact, a genuine mummy – and the property of the British Museum?'

With a low moan, Mr Henderson staggered back, clutched for support at the nearest bit of furniture and landed beside me on the hard settle seat.

Startled, I jumped up and moved out of his reach as his shoulders slumped and his head sank into his hands. Although he looked a helpless, defeated man, I thought of Mr Leary and went to stand beside my partner, who was looking stern.

'I suppose you hired Leary to be your inside man. Never mind your protest that he would never steal from the great institution of which he had been a part—'

Henderson's head jerked up. 'You have no right to call it *stealing*. The so-called owner of the remains was a thief himself – or at the very least, he was willing to purchase from thieves and grave-robbers. On top of that, he had made up his mind not merely to desecrate, but to destroy the corpse. No, no, I am neither a petty thief nor a prankster. I acted from the most pure and noble motive: to save her body from the dreadful fate he had in store for her.'

He groaned again. 'And now you will deliver her unto a minion of Mammon. You too must be worshipers of Mammon if you believe in the terrible rights of *ownership*. Does money put anyone, everyone, above the demands of religion, of morality, of common humanity and life itself?'

Jesperson appeared to give this argument serious consideration. After a moment, he said, his voice a little less harsh, 'I understand what you say, but there is no life here, Mr Henderson, only the earthly remains of someone who once lived. That is no more than the empty shell of what was once a living human being.'

'Was once, and might be again!' Henderson almost shouted. 'There was a reason why the ancient Egyptians devoted so much time and energy to the preservation of dead bodies. It was because, like us, they believed every living being has a soul – a potentially immortal soul – which survives the death of the body. Their conception of the soul was different from ours, for they divided it into five parts – but who are we to say they were wrong? And they believed most sincerely that the soul could be reborn to live again, but in order for that to happen, the body *must* be preserved. Budge knows that very well, and still he is willing to commit murder, to risk the destruction of a still-living soul.'

I was certain, hearing Mr Henderson speak and seeing the anguish etched into his face, that he absolutely believed what he said. I remembered Mr Budge's brief burst of annoyance at 'those people' who objected to the desecration of long-dead bodies, and suspected he had had this man in mind.

'I tried to stop it,' Henderson said sadly. 'I tried to save her, and I failed.' He sighed. 'I am done for, but what does it matter? What does anything matter, since my dearest Emma is gone? So what if my reputation is destroyed, if I end my days in a gaol cell—'

Jesperson's voice cracked like a whip, cutting short Mr Henderson's lament. 'Tell me about Patrick Leary.'

Henderson looked up, blinking. 'Tell you what?'

'What was his involvement?'

'You have said it. He was the inside man.' He gestured vaguely with both hands. 'He had the keys, he knew the best time to take it out . . .'

'You worked together?'

'I waited outside by the back entrance with my trap. He brought the mummy out, wrapped in a canvas sheet. He returned to his usual work and I drove home. It was three o'clock in the morning; there were no witnesses and no trouble.'

'And afterwards,' Jesperson prompted, when the man fell silent, 'you gave Leary a job.'

'He thought it best to resign his position. Maybe he felt guilty, afraid of being named a criminal. I had managed to convince him it was not really a crime, you see. He saw it as a blow against Budge, who kept the mummy in his office as if it were his private property. I had explained to him that it never would be part of a public display in the Museum because Budge intended to dissect her and dispose of the remains. He thought it was a great joke on the man he secretly despised. Afterwards—'

Jesperson continued where Mr Henderson had left off. 'Afterwards, he blackmailed you.'

'No!' The dark, mournful eyes widened with shock. 'Never! I am sure he never considered it – in any case, he was quite sharp enough to realise he could not threaten me without exposing himself, and he would most likely get the lion's share of the blame if it did come out.'

'Of course, Mr Budge – and probably the court – would have more sympathy for a gentleman like you,' Jesperson said with distaste. 'So what did you mean by "afterwards"?'

Henderson sighed. 'He began to speak of returning the mummy. He liked the idea that Budge should be shown up on stage, before a great crowd, when he opened the case to find it empty. But after that, he maintained it ought to be returned to the Museum, where it belonged. He thought the joke would be even better if Budge went in to his office to find the mummy waiting for him, perhaps resting in his chair.' His lips thinned in disapproval.

'That might have been somewhat difficult to accomplish, I would have thought, since he no longer had easy access to Mr Budge's office,' I suggested.

'Oh, this was before he left their employ. It was only when

I refused to countenance such a plan that he decided he would have to give up his position. He said he could move in with his daughter and look for work locally, which was when I suggested that if he was handy, there was some work in my garden and about the house that needed doing.' He sighed. 'Poor Leary! He was willing enough, but a bit of a bodger, and awfully slow about the simplest of tasks. I thought it was laziness, but now . . . now I wish I had been more sympathetic. He must have already been feeling the weakness that would kill him.'

'You know you must return the mummy,' Jesperson said. 'I think Mr Budge will be sympathetic if you make amends, and if you can explain what drove you to this desperate act. Can you explain?'

Henderson stared past him at the mummy and his features softened. 'I do not know if you can understand it, but something happened, the first time I saw her. When Budge opened the coffin and I looked, I had a strange thought – it was almost like a voice whispered in my ear, saying, *You must save her.* Budgie was telling me about the mystery, that no one knew who this mummy had been, or why it had been hidden in a secret chamber – and all of a sudden, I knew *everything.* Somehow, I was certain the mummy had been a female of royal birth, married to a pharaoh who was too young to rule on his own, and that she had been caught up in a power struggle and murdered. Her supporters managed to spirit away her body in time, and they performed all the necessary rites and procedures for its preservation before they hid it. If they had not done so, her enemies would have destroyed the body in addition to wiping out every mention of her name in the public records, thus ensuring that she would be forgotten and that her soul could never be reborn. That would have been even more cruel and extreme than her initial murder.

'But she had been saved, kept safe for millennia – only for a man I had considered to be my friend deciding to undo all that good work by unwrapping the body, dismembering and dissecting it and thus ensuring her final, absolute and total destruction, not for political reasons, not because he had any cause to hate her, but simply out of curiosity.'

He seemed to shrink into himself and his voice grew softer as he murmured, 'I saw it happen once. I witnessed an unwrapping when I was in Egypt, years ago. I know how destructive it can be. It was a dreadful thing . . . I could not let it happen to her . . .'

We waited, but he had come to the end of his confession.

At last, I said, 'I understand your feelings about the ancient princess, Mr Henderson – but why steal those animal mummies?'

'What?' He blinked at me, pulled out of his reverie and clearly bewildered by the question.

'Some small animal mummies are also missing from the Museum's storeroom.'

'That has nothing to do with me.'

'What about the stolen papyri?'

That question did strike home, for he blanched.

'You do know,' said Jesperson sharply. 'You took them.'

'It wasn't stealing—'

'You were saving them too, I suppose?'

'I only borrowed them,' he said defensively. 'I suppose I should not have taken them, but Budgie had let me borrow things before, and it was only because these were not catalogued that he wouldn't agree . . . but I took good care of them, and I had them for only a few days before I returned them.'

'Oh? What about the iron *tyet?* And will you say you only "borrowed" this mummy, too, when you return it? As long as we are on the subject, is there anything else you would like to confess to having taken without permission?'

Mr Henderson scowled. 'You are coming very near to libel, sir.'

'I think a self-confessed "borrower" has no grounds for complaint. Come, come. Is there anything else in your possession that belongs to the British Museum?'

'Nothing,' he said sullenly, adding, 'and not even the mummy, in my opinion. It was taken without permission and transported out of Egypt by grave-robbing thieves.'

At first, when caught out as a thief, Henderson had been cowed, but he was regaining confidence, which I thought might lead to trouble.

Jesperson and I exchanged a look of complicit understanding before he turned the full force of his personality upon Mr Henderson.

'I do take your point, old chap, but as we live not in the pure realm of spirit but in materialistic nineteenth-century London, we must abide by the laws of *this* land. Our job was to find the thief and return the stolen goods. We have done one half of that, and you would be well advised to help us carry out the second. Then, indeed, you may have the right to speak of something "borrowed", rather than stolen.

'We will return it in the way that it was taken, wrapped up – you have something that will do the job? Good, good. It can be transported by trap once again. The Museum is closed today, of course, and that should make it easier. I'll have to wire Budge to meet us at the back entrance, but if he is not at home or cannot otherwise make it, Miss Lane and I are known to the guards. But it will be best if we can keep this between us and Mr Budge. If you will allow us, I think we can manage to explain your actions in a way that should cause him to respond more sympathetically than otherwise. You are not his enemy, you are not a thief and you have not benefitted from what you did in any way. All right? Will you leave that in our hands?' Jesperson had moved closer to the seated man as he spoke and now thrust out his hand.

Mr Henderson took it automatically, and Jesperson hauled him to his feet. 'Good man! Where do you keep your carriage? And the horse?'

'There is a stables nearby – only a few minutes' walk,' he replied, dazedly.

'Good. Let us go – you will not mind Miss Lane waiting here for our return?'

It was obvious from his expression that Mr Henderson minded very much. 'But will you not come out with us, Miss Lane? I should warn you that my trap is only a two-seater, which will make it an uncomfortable journey for three, especially with our immobile passenger. You might prefer to travel back to town by tram or omnibus.'

'Your trap will suffice,' Jesperson said. 'I grant you, my legs are extraordinarily long, but they do bend, you know: I can fold myself up quite comfortably in the back, and I will be on hand to keep the mummy safe and steady.'

'Ah, whatever you say. But if we all go now—'

Dropping his genial tone, Jesperson said, 'This is not a social call, Mr Henderson. We came to find a missing mummy and having found it, it is our duty to keep both it and you under observation until it has been safely returned. You will come with me, and Miss Lane will await us here.'

Moments later, I was alone in the room – yet I did not feel entirely alone; the presence of that immobile, silent human form wrapped in bandages was unsettling. Who had that person been in life? Was she truly, as Mr Henderson imagined, a woman of royal birth who had been murdered as part of a political plot? Or was the cartouche on the coffin case in Mr Budge's office correct and he had been a man with a far more ordinary life?

I resisted the strong urge to replace the lid. When the men returned, they would have to take it off again, and they might suspect the childish fear that had driven me to close it. I told myself not to be silly – after all, how often had I lingered in the Egyptian galleries at the British Museum, passing before the unseeing eyes of the dead without a shudder? This was no different, surely; had I not been struck from the first by how much like a museum this room was?

I prowled around the room, examining objects and works of art from ancient Egypt, and other things in the Egyptian style, but I saw no other mummies of any shape or size, and nowhere they might be hidden, apart from an escritoire in the French Egyptian style, and that was locked.

I examined the keyhole. I did not have the tools, nor Mr Jesperson's skill at lock-picking, but these were simple; a steady hand and a small flat blade of the right size might do it . . .

Some small noise made me turn sharply. The girl – Matilda – froze in the doorway at the sight of me, mouth fallen open and her heavy-lidded eyes wide in surprise.

I was just as startled, but I had more experience in disguising my feelings and sounded perfectly calm when I told her, 'Mr Henderson has had to step out.'

'But I saw . . . that is . . . I saw your – that very tall young man – go past our house, and he was speaking, I thought, to you, but – if Uncle was with him, why are *you* here?' Emboldened, she came into the room as if to confront me.

I moved away from the escritoire, giving it a final glance as if to suggest I had been doing nothing more than admiring the marquetry work. 'They have gone to fetch the horse and trap. Mr Henderson has been called away – he wished me to tell you he may not be back in time to dine with you today.'

Her heavy brows, which were surprisingly dark in contrast with her golden hair and pale skin, came together as she frowned.

'He could not tell us that himself? He let a *stranger* stay alone in his house to tell me? And what if I had not come by?'

'I am certain he would have found another way to let you know.' I gave her a knowing look and a smile. 'I think he guessed you would be along shortly, dying of curiosity about the visitors you did not stay to be introduced to.'

Her cheeks flushed a fetching shade of pink. 'You all looked so very business-like – even a little secretive – that I did not wish to intrude,' she admitted. 'I meant no affront. I apologise. I am Miss Verver.' She thrust one pale, elegantly long-fingered hand at me.

I did not take it, only replied coolly, 'Miss Lane.'

'*Miss* Lane,' she repeated, with extra emphasis and arched eyebrows. 'So that very tall gentleman is not your husband. And I think, from his red hair and general appearance, he is not your brother. Is he your sweetheart?'

I responded coldly. 'Did your governess never instruct you in the finer points of conversational etiquette?'

She drew back as abruptly as if I had slapped her. 'When I had a governess, she encouraged me to ask questions, for how else am I to learn anything?'

I stopped myself asking her how old she was and said instead, 'When you have just met someone, such very personal questions are rude. I supposed you must be younger than you look, which would excuse your lack of social skills.'

'I turned sixteen last month,' she said proudly. Then, her face falling, she added, 'But I have not yet been out in society, and I do not have many friends – none, in truth, not since poor dear Emma passed away.' She swallowed hard.

'Do you refer to Mrs Henderson?'

'Yes, indeed. There was a very close bond between us – we read each other's hearts and I loved her deeply. Maybe I loved her more like a mother, but Emma was the dearest friend I have ever known.' Blinking away tears, she went on, 'If she had not been so ill, I could have learnt more from her. She was so good and gentle, and she cared for me, too. When my last governess said I was impossible to teach, Emma told her that was nonsense. But when the governess left, Grandmama said it would be a waste of money to hire another – she said I had probably learnt as much as I was able – and in any case, what would be the point, for more education will not help me make a better marriage.'

'That sounds very old-fashioned and short-sighted of her,' I said, as calmly as I could, for that attitude, the assumption that marriage should be the only thing on a girl's mind, her only goal and ambition to be some man's wife, easily stirred me to rage. 'Education is important. It matters, whether you marry or no—'

'I shall marry,' she said complacently. 'Of course I shall. And I was never any good at lessons, so I do not mind the lack. I am quite happy never to be required to conjugate French verbs or do long division or name the rivers of Africa ever again.' She sucked in her lower lip, dipped her chin and gazed up at me through her lashes. 'You are not married. Is it rude to ask if you mind? If you are happy as you are?'

I elected to ignore the first half of her question and said warmly, 'I am happy as I am.'

'I am glad.' She dropped the coquettish look. 'I should like to know you better, Miss Lane. Do you think we could be friends, you and I?'

It would have been cruel to be honest, so feeling a hypocrite, I assured her that we could.

'When may I see you again?'

'That may be difficult, for I live a good distance from here and my work keeps me very busy.' I spoke almost without thinking, half my attention on the possible location of the clock I could hear ticking somewhere nearby.

'Work? Why, what is it that you do? Is that what brought you here to see Mr Henderson? Do you have a profession? What is your occupation?' Her eyes sparkled with interest.

At that moment, a little carriage clock on a corner table began to chime the hour and I seized it as an opportunity to escape her questioning. 'You must go now,' I said, and I walked towards her until she was forced to retreat.

'Please, I do want to know,' she said, backing slowly out of the room. 'Or I shall have to ask Mr Henderson!'

I laughed. 'Of course you would. But you might get more details from me if only you can wait until our next meeting.'

'When will that be? Soon, I hope. Will you be calling on Mr Henderson again? When you do, you could call on me – I don't mind if you bring your friend – is that right, should I call him your friend? It is difficult to speak of him otherwise, as I do not know his name.'

We were both in the entrance hall now. 'My friend – who is also my partner in business – is Mr Jesperson.'

'Partner in business.' She imbued the words with awe, pronouncing them as something rare and exotic. 'So, you are in business.' She lowered her voice and leant closer to me. 'Are you a New Woman?'

'That is not a term I would use.'

'Why not?'

'It is a meaningless phrase – or at least, no one agrees on what exactly it means. I believe it was invented by some Grub Street hack. I am a single, independent woman, although as I am not independently wealthy I must depend upon myself and take whatever honest work I can in order to survive.'

'But what is your work? You have not said what you and Mr Jesperson do.'

'I am afraid I do not have the time today.' I opened the front door. 'Good day, Miss Verver.'

'Wait – you haven't said when I shall see you again. Will you write to me?'

'Yes.'

'Please address it to Miss Verver, care of Mrs Munro at The Laurels, Swains Lane, Highgate.'

'I will remember. Run along home now, Matilda Verver, and wait for my letter.'

Shutting the door firmly on her, I went back into the sitting room, where the first thing that caught my eye was the baleful sight of the mummy, erect and exposed in the open case. I realised Matilda had not given it a second glance – nor, indeed, a first. Was it possible she had not noticed it? Or had she seen it before? She had appeared to be far more interested in me than in Mr Henderson's Egyptian collection.

As I waited for Jesperson and Mr Henderson to return, I was moved to examine the contents of the room again, many items displayed under glass as if in a museum. They included a nice collection of amulets, particularly the scarab in a variety of colours. There were also half a dozen tyets, all roughly the same size and all of some reddish material, although I could not make out if it were of stone, clay, wood or glass. Not a single one was metallic – but, then, if the owner of this collection had stolen the iron tyet, would he have put it on display? I felt strongly that if he had been impelled by the acquisitive feelings of a true collector to steal one especially rare example, Mr Henderson would not have been satisfied to hide it away. He would have treated it in exactly the same way as those treasures he had purchased legally – or illegally smuggled out of Egypt; after all, I had no idea under what circumstances he had acquired all his treasures – and put it inside this case where it could be admired.

Mr Henderson did not consider himself a thief, because he could explain the papyri that had cost poor Mr Campbell his job as only 'borrowing', and he had enlisted the aid of Mr Leary to take the mystery mummy for the noble purpose of saving it from destruction. That meant Jesperson was right when he maintained someone else was behind the thefts that Mr Sand had asked us to solve.

The men returned shortly thereafter, carrying a roll of canvas between them. This they spread out on the floor, then Mr Henderson alone lifted the mummy tenderly from its case. There was something so careful, even reverent in the way he handled the swaddled, ancient body that it touched a chord of sympathy within me. Observing how gently he placed it down on the canvas, I felt the truth of his horror at the idea that this once-living human being, however long dead, should be laid out on a table and stripped of its wrappings, all privacy and modesty denied, merely to satisfy the curiosity of people who called themselves scholars, for all they apparently had little true, empathetic understanding of what that life had been for the deceased. In despair because he could do nothing to save the beloved wife who was slipping away from him, soon to be claimed forever by death, unable to take comfort from the religion that said she was going to a better life beyond, had he transferred some of that emotion to the mummy in Mr Budge's office? Had the idea that here was something he *could* save from destruction given rise to the plan he devised with Mr Leary? Unlike death, human designs could be thwarted: a thing could be stolen and kept safe, unlike a loved one in the grip of death.

Imagining myself in his position sent a wave of sympathy through me for this poor man. He had been so devoted to his wife that his life must now feel sad and empty. Without children, with no demands placed on his time by some regular occupation, what would he do? Perhaps he would marry again – many men in his situation married again in haste, often a woman much younger than themselves . . .

Like Matilda, already so at home, here calling him 'Uncle', a naïve young girl who came and went without even bothering to knock. He'd been the husband of her dearest friend, but now that friend – that wife – was gone, would Mr Henderson's avuncular feelings towards her undergo a change? It was entirely possible, I thought, and she, having been raised to believe that the only purpose of her life was to make a 'good' marriage, might be fond and foolish enough to accept her first marriage proposal, from a man more than twice her age . . .

I must write to her without delay. My promise to do so had been given carelessly, but now I was happy to think I might be a positive influence, a better guide than her old grandmother—

'Miss Lane?'

I surfaced from my thoughts to find Jesperson looking at me quizzically. The mummy was tidily wrapped and ready to go.

Although light enough to be carried by one man, the length of the canvas parcel and the need to keep it steady made it a difficult job, so it was as well I was there to deal with doors and gates for them.

Just as we reached the trap, a charabanc went past, pulled by heavy shire horses and filled with holiday-makers on their way . . . to where? I wondered. Did they intend to go picnicking in the cemetery?

'Waterlow Park,' Jesperson murmured as if reading my mind,

looking at the flushed, jolly faces turned our way, smugly pleased by their own leisure and pitying the men who must grapple in the heat with removals on a Sunday.

And then they were past and Jesperson was vaulting easily into the back. He swiftly demonstrated he was every bit as skilled as he had claimed at compressing his long frame into a remarkably small space. I took my seat beneath the sunshade as Mr Henderson picked up the reins and, with a heavy sigh, instructed the bay mare to walk on.

CHAPTER TEN

The Return of the Mummy

Much of the journey passed in silence. Small talk has never been my forte, and it was certain that Mr Henderson did not regard either of us in a light that would make for conversation either natural or friendly. Looking round, I saw Jesperson was comfortably lost in his own thoughts, so I sank into mine, although they were tending towards the worrisome: what if Mr Budge were away and had not received the telegram Jesperson had sent? How long should we wait for him at the Museum? Would we have to take the mummy into our own keeping?

Determined to put aside such unhappy thoughts, I found myself thinking once more of Matilda. Perhaps I should make a gentle suggestion to Mr Henderson, that it was not right for the young lady to treat him like her favourite uncle – but no, that might do more harm than good, if my unasked-for concern opened his eyes to the fact that she was no longer a child and gave him ideas . . .

No, it was better to stay out of it. Once we'd returned his

missing mummy to Mr Budge, we need never have anything more to do with Mr Henderson again.

Unless, of course, he was responsible for the death of Mr Leary. In that case, we could not let a murderer get away with his crime.

Trying to look unconcerned, I glanced in the driver's direction. Mr Henderson had his attention grimly fixed upon the road ahead, and I think he would not have noticed even a basilisk glare. It would be idiotic to say that he did not look like a murderer, for what does a murderer look like? For all the claims made for phrenology and the categorisations of physical and facial traits, there is no one established type of cranial structure called 'the murderer'. All manner of people kill for all sorts of reasons. And this was such a strange murder . . . if, indeed, the death had been an act of deliberate, calculated murder and not in some way accidental. And what if the doctor was right and the marks on Leary's wrist bore no connection to his death? I was not in the habit of doubting my partner's insights, but all the same, I had to wonder.

As we drew nearer to our destination, Mr Jesperson emerged from his silent contemplation. He leaned forward, poked his head in between Mr Henderson and me and said, 'If you will take my advice, Henderson, when you see Budge you will confess all your crimes.'

Henderson replied with obvious sarcasm, 'Why, it appears that you have mistaken Wallis Budge for a priest, and me for an adherent of the Catholic rites.'

'Not at all. Your sins may be manifold, but I refer to something specific: that is, the *other* things you took from the Museum.'

Henderson's hands tightened on the reins. 'I told you, Mr Jesperson, I *borrowed* some papyri – it was wrong of me to take them without permission, I admit, but it was very important that I read them and I kept them no more than three or four days. I am surprised Budgie even noticed they were missing – his office is so chaotic, it is a wonder he ever finds anything he wants – but that is hardly my fault.'

Jesperson pounced. 'But in this case, it is your fault, if you left them in Budge's office, for that was not where you found them.'

'It was the best I could do,' he said defensively. 'The storeroom was locked and Budgie had no time for me that day – he would not let me go in whilst the room was unattended. He had no assistant at that time, and—'

'But that was your fault, too,' I said, interrupting his pathetic attempt at self-justification. I explained clearly that his supposedly insignificant act had ended with an accusation of theft laid against the entirely honest erstwhile assistant, who had lost his job and been lucky not to be charged with Henderson's crime.

My words hit home, and I was a little ashamed that I took a vindictive pleasure in seeing how he paled and shrank into himself. 'Oh, dear. How dreadful. I had no idea. I am so sorry. Certainly I will do whatever I can for that poor fellow. I will explain it to Budge. I will confess all.' He gave a small moan. 'Oh, what can have possessed me? Why did I behave in such a reckless, foolish way? I was once an honourable man – I have forfeited Budgie's good opinion and he will never forgive me. And that is only what I deserve.'

No one spoke again before we reached the service entrance at the back of the British Museum, where we found Mr Budge, pacing back and forth. When he saw Jesperson jump off the back of the trap, he rushed forward.

'You have found it?'

'Indeed, and brought it back.'

'Unharmed?'

'Mr Henderson has taken good care of it, and bearing that in mind, I hope you will listen to him with an open mind and some sympathy, Mr Budge. He did it not out of any animus against you, but while he was in a disordered state of mind, half mad with grief . . .'

Mr Budge blinked perplexedly. 'Who? You mean it was not Leary after all?'

'Leary was working for Henderson, and as the lawyers say, *qui facit per alium facit per se*. Henderson takes full responsibility and now can only throw himself on your mercy. I hope you will listen to him, and find it in your heart—'

'Henderson?' He said the name in a tone of utter disbelief. 'But we are *friends*; he is a friend to the Museum; he has donated items to our collection. Surely you must mean someone else?'

Jesperson turned and called softly, 'Mr Henderson, come down here.'

Sitting so close, I could see how Mr Henderson was trembling, fumbling with the reins before he climbed down, looking like a man going to meet his doom.

But Mr Budge was not the ogre he might sometimes appear; for now he was all concern and gentleness, taking Mr Henderson by the hand and expressing his deep sympathy and condolences on his recent loss. Only then did he turn his attention to the rolled canvas in the back of the cart. 'Is that—?'

At his nod, Mr Budge said gently to Mr Henderson, 'I wonder if you would oblige me by helping me to carry it into my office?'

It was a clear expression of trust and, I thought, forgiveness was surely not far away.

Jesperson and I stayed behind to allow the men privacy, although we did not have long to wait before they came out again. Mr Henderson was walking like a man who had been released from heavy chains. He actually smiled as he shook hands with Mr Budge, saying quietly but ardently, 'Thank you, thank you. You have my eternal gratitude.'

'We will not speak of it again,' Mr Budge replied. 'I hope you will take my advice and go away for a few months. A complete change of scene is the tonic you require. Spend the summer abroad – in the mountains of Switzerland, perhaps. Hiking in fresh mountain air will clear your mind and help restore your spirits. Do not put it off, dear fellow! If I were you, I should pack a few things and be off tomorrow.'

'Yes, thank you, I'm sure that is a very good plan,' he said rather vaguely.

'It is! Do not hesitate. And be sure to send me your address as soon as you are settled. Send me a postcard with a view of lakes and mountains – I shall envy you your freedom every time I look at it.'

Mr Henderson did not bother with more than a cursory nod of farewell to Jesperson, but he did tip his hat to me before returning to his seat. He slapped the reins against the neck of his patient mare and we watched until he had trotted out of sight.

At his invitation, we accompanied Mr Budge to his office, where the mummy was once more nestled within the confines of its open coffin.

'Words cannot express my gratitude,' said Mr Budge, gazing happily at the mummy. 'Indeed, I am amazed at the speed with which you solved this troublesome matter! Thank you. If I am ever in a position to recommend your services to someone, you may rest assured that I shall do so.' He paused, and I saw a slight cloud covering his evident delight. 'I hope I may depend upon you to say nothing to anyone else about this little . . . er, problem?'

'Naturally. Discretion is part of the service,' Jesperson replied. 'This is your secret, to share or keep buried as you decide fit.'

'Good, good. It remains between us, then. Henderson will say nothing, poor chap, and as for the man who actually stole it . . .' He grimaced. 'Poor Leary can never speak of what he did, or attempt to justify it. Henderson nobly insists it was all his doing, but I think not. Even with the balance of his mind disturbed by grief, Henderson is and always will be a gentleman, not one who would turn to crime without some strong encouragement.

Would it be fair to say Leary pushed him to it? I know he had his own reasons for wishing to thwart me however he could.'

He stopped himself there, and after a sorrowful shake of his head went on, 'I should not speak ill of the dead. Patrick Leary is beyond mortal judgment; God, knowing his heart, will judge him. What is important to me is not the reason behind the disappearance of Mummy X, but the fact that you have returned her – or him – to me, and no harm done.'

Crossing the room to his desk he said, 'Would you like your payment now? Will a cheque be acceptable?'

'We will send you our bill,' Jesperson replied. 'It will not be a very large one, as we incurred so few expenses, and your mystery turned out to be easily resolved.'

He looked a little embarrassed. 'I trust you will not include too many details in regard to what the bill is for . . .'

Jesperson answered with a conspiratorial wink, 'For research, parcel delivery and sundry other services rendered?'

He chuckled. 'Something like that. And I shall add on a bonus, for *expedited delivery* – and on a Sunday. Not many companies offer that. We shall keep the firm of Jesperson and Lane in mind should any future occasions arise requiring your specialist abilities.'

'I assume you are content with the condition in which the parcel arrived? It appears to you to be the same as when you saw it last?' Jesperson gestured to the swathed figure within the coffin.

'Why, yes. Do you not think so?' A small crease in his forehead indicated Budge's concern as he moved closer to peer at the mummy.

134

'We never saw it before,' Jesperson reminded him. 'If not for the fact that Henderson broke down and confessed, it would have been difficult for us to prove that this was indeed your property and not something he had purchased – legally or otherwise – and brought back with him from Egypt.'

Mr Budge let out a small sigh of relief. 'I see – I thought you had noticed some damage. That could only have happened if Leary had been clumsy. I am quite certain after speaking to him that Henderson would never deliberately do anything to harm it – or allow it to be harmed. After all, his motive was to keep it safe from *me*.' He chuckled.

'And now, presumably, you will keep it safe and intact in the Museum for many years to come.'

Mr Budge had eyebrows as expressive as Jesperson's. 'You should not so presume.'

'But I saw the great change in Henderson when he left you, and heard the emotion in his voice when he thanked you. Is it not the case that you told him you had changed your mind – even, that *he* had changed it for you? – and that there would be no unwrapping?'

'You are very perceptive. Yes, he left – well, I allowed him to leave – with the impression that his heart-felt plea had moved me to alter my plan. In fact, everything he said has convinced me that his mind is still not right. The theatre at University College has been reserved for the evening of the twentieth – that is on Wednesday week. I mean to send out invitations tomorrow or the day after. It will all go ahead according to plan.'

135

'What if Mr Henderson hears about it?' I asked.

'I hope he will not – and if he takes my excellent advice and leaves for the Continent very soon, there is little likelihood that he will know anything about it for quite some time. And if, on his return, he comes to the Museum wishing to pay his respects to the ancient lady, well, then . . .' He shrugged. 'He may look upon her sarcophagus. If he presses me, I shall not lie, of course. I hope he will have come to his senses by then, but, if not, then he will simply grieve for her as he now grieves for his wife. In the end, he will get over it.'

'You think it is a woman?'

Mr Budge gave a short, embarrassed laugh. 'I said "her" in error, no doubt influenced by my conversation with Henderson. He is convinced that he knows the whole story of our mystery mummy – indeed, he was willing to tell me far more details than a mere unwrapping could ever reveal. He thinks this is the mummy of a princess, a member of the reigning family of her day, whose attempt to rule, rather than to concede the throne to her young husband when he came of age, could not be allowed. She threatened the established order, which is why he imagines she was murdered and her body subsequently spirited away by her followers and hidden, for otherwise it would have been destroyed, along with every other trace of her existence. She would have been stricken from the records. Imagine, if that had been the response to our own dear queen!' He laughed again. 'No, no, for myself, I admit I know nothing. I will wait and see.'

He moved towards the mummy, his gaze becoming more intent, almost ardent. 'And yet, despite the imperative to keep an open mind, I cannot help feeling that beneath all those layers of cloth lies the body of a woman. I seem to make out the faintest suggestion of the feminine form,' he added, inscribing curves in the air with his hands. 'Tell me, Jesperson, what do you think?'

The way he stared at the wrapped body made me a little uncomfortable, for it reminded me of occasions in art galleries when the hungry gaze of a man in front of a statue or a painting of a naked woman had made me hurry to another room. But surely Mr Budge's hunger was that of the scholar seeking truth. To my eye there was nothing distinctively female *or* male in the swathed and motionless form, but he had not asked for my opinion.

'I lack your experience in these matters,' Jesperson demurred. 'I see a smallish person, nothing more.'

Mr Budge sighed. 'Maybe it is only my imagination. And perhaps I have let myself be swayed by Henderson's conviction after all. Well, we shall know soon enough. I hope you intend to be there for the unwrapping?'

'We would not miss it for the world.'

'Excellent. Now, will you give me a hand with the lid?'

Together, they lifted the carved wooden lid (it was, of course, considerably weightier than the cartonnage coffin in Mr Henderson's house) and put it back in place, once more hiding the mummy from view.

'If it was a woman, then the face we see painted there is her

137

portrait, and it tells us she was both beautiful and a figure of high rank. But then the mystery deepens. Who was this woman in her lifetime, to have been so honoured, but after death, to have had her body hidden by her friends or followers, to save it from destruction by her enemies, even as her name was stricken from the public record? She was surely no common woman. Was she the mother of a pretender to the throne? An unofficial wife of a pharaoh? Herself a reigning monarch? Or perhaps the priestess of an outlawed cult? Whatever we find when we unwrap this mummy will be only the beginning of a deeper mystery to be resolved . . . unless it was a man.'

'There will still be a mystery about who that man was.'

'Not so much, for we have his name there on the cartouche already.'

It was obvious that Mr Budge dearly wished for the mummy to be proven female. An unknown woman surrounded by suspicions of danger, murder and warring factions at the highest level of society was far more exciting than that of an ordinary man (even if he had been a figure of some wealth and importance in his day), but either would add only a small footnote to history. I found I did not care very much whether we ever knew the identity of the body beneath those wrappings.

We said our goodbyes, and Mr Budge, in thanking us once again for our help, reiterated, 'It shall remain a secret between us, of course.'

Jesperson tapped the side of his nose.

'Oh – what of Miss Dawes?' I said, suddenly recalling that

she had been with Mr Budge when he had discovered that the mummy had gone.

'Oh, yes – poor little lady. She was most upset. It would be a kindness to let her know it has been safely restored—' He stopped and frowned, then shook his head. 'Or perhaps not. She is another one of those sensitive souls who considers scientific examination of ancient bodies to be a desecration that should not be allowed.

'Dear Miss Dawes, despite her genuine interest in ancient Egypt, is neither a scholar nor a scientist. Her sympathies are all with the ancient Egyptians. No doubt if she knew about Henderson's actions, she would take his side.'

He sighed. 'I think that I had better keep out of her way until the unwrapping is over and done with. And after that, no doubt I shall be in her black books for ever.'

CHAPTER ELEVEN

To Hampstead Heath

Walking home, I brought up Mr Sand's as yet unsolved case, but Mr Jesperson's mind was on the snake.

'It is more important for us to discover where the cobra came from, and where it is now,' he said.

'There are more than a hundred dealers in exotic animals in London alone,' I pointed out, 'and that is not even considering all the private menageries, personal collections and zoological gardens.'

Jesperson interjected, 'There might even be an assassin-for-hire who uses a cobra as his favoured weapon ... but surely, unless Leary was his first victim, I should have heard rumours of such a one already. No, I think we had better stick with what little we do know, and begin our search closer to home – Leary's home, that is.'

We had reached Gower Street as he spoke, and when he opened the door, the savoury smell of roasting meat wafted out. He inhaled deeply, smiling. 'Roast beef – and Yorkshire pudding! My favourite!'

The prospect of Sunday dinner, appealing though it was, did not soothe my nerves, which had prickled uncomfortably at Jesperson's words. Did he mean us to set forth on an *actual* snake-hunt in Hampstead?

Not exactly. Edith told us dinner was still half an hour away, so we adjourned to our office, where Jesperson took down the London trades directory. After a short perusal, he exclaimed, 'Here it is: J.P. Conrad and Sons, on the Heath Road in Hampstead. They are the nearest dealers for anyone in Hampstead or Highgate, so they will be our first port of call. Even if the snake was not sold by them, they may be able to help.'

The next morning we went by cab to a square brick building on the Heath Road that was the headquarters of J. P. Conrad and Sons, Dealers in Exotic Animals.

When Jesperson rang the bell, the jangling sound was quickly drowned out by a cacophony of shrieking, squealing and raucous cries that threatened a nightmarish assembly awaiting us within. After a few moments, the door was opened by a red-faced, perspiring young man in shirt-sleeves whose, 'How may I help you?' was anything but friendly. Behind him the wailing and screaming continued, putting me in mind of prisoners begging for release.

Jesperson doffed his hat. 'Mr Conrad?'

'John P. Conrad the younger. If you want my father, he is travelling abroad. What is this regarding?'

'Perhaps we could come in?'

141

He frowned. 'We are not a public menagerie.'

'I understand that. I wish to enquire about a purchase of – a particular imported creature. You do sell to the general public?'

He relaxed a little. 'Yes – however, customers are encouraged to contact us in the first instance by post or cable.'

'Do you never get any passing trade?'

'Occasionally. Recently, however, our hospitality has been abused and we are forced to be . . . more selective . . . in whom we admit.' He looked at us more closely and I had the distinct impression he was trying to assess our social status by the probable cost of our clothing. Evidently he decided we looked as if we could afford to become customers, for his manner thawed and he favoured me with a smile. 'What is your interest? An exotic bird, perhaps? You ladies do love them. We have some very fine and unusual specimens from Africa and South America that I would be more than happy to show you.'

'What about snakes?' said Jesperson. 'Cobras in particular – have you any in stock?'

His gaze slid quickly back to Jesperson and his manner was noticeably cool again. 'That is quite a specialist interest. Yes, we have some. Are you a collector? You are too late for the king cobra – that went to Wombwell's only last week.'

'What about the Egyptian cobra, *Naja haje?* I understand a gentleman in the neighbourhood recently purchased one.'

'Not from me, he didn't.'

'No? Perhaps it was another type? African, or even an Indian cobra.'

'We have some customers in Hampstead and the surrounding area, but none with an interest in keeping poisonous reptiles. The gentleman must have acquired it elsewhere,' he said firmly.

Jesperson was watching him closely. 'Did you sell a cobra, or any sort of poisonous snake, to anyone, this past week? On Friday, perhaps?'

Anger flared in the young man's eyes. 'What are you playing at?' He stepped forward, hands curling into fists at his sides.

'I had hoped you might be able to help us,' said Jesperson. He stood there calmly, not moving.

Mr Conrad stopped very close to Mr Jesperson and peered up at him. 'What do you know about it?'

Jesperson's voice was quiet. 'A man died on Friday night from the bite of a venomous serpent. It is likely that the snake was acquired from these premises. We have not come here to accuse or to blame or to threaten, but to ask for your help. You might aid us very greatly in our enquiry if you can tell us of anyone who recently purchased such a serpent.'

The clenched fists relaxed, but Mr Conrad was still wary. 'You are not the police.'

'That is correct. This is a private investigation. Will you help us?'

His shoulders slumped. 'I wish I could. We did not *sell* it to anyone. And whoever stole our Egyptian cobra neglected to leave his calling card.'

'Tell us what happened – everything that you know.'

Mr Conrad took a step back and obliged us with his account.

'We think it must have been on Friday – but we only realised the snake was gone a few hours ago. My brother and I had not yet made up our minds to report it to the police. There's a problem, you see—'

Jesperson interrupted. 'What happened on Friday?'

'I was with a customer – a gentleman well known to us – in the back office. Matthew – my brother – answered the door. Some ladies had seen our sign and stopped out of curiosity. He let them in and showed them around – he believed they might become new customers,' he added quickly. 'We do let people in to look around, only not too many at a time. But we shall be more careful now.'

'You suspect the ladies?'

'Dear me, no!' Mr Conrad looked quite shocked. '*They* never even looked at the reptiles. They were chiefly interested in the monkeys, and particularly the potto. Have you ever seen a potto?' He half turned back towards the shop and I thought he might be about to lead us inside and show us the unknown creature, but instead, he pulled the door firmly shut. This made the bell ring, which set off a renewal of the squealing and squawking that had only recently died away.

He grimaced apologetically. 'I meant to say that while my brother was occupied with the ladies and I was in the back office, someone else entered – the bell alerted us to this fact. Whoever it was did not call out, and neither of us saw anyone before the bell rang again, when the door was closed. We might have forgotten it entirely, except that today, when we discovered

144

our loss, we went over every single thing that had happened recently – that is how we worked it out.'

'I suppose there is no way the snake could have escaped on its own?'

'Absolutely not,' he said indignantly. 'We take every precaution, and – well, you had better come in and see for yourself.'

When he let us inside, the now-familiar uproar enveloped us – along with a most unpleasant, quite overpowering stench of too many birds and animals crammed together inside solid walls: a mixture of excrement, rancid food, fur and feathers, dust and mould, and emotions, too, I thought, the boredom and fear and despair born of captivity, for whatever people said about mindless, soulless beasts, I had read Darwin on the subject, and knew it was not mere sentimentality to believe they had feelings not so very different from our own. I imagined that this would have been similar to the smell on Noah's ark after several weeks afloat, but those animals were being saved; their captivity had an end date. The hapless animals confined here would be sold, only to be locked up in yet another cage, far from their natural homes. They would never taste freedom again.

I made an effort to screen out the unpleasant surroundings, but when Mr Conrad locked the door I could not help but feel that we too now were trapped within this unhappy place.

'The snakes and reptiles are at that far end,' he said. 'You cannot see them from the front. Follow me, please.' He led us past several cell-like aviaries stuffed with brightly coloured, bedraggled-looking birds and around a corner where we were confronted by a cage of small monkeys. They began running back and forth, emitting strange, excited cries. Raising his voice to be heard above their hubbub, Mr Conrad said, 'My brother and the ladies were here, from where, you will note, neither the front door nor the reptiles can be seen.'

Jesperson had to raise his own voice almost to a shout to be heard. 'I am surprised you could hear the bell.'

'Ah, it is a matter of what you are used to. To me, the sound of the bell cuts through everything else. If only Matthew had thought to lock the door – oh, here is my brother now.'

A younger, plumper version of our Mr Conrad approached.

'Mr Jesperson and Miss Lane have come about our missing snake,' said his brother.

Mr Matthew Conrad's pale eyebrows shot up. 'She has been found? Is she all right?'

'The cobra is still missing, unfortunately,' said Jesperson, 'and the man who probably stole it is dead. Would you care to show us where the theft occurred?'

Snakes and reptiles were kept at the far end of the long room, the snakes in the furthest reach, screened from view from the birds and smallest mammals for whom, as the Conrads explained, the sight and smell of their natural enemies might have induced heart failure. Instead of bars, solid glass walls served to enclose the serpents.

'You see this cobra?' Our guide indicated one of the larger glass-sided cases. 'Yesterday there were two.'

I tried, but as hard as I looked, I could see nothing but sand

and stones. I glanced at Jesperson, who was gazing through the glass with intense interest.

'I understand that in their natural environment they make their homes amongst the rocks, or in abandoned animal dens,' he said. 'I believe they prefer to stay safely hidden during the day, for they do their hunting at night.'

Following his gaze, at last I could make out something brownish-grey coiled between two rough piles of paler stones. It was as still as its surroundings.

'She – the one he stole – was not hidden,' said Matthew Conrad. 'She'd recently fed – they swallow their prey whole and that great bulge makes it not so easy to coil up into a small space. She was lying out on the sand, letting her meal digest, probably feeling a bit sleepy. The lid is simple enough to lift off. I expect he would have worn thick gloves for protection, but with a full belly and half-asleep, she likely put up no resistance. He must have put her into a basket, replaced the lid, and was gone before we had any idea what had happened.'

'You did not check this cage again until this morning?'

'We were very busy on Saturday,' said John Conrad defensively. 'And there's always the cleaning up to be done on Sunday, after church, of course. Most of our stock need care and feeding every day, but not the snakes and reptiles.'

'They didn't need feeding today, either,' said Matthew Conrad. 'I just wanted to take a look at the female. I was curious how quickly she'd manage to digest the chick – I had read that heat speeds up the process, and as the weather has been so warm recently – well, I take note of these things out of scientific interest. So first thing this morning, I looked – and she was gone.'

'Johnny wouldn't believe me at first,' he added, with a sideways look at his brother. 'As if I couldn't tell the difference between one snake and two!'

'It did not seem possible,' John Conrad admitted, 'but there it was – the lid firmly in place as ever, but one of the snakes gone. So then we went over everything that had happened, and I remembered hearing the bell, and we understood how it must have been. I thought he must have stolen it to order.' He shook his head, disgusted. 'Down by the docks, there are all sorts of law-breaking ruffians, but we never expected anything like that up here.'

His expression changed and his face paled as he remembered. 'You said the thief died from a bite? Where is our snake now?'

'That is a good question,' said Jesperson.

'Could you find her for us?' Matthew Conrad asked with sudden hope.

'You had better inform the police.'

'The police! If they happened across her, they'd kill her as soon as look at her. I don't trust them.'

'I'm afraid they'd be no help at all,' his brother agreed. 'They'd fine us for carelessness – or try to shut us down. And if word spread that there was a cobra on the loose, local people would panic. There would be calls for us to be closed, or force us to locate somewhere further out. As if we aren't "out" far enough already! If the snake has got into the village, it is only because a thief took it there – not because of anything *we* did. And it's not a rampaging beast, you know. If it is not still wherever the thief took it, it will be close by, curled up somewhere dark and warm and quiet. It will come out when it gets hungry, but that may be a few days yet. I'd look for it under a hen-house or some out-building infested by mice.'

Then he put the same question to us that his brother had.

Once more, Jesperson declined. 'We are not snake-hunters.'

'Maybe not, but you know where the thief took it before he died – and you clearly know something about snakes.'

He demurred. 'Only a little. We have other business to attend – oh, very well. I promise nothing, but if we do find the cobra – and if it is still living – I will tell you, so you may go and capture it yourselves.'

They thanked us, we thanked them, and left.

Heath Road was not a good place to find a hansom, but although the sky was now filled with heavy grey clouds, it was still a warm, dry afternoon and a walk offered the chance to talk over what we had learnt.

'But what made you think it was Leary himself who stole the snake?' I asked.

'It was obvious. First, the bite from a cobra does not cause death at once, and nor does it instantly incapacitate the person. Death comes inevitably, but usually after an hour or more, although the process may be speeded by stress or strenuous activity. If the snake had been introduced into Leary's room while he slept, it would not have been likely to bite until he moved, and then, as soon as he became aware, surely he would have sought help.'

'If the killer locked him in . . .'

'The room was not locked. And remember, there was an open window, and neighbours to hear if he shouted for help.'

'And you conclude therefore there was no killer? But why did he steal the snake?'

Slowing his steps so I would not have to struggle to keep up, Jesperson said, 'If we knew that, we should know everything. The snake bit him when he committed the crime, or soon after. The Conrads imagined the thief must have come prepared with heavy gloves and a basket or other secure carrying case. There was nothing like that in his room – remember, I had plenty of time to search it while you were downstairs with his daughter. There were no gloves, no forked stick such as a snake-hunter uses, and, most tellingly, no basket or sturdy case, nothing except a dirty sack that I found under the bed along with his discarded shirt, that he could have used to carry home a six-foot-long serpent.'

'You mean to say Mr Leary set out to steal a large and deadly snake without taking any precautions for his own safety? It sounds to me like a very elaborate means of suicide.'

'I doubt that he was bent on self-destruction.'

'Then he must have been a very great fool,' I said. 'And nothing his daughter said – or his employers – indicates that. Quite the contrary. He may have been lazy, but he was a practical, competent man. Surely it is more likely that the snake was put into his room by someone else. The Conrads did not see the thief, and as there was nothing in Mr Leary's room in which he could have carried it—'

'Nothing but the bag I mentioned – empty, but reeking of snake.'

I shuddered. 'Maybe someone else left it there?'

But Jesperson did not bother to repeat his argument that a snake would not strike an unmoving, sleeping person for no reason. He went on as if I had not spoken, 'We can agree that Leary would not have stolen a cobra on a whim. He must have been commissioned by someone else. And I think that person gave him no instructions on how to handle the deadly snake – perhaps they even lied about what type of serpent it was.

'Cobras are sluggish when digesting a meal, so that is when they are safest to handle, but only if you know what you are doing. It is likely that Leary, trying to work quickly, was clumsy. He may have startled the creature, or been too rough when he thrust it into the sack, and he received the fatal bite then. Did you know that snakes can bite without injecting venom? It is painful, but relatively harmless. Maybe he had been told this might happen, and not to worry. Even if he meant to see a doctor, he wanted to go home first, to hide the snake, or deliver it to someone.

'You remember he wore no shirt. But the fact that he was wearing shoes indicates that he had come in from the outside, rather than having just risen from his bed. He probably took off his shirt to inspect the wound. But it was too late – it would always have been too late – for that was when he collapsed, and he died almost immediately afterwards.'

'And what happened to the snake?'

'Sooner or later it escaped from the bag, which may not have been tied tightly, if at all, and slipped out the window, and went to earth not far away . . . perhaps even beneath that shed in the Balmers' garden. Wherever it went, it is probably still there. Unless . . .'

'What?'

'Unless he had already delivered it to his employer.'

My skin prickled. 'Mr Henderson?'

'I find that hard to believe. His surprise when he learned of Leary's death struck me as genuine. And he had little reason to want him dead – maybe enough to wish him out of the way, but if Leary was threatening blackmail, they both knew he could not reveal Henderson's crime without implicating himself. And if this other crime went wrong, as it so easily could have done, what was there to stop Leary from dragging Henderson into it?'

We paused by Whitestone Pond to catch our breath and take in the view of London, although our talk of murderous plots made it difficult to attend to anything else.

'Who else could have wanted to kill poor Mr Leary?' I wondered aloud.

'Of course, we do not know for certain that his death *was* intended. It might have been down to his own stupidity. We must try to learn more about Leary – his character, his circumstances and his associates. But there must have been someone else behind the theft, just as Henderson was behind the theft of the mummy. And even if his death was an unintended consequence, it indicates a criminal lack of concern for the man's safety. It would have to be a person who thought nothing of using another human being as a disposable tool – and to acquire something which could more easily have been purchased.'

At that, he walked on, and as usual, I had to hurry to catch up.

He was muttering to himself, 'Who goes into a menagerie and picks up a deadly snake as if he was taking a loaf of bread from a market stall? People who know nothing about snakes are usually *more* fearful: they would take more care rather than less. There is a sort of instinctive recoiling from serpents that is surely inborn . . .'

Suddenly aware of my inevitably doomed attempts to keep up with his long stride, he slowed and turned to include me in the one-sided conversation. 'I am sure you agree that in this case Leary's behaviour was eccentric in the extreme, very different from the earlier theft.'

'Yes. It's as if he had gone mad. Could it be that, after years of abiding by the law, the commission of his first crime tipped him over the edge of madness, or perhaps made him believe he could get away with anything?'

'No.' Frowning thoughtfully, he rubbed his chin. 'My dear Miss Lane, do not imagine I dismiss your suggestion out of hand; it might make sense in other circumstances – if he had tried to rob a bank or a jeweller's shop. But he no more wished to possess a snake than he wanted the mummy for himself. And although he disliked Mr Budge, there is no reason to think he had any personal animus against the Conrads. Therefore, what he did could only have been for the benefit of someone else – some unknown, sinister and clearly very dangerous villain who wished for purposes as yet unknown to acquire a deadly snake.'

'But why take the risk of hiring someone to steal something that the villain could have purchased for himself – if not in person, then through some intermediary? Mr Conrad had a list of prices – it does not require riches beyond the dreams of avarice to buy a cobra. If this villain could afford to pay Mr Leary—'

We were walking into Heath Street when Jesperson stopped short and faced me. 'I do not suppose for a moment that Leary was paid. It is more likely that he was compelled.'

'Compelled? How? Blackmail? A threat against his daughter?'

'Nothing so ordinary. And it could explain why Leary acted as he did, with such utter disregard for his own safety.' Blue eyes blazed in the long, pale face. 'We have seen this power before, experienced it at close hand, only last year, in the case of the somnambulist and the psychic thief.'

A thrill of horror ran through me. 'You mean—?'

'Indeed. Hypnotism.'

CHAPTER TWELVE

The Search Continues

But who was the hypnotist? And what was his purpose? Who wanted Leary dead? Why use a snake?

By the time we reached the stop for the regular omnibus into London, Jesperson had made up his mind to return to Highgate and look for the cobra. If he could find it hiding somewhere near the Balmers' residence, it might suggest murder had been the intention, the snake a discarded weapon like a pistol thrown into a ditch after the killing shot was fired.

The idea of a snake-hunt made me nervous, but nevertheless, I agreed. To my relief, Jesperson told me he thought it better that he went alone. 'I shall find it easier to skulk about in odd places and strike up conversations with the neighbours if I am on my own. If you will oblige me, write to Mr Sand – ask him if he can give us any more details about the missing items, or if anything else has come to mind that might be connected, such as the names of anyone who was given a tour of the storeroom, or came to visit him there, in the week before it happened.'

I was pleased to be assigned a task that could not possibly involve close proximity to a deadly cobra, but I could not entirely still my apprehension on Jesperson's behalf.

He smiled and reassured me. 'I will not try to capture the beast. I had rather leave it in peace, and send the Conrads to fetch it. But if it threatens any harm . . .' He raised his walking stick, and I saw it was his sword-cane.

The rain came on shortly after I arrived back at Gower Street. My partner did not return for many more hours, and when he did, he was in such a state of dirty, wet dishevelment that his mother cried out in horror. After scolding him for dripping all over the carpet, she ordered him to bath and change, speaking to him as forcibly if he were still her little boy. 'No, Jasper, not another word! You can tell us all about your adventures when you are clean and warm and dry. I will not have you catching cold – remember what happened to your father. Now, go. There will be a hot drink and something to eat when you return.'

Edith went so far as to set a fire in the grate – a rare luxury in June. Even if it was not strictly necessary, it certainly did make the big room feel much cosier. By the time Jesperson returned, virtuously clean and attired in his thick scarlet dressing-gown, his mother had made him a plate of scrambled eggs and toast and a hot rum toddy.

'You will not eat?' He looked at me in surprise.

'Your mother and I dined earlier – we had the rest of yester-day's soup with some bread and cheese.' (I thought he would like to know he had not missed anything special.) 'Now, tell me – did you find the snake?'

His mouth full of eggs and toast, he shook his head. When he had swallowed, he said, 'I was quite thorough. There are not many places for a large snake to hide on such a street, with its modern houses set in such small and tidy gardens. I knew I must look into and beneath all out-buildings, so I pretended to be from the local authority, concerned with health and sanitation. When I found a hen-house, I said we'd heard reports that a ferret might be loose in the neighbourhood. Everyone was very helpful.'

'Including the Balmers?'

'Of course, although that was a bit trickier. I am afraid I led Mrs Balmer to believe that I was in the habit of doing favours for people – that mine was a rather precarious, hand-to-mouth existence, but I could turn my hand to almost anything, and I was someone in whom trust was well-placed.' He paused to sip his hot toddy before going on, 'I hoped, you see, that this revelation from me might lead her to sympathise, to say that her father had been the same, and that he had been employed by others besides Mr Henderson . . . But I hoped in vain. In the end, I had to ask her outright if he had recently done any work for anyone else.'

'And had he?'

'Not to her knowledge, and she thought he would have told her, especially if it had to do with money. But of course, she had been away all that week, so if someone other than Henderson had hired him to do some little job or other, there would have been no opportunity for him to tell her. And if he was acting under hypnotic suggestion, he would not have known it himself.'

He set down the empty mug with a sigh. 'If it *was* someone new, they probably met in the local hostelry. That was where he spent his evenings. So after I had prowled around the garden, and investigated the shed—'

'How did you explain your interest?'

He coarsened his voice. 'Mate of mine lost his ferret, didn't he.' He laughed, and in his more usual tones went on, 'As I was saying, I met some of Leary's former drinking companions, but no one who looked at all likely to be our mysterious villain.'

'Do you think it was Henderson after all?'

'I went to his house next – you will be unsurprised to learn that he is still there, and has no intention of travelling abroad. "Mr Budge is very kind, but what should suit him would not suit me," he said. "Perhaps, in August, I might go away for a few weeks." I sounded him out on the subject of snakes, but he was nonplussed, wondering what had made me think he knew anything about the subject? He had no interest in reptiles. I tried to make a connection with Egypt and his collection of art and artefacts, but it was only when I asked if there were any Egyptian serpent gods that he was able to tell me anything. Like many self-taught amateurs, I believe he was happy to demonstrate his knowledge. There are several, it transpires: Mehen, depicted as a coiled serpent, protected the great sun-god Ra; Nehebu-Kau was another helpful and benevolent god in the form of a man with a snake's head and tail – these he could only describe, but he was able to show me Apophis, an enormous snake who embodied the powers of darkness and dissolution and was the enemy of Ra. He showed me an illustration in one of his papyri – it was part of that innumerable collection known as the Book of the Dead – and the same picture, he said, was frequently painted on the walls of tombs. The evil snake was always depicted bleeding, in the process of being decapitated, as it was here, coiled around a sacred sycamore tree and being attacked by a large, furious cat.'

Jesperson leaned back in his chair. 'After that, I asked him about real snakes: did they frighten him? He said there was no need to be afraid, only cautious. During his residence in Egypt, he had encountered quite a few deadly vipers and cobras – the Egyptian cobra especially, as it liked to live in the places people were, unlike the snakes which populated the desert wastes. Even there, he maintained, one should remember that a snake was only likely to strike if you frightened it or you posed a threat.

'When I asked if he had ever thought of keeping snakes, or if he knew anyone who did, he was by this time understandably suspicious, so I told him one had gone missing from a local menagerie and could be hiding almost anywhere; that I thought someone with knowledge of snakes might have some idea as to where it might be lurking.'

He smiled rather grimly. 'Not surprisingly, Henderson immediately assumed that I suspected him of stealing it. I saw the emotional struggle he had with himself, torn between the natural indignation anyone would feel at being accused of a crime, and the awareness that he had, by his own criminal actions, forfeited the right to take offence. I could see he was holding himself in check, and he was very stiff with me, but he immediately offered to show me around the house to satisfy myself there was no snake and no serpentarium hidden about the place.'

'Did he let you look everywhere?'

He screwed up his face. 'Nearly. By the time we reached his bedroom – you would not have been pleased, Miss Lane, to see a bed unmade and clothing strewn about! – he was so uncomfortable that I only poked my head in quickly. After all, what sort of man would keep a cobra in his bedroom?'

'What sort of man would *steal* a cobra?' I retorted, which made him look worried.

'Ah, you put me to shame! Oh, Miss Lane, if you had been with me, you might have kept Henderson engaged in conversation downstairs whilst I pried into every nook and cranny upstairs – or at least inside the wardrobe and under the bed.'

I shuddered. 'Surely he would not keep a live snake anywhere near his own bed. I did not mean to imply you should have done more, truly.'

'Miss Lane,' he said solemnly, 'I rely on you to be vigilant and keep me up to the mark. But I think I may say that even if Henderson had something hidden in his house, it was not a snake.' He tapped his nose. 'The bedroom had a pungent, unpleasant reek, but it was the smell of human occupation, of unwashed linen, old books, body odours, dust and dirt – but in the entire unholy mixture, I would swear, not even a whiff of the ophidian.'

'I would never doubt your nose,' I replied, matching his solemnity.

He grinned. 'You will be pleased to know I also explored the grounds, rather more at my leisure. There was no sign of any snake, although it offered many potential hiding places. I gained the impression that Leary had not done very much towards rescuing a garden that had been left untended for so many months.'

He stood up abruptly. 'Henderson *must* be involved in some way, and yet I cannot believe him a murderer . . . and unless I completely misjudge him, or he is the most astonishingly talented actor I have ever seen, he was genuinely surprised when we told him about Leary's death, and I would swear he knew nothing about the stolen cobra. I am afraid all my exertions today have brought us no closer to the question of why and for whom Leary took that snake.'

It was difficult to know where to look next, but, when in doubt, it was Jesperson's habit to turn to the printed word, searching for suggestions in everything from the popular press to scholarly journals. The news-agent next door was happy to supply us with whatever was current, and for back numbers, there was the Reading Room just down the street, or the London Library, also not far away.

I joined in, although my faculty of intuition – or 'unconscious logic', as my partner had recently begun to term it – was not as finely tuned as his when it came to sifting through the news-sheets for anything which might have some bearing on our own mysteries but Jesperson said it was like any muscle and needed to be used regularly, and hard, to grow stronger.

Death by snake-bite was not the commonplace event here that it might be in India, Australia or the Americas, and villains who used venomous snakes as murder weapons were the stuff of fiction, at least in England in 1894.

As for hypnotists, those currently in the news were the usual stage sort, and a French doctor intending to de-mystify the process. The only reported criminal case involving hypnotism that I could find had taken place abroad.

On Wednesday morning, my partner announced his intention of going to the Museum, in the hope that the relics of ancient Egypt might provide some inspiration. I declined his invitation to accompany him, although I had no particular reason to stay in, but as it turned out, hardly a quarter of an hour after Jesperson left, I received an unexpected caller.

CHAPTER THIRTEEN

A Warning from Seshemetka

'Miss Dawes!' I exclaimed in surprise.

'My dear Miss Lane, I do beg your pardon for turning up out of the blue like this. I hope I am not intruding,' she said anxiously, 'but as your Mr Jesperson was kind enough to invite me to drop by whenever I might be passing, I hoped you might not mind.'

'But of course — such a pleasant surprise. I am delighted to see you,' I said, already ushering her through the door. 'Please, do come in.'

She was still regarding me, I thought, with some anxiety, so I did my best to reassure her. 'May I offer you a cup of tea?'

'Oh, no, thank you. I really cannot stay long. I came because I have something very particular to ask you.'

Something about her words made me wonder if her visit was professional, rather than social. I showed her in to the front room that was our office; there was no obvious reason to interpose the length of a desk between us, so I gave her a choice of the sofa or one of the several comfortable chairs at the other end of the room. Taking a seat close to hers, I said, 'I'm afraid Mr Jesperson is out at the moment, but I hope I may be of help.'

Her gaze sharpened. 'In fact, it was *you* that Mr Budge told me to ask. I must say I was puzzled, for what could you know about the missing mummy? But then I read the placard on your door. "Jesperson and Lane, Private Investigations."' Her voice lifted in excitement. 'Does that mean what I think? Are you truly detectives?'

'Yes, indeed we are, so you may trust me with whatever you wish to ask.'

At my warm words, she relaxed. 'Ah! Now I understand – Mr Budge asked you to find the missing mummy?' I dipped my head in affirmation and she went on, 'Then you will know that I was with him when he discovered the loss, so you may speak freely to me about it. I have been worried ever since, but naturally, I have told no one. And today, when I saw him at the Museum – he was in a hurry; he could not spare me even a few minutes of his precious time – he told me, "You may ask your friend Miss Lane. She knows all." Well!' Miss Dawes pulled a fan from her reticule, snapped it open and rapidly fanned her flushed face.

'What was I to think of that? After he had been so clear in his instruction to me to say nothing to anyone about the matter, after he had declared that no one else must know, he had gone and confided in *you*? Surely he was not saying, despite his jolly smile, that Miss Lane was the thief?' She snapped her fan shut with a little laugh. 'Of course, I did not really think such a thing for a moment. But I was utterly in the dark about why Miss Lane should "know all" – but, knowing your home was only a short walk away, I came here at once.'

Leaning towards me, she lowered her voice. 'Have you solved the case of the missing mummy?'

'Indeed, we found the culprit, who repented of his crime and returned it unharmed to the Museum.'

'And what will happen to it now? Will Mr Budge unwrap and destroy it?'

It made no sense to lie, but I said merely that I was sure Mr Budge would treat the remains with respect, and make every effort to preserve as much as possible.

Her body went suddenly rigid and with suddenly staring eyes, she said urgently, 'No, he should *not*. I wish he would destroy it utterly, along with every other trace she left behind. May her name, her spirit, her shadow and every remaining memory and relic of her despicable being be struck from the earth.'

The hairs on the back of my neck lifted – it was as if I was hearing someone else speak through this woman's lips, a feeling I'd had so powerfully only a few times in my life, despite the numerous séances I had attended at which the dead had been invited – even exhorted – to speak.

But I controlled myself and said calmly, 'I am surprised to hear such sentiments from you, Miss Dawes.'

Abruptly she relaxed and smiled, herself again. 'Oh, do please call me Violet. I hope we are friends?'

'I hope so, too, Violet. My friends call me Di.'

'Vi and Di,' she said with an unexpected giggle.

Her laugh was so infectious, I joined in, 'Do or die!'

After laughing together, we really did feel like friends. I gestured at Miss Dawes for her to continue.

'You were saying, Di? That I surprised you?'

'I had thought you opposed the practice of unwrapping as a desecration.'

'I do, and it is,' she said firmly. 'Why should the buying and selling and putting on display the dead of another land be acceptable when such treatment accorded to our own ancestors would never be allowed? Only imagine the feelings that would be aroused if someone announced that, in the name of scholarship, he intended to exhume and examine your grandfather's corpse?'

'Well, for one thing, our grandparents – even our *great*-grandparents – are much closer to us in time. Stronger sentiments attach to people we have known, or whom our parents may have known. But the mummies displayed in museums died so long ago that no one – or perhaps anyone – could claim kinship.' Struck by a happy thought, I added, 'And it is not only the bodies of foreigners that are put on display. Consider Jeremy Bentham, whom you may see – he is but a short walk up the road.'

She looked surprised. 'Oh, you mean the philosopher? I remember now: he left his body to the college, did he not? But that is quite different – no one robbed his grave; he left instructions for how his corpse should be dressed, and that it should be allowed to attend regular meetings, so the members of the college are following his wishes. The ancient Egyptians would be horrified by the treatment accorded to their physical remains, and especially by the casual destruction of what they intended to be preserved forever. Without bodies, they had no hope of immortality.'

She settled more comfortably in her chair and began to lecture me on the subject.

'I see I had better explain. To begin with, they conceived of the human soul as consisting of five parts. The *Ba* was closest to our idea of a soul. *Ka* was the life-force; *Ib* the heart, which they thought of as we do the mind, as the site of memory, thought and emotion. *Ren* meant the name, because a person continues to live, in some sense, so long as their name survives in the memory of others. Finally, *Sheut,* which is translated as "shadow"; that remains something of a mystery to my modern British mind, but perhaps was the hidden side of the personality, visible only in a particular light.'

Taking a deep breath, she went on, 'These were the aspects of the human being that survived the physical death of the body. After death the Ba – accompanied by the Ib and Sheut – set off on a long and dangerous journey through the Underworld, for which everyone in Egyptian society had been prepared throughout their lives. I need not go into detail just now, but there are tests they must pass along the way. Meanwhile, the Ka stayed home in the body; it required a permanent residence in this world. Therefore the dead body was carefully prepared to withstand the ravages of time before being hidden away from the possibility of destruction inside a coffin carved and painted in the person's likeness, then interred in a tomb filled with painted images and carved replicas of everything required to please and nourish the Ka for however long it might take before it was reunited with the other parts and could be born again.'

'That is fascinating. I can understand why the mummy was so important to ancient Egyptians, and why you feel sympathetic to their beliefs – but you have not explained why you have changed your mind.'

She opened her eyes very wide. 'I have not changed my mind.'

'So it is only this particular mummy you think should be destroyed?'

'Yes! It should have been done long ago.'

'Why?'

Sternly she replied, 'Some people do not deserve a second life.'

I waited, and after a pause she went on, 'She was a terrible woman – she would stop at nothing, not even murder, in her pursuit of power. I do not know that she ever killed anyone with her own hands, but she was certainly responsible for several deaths, and one of them a child. She was dangerously ambitious, and even death will not have changed her.'

'Who was she?'

'She was called Meretseger. She was the daughter of a high-ranking officer in the Pharaoh's army; his position gave her entry to the royal household, where she managed to seduce the Pharaoh's younger son – he was only a child at the time. But he loved her dearly, in his childish way, and he vowed to marry her. However, royal protocols meant he must first marry his sister; his lover would at best be a secondary wife – not that there was any shame in that, not in those days. It would have been honour enough for most women, but it did not satisfy Meretseger. The Pharaoh's older son, his heir, died in a hunting accident contrived by her. It was part of her plan to have the younger son succeed to the throne, and that was what happened in due course, when his father died.'

'Was she accused of killing the Pharaoh, too?'

'Oh, no. Pharaoh was worshipped as a god – even she would not have dared to harm him. And it was unnecessary, for everyone knew he had been ailing for some time, and all the prayers and magical spells in the world could not have staved off his demise forever. The younger son and his sister-wife were still little more than children, so a regent had to be appointed. Usually, that would have been the boy-king's mother, or the widow of the Pharaoh, if they were not one and the same, which in this case they were not. But for some reason, neither of those women were made Regent; this time, the unofficial wife became the unofficial ruler in the name of the young Pharaoh.' Violet gave me a long, meaningful look.

'And then?' I found myself strangely fascinated by this ancient story.

'The young Pharaoh adorned his mistress with every title he could think of, including one used very rarely: that of the God's Wife. At a stroke, Meretseger outranked everyone except her royal husband. She was promoted to the title of Royal Wife while the Pharaoh's sister faded into the background – I do not know what happened to her, but she must have recognised it would be in her best interest to step aside quietly if she wanted to avoid an early death.'

'And what happened to Meretseger once she'd attained her prominence? When her husband came of age – surely, as he was married, he cannot have been a very young child? Did he take over? Was there a struggle between them? When did she fall from grace? What happened to her?'

'That I do not know. She was still in power alongside her husband – two thrones, twin rulers – when I died—'

At my gasp, she quickly clarified, 'I mean, when I died in *that* lifetime. Seshemetka was carried off by a contagion that fell upon the city like a poisonous miasma. How or when Meretseger's wickedness was revealed, I do not know, but the need to hide her body away and disguise her coffin shows that although she still had some loyal servants, she was no longer deemed worthy of respect.'

There was no arguing with that. 'And you have learned all of this from Seshemetka.'

'Yes, but not easily. It has taken time, and there are still many gaps in my understanding. I cannot simply speak with her and ask questions and hear her reply as in an ordinary, comfortable conversation with a friend, the way I can with you.'

'So how do you communicate?'

'Chiefly through dreams. Sometimes in them I *am* Seshemetka, experiencing moments from her life, and when I wake up, I know much more. But you know how unreliable dreams can be; the way that memories of real events are scrambled up with fantasies, the ordinary mixes with the impossible, and even scenes from plays and books feel as if they have happened to oneself.'

'And you are quite certain this Meretseger really was so very wicked?'

'Oh yes! There is no doubt about it.'

'It is a bit surprising that her body was preserved at all, in that case.'

'Not at all. She had friends in high places. One in particular, her staunchest ally, was a powerful priest, the head of an important local cult. He would have been sure to protect her and take care of her, even after death. Perhaps *especially* after death.'

'How did Seshemetka come to know this woman?'

'We grew up together. There were some family connections . . .' She waved her hand vaguely. 'As children, we saw a good deal of one another. Although we were never really friends . . . she was too ambitious, and there was something in her, even as a child, that repelled rather than attracted me. And she . . . well, she had her eyes fixed on the throne from a very early age and she used all her beauty – for she was very lovely – and wiles to get closer to the royal household.

'As for me, at the age of twelve I was dedicated to the service of the goddess Bastet, and I spent most of my time in the temple. After that, I had little contact with Meretseger, and I saw her less and less once she became part of the royal family.

'But I knew about her doings, and her schemes and

171

machinations.' Her mouth took on a grimmer set. 'My father was a scribe, and very close to the royal scribes, so he heard all the news and palace gossip, and I had it all from him.

'When Mr Budge showed me her coffin, I felt *something* – a strong sense of unease. He let me touch it . . . and it gave me such a shock, I nearly collapsed! I should like to say I knew her at once, but at that point the only thing I was certain of was that this person had been known to me when I was Seshemetka. It was some time before the memories began to emerge, bit by bit, in my dreams, and even then, I was not aware of the importance – it was all so far away and long ago. It has always been exciting when more of my memories as Seshemetka surfaced, but this . . . this was different.'

She pressed a hand to her chest as if she was having difficulty drawing breath.

'Violet, are you all right?'

'Yes . . . yes, you must forgive me. Sometimes my emotions get all mixed up with hers . . . Violet and Seshemetka, tangled up – *She* was worried – terrified – and although I tried to tell myself it was really nothing to do with me, only left-over feelings about events that had happened thousands of years ago and could have no possible relevance today – well . . .' She smiled weakly.

'Would you like a cup of tea? A glass of water?'

'No, no thank you. Honestly, I will be fine. I will get through this. I want to explain. I knew that something was bothering Seshemetka. Without understanding why, I was compelled to go to Mr Budge and ask him to show me the mystery mummy – not merely the sarcophagus, but the mummy inside. I knew this was vitally important, even if I had no idea why. I just had to do it, and it was for Seshemetka's sake that I persisted, knowing I risked angering Mr Budge, who has always been so kind and generous with his time. And when he opened the case – and the mummy was gone— Oh!'

She stopped, pressed a hand against her breast for her breath was now coming in little pants.

This time I said nothing, only waited for her to calm, and, after a few moments, she gave me a weak smile.

'That was when I realised . . . I understood . . . it was not only what had happened in the past that worried Seshemetka, but what might happen in the future – or rather, the present – *our* present. She feared that Meretseger had been reborn in our day, just like Seshemetka herself had – but not only Meretseger, with her terrible thirst for power, but someone else, that powerful priest also lives again, and he is still her willing servant. *They* were behind the theft of the mummy. It was part of a greater plan, to return not only to live again, but to *dominate*.

'I could feel Seshemetka's fear and agitation, even without understanding the cause. Such dreadful nightmares I had! I woke time and again – until finally, I had my idea.' Her eyes wide, she leaned forward and gripped my hand. 'If Seshemetka could speak to me when I was in a trance, why not another way? I wondered if automatic writing might be the answer – and it was! It worked! Seshemetka came through and used my hand to write, page after page – and much of it was what I have just told you about Meretseger.'

She lowered her voice and I moved closer to hear. 'And the most important thing of all was her warning that we are in danger.'

'We are?'

'I do not mean personally – although personal danger is not excluded! – I mean our country, everyone now living – is in danger so long as that mummy exists. The Ka of Meretseger still inhabits it – and if it is ever able to be reunited with the other parts of her soul, she will truly live again.'

I could see she was deeply serious in her conviction that the unquiet spirit of a woman who had died thousands of years ago posed a real threat to our world today. 'But how could that happen, Violet? Does she think the Ka could escape the ancient body that holds it and enter into a living person?'

I stopped, for the image from Jesperson's Egyptian tale had just come to mind: something that might have been a winged beetle or a cloud of dust emerging from the mummy's unwrapped mouth, and the man standing closest to it suddenly collapsing in a dead faint. 'But then, unwrapping might be the biggest risk,' I said. 'That might allow the Ka to be released – so it might be best to try to stop it. After all, it does not seem to pose much of a threat where it is now. If it could be kept away from the public . . .'

Violet looked unhappy. 'I can only tell you what Seshemetka thinks. If the body is destroyed, the Ka will no longer have a home and it will die. As long as her mummified body survives, there is danger. There is danger now, as there has been ever since it was brought to this country. Meretseger is not dead and she will remain a threat until her mortal remains are finally and utterly destroyed.'

CHAPTER FOURTEEN

Introducing Pagan Brown

Mr Jesperson returned later in the day, just as Edith and I were clearing away the dishes from the afternoon meal.

'There's plenty left for you on the table,' she told her son. 'Salads and cheese and bread – it was far too hot to cook. I'm going upstairs to have a little rest now – perhaps you might help Di to clear away when you are done? I will do the washing-up later.'

'Are you unwell, dearest?' He bent down to peer into her face with concern, but she gently pushed him away, assuring him that she was perfectly well, only a little tired.

'You can leave everything to us,' I told Edith. 'Including the washing-up. Now, if you protest, I shall think you do not trust me with your precious porcelain.'

That made her laugh, for the dishes were a common variety, and cost little to replace, and so I won her agreement.

When Edith had left the room, I sat down again. Jesperson was already filling his plate. 'I had a visit today from Miss Dawes,' I said. 'Shall I tell you all about it, or have you found something interesting from your reading that you'd like to discuss first?'

'Not about my reading, but my conversation with Pagan Brown may prove useful.'

The name was familiar, but I could at first not think why. 'Pagan Brown?'

'A chap I have often noticed in the Reading Room, and the man who came to mind when Mr Campbell spoke of "a shabby gentleman who spends his days divining mysteries from a close study of hieroglyphics" – you remember?'

I did, but, 'I supposed there must be more than one.'

He gave a snort of amusement. 'No doubt. But catching sight of Mr Brown in the courtyard this morning, I thought I should take the opportunity to make his acquaintance. I realised almost immediately that he is a mine of useful information on all things Egyptian. He is something of an expert on ancient Egyptian magical practices, but he is not – as he was quick to inform me – a believer, and certainly not a practitioner, despite having encountered a few of that sort in London.'

'Indeed?' I was alert to the possibility that a new direction for our investigation had opened up.

Jesperson made a noncommittal noise as he carved off a chunk of cheese and added it to his plate along with a heaping spoonful of tomato chutney.

'Well, who are these modern, would-be Egyptian magicians? Members of the Golden Dawn?'

'No, no. As I understand it, although they use Egyptian

imagery and name their temples after Egyptian gods, in the
Golden Dawn their magical practices are derived more from
the Kabbalah by way of the Rosicrucians. In any event, Mr
Brown is of the opinion that there is no single united magical
order to which these modern mages belong. Rather, they hew
their own paths, working in isolation; if they are aware of the
existence of others, they have no desire to share their own
discoveries with them.'

He began to eat, attacking his food with his usual enthusiasm.

'Did he give you any names?'

After finishing his mouthful, he explained, 'I told him, in
strictest confidence, that we were conducting an investigation
into the theft of several small items, none of them with any
real marketable value, and although there was the possibility
that it was simply a prank, it was more likely that they had
been taken by someone with a purpose for them, someone
for whom they had more worth than would be perceived by
the common man.'

I wondered if it had been entirely wise to tell a stranger – and
a potential suspect – anything at all about our investigation.
Although I thought I showed nothing of my unease, Jesperson
evidently sensed it, for when he spoke again it was to say, quite
casually, 'I knew Brown to be on friendly terms with Budge,
who has often allowed him to inspect items not on public display. And, I confess, I took to the fellow: he strikes me as an
honourable man, far more straightforward than Mr Henderson.
Now, if *Brown* had wished to examine something and Budge

had turned him down, I do not believe he would have felt entitled to "borrow" anything, as Henderson did. But scholarship, like the acquisitive desires of the true collector, may lead to obsession and if, in a moment of weakness, Pagan Brown had taken anything that was not his, perhaps my turning to him for help would prick his conscience and lead to a confession.' He shrugged. 'Or at least the things might turn up again, quietly returned by the penitent borrower. Anyway, I decided to tell him what the missing objects were: the tyet, a papyrus, contents unknown, and the mummies of some small animals.'

I gestured at him to continue and he went on, 'He said he could not speak to their moral natures, but he found it hard to believe that anyone would bother to steal such small mummies when they are easily available and very cheap to purchase. Cats are common – they are found buried en masse; they are, I have discovered, now being sold in bulk as fertiliser. Something unusual, like a crocodile, or a well-preserved ibis, might be tempting, but on the whole, he thought it unlikely. As for the tyet – they are also very common, and would present no temptation to a magician.'

'Not even if it was made of iron?' I interrupted.

'Well, he had never heard of such a thing, but the material did not change his opinion. He asked if there were any symbols carved into it, and when I said I believed not, he said he could not imagine why a magician would want one. The tyet was supposed to have been a prophylactic against certain ailments, and it was traditionally interred with the dead, its usual place being at the throat; but without an accompanying word of power, he could think of no reason to steal something so easily bought or made. Now, if it had been a scarab, that would be another matter entirely, for the scarab was believed to possess great power. Depending on the size, the material it was made of, the age and provenance, and most especially if it had been inscribed with words of power, a magician might very well be fired with the desire to possess it at any cost. Likewise, if the papyrus contained a spell or instructions for a magical ritual, then a would-be magician would seem a likely thief . . . but, of course, we do not know the contents. In sum, Pagan Brown thought there was no reason to think the thief was a magician or a scholar, and I am inclined to agree with him.'

He picked up his fork. 'Now, tell me about your visitor.'

'Miss Dawes thinks the mystery mummy had better be destroyed,' I said, and gave him a quick summary of the latest news from ancient Egypt while he ate and listened with equal intensity.

'Interesting,' he said when I had finished. 'Pagan Brown said it is a widely held belief that the ancient Egyptians were the greatest magicians of all time, and that their most powerful priests had the ability to restore the dead to life. I do wonder about that ancient priest . . . perhaps we should try to get a bit more information about him and his present whereabouts, if Seshemetka would be so obliging.'

Despite Violet's firm belief in the existence of Seshemetka, I was not so convinced of the reliability of evidence obtained in this way. Even if Violet really was the reincarnation of an ancient Egyptian temple maiden and able to call on her actual memories, I did not see how it could help us solve Mr Sand's mystery, and I said so.

'But someone living must know what happened to those missing items. We should question all the guards, and the night-watchmen, too. And the cleaners.' With sudden inspiration, I added, 'Perhaps one of them has a child and brought him to work after closing time, and that child just happened to carry off – or simply play with and then hide? – a few odd articles. And if we could ask Mr Budge about any visitors he had on that particular Wednesday evening . . .of course, only if Mr Sand gives us permission . . . I might write to him tomorrow to raise the question.'

My letter turned out to be unnecessary, for the first post the following day brought a letter from Mr Sand himself, writing to say that he was happy to pay us for our work to date, but our services were no longer required. He had made a clean breast of everything to his employer and so the missing items, although still missing, were no longer his responsibility.

He was pleased to inform us that Mr Budge no longer suspected Mr Campbell of any wrongdoing. The missing papyri had been returned and the man who had taken them (whom he preferred not to name) had confessed to stealing something else (unspecified) from the Museum, which a 'superior private detective agency' had recovered without attracting any undesirable publicity.

'I deduced at once that yours must be the detective agency,' I read aloud, and Jesperson snorted.

'Deduced, did he? Everyone is a detective nowadays.'

Smiling, I continued reading aloud, 'Mr Budge is of the opinion that the same man must have been responsible for taking my tyet and the papyrus from my work-table, and probably the two mummies, one of which, as I think I said, was a cat, and the other, according to Mr B (who has a stronger recollection of the contents of those shelves) was an oblong sort of parcel that, having unwrapped a few in his time, most likely contained a very long but tightly coiled snake.'

I stopped abruptly and we stared at each other. I felt distinctly uneasy, but Jesperson looked rather pleased, as if this confirmed his own suspicion.

'Go on,' he said, and with a deep breath, I continued, 'To make up for the loss of the tyet, Mr Budge was kind enough to give me another small gift from his personal store of amulets. I hope you feel, as I do, that all is well that has ended well. Thank you for all your help. I remain, yours sincerely, E. M. Sand.'

I put the letter down. 'Well, that is the end of that affair.'

Jesperson laughed. 'On the contrary. It is barely the beginning.'

CHAPTER FIFTEEN

An Unexpected Visit

Later in the day, I answered a knock at the door and was greatly surprised to discover Miss Matilda Verver on the doorstep, looking more grown-up than at our first meeting, and even more wonderfully Pre-Raphaelite in a flower-printed Liberty gown, her hair flowing free beneath a smart straw boater.

She so compelled the eye by her vivid presence that I only realised she was not alone when I heard a soft voice with a gentle Scottish burr say, 'I beg your pardon – I hope we do not intrude?'

'Mrs Munro?' I guessed, smiling at the little grey mouse of a woman at Matilda's side.

'Yes, this is my grandmother,' said Matilda, before the woman could reply. 'And I told her there was no need to write and wait for an invitation before we came – you are in a *business*, one where people must call in at all hours, and without an appointment, isn't that right?'

I gave her a cool reply. 'To an extent, you are right, but

we are not shopkeepers, you understand. Sometimes business calls us away. And this is our home, as well as an office. Most people *do* write to arrange an appointment, unless the matter is quite urgent.'

'Oh, dear,' murmured Mrs Munro. 'I did try to tell you, Matilda . . .'

At once I regretted my tone, for it had not been my intention to cause the elderly lady any distress, but only to mildly rebuke her granddaughter.

'I beg your pardon, Mrs Munro, but it really is of no consequence, for we are in fact quite free at the moment and it is a pleasure to have company. I have kept you standing far too long. Please, come in.'

I relieved Mrs Munro of her superfluous umbrella before ushering both ladies into our consulting room – perhaps today it was the parlour, for I thought it unlikely that any genuine business had brought them to our doorstep. Jesperson was where I had left him, lounging in his chair, nose buried in one of his many newspapers.

He glanced up, then lurched to his feet, scattering the pages of the abandoned paper around him.

'Miss . . . Matilda,' he said. There was a note in his voice I did not recognise, and a glazed look in his eyes as he stared at her. I had often seen his gaze sharpen and fix with fascination on others, but that was nothing like this. His dazed, almost sickly expression gave me an unpleasant tightness in my chest; for a moment, it was hard to breathe.

I calmed myself, and performed the necessary introductions.

'How do you do, Mr Jesperson,' said Mrs Munro. 'It is a pleasure.'

'The pleasure is ours,' I replied for us both, as my partner appeared to have been struck dumb. 'Please, won't you sit down?'

In silence, Jesperson directed Mrs Munro to the most comfortable chair, and, when Matilda sat down nearby, pulled two other chairs closer, to form a cosy circle.

Matilda chose to begin with a combative statement, and a frown someone other than me might have found adorably fierce. 'You have let me down, Miss Lane. You said that you would write, but you did not. And so I have had to come to you.'

Her grandmother sighed, casting a helpless look in my direction.

I was neither charmed nor amused. 'You are an impatient young lady. I have been busy with other things.'

'Busy! With your work?'

'If you like.'

'I should like to know more. Now I know what your work is because Uncle – I mean, Mr Henderson – told me. You and your friend are detectives. Why did you not tell me before? That was very bad of you. You must have seen how interested I was in the subject of women and work. It was not very sisterly of you to keep your work a secret.'

'Sisterly?' I laughed. 'I am not your sister.'

She scowled. 'All women are sisters – or we should be – because we suffer the same injustices and oppressions, and unless we stand together and help one another, how shall we advance? You, a successful, self-supporting, working woman, have a duty to help younger women like me.'

'Oh, dear,' Mrs Munro murmured.

I hardly knew how to reply, but when I turned to Jesperson, he did not notice, too absorbed was he by the sight of Matilda Verver to pay any heed to what she was actually saying. Or was that mere pretence? There was something very odd about his manner. In any case, I saw that I could not rely on him for help, but must answer her myself.

Quietly, and more kindly than I felt, I said, 'If you think it would help you to talk to me about possible opportunities in your life ahead, and to hear about my own experiences, of course I will help you. But now is not the time. Let us make a plan to meet again, just the two of us.'

She brightened at once. 'You will call on me?'

Clearly, this was my duty. I remembered the things I had meant to say to her in the letter I had not written: a warning against treating the widower next door as a harmless old rela-tion, and encouragement to think of something other than her marriage prospects in the future. Her remarks about the need for women to support one another were true, even if she *had* only said it to annoy. 'When would suit you?'

'Could you come to tea tomorrow? Or would Saturday be better for you?' She glanced at her grandmother, who nodded her acceptance.

I knew there was nothing in the diary; Mr Sand had terminated our case and there was nothing new on the horizon. I decided I should get my dutiful visit over with as soon as possible, and agreed to her first suggestion.

Once we had settled on the time, Matilda sat back in her chair, her full lips curved in a contented smile, and looked about the room. 'This is your office, but also your home? How interesting. So many books! I love to read, but it is all novels and poetry for me; anything too difficult makes my brain hurt. That desk is very large – and so untidy. I suppose you share the desk between you, but—'

'Miss Verver.' Jesperson's voice cut across her prattle and made her pause and look at him.

He spoke softly, and I noticed he did not quite meet her eyes, despite addressing her directly. 'Why not admit that you had another reason for coming here today? A letter would have done as well to initiate the friendship you so desire; once you had Miss Lane's address, you might have written. Why did the fact of her profession affect you so strongly? Tell the truth: you wish to hire a private detective. There is some mystery you want us to solve.'

'Nonsense,' said Mrs Munro, sounding uncharacteristically forceful. 'There is nothing of the sort. Matilda was cross when she did not hear from Miss Lane, and too impatient to wait. She is a very headstrong, stubborn young lady, and when she gets an idea into her head, she will not be baulked. There is no mystery; her life, like all virtuous young girls, is a pure, blank page.'

But Matilda was still staring at Jesperson. 'However did you know, Mr Jesperson? Of course, you are a detective – and clearly a very good one indeed. Yes, there *is* a mystery in my life, as Grandmama knows very well, but I do not know if it is one for you to solve.'

'Try us. I enjoy a challenge.'

'Very well.' She sat up straight and glanced at the ceiling. 'I should like to know where I go when I am asleep, and why I do not stay in my bed as I ought.'

I was gripped by a powerful sense of *dèjá vu* as Jesperson asked, 'Are you a somnambulist?'

Her grandmother answered for her. 'Matilda occasionally walks in her sleep. Not often. It is not a big problem. And there is no real mystery about it.'

'It is very mysterious to *me,*' said Matilda, giving her guardian an irritable glance. Then, to me, with a more docile expression, 'I remember nothing about it afterwards. And I have no idea what it is that makes me get up out of my bed and go wandering abroad in my night-dress!'

'You have done it from time to time since you were a child,' her grandmother said. 'The doctors said you should outgrow it, and you will. I know you think of yourself as fully grown, but you are scarcely out of childhood, my dear.'

'I do not remember that.' Her voice was petulant now. 'No one ever told me so.'

'We did not wish to upset you, and we took the advice of the physicians, which is why no one spoke of it to you.' Mrs Munro leaned closer to her granddaughter and patted her hand.

'After your father died, when you came to live with me, it began again, but the doctor said there was nothing to be concerned about. He said it was quite natural, that it was inspired by your grief and mental turmoil as you were forced to adjust to a new life in a strange place. He told me the sleep-walker should never be disturbed, and this would soon pass, so I should try not to worry. And as long as you stayed in the house—' She stopped herself, and, turning to Jesperson, her voice firm, said, 'But this is no concern of yours.'

Matilda frowned. 'It could be, for it *is* a mystery.'

'Not one for any detective.'

Jesperson turned his limpid blue gaze upon Mrs Munro. 'Ah, but we are not "any" detectives. One of our most significant cases began with the request to keep watch and be ready to follow a somnambulist, should he leave his house, to discover where he went.'

She glared at him. 'I make no such request. I am entirely capable of keeping watch over Matilda myself.'

'Night after night? That must be exhausting – it could even be injurious to your own health.'

'Matilda does not get up every night.'

'She's put a bell on my door,' said Matilda helpfully. 'So her poor maid doesn't have to stay up, or sleep with me.'

'I could not bear the thought of locking the child in,' said Mrs Munro, 'and I dare not hide the key to the outer doors, for that would be too dangerous, in case of fire.'

Jesperson rubbed his chin thoughtfully. I wondered if our

guests were also aware of his mounting excitement. When he did not speak, I said, 'So your granddaughter has left the house? Do you know where she goes?'

Mrs Munro gave me a chilly glance. 'I certainly do. I told you there was no mystery. It is the same routine she follows every day in her waking hours. I followed her to the house next door, where she tried and then failed to open the door, for naturally, it was locked. I thought that she might knock, and I wondered if, despite the advice I was given, I should try to stop her, for I disliked the thought of causing any disturbance, or waking poor Mr Henderson, but fortunately, when the door did not open, she turned around and went straight back home again. In the morning she remembered nothing of it.'

She looked at Mr Jesperson. 'So you see, there really is no mystery. The return of her childish sleep-walking habit came about as Mrs Henderson lay dying. The poor lady was very dear to my Matilda, who visited her faithfully every day. Naturally, she was much on my granddaughter's mind, when every hour could have been the poor lady's last. And since she has died . . .well, it is no wonder if Matilda is haunted even in her sleep by the memory, and imagining her dear friend is still alive, tries to visit her one more time. You see,' she repeated, now speaking directly to her granddaughter, 'there really is no mystery about it.'

Matilda's brows drew together and she wore the stubborn look that was already becoming familiar to me. 'No mystery about the times you followed me – but what about when you did not?'

'The doctor explained to me the influence of regular habits on the activities of the sleep-walker. Even when I did not follow you out of the house, I was awake, and I heard you return. Perhaps instead of going next door you only walked up and down our own garden. You were not outside for long enough to go any further.'

'You are wrong.'

'You are very rude to contradict me like that.'

'Forgive me, dear, wise Grandmama, but I am obliged to point out that despite your great wisdom, what you have said is incorrect,' she said, her words slow and heavy with sarcasm. 'You only know about the times when the bell woke you, not about what happened when I took the bell off the door – in my sleep.'

'When was this?' I asked.

'Just after Emma's funeral. I don't remember what day it was . . . but I wrote it in my diary, and if you do take this case, I will tell you.'

'Matilda, this is not a *case*. There is no need to hire detectives. If you are so willing to share such personal details with them, why did you never tell me about it?'

The girl looked troubled. 'It frightened me . . . I did not want to think about it. It is always the same: afterwards, I wake feeling unrefreshed, and there is a certain oppressive mood, like a headache that never comes but just hangs over me all the day. On *that* morning, though, there was something worse, for my feet were all scratched and sore and filthy, and the hem of my nightgown was stained and damp. And I had a patch of nettle rash on one leg – but there are no nettles in our garden, nor in Mr Henderson's garden, so where did I get that from? The bell you had tied to my door was lying on the floor – if it had fallen off, you would have heard it, so I must have removed it myself. You did not hear me go out, Grandmama, and but for the sad state of my poor legs and feet, I might have thought that even if I did get up, I never left the house.'

Mrs Munro was evidently disturbed by this, but she tried not to show it as she said, 'Oh, my dear, how very unfortunate. But it will not happen again, I will make certain of it. These incidents are upsetting, but they will pass as you gradually adjust and accept the loss of your friend. Time is the great healer. And a change of scene will help, for you will have other things to think about, which will allow you to sleep more soundly at night. A few weeks breathing in the good, clean Highland air will work wonders, you mark my words.'

'When do you go to Scotland?' I asked, feeling it was time to move the conversation along from such personal matters that were surely no concern of ours.

Mrs Munro sounded grateful for the change of subject. 'Just over a fortnight from now. We intend to depart on the third of July. My brother-in-law has a house near the River Dee, and we have been invited to stay for some weeks, or longer, if we like.'

To her granddaughter, she said briskly, 'Now, I am sure we have taken up enough of these good people's time. You'll have a visit from Miss Lane to look forward to tomorrow.'

Matilda made no attempt at argument but was on her feet before her grandmother had finished speaking.

'Oh, please, stay a little longer,' said Jesperson as he also stood. 'At least take a cup of tea – and there is cake—'

But Matilda paid him no heed, for her attention had been caught by something on the mantelpiece. I wondered if it was the green jade Buddha, or the garishly coloured elephant, and waited for another of her artless, gushing outbursts. I admit I was surprised when she said nothing, only continued to stare in silence.

Mrs Munro politely declined both tea and cake, holding fast to her decision to depart. 'We are due at the dressmaker's and it would be very wrong of us to be late for our first fitting. Come along, Matilda; no more of your dawdling, if you please.'

Matilda responded to her summons meekly, and smiled at me as she crossed the room. 'Thank you so much for everything. I shall return your hospitality tomorrow, Miss Lane, at four o'clock. Remember the time! I shall be waiting.'

As Jesperson saw them to the door, I looked again at the mantelpiece, and with a sinking sensation, noticed the card inviting us to the unwrapping of 'the Mystery Mummy'. I could only hope that it would have slipped Matilda's mind by the time she got home, and that she would not rush to share the information with her 'Uncle' Henderson.

When Jesperson came back into the room I saw from his expression that he had noted what I had, but before I could open my own mouth, he was already speaking.

193

'Well, no matter. Henderson is bound to find out sooner or later. There is nothing he can do about it now that his accomplice is dead. It is not impossible that he might turn up on Wednesday evening and create a fuss, but forewarned is forearmed. I shall make Budge aware of the possibility. Perhaps Henderson will try again to talk him out of the unwrapping, but' – he grinned suddenly – 'we know Budge won't budge.'

CHAPTER SIXTEEN

Matilda

'Miss Lane – no, that won't do,' Matilda said as we sat down at the table that had been laid for us in the shade of a large, leafy tree in her grandmother's garden. 'You call me Matilda – and that is unfair unless I can use your Christian name also.'

Clearly, she did not accept the convention that children should not address their elders by their Christian names – but then, I had to admit, she was no child.

'My friends call me Di.'

'Di – because with you it's "Do or Die"?' she said, with a burble of laughter.

Her laugh was as lovely as her face, yet I did not find it as congenial as Violet Dawes' giggle. 'No. It rhymes with pie, and, as a child, I was mad for eating pies.'

She cocked her pretty head and gazed at me flirtatiously from beneath lowered lashes. 'I cannot believe it.'

'Cannot believe I loved pies? Why not? I still do.' Then, looking at the tea-table, which was spread with an array of small iced cakes, shortbread fingers and elegantly cut crustless sandwiches, saw there was not a single pie in sight and regretted my casual reply. Trying to make amends, I added hastily, 'And all sorts of other good things to eat. How delicious this looks.'

'I cannot believe you were ever a child.'

For some absurd reason, the foolish remark stung. 'How absurd.'

'No, really. You are so sure of yourself, so poised, so wise, I think you must have been born knowing who you were and what you wanted.'

'Like Athena, sprung from her father's head? In fact, that is my sister's name, but she, like me, grew up in the usual way, as we all do, by making mistakes, and gradually learning to be an adult.'

'I meant it as a compliment.'

'No doubt. But stop and think for a moment: how is it a compliment to imply that wisdom, poise, intelligence or whatever it is you admire about me came naturally, none of my own doing, but as a gift from the gods?'

Now she looked sulky. 'I suppose you think I should despise all the compliments I get on my looks?'

'Compliments are never to be despised, if they are sincere. If someone admires your hat, you recognise the compliment is not only to the milliner, but to your good taste in choosing it, or they mean that it suits you. If they praise the beauty of your eyes, or the shape of your nose, they might as well compliment you on this fine weather, for you had nothing to do with either.

By all means, take pleasure in such praise, but I hope you will learn that it is more gratifying to be praised for something you have *done,* and not for the circumstances of your birth.' I looked at my still-empty cup, and then at the teapot, but she took no notice.

'Good looks and the circumstances of one's birth *are* important,' she said stubbornly. 'It would be dreadful if my family had been poor, but at least I would have my looks to help me move up in the world – the looks God gave me, just as he gave you brains. Or do you mean to pretend that I could be as clever as you if I only tried harder?'

'I think you are at least as clever as I was at sixteen – in your own way.' I looked again at the teapot. 'Would you like me to pour?'

'Yes, thank you.' Her placid acceptance reminded me again of how young she was, and how accustomed to having everything done for her.

'So tell me,' she said, as I offered her the sugar bowl, 'when did you decide to be a detective?'

I smiled. 'It was the decision of a moment, not something I had planned. I happened to see an advertisement from Mr Jesperson, who was just starting out on the career he had chosen for himself. I was in desperate straits financially and had to find some way to support myself. Mr Jesperson's advertisement held out the promise of interesting work that I knew myself to be capable of doing.'

'Had you worked at something else before that?'

'Oh, yes. For several years I wrote and conducted investigations with the Society for Psychical Research.'

Her eyes widened. 'I should so love to hear stories about that!'

'Perhaps another time. For now, I thought you wanted some advice regarding your own future? Or did you want to discuss your somnambulism?'

She wrinkled her nose. 'Not *that*. I wish I had never mentioned it. But I thought it might interest Mr Jesperson and you, as detectives.'

'Did you really mean to hire us to investigate?'

She took a sip of tea before she replied, 'It does not matter what I meant. I should not be able to hire you or anyone else unless my grandmother agreed to pay.' She put down her cup. 'Is there much money to be made as a psychic investigator?'

'It is not exactly a career,' I said cautiously. 'Most of the ladies and gentlemen active in the Society have private incomes, or see it as a side-line to their chief occupation. But if the subject really interests you, and if money is not an issue . . .'

'It is only an issue for me for now. I know I should not complain, because Grandmama does give me everything I need, but sometimes, there are things that I *want*.'

I waited, expecting her to tell me something about these things, but she only stared moodily into her teacup.

Hoping to draw her out, I asked about her hopes for the future.

She groaned. 'The future! What is the future? I am *so tired* of waiting, always waiting. I am not a child any more, but

Grandmama treats me like one. And it seems that will never end until I get married, or come into my inheritance. Twenty-one! That's . . . that's' – she counted on her fingers – 'five years! Why, five years ago I was a little girl – it feels like forever!' She reached for one of the dainty sandwiches, but did not offer me one.

Well, I was not her governess and there was no one else at the table to be shocked by my bad manners, so I reached out and took one for myself.

'I am not like you,' she said. 'I shan't have to work for my living. My inheritance is not so large as to attract fortune-hunters, but enough to ensure I may marry whomever I like, Grandmama says.'

'Or even not marry at all?'

She frowned. 'And be an old maid? What sort of life is that? No, of course I shall marry.'

'Be careful how you choose your master, or you may wish you were back with your grandmother,' I said quietly.

She stared at me for a long moment. 'I would not marry a man who would not let me do just as I like.'

I raised my eyebrows.

'Of course, I must love him – and he will love me – and that means we will each want to make the other one happy, so there will be no problem, I am sure,' she gabbled. 'Oh, Di, just because *you* have made a good life for yourself – you have an interesting occupation, and freedom – that doesn't mean that I could. Most women cannot. There are so many restrictions on us.

Men have it all their way. Only men have power – well, except the Queen, of course. But I cannot hope to become Queen.'

Her sullen expression made me laugh. 'Would you want to be?'

'To have such power? Who would not?'

'I, for one. Oh, Matilda. I would not be so quick to envy the Queen. Royalty comes with many privileges, but many more duties. The Queen's power is largely ceremonial. Surely you were taught that the Queen is the head of state, but not of government. She does not make the laws.'

Matilda sat up at that. 'Even the most important woman in the country – the world! – has to do what others tell her?'

'It will be the same for her son,' I said.

'But it is always harder for a woman,' she said darkly.

Hoping to inject a more cheerful note, I said, 'Did you know, women in New Zealand recently won the right to vote? Surely that will happen here, too. It could be your generation that brings about that change. Not that having the vote would be enough – but it is a necessary beginning.'

Despite having expressed concerns about the rights of women, Matilda was clearly uninterested in the democratic process, so I turned to the subject of work, and the possibility that her future need not be defined entirely by marriage. This was more to her taste, especially as it allowed her to talk about herself.

From what she told me, it was clear that Matilda's education had been haphazard. If she disliked a subject, she was usually allowed to drop it. She was proud of her ability to read and converse in both French and Italian; she could ride a horse, enjoyed singing and dancing, and could play the piano, a bit, but professed no special talent nor any passionate interest in anything specific.

'What would you like to do?' I pressed her. 'If you were free, right now, and your grandmother could not stop you from doing as you liked – as will be the case when you are twenty-one and in possession of your own fortune – what would you do?'

She blinked as she nibbled an iced cake. 'I don't know. My life is so boring.'

I struggled against my rising annoyance with this over-indulged young woman who could not appreciate her own good fortune. Had she been born into a different class or country she would already be handling adult responsibilities. 'You are a very lucky girl. You have the freedom of choice: you will not be forced to marry or to do uncongenial, difficult work simply to survive. And now you're about to go to Scotland. Are you looking forward to that?'

She frowned into her lap and toyed with the fringed end of one loose sleeve. 'I suppose so. I will meet new people. I might fall in love.' She gave a little laugh. 'Or someone will fall in love with me.'

She sipped a little tea as she reflected on this likely prospect. 'I might find myself engaged by September. I must be careful, though. I cannot afford to make a mistake and throw myself away on the wrong man. My marriage will be the proper beginning of my life, not the end of the story, as it is in books.'

Her narrow view of life was so dreary, I thought, but was that her fault? She was unlucky to have been raised as she had been, well-cared for physically, but intellectually and morally stunted, shielded by money and some old-fashioned ideas of propriety from having to ever think for herself, or even look after herself.

'Yes, marriage is a very important decision,' I said. 'But do you truly dream of nothing else?'

She looked blank. 'I never can remember what I dream. When I wake, it is like I have just come back to life.'

'I mean another kind of dreams. What you wish for. What would you like to do?'

'Oh, anything. Everything!' She set her teacup down so hard it rattled the saucer. 'Living here, I can do nothing except what Grandmama tells me. I read books, play with the cat, beg Grandmama to let me go for a walk or for a ride, but of course I cannot ride alone. I have no friends since Emma is gone. I meet no one but a few old ladies. Grandmama won't even let me go into the city by myself.'

To my astonishment, she suddenly reached for my hand. 'Please, Di, be my friend. If you talk to Grandmama, she will trust you to look after me, and not worry. You are older. We could go places together, and you could introduce me—'

'Matilda. Stop.'

She stared at me, her mouth open.

'You have a peculiar notion of friendship. It seems to me that what you want is a paid companion. Or a new governess. Perhaps your grandmother would send you to a class where young ladies are taught deportment and court etiquette and how to dress for their presentation. You might find some friends there, young ladies of your own age and class.' I saw there were tears in her eyes. 'I am sorry. I did not mean to upset you.'

'You don't like me,' she wailed. 'Why? I thought you liked me. Why don't you?'

I took a deep breath. 'I do not dislike you, Matilda.'

'Yet you won't be my friend.'

I sighed. 'I have tried to explain that you are not asking for friendship, but for service. You want a woman who would be trusted by your grandmother to look after you, while supplying you with more freedom and interesting companionship than you get at home. If I had nothing better to do, and if you were better company—'

'How could I be better company?'

She stared at me, wide-eyed.

'Well, for a start, you might attempt to think more about others than always about yourself. Actually, I think that would answer your problem. You are bored and unhappy because you dwell too much on your own feelings. In your friendship with Emma Henderson, for instance – weren't you always thinking of her? Doing things to make her more comfortable, trying to cheer her and ease her pain? You cared for her.'

'That is true,' she murmured.

'*That* is friendship.'

'But you're not ill.' She gazed at me speculatively. 'What can I do for you?'

I was horrified by her misunderstanding, and quickly told her so. 'That is not at all what I meant.'

'Then . . . perhaps I should try to do more for Mr Henderson? That poor man—'

'No, Matilda,' I said earnestly, leaning towards her and touching her hand. 'In fact, quite the opposite. You should stay away from him.'

She looked shocked by my blunt warning. 'But he is my friend! Perhaps my only friend, now.' Her look challenged me to protest.

Instead of an assurance, however hypocritical, what came to my lips was a question – the first of many I wanted to ask. 'Do you spend a great deal of time in his house?'

She was cautious. 'Why?'

'I suppose you see him every day. Your grandmother does not mind?'

'Why should she mind? It is only next door. I have always gone there, ever since I came to London. You know Emma was my friend.'

'Yes, but now . . .'

'Mr Henderson was her husband. He is my friend as well.'

I shook my head. 'You talk like the child you were when you first met the couple next door. But you are a grown woman – a beautiful one – and your best friend's husband is now a lonely widower. Your visits to him could be misconstrued, or lead to consequences you do not want. I am surprised your grandmother has not said something about this to you already.'

'She doesn't see any harm in it, and nor do I,' she muttered, pouting. 'It would be wrong, and hurt him very much if I stopped my little visits. Besides . . . I like to go there.'

'Why? Do you find his collection of antiquities so interesting?'

She wrinkled her pretty nose. 'Heavens, no! Those ugly beetles and other rubbish Uncle brought back from Egypt are of no interest to me. But . . . It was *Emma's* house. When I am there, I can believe she is still nearby, upstairs asleep. I like to look at her picture. Did you see it on the wall? She was so beautiful.'

'Yes, I thought so, too. And what do you think of the sarcophagus? With Mrs Henderson's face painted on it in the Egyptian style?'

'Sad,' she said flatly. 'Do you know, he commissioned that thing as a coffin for his wife? It would have turned a few heads when they carried it into the church, for certain. But they — I mean the people at the cemetery — they said it would not do. You called it a sarcophagus, but I know a *real* sarcophagus is made of stone. That one, the one he still keeps, is only *papier-mâché*. Isn't that funny? But Emma's body could not be buried in it, because in her family's vault all the coffins are made of lead.'

She stopped to wonder at this. 'Lead — imagine! They have very strict rules. But in a way it is just as well they do, because otherwise I do not know what would have happened. Emma's brother was furious when he found out what Uncle meant to do. He raged at the idea that a pagan creation could be used for a Christian burial. He refused to believe that Emma had agreed to it — even though she *had* — and he said that since it was the

Coverley family vault and *he* was a Coverley, it was his decision. Of course Uncle – I mean, Mr Henderson –did not like Mr Coverley telling him what to do, and there would have been a huge row over it and I do not know who would have won – except that it turned out the cemetery had these very strict rules and there was no getting round them. As it is, I shouldn't think Uncle will ever speak to his brother-in-law again.'

She touched the teapot. 'It is still warm. Would you like some more?'

'Thank you.'

She refilled both our cups, then offered me the plate of scones.

Taking one, I said, 'You need something more to occupy your days.'

'I need a friend.'

I grimaced. 'Then put yourself into situations where you will meet them, and develop interests, learn something new. Don't brood – *do* something.'

'What? How?'

'Well, since you are still in your grandmother's care, you must abide by her rules, but perhaps you can make her see that you are no longer a child, and can – indeed *must* – be trusted with more responsibilities. I am sure she does not wish you to be lonely. It would be good for you to take up some pursuit that would get you out of the house and allow you to associate with others. I am sure you will make new friends during your forthcoming visit, but while you are here . . .'

Seeing how interested she looked, I suggested, 'You might

join an organisation, or go to public lectures on some topic of interest. You could do charitable work, perhaps. Look at the notice board in your church and read the advertisements in your local newspapers. Surely your grandmother would not object to you being involved in something organised by the church, or attending the occasional lecture?'

She was glazing over. Maybe I had given her too much to think about.

'One step at a time,' I said encouragingly.

'May I see you again?'

'Of course – I shall look forward to hearing all about your adventures in Scotland. I hope you will not rush into a formal engagement, though, no matter how hard some charming young man presses you.'

She flushed becomingly, then looked down and fiddled with a teaspoon. 'I meant – I really meant, before I go. We did not get off to a good start, you and I, and I know it was my fault. But I wish you would give me another chance.' She looked up. 'May I call on you? When Grandmama and I are in town, Gower Street will not be out of our way. I promise to let you know beforehand.'

I remembered the look on Mr Jesperson's face when he saw her, and quickly said I had rather call on her. 'Then it will be just the two of us, talking together in confidence.'

Her face lit up. 'Oh yes, that would be lovely! Call whenever you like. No need to stand on ceremony.'

CHAPTER SEVENTEEN

The Great Unwrapping

The evening of the great unwrapping arrived.

I asked Edith into my room to help me fasten my dress. 'Will we ever have clothing fashioned so that we women may dress ourselves without assistance?' I wondered aloud. 'Or must we evolve as a species with more, longer and more flexible arms?'

Rather than the laughing agreement I had expected, she said soberly, 'We are not meant to live alone. Someday I hope you may have a husband to help you.'

Her reply gave me a twinge of discomfort. I had never known Edith in any role other than that of a devoted mother, and it had not occurred to me that she might still, even after so many years of widowhood, miss her husband. Rather than say anything about living alone, I replied, 'Yet *men* do not require the assistance of a valet or a wife to look respectable.'

'There you are,' she said, ignoring me as she settled the last silk-covered button into its slot. 'All neat and respectable.'

Her pragmatic assessment was not entirely encouraging. I

stared into the looking-glass. 'But I hope not entirely dowdy and unfashionable. Although it is hard to know what might be the most appropriate attire for observing the unwrapping of a mummy in an academic hall.'

'I imagine it will attract all sorts, if largely of the scholarly class. Mr Budge wishes for it to be regarded as a serious scientific investigation, does he not? Rather than the piece of theatre it will be.' With a gentle smile, she patted my shoulder. 'You have nothing to worry about, my dear. That dress is becoming, and suits you very well.'

Jesperson was in the hall with his hat on already, pacing impatiently in the small space. He looked up as I descended the stairs and I wondered if he might comment, or pay me some small compliment on my appearance, but he said only, 'At last,' and turned to open the door.

'We shall be early,' I warned. The hall that Mr Budge had hired for his demonstration was a part of University College, just a few minutes away.

'I want a seat with a good view,' he replied as he ushered me out.

It was a warm, dry evening, so there was no need for even the lightest wrap. We walked the short distance in silence. Early as it was, there was already a small queue waiting to get in, but, as it turned out, there was no need to worry about the seating, for we discovered when we reached the door that our names were on the list of special guests for whom Mr Budge had set aside the front row.

We were directed upstairs to the viewing chamber above the operating theatre below. This was part of the medical school; we were sitting where students would normally watch a dissection or other surgical procedure. Below us were two empty tables with a work-bench between them, upon which were set out a bowl of water and a towel, and the equipment deemed necessary for the grisly work ahead, including shears, scissors, a scalpel and two small saws.

We took our seats beside a couple of elderly gentlemen who were chatting together in German. I surmised from their appearance that our colleagues in the front row were likely patrons of the Museum, scholars and journalists, for I recognised one newspaper reporter. When I craned my neck to scan the rapidly filling chamber, I spotted Mr Campbell near the back, but there was no one else that I recognised in the overwhelmingly male gathering. If Mr Henderson knew about it, he had elected to stay at home – or perhaps he had been turned away at the door.

At last, with nearly all the seats filled, I allowed myself to relax, relieved to think there would be no trouble this evening.

The show began with Mr Sand and another man carrying in the gilded and painted case of 'Mummy X' between them. The gentle roar of conversation died away to a general rustle of clothing and creaking of chairs as members of the audience sat up or leaned forward attentively.

The men carefully laid their burden down on one of the tables and removed the lid.

The audience reacted with more rustling, sighs and murmurs at the revelation of the mummy inside.

Mr Budge now stepped into our view. With a few words and gestures he instructed his assistants to lift the mummy out of its case and place it on the other table, ready for him to take charge of the unwrapping. He positioned himself near the head, looked up at the audience and began, 'Good evening, ladies and gentlemen. It is a pleasure to see so many familiar faces, and to be assured of your serious interest in tonight's investigation. Unlike the unwrappings so popular in days gone by, this one has a specific purpose, and it will, we hope, provide us information of historical significance. As most of you already know, a mystery hangs over the identity of this particular mummy. We hope to be at least halfway to solving it once I have completed tonight's investigation. Before too long we shall know if the mummy is that of the man named on the cartouche, or a female, as indicated by all the clues showing that the coffin was originally intended for a woman – and a very beautiful woman at that. If the body is that of a man, many details about his life, including his name, are known to us from the hieroglyphics here, and here—' He stepped around the case, pointing to symbols on the painted lid.

'If, however, the body is that of a woman, our mystery will deepen. Who was she, and why was her name so effaced? What dreadful crime had she committed, to rouse the fury of powerful people so that, in order to save her immortal soul from destruction, her friends must hide her body in a concealed chamber to keep it safe? But I am getting ahead of myself.' He rocked back and forth on the balls of his feet, hands thrust into his pockets, and beamed a modest smile up at his captive audience.

'Prior to this evening, we could only speculate, and speculation, in the absence of hard evidence, is nothing more than dreaming. After this evening, we shall know – *something*. At the very least, we shall have one solid fact about the identity of Mummy X. With luck, we may have more information, gleaned from whatever we will find secreted within the layers of wrappings. My hope is that we shall find amulets, jewellery and a scroll of papyrus, all or some of which may be inscribed with the name of the deceased.

'If there are any amongst you who still doubt the necessity for this unwrapping, let me assure you that this is a serious, scholarly endeavour and not the publicity stunt that one unkind journalist has suggested. That it is not designed to pander to macabre or ghoulish interests will be obvious, I hope, from the presence of so many esteemed scholars, historians, archaeologists and Egyptologists in the audience this evening.

'Gentlemen – and ladies' – he inclined his head very slightly in my direction – 'what we do here today will open a small window into the dim and distant past.'

His solemn expression turned to the beginnings of a smile as he spread his arms open invitingly. 'Now, with no more ado, let the unwrapping commence! The large shears, if you please, Mr Sand.'

Prolonging that first moment, Mr Budge brandished the shears, the blades sparkling as they caught the light. Then he turned and in two steps was standing over the mummy. As gently as a doctor solicitous of the feelings of a living patient, he slid a blade beneath one of the outer layers of bandaging around the neck and made the first cut.

'This may take some time,' he announced cheerfully as he began to unwind the long strip of old linen. 'The purpose of mummification was, of course, to arrest bodily decay and preserve the corpse for a long time, perhaps for ever. The ancients believed that only so long as the body was still in existence could the soul of the deceased retain the possibility of being reborn.

'After death, all the internal organs were removed, the body cavity was cleaned out and sewn up again before the corpse was bathed in a special solution to . . . to . . . well, one might compare it to the pickling or preserving of fruits and vegetables.'

He laughed, but there was something slightly off about it, I thought. Because he was looking down at his work, I could not see his facial expression. My sense that something might be wrong was amplified when I felt Jesperson shift in the seat beside me to lean forward over the railing, keenly alert to what was happening below.

The linen strips were piling up on the floor at Mr Budge's feet, but as he continued to pull them free of the body, his voice had changed. No longer was he the confident lecturer reciting well-known facts; now he sounded almost hesitant. 'Well, this is odd, I must say. The usual practice was to cover the linen strips with gum – understand, they were not merely wrapping the corpse, but gluing each new layer to the one beneath. Over time, the layers adhered together, and to the body they were meant to protect, to form a single indistinguishable mass of gum, cloth and skin. Unwrapping a mummy after several thousand years is not easy – indeed, it can sometimes be practically impossible. That is common – but this . . . I have never encountered anything like this. What has happened? Could there have been something in the air of the tomb that caused a chemical reaction, dissolving the glue at an early stage?

'Here, now, I have reached the throat – can you see? And on it, as expected, is the usual protective amulet, the tyet, also called the girdle of Isis – goodness! I have seen only one other like this . . . most unusual, I should have said unique if not for the one other – made not of stone or wood or even glass, but *iron*, an iron tyet, d'you see?'

He held up the small iron figure, raising it above his head so that it caught the light. A wave of subdued excitement ran through the audience at this discovery; there were murmurings, and one or two people went so far as to clap their hands.

Mr Budge handed the treasure to his assistant, who gazed at it in obvious astonishment before turning away to put it down very carefully on the table.

'I think I had better use a smaller implement. The scissors, please, Mr Sand,' said Mr Budge, handing him the shears. 'This is like no other mummy I have had to deal with before. Brute strength is not required here but delicacy – and – what can I say – this is all quite unexpected—'

214

He was almost babbling now, and beads of sweat breaking out on his brow were catching the light, like the tyet had done.

'Thank you, Sand,' he said as he received the scissors. 'Stand right beside me, if you will. Come closer. I know you are new to this, but you've seen other mummies, you know how the flesh takes on the feel of old, dry leather; how it shrinks against the bone; how dark in colour – whereas this – there is no comparison to *this*.'

Around us people were leaning forward, all trying to see what was evident only to the two men below. Jesperson got to his feet and leaned over the railing so far I was afraid he might topple over. I stared at the lower half of the mummy, still swathed in bandages; the upper part of the body was still hardly visible, hidden from our view by the bodies of the two men leaning over it.

'Perhaps it is only the throat, only one small piece of flesh that was missed, or reacted differently, resisting mummification?' Mr Sand sounded nervous and uncertain as he offered this suggestion. 'Could it have been a chemical reaction caused by the touch of iron?'

'Nonsense! What sort of chemical reaction do you imagine that could be? Besides, the amulet would have been placed there at the *end* of the drying process, when the body was being wrapped. And if it – if any part – had not been preserved, no prayers or touch of iron could stop the rot from setting in. That is not . . . that is . . . Feel the flesh, touch it! That is flesh, not bone. Cold dead flesh, but soft still, not utterly rotten, and certainly not desiccated.'

215

Mr Budge had apparently forgotten the presence of the audience and was thinking aloud. 'How is it possible? Here, let me get the rest of these wrappings off – we must see more. Perhaps it is only a skull beneath the bandages – look, it comes away so easily – only the first layer was glued, the rest has been merely wrapped about the head – one more pull and—'

His voice rose to a shriek and he cried, 'Dear God!'

Reeling back from the table, Mr Budge dropped the scissors to the floor, but the swathe of linen continued to come away in his hand. Mr Sand stared, ashen-faced, and at last we could all see the mummy's face.

The body of a woman was revealed, no ancient corpse, but one who, judging by the appearance of her pale, waxen face and long grey hair, had been alive until a few weeks ago.

'Emma Henderson,' said Jesperson softly.

Staring down at the dead face, I remembered the portrait on the wall of Mr Henderson's parlour, the smaller framed photographs and the faux-Egyptian mask on the replica mummy case. I could see very little resemblance to any of those memorials, but I knew Jesperson was right. There was no one else it could be. Now Henderson's care for it and his anxiety that it should not be unwrapped made more sense – and at the same time, it made *no* sense at all – for why had Henderson been willing to sacrifice the corpse of his beloved wife to keep us from finding the ancient mummy he'd stolen from the Museum?

Around us, the audience was buzzing, exclaiming and muttering. One of the men in our row got to his feet and leaned over the railing to call down to Mr Budge, 'Sir! Explain yourself, sir – what is the meaning of this absurd spectacle?'

Mr Jesperson gripped my arm. 'Come on,' he murmured. 'We must find that mummy.'

CHAPTER EIGHTEEN

Highgate Cemetery

We hurried back home and gathered the tools Jesperson considered necessary: a bulls-eye lantern (the sort carried by policemen), his set of lock-picks, a chisel and – a shiver of trepidation ran through me – a loaded pistol.

Outside, he hailed a passing hansom cab and instructed the driver to take us to North Lodge, Highgate. 'It's between St Michael's Church and the cemetery.'

'Got it, guv'nor.'

I wondered if my partner intended to break in to the cemetery. Although I said nothing, he sensed my doubts and, once the door was shut and we were away, he explained, 'Most of the cemetery employees live on-site. I hope Bert Garnett is still there, for he was a good friend to me in my younger days and he may be willing to help.'

His friendship with Bert Garnett must have started in Jesperson's childhood, before his mother took him abroad. I wondered if his father was buried in Highgate Cemetery, but I did not like to ask, for neither he nor Edith mentioned Mr Jesperson very often. His mother's silence on the subject had surprised me – that she remembered her late husband fondly, I did not doubt, but if she ever visited his grave – or regretted her inability to do so – she never spoke of it. From my experience with other widowed ladies of my acquaintance, this was most unusual.

'My grandparents are buried there,' Jesperson remarked suddenly, almost as if reading my mind. 'I was taken from time to time to pay my respects, but I'd get bored and wander off – that is how I came to meet Bert. I hope he will remember me.'

'I hope he will still be living there.'

'Oh, I think he will. He was quite a young man then, and he loved the place. He took pride in his work, and had no other aim in life than to continue there. Of course, one never knows what may happen to change one's plans.' He sounded wistful. 'I should have called upon him before now. If he treats me as an importunate stranger, I will have only myself to blame.'

As we moved further away from the centre of London, the traffic lightened and we made good time, until I could see the steeple of St Michael's, higher than any other church in London, growing larger with every minute. At last we pulled up before a handsome Gothic building on the slope of the hill below the church. Jesperson paid the driver and led the way through an arched entranceway into a covered yard. There were four doors, but without pausing long enough to read the engraved brass name-plates, Jesperson rapped smartly on one of the doors.

Almost at once we heard a deep male voice asking, 'Who is there?'

'Jasper Jesperson, here to see Bert Garnett.'

The door flew open to reveal a small, lean, but powerfully built dark man in shirt-sleeves and braces. White teeth gleamed in his smile through a thick, curling black beard. 'Is that really you, young Jasper? Only not so little now! On my life, how you've grown – like Jack's beanstalk – and still skinny as a beanstalk at that! Come in, come in!'

As I stepped forward, Mr Garnett exclaimed, 'And who is this charming young lady? What's a fine woman doing in the company of such a wild, beardless youth?'

'Mind your tongue, you old reprobate,' Jesperson replied with a broad grin. 'Miss Lane, this is the man I have told you about, a staunch companion of my youth, Mr Bert Garnett.'

'How d'ye do, Miss Lane? No offence intended, or taken, I hope. Jasper and I always did tease each other and in my mind he's still a little boy, though he always was advanced for his years, to be sure. Please come through.' He ushered us into a rather cluttered but comfortable sitting room. 'I'll put the kettle on – or will you take a glass of beer with me?'

A gesture from Jesperson kept me on my feet. 'Very kind of you, Bert, but Miss Lane and I are here on business. I've a favour to ask.'

He rolled his eyes and gave a theatrical sigh. 'Young people today! Nothing, not a word or a letter for I don't know how many years, then you turn up without warning, asking for my help. No, no, no need to apologise! Of course it's all right. I told you that you could always come to me for anything, at any time. So what can I do for you?'

'Let us in to the cemetery, if you would be so kind.'

Bert Garnett gave a start, glanced quickly at me and then back at Jesperson. 'Now? Tonight?'

'There's no time to waste. I can explain—'

'You are a silver-tongued devil. I had rather hear Miss Lane explain – why tonight, when you could enter freely during the daytime?'

There was nothing to take offence at in his words or manner, but I understood the direction his thoughts were tending and dealt with it forthrightly. 'Sir, Mr Jesperson and I are part-ners in detection – here is our card. Our present investigation has brought us here because of something that happened this evening; we have good reason to suspect that a piece of stolen property has been hidden in one of the vaults.'

Mr Garnett looked from the card to Jesperson. 'What sort of stolen property? Jewels, gold, that sort of thing?'

'Something very different,' Jesperson said. 'An Egyptian mummy was stolen from the British Museum – the man who took it swapped it for the body of his wife and, we suspect, interred the mummy in her place in the family vault.'

'A very strange sort of prank,' Mr Garnett commented. 'Is the fellow mad?'

'Probably. He wrapped his wife's body like the mummy he had

taken and gave it to the Museum. His deception was uncovered about an hour ago.'

Bert Garnett sighed heavily. 'Jasper, I cannot help you, much as I should like to. The only person authorised to open a vault is a key-holder – a member of the family, or in special circumstances, one of the partners in the corporation. I do not have that right, nor do I hold the keys. And any exhumation can be done only by permission of the Home Office. You must wait until tomorrow, I fear.'

'Tomorrow will be too late – Henderson may be on the move already; we might be too late to stop him from hiding it somewhere else. I am not asking you to open the vault, Bert, just to open the gates and let us in to the cemetery, so that we can keep watch until morning, by which time we can hand the matter over to the police.'

'Henderson, you say? Is that the name of the family?'

'Yes. The funeral was—'

'No.' Mr Garnett looked relieved. 'You must be mistaken, Jasper. There is no vault for anyone of that name.'

'Mrs Henderson was a Coverley before she wed.'

I saw him recognise the name. 'Yes,' he said, 'there is a family vault for the Coverleys. It's in the Egyptian Avenue. Only let me put on my boots and I will take you there.'

In addition to his boots, Mr Garnett put on a jacket and picked up a lantern and a stout stick, 'In case someone tries to give us any trouble,' he said with a wink.

The warmth of the day had completely gone from the air when we emerged onto the darkened street and there was a faint mist, a premonition of the fogs that would come later in the year. Although it was not very late, it might have been the middle of the night out here, so still and silent was it, far from the bustle of city life. We met no one, and not a single cab or carriage went by during our walk down Swains Lane.

Bert Garnett unlocked the black iron gates with a big key and pushed one open just wide enough to admit us. I jumped a little as the hinges gave a low wail, like a child's protesting sigh.

'I am surprised at you, Jasper, asking me for help in this way,' he said, following us inside. 'Surely you have not lost your skill at climbing? Tall as you are, you'd be even better at it now – and I'll bet you haven't forgotten the best place for getting in when the gates are locked. Although' – he glanced at my fashionably narrow skirt. –'it would be considerably more difficult for a lady.'

'Do not make the mistake of underestimating Miss Lane,' said Mr Jesperson, then, just as the custodian turned away to push the gate shut behind us, he said, 'But, Bert – may I call you Bert?'

Mr Garnett, who had been about to insert the key in the lock, turned back in surprise. 'Why ever not, when it's what you've always called me? I suppose I may still call you Jasper, even now you've grown up into *Mister* Jesperson?'

'I hope you will,' he said, his voice warm. 'I was afraid you might be cross with me for not coming to see you before now – in truth, I thought you might not remember me at all, after so many years away. And . . . well, for me to turn up out of the blue only because I wanted something from you is . . . is not very . . .' Jesperson looked and sounded unusually humble, his voice dropping so low that Mr Garnett moved closer to hear him, tucking the key away in one of the capacious pockets of his jacket as he did so.

'Oh, come now,' he said gruffly. 'I'm your friend Bert and you're my friend Jasper, and there's nothing to be said about your long absence but that I am glad you're back and happy to be able to help. Now come along, and mind how you go.'

We followed him through the colonnade and down a flight of steps onto the gently rising main path through the west cemetery. I had visited this place in the daylight hours, but now the darkness, broken only by the lights of our two lanterns, made it a very different place. The Egyptian Avenue, one of the great cemetery's best-known attractions, took longer to reach than I remembered, but we were walking slowly in tense silence, with no idea what might await us at our destination.

At last the entrance to the Egyptian Avenue loomed just ahead, looking bigger and more ancient in the lantern-light than it ever did by day. The entrance, based on a tomb at Luxor, was striking at any time, but now, shadow-haunted, it had a more sinister aspect, though I had spent too many years of my life searching for proof of an afterlife to be disturbed by mere appearances – any threats it held would come not from the ranks of the silent dead around us, but from living interlopers intent on their own selfish, violent pursuits.

Once past the twin obelisks and through the column-flanked archway, we left the path beneath the night sky for the deeper darkness of a short tunnel lined on either side with individual family vaults. Each was guarded by a heavy iron door decorated with an inverted torch, which Mr Garnett told us symbolised a life extinguished here on earth, but still burning in another realm.

'There is room inside each one for twelve coffins,' said Mr Garnett. 'None are filled, nor likely to be soon. In all my years I have been present for only two interments in the Egyptian Avenue. Mrs Henderson was to join her parents, and there is space enough for her siblings, their children and her husband when his time comes – but he does not deserve it, not after what he did. What was he thinking, to put some rotten old mummy in her place? Pah!'

He raised his lantern so the light shone on the name incised above one of the middle doors.

COVERLEY

Having given us time to read the name, he lowered his lantern at the same time that Jesperson turned ours to direct its beam on the great cast-iron doors, illuminating the regularly spaced set of holes – six near the top and six at the bottom – that had been made to allow for the escape of gas.

'No signs of mischief. It does not appear that anyone has tried to break in.'

'The keyholder would have no need to break in,' Jesperson said grimly.

'Oh no, of course. Yet I can scarcely believe such desecration from a husband and son-in-law. But you have found the villain – good for you, Jasper! Well, what now? We stand guard over the tomb all night?'

'You are kind to offer us your help, Bert, but there is no need for you to stay. It is our affair; you may safely leave us to our business.'

'I am not leaving,' he answered firmly. 'This may be your "case", or whatever it is you detectives call it, but it is my cemetery. I have my own responsibilities.'

'Of course – I am only sorry to have dragged you into this—'

'Nonsense! I am glad you did, rather than taking matters into your own hands and breaking in one way or another – as I have no doubt you could.'

'If Henderson has not already been and gone, it is likely that our vigil will be entirely unnecessary. He has a key to the vault, but not, I presume, to the cemetery gates?'

'No, of course not. We do not hand out keys to just anyone. Only employees who—' As he was speaking, his face changed; he patted the pocket where he had put the key and it was clear that he was thinking back to the last time he had used it.

Mr Jesperson responded at the same time, saying sharply, 'Did you lock the gate behind us?'

'Of course I did – I must—' Mr Garnett looked nonplussed.

'Or did I?' With an oath, he turned and hurried away, almost running back up the path.

Jesperson smiled with satisfaction. 'I was beginning to think he would never go.'

All business now, he handed me the bulls-eye lantern with the instruction not to shine it in his face as he worked but to keep it directed at the doors. He pulled out the small, flat leather case that contained his pick-locks and crouched before the keyhole. 'Inverted – odd, but it should not be a problem. Ah! There.'

He straightened up and took a step back, gazing at the doors as he replaced his tools in his pocket. 'Now then, before our friend returns to raise objections, let us see what waits within. Will you stand back and direct the light?'

There was no handle on the doors, but when Jesperson pushed, heavy as they were, they moved easily, almost soundlessly.

I extended my arm, directing the lantern's beam to reveal the space inside. It was larger than I had imagined, but only three of the twelve stone ledges held coffins. A human figure, utterly still and wrapped in bandages, was lying on a folded quilt on the lowest ledge. It was a strange, disturbing sight.

'There she is,' I murmured. I cannot explain what came over me at that moment at my first sight of that weird, white figure; I felt in the grip of an awed fascination, like someone encountering the aura of a powerful supernatural being. I had seen mummies before, many of them in the British Museum, as well as photographs recording the discoveries made beneath the sands of Egypt, but never had I felt like this. The mummy in this cemetery vault, although it was out of place, was neat and inoffensive by comparison with other, more disturbingly decayed bodies that I had viewed with barely a flicker of unease, and although I had been prepared for the discovery, the actual encounter affected me in a way I could never have imagined. I was both unnerved and fascinated, and determined to know why. All at once, I was seized by the conviction that the thing lying on that ledge beneath other coffins, surrounded by the invisible dead, was *alive*. But it was no natural life. Something within it pulsed with a strange power that called to me, a magnetic compulsion to go nearer, close enough to touch it. Indeed, I longed to put my hands on it, to feel the physical reality that would assure me this was no dream. I would learn so much, I thought, if I could only get closer.

When I stepped into the vault, a strange shadow loomed up from the dark recesses. I thought it must be a trick of the light and was undeterred even when Jesperson shouted, 'Get back!'

His words did not cut through my strange detachment, and I continued to move forward until he pushed me aside, stepped in front of me and fired the pistol.

The noise of the shot in that enclosed space was deafening. I thought I heard a high shrill scream, but the echo of the gunshot was resounding still and it might have been only a trick of acoustics.

'What—?' I started, but Jesperson had gripped my hand and was making me lift the lantern until it shone on the headless body of a large snake writhing on the floor.

A cobra.

I felt a little faint.

'It's dead. You're all right. Come outside – the air in here is foul.'

Feeling weak and dizzy from the rapid rush of emotions, I was grateful to lean on him for a moment as he led me out. Although we were still within the tunnel, the air was cleaner and I gulped it in, hoping it would flush away the stench and the lingering trace of that weird, dreamlike compulsion that had gripped me. I did not want to think about how near death I had come. If I had reached the mummy, if Jesperson had not stopped me . . .

'Was that the snake that killed poor Mr Leary?' I asked, still gasping.

'I should think so. *Two* poisonous snakes on the loose in north London would be one too many. It cannot be here by accident. Someone put it there, to guard the mummy.'

'Jasper! What the devil?'

The angry shout came from Mr Garnett, who had come racing back. 'What happened? Was it your man Henderson? Do not tell me you've killed him!'

'Calm down, Bert. There's nobody else here. It wasn't a man I shot, but a cobra. Yes, a venomous snake – see for yourself.' Putting his hand on the other man's shoulder, Jesperson turned him towards the open vault.

The sight did nothing to calm Mr Garnett. 'Who opened that vault? Did you break in? What are you playing at? You've gone too far this time, son, detective or no detective. Exhumations are strictly by permission—'

'Hardly an exhumation,' Jesperson cut in. 'As you will be able to confirm, all three coffins are still in place, unopened. The mummy is just where I thought it might be.'

'You broke in! As soon as my back was turned—'

'Now you are leaping to conclusions, and really, it is awfully unfair to call it "breaking in" – I broke nothing. I did no more than give the doors a little push – something I thought *you* might have done, when you declared on such a superficial inspection that there was no sign of disturbance. I mean it was hardly even a push, I only *leaned* on them a bit, and blow me if they didn't fall open.'

He was over-doing the wide-eyed innocent act and Bert Garnett was not taken in. 'Now see here, young man, don't give me that nonsense. Them doors are always locked and I would have noticed—'

'Indeed, I was as surprised as you,' Jesperson pressed on. 'They were shut, but whoever was here last – whoever put the mummy and the cobra inside – was careless and forgot to lock up afterwards. Easily done, don't you think? Like you forgetting to lock the front gate? I hope you did it this time before you came rushing back here.'

But before he could respond to Jesperson's accusation, Mr Garnett was startled into silence by a sound that made the hairs rise on the back of my neck: someone not very far away was singing.

The voice was high and eerie, the song was dirge-like, the words impossible to make out, and the singer was coming closer by the second.

Jesperson started towards the entrance to the enclosed avenue, with Mr Garnett and me close on his heels – but we all stopped abruptly at the sight of the woman dressed in long, pale fluttering garments who was walking down the path towards us, singing an incomprehensible, almost tuneless, song of mourning.

As she came within the reach of our lantern-lights, she was revealed as no spectre, but a tall young woman with rippling golden hair, wearing a white night-dress, a sprigged cotton dressing-gown and a pair of dirty pink slippers. Her face was both beautiful and familiar.

'Matilda,' Jesperson breathed.

It was indeed Miss Matilda Verver, walking and singing in her sleep, inasmuch as such a tuneless dirge might be dignified by that term. The words, if they were not nonsense, I guessed were in a language no living person had spoken for thousands of years.

'Do you mean to say you know this person?' Mr Garnett demanded, but Jesperson was already walking silently towards the somnambulist.

Left to explain, I said, 'That young lady lives in the house next door to Mr Henderson. We have been told she suffers from somnambulism, but . . .'

'I never heard the like. If this is some more of Jasper's mischief—'

I turned to him, frowning. 'Whatever do you mean?'

He shook his head. 'There was no mention of a girl, yet here one is, and no stranger to Jasper. See how he looks at her, making calf's eyes! And he made certain the gate was left unlocked. Oh, yes, I see it now, the way he distracted me – he wished the gates left open for *her*.'

'No! Certainly not!'

But I could not tell him the *real* reason had been so he could unlock the vault. And I wondered if Matilda would have been forced to turn back if the gate had been locked – perhaps she had come over a wall, or knew some other way in. Jesperson and I had some experience of somnambulists, after all, and they have been known to perform feats far beyond their usual abilities. But in any case, here she was and we must see that she came to no harm.

At least she had stopped that terrible wailing. She came to a sudden halt, just inches from Jesperson, who was now blocking her way towards the avenue, then she turned on her heel and walked unhurriedly away.

As Jesperson followed her, I was suddenly anxious about being left behind. Mr Garnett, perhaps sensing my mood, said, 'Go on, Miss Lane. I'll stand guard here. If anyone else should come, my stout stick will see him off.'

'Is the gate locked?'

'Never had the chance – I ran back the moment I heard the shot.' He dug into his pocket and handed over the key. 'Be a good girl and lock it behind you, will you? And give it to the police. I'd rather not have to spend the whole night here on me own.'

'You are a treasure to help us like this.'

Ducking his head, he gave a bashful grin. 'Not at all. Strikes me that you are the treasure, Miss Lane. I hope that scamp Jasper knows how lucky he is.'

My cheeks were burning as I hurried to catch up with my partner. Thinking over what I had seen in the vault, I realised there was something else wrong with it. Reaching his side, I blurted out, 'That cannot be Mummy X.'

Jesperson had his eyes fixed on the sleep-walker, but my words broke his concentration. He looked down at me. 'Why do you say that?'

'Because Mr Budge saw no difference!'

He understood me at once. For the sake of my readers, I should explain that the usual 'mummiform' shape – it was reflected also in the design of the sarcophagus – was imposed upon the corpse at the end of a long process. After the limbs had been individually wrapped in strips of linen, it was usual for the hands to be crossed upon the chest and the legs bound together as the body was swaddled in one final layer to create a smooth, unitary outline. But the mummy we had seen in the vault had limbs that were separately wrapped, and the arms were positioned straight down at the sides.

Falling back slightly from the somnambulant Matilda, Jesperson spoke quietly. 'Another detail that makes me realise Henderson is more dangerous than we thought. I fear we have underestimated him.'

I did not understand. 'Why?'

'Henderson removed the outer wrappings to avoid detection. If he had tried to disguise his wife's body using bed-linen or some such, he could not expect to fool an expert like Mr Budge. But with authentic Egyptian material he was safe so long as the outer wrap remained undisturbed. Probably he did not expect to be found out, but if he did fall under suspicion, it would be safer for him to explain away the presence of another mummy in his house if it did not resemble the missing Mummy X.'

We followed more than escorted Matilda back to her grandmother's house in Swains Lane. I thanked the heavens that the steep road was dark and deserted at this hour of the night, with no one around to see and wonder at the odd procession we made.

We found the old lady playing cards with her maid; she was so shocked by the appearance of her somnambulant granddaughter in our company that she swooned and had to be revived with smelling salts and the massaging of her extremities.

Matilda, in the usual style of somnambulists, made her own way back to bed, even divesting herself of her dressing-gown and filthy slippers before climbing between the sheets. In the morning, I knew, she would remember nothing of the night's adventure.

Of course we could not rush away at once; we must wait to see Mrs Munro conscious and settled, then explain the situation and try to calm her fears. That delay, however, turned out to be fortunate, for it meant that we were just in time to meet two police constables as they left the house next door. One of them, recognising my partner, was happy to tell us what had transpired.

'Poor fellow – he confessed all, though he was unable to explain why he had done it. No doubt he was at least half-mad with grief and exhaustion, for he had been his wife's constant nurse for years, with no thought for his own health.'

'You have left him there alone?' Jesperson asked sharply.

The two constables, one a handsome young fellow in his twenties, the other a rather stout man of perhaps fifty years, exchanged a glance. 'He lives alone – do you think he is a danger to himself?'

'Not to himself, but to others. Why was he not arrested? He should have been charged with his crimes and locked up until he can be brought before a judge.'

There were more uneasy glances, then the older constable replied, 'His crime – well what harm there was is done now, but to no one living. He poses no danger – he will have to pay a fine, perhaps, but the court will likely be lenient, under the circumstances. There is no reason to lock him up.'

'There is every reason,' Jesperson answered sharply. 'You speak of one crime, by which I suppose you mean preventing the proper burial of his wife, mis-use of a human corpse, however the law wishes to define that. But he also stole a mummy from the British Museum, and practiced deception by wrapping his recently deceased wife's body up like a mummy and pretending that it was the thing he had stolen – were you not told about that?'

'N-no sir, there was nothing said about any theft. We were sent to interview Mr Henderson about the discovery of his wife's

body, wrapped up like a mummy in a theatre where it seemed—
Oh.' He stopped, understanding his mistake. Of course they
had been told about the missing mummy; that was the whole
reason why Mrs Henderson's body had been found where it was.
But somehow, as they had confronted Mr Henderson and he
confirmed his culpability for this strange crime, the one behind
it had been obscured, perhaps deliberately.

'We never asked him about the mummy,' said the younger
constable with a frown of annoyance. 'He started weeping,
and talking about his wife . . . he got us all sympathetic and
we never thought of it. I suppose it's still in his house.' He
turned as if to go back to Henderson's house, but Jesperson
stopped him.

'You won't find it there. It is lying on a shelf in his wife's
family vault, not in Mrs Henderson's empty coffin. Bert Garnett,
who works for the cemetery, is there now, standing guard while
he awaits the arrival of police. You have the key, Miss Lane?'

I gave it to the constable. 'This is for the main cemetery gate.'

'We believe it is vital to secure the mummy tonight,' Jesperson
added, 'and to ensure that neither Henderson nor anyone else he
may have employed is able to seize it. There is no telling what
evil consequences may result if the wrong people get hold of it.
There is no time for me to explain the reasons; you must take
my word for it and act immediately. And take care – there was
a deadly cobra in the vault, stolen to order, which operated as
a sort of watch-dog. I despatched it with my pistol, so I don't
think there is anything else to worry about, but without the

time to conduct a thorough search, I can only advise you to act with the greatest caution.'

The police constables were staring at Jesperson with open mouths and wide eyes. I thought of children listening to some fantastic tale and believing every word – at least, for as long as the story-teller held them enthralled.

'What about Henderson?' the elder asked.

'Arrest him – take him into custody. He is unlikely to resist, but even if he tries, he'll be no match for you,' said Jesperson, and the burly constable straightened his back and stood as if to attention.

They responded unquestioningly, as if Jesperson had been a much-admired superior officer giving them their orders. I had seen others do his bidding in this way, and I was both impressed and puzzled, maybe even a little bit envious, wondering how he had come by what seemed an innate power of command. Was it something some men simply were born with, or was it a convincing act he had perfected?

CHAPTER NINETEEN

The Other Mummy

'Was it hypnotism?'

We were in a hansom cab, speeding back to Gower Street, and no one could overhear our conversation, yet still I whispered.

In the dimness I saw him frown and thought he had not understood, but before I could repeat my foolish question, he answered it.

'No. How could it be? That requires close contact, so Henderson certainly could not have done it. Only her grandmother or the maid could have sent Matilda out tonight; surely you do not suspect one of them?'

Remembering past experiences, I argued, 'There is such a thing as a post-hypnotic suggestion.'

'That seems unlikely. Who could have known the mummy was in danger? She arrived too late, but it was surely not by chance that Matilda came when she did.'

'She may have gone there before. It might be a regular event.' But even as I spoke, I remembered the mournful song and the tears I'd seen shining on her pale cheeks, and conceded. 'I suppose Henderson must be our villain.'

'Henderson may be as much a victim as Matilda. We are dealing with something more – or less – than human. Ancient spirits restored to life. Of course, it is what we have long suspected—'

Have we? I wondered.

'—but now I realise there must be two of them. Two ancient Egyptians working together. Miss Dawes was right. You remember, of course, the story I told you about Henderson and the mummy in Egypt.'

'Of course.'

'What people saw emerging from the mummy's mouth must have been the Ka, and when Henderson passed out, it was caused by the shock of another entity passing into his body. Then, I suppose, the Ka may have joined with the man's soul or gone into a sort of hibernation, similar to the state in which it had survived within the mummified remains of its original body. I suspect it has been lying in wait all these years for the right concatenation of circumstances. If Henderson was the reincarnation of that particular ancient Egyptian it could have been simple to awaken that sleeping consciousness within. If not, perhaps the Ka, being the surviving force of a powerful magician, was able to enslave the weaker, living soul and make Henderson his puppet. This is speculation, of course, but I believe it fits with what we know. I should like to understand more about how and why such a strange thing could happen, but we live and learn.

'We know from Miss Dawes that many considered Meretseger

a wicked usurper, and from the fact that her mummified body was hidden and preserved, we know, too, that she had others on her side, determined helpers. The Ka that has been guiding Henderson's actions was evidently one of Meretseger's supporters – and didn't Miss Dawes say there was a very highly ranked priest on her side? He may have been one of those priest-magicians with power over life and death. Everything he has made Henderson do has been to aid Meretseger.'

'Matilda – do you think she is the reincarnation of Meretseger?'

He hesitated. 'That must be considered a possibility. Has she said anything to you that would indicate an awareness of a past life, or a second soul?'

I shook my head. 'Nothing. She expressed a positive lack of interest in anything to do with ancient Egypt. And she told me she never remembers her dreams. It was through dreams that Miss Dawes became aware of her own earlier life as Seshemetka, of course.'

'Then I should say the girl is unaware.' He looked rather relieved by this conclusion. 'And the situation may not be one of reincarnation,' he continued rapidly. 'I have had another thought about that. The Ka of the ancient priest – I wonder if Miss Dawes could tell us anything more about him? – may have been roused to action by the arrival in London of the mystery mummy. As Meretseger's supporter, it would be his duty to find an appropriate living body to house her soul. A beautiful girl, young enough to be malleable, without the defences that an older person might have to protect the self . . . He did not have to look far for what he wanted. It was Matilda's misfortune to be living next door to his new home.'

Since entering into partnership with Mr Jesperson I had encountered genuine instances of psychic phenomena and what has been termed 'the night-side of nature' far stranger than any I ever witnessed under the auspices of the Society for Psychical Research, so by now I should have been accustomed to accepting as fact events that most intelligent people would dismiss as fantastical. Yet something in me baulked at the idea that someone who had died several thousands of years ago in Egypt could be controlling modern-day Londoners and bending them to his ancient Egyptian will.

So although I did not usually argue when Jesperson was so certain of his theory, I protested, 'Surely there is a more rational explanation?'

'I should like to hear it.'

I took a deep breath. 'Perhaps Mr Henderson is mad. It could be his own spirit that is divided, and at times he imagines himself to be an avenging devil from the past. Such things have been known. Matilda has suffered from somnambulism for years, and we have learned from an earlier case about the connections between somnambulism and hypnosis.'

'You propose Henderson as the hypnotist, I suppose?'

'You disagree?'

'Not about that, at least. The only question is whether we are dealing with a madman, or one who is in fact possessed, and I cannot see an easy way to answer that.'

I had an idea. 'Perhaps we should hold a séance?'

He frowned. 'Not with Henderson.'

'Why not?'

'If he is mad, he will string us along, tell us what he thinks we want to hear, like any false medium. But if he is, as I suggest, the host to a powerful undead magician, that would be worse. It could be disastrous. Who knows what damage he might do if allowed to communicate with us directly? This is no biddable, helpful spirit like the one Miss Dawes is in communication with.'

More gently he said, 'I fear your years of attending séances in genteel English drawing rooms have not prepared you for the realities of a much darker sort of spirit. Prior to the rise of the Spiritualist movement, and still outside of it, most people are afraid of ghosts, vampires and other such unnatural presences. If, instead of moving on to another realm, the dead cling to this one, it means danger to the living. It might sound a reasonable idea to ask them what they want – as if they were reasonable. But they are not, and what they desire is nothing we could want.'

I remembered the strange impulse that would have brought me into striking range of the cobra and knew Jesperson was right. Whatever the reason for Mr Henderson's actions, they put others in danger. We could not afford to take any more risks. We were up against someone – or something – that would stop at nothing.

'Then what do you propose to do about it?'

'Miss Dawes has already told you what must be done.'

'Destroy the mummy,' I said, and then, with a gasp, 'but

now that the police have been informed, it will be returned to the Museum – it will be impossible now.'

He smiled. 'Not impossible, and not so very difficult. But that can wait. Our first task will be to get rid of the other mummy.'

'What other mummy?'

'Henderson must have brought it back from Egypt, so it must be somewhere in his house. Why didn't I find it when I searched his house and garden? Because I was not looking for a mummy, only a snake. It is probably in the wardrobe. If only I had gone into the bedroom and looked properly.'

'Perhaps it is just as well you did not. He might have put up a fight.'

His eyebrows rose precipitously. 'Do you mean to imply that *Henderson* could have bested me?'

'Not Henderson alone – if you are right, it would have been two against one, and one armed with magic,' I said quickly.

'Hmmm.' He gave me a doubting look. 'Anyway, we shall have an easier time of it tomorrow morning. We will seize the opportunity to search his house while the man is in gaol. The judge may decide to impose a fine and release him on his own recognisance, so we must act swiftly. And this time, I intend to search every inch – there may be a hidden safe, or a box in the attic where the missing papyrus and the animal mummies are kept safely out of sight.'

I blinked in surprise. 'But – I thought you had decided there were *two* thieves – and we know that Mr Henderson returned those papyri he stole – or *borrowed* – so—'

243

'Well, I was wrong,' he said easily. 'I do, on occasion, get things wrong. Discovering the iron tyet on the throat of the late Mrs Henderson was the first indication that I had not yet seen the full picture. Now, I think we shall find the mummy of a snake – the magician may have found it easier to control the spirit of an Egyptian cobra from his own time, magically transported into the body of a modern reptile. An ordinary snake might not have been as responsive to his will.'

'And the cat's mummy?'

'I confess, I find that theft rather more difficult to fit into the whole picture. But never mind. We will surely find the other mummy and the missing papyrus scroll, and I have a feeling that when we know what is in that, we shall understand a great deal more about the whole curious affair.'

Next morning, just as we were about to leave for another trip out to Highgate, Violet Dawes turned up on our doorstep in a state of agitation.

'Oh, whatever has happened?' she cried. 'Forgive me for disturbing you like this, but Seshemetka has kept me up half the night. Is it true that the mummy was not destroyed, not even unwrapped last night?'

'It is true,' Jesperson responded crisply. 'The intended unwrapping did not take place as planned, and you may read about it in more than one newspaper today. There is no time for me to explain now, and you must forgive us for not inviting you in, but we are in a hurry – it may console you to learn that our urgent business is closely tied to your worry about Meretseger.'

Violet's daintily gloved hand covered her mouth. 'Oh! Do not say that name – the name is one part of the soul, and for as long as it lives, she will survive. I think too that she gains power every time it is said.'

I saw Jesperson's lips tighten in exasperation, but he apologised. 'Now, if you will excuse us, we really must go.'

She didn't move, apparently unaware that she was blocking our way. 'Just one more thing, I beg you – it is a great weight upon my mind – I cannot understand it, but Seshemetka is most unhappy, indeed, grieving – she believes that someone died, suddenly and violently, last night. Can you tell me who it was?'

'I am sorry to be unable to enlighten you,' Jesperson said, rather shortly, I thought. 'Perhaps you should buy a newspaper rather than come to us for answers on everything? Look, there is a news-agent next door.'

She gave him a reproachful look. 'But this death is connected to *you*, Mr Jesperson. You *must* know about it. Indeed, Seshemetka holds you directly responsible. I am certain this is either a misunderstanding on her part, or connected to some unintentional action on your part, and I certainly do not mean to imply any blame . . . Do you really not know what I am talking about?'

He met her question with a most eloquent silence.

'Oh, there must be a reasonable explanation, no doubt,' she said quickly. 'But someone died last night, and you know something about it.'

245

I had been racking my brains to understand what Violet could possibly mean when I had a sudden memory of Matilda's mournful dirge. A bit hesitantly, I told Violet that Mr Jesperson had been obliged to kill a deadly snake.

She looked at me, her eyes wide. 'Oh! The sacred cobra?'

'I don't know about sacred,' Mr Jesperson said dryly. 'The creature was keeping guard over the stolen mummy, and had I not shot off its head before it could strike, it would have been Miss Lane who died last night and not merely that low reptile. Would your precious Seshemetka mourn as much had your friend died instead?'

'Oh, my dear Di,' she exclaimed, grasping my hand, and I was startled to see there were tears in her eyes. 'Thank goodness you are safe! And how grateful I am to you, Mr Jesperson,' she went on, smiling through her tears. 'Thank heaven for your quick reflexes, accurate aim and courage. I do not share my earlier self's religiously inspired attachment to snakes – indeed, I am glad to hear that it is dead. No doubt it was controlled by – by the evil soul still lurking in the mummy it was guarding.'

Dropping my hand, she stepped away from the door, out of our way. 'I am sorry to have detained you. God speed. And if there is anything I can do to help, anything at all, please send for me at once.'

We approached the house in Swains Lane with caution, keeping an eye out for Matilda or anyone else who might be around to see us, all too aware that what we planned was a criminal activity. We had won the respect of the police before now, but should they discover our plan, we might well forfeit that high regard.

Even once we were through the gate and knew ourselves to be invisible from the road, we could hardly relax. Jesperson knocked and called out, to be certain the house was truly unoccupied, before he quickly picked the lock. Inside, I bolted the door, to prevent anyone from surprising us at our work, before we began a methodical search.

The painted coffin case was empty. There was nowhere beneath or behind any of the furniture to hide something as big as a mummy, but Jesperson tapped the walls and carefully inspected the floorboards for signs of access to secret compartments. While he was thus occupied, I searched for animal mummies and the missing papyrus.

I tried my own hand at picking the lock on the writing desk, and was pleased by my success, although there was nothing inside but the sort of papers and other items one might find in any man's desk. A booklet of picture postcards was the only thing that had any obvious connection with Egypt.

On top, as I had previously noted, stood a silver-framed portrait of the Hendersons on their wedding day, and beside it, a humidor, very like one made of Spanish cedar owned by my father. I had happy childhood memories of standing close by, watching as he carefully selected a cigar, rolled it between his fingers and then clipped off the end with a special silver cutter, waiting for him to light it and take his first puff . . .

Jesperson's voice broke into my reverie. 'When you are done here, join me in the dining room.'

Something about the familiar box nagged at me, and after a moment, I realised too much was missing from this scene. Perhaps the cigar-cutter, matches and ash-tray were all kept elsewhere, but where was the distinctive odour of cigars? And why, if he was not a regular smoker, did Henderson keep the humidor so readily to hand?

I lifted the lid.

Inside, there was a dark, shrivelled human hand with a black stone scarab set in a silver ring on the smallest finger.

I called out to Jesperson, who came racing back to my side. 'What is it—? *Oh!*'

Less squeamish than I, he did not hesitate to lift the grisly thing out of the box.

'This must be an object of power,' he said quietly. 'Well found, Miss Lane! I would venture to guess that it is *this* that allows the ancient Egyptian magician to take control of Henderson and use him as his puppet.'

He tried to pull off the ring but had to give up, for it was stuck tight. 'Never mind that now,' he said to himself, putting it back in the box. He shut it and gave to me. 'Do you mind? Once a magical object is found, it is best to keep it close. We must not risk losing it now.'

As long as I did not have to actually touch it, I did not mind. The pleasant memories stirred by the appearance of the box went some small way to alleviating the thought of what it actually contained.

Our search of the dining room did not take very long, and as he had explored the kitchen and scullery thoroughly in his earlier search for the snake, we decided we could proceed directly upstairs to Mr Henderson's bedroom.

It was indeed a dirty, foul-smelling nest of a room, even worse than Jesperson had described. Once we had entered, I had to force myself to stay there and resist the urge to open a window to let in some fresh air. The thought of digging through the piles of dirty clothes strewn about on the floor was too horrible. I clutched the humidor tightly and searched only with my eyes, hoping for a sight of a papyrus scroll amid the clutter on the dressing-table, while Jesperson opened the doors of the big oak wardrobe, pushed the hanging clothes aside and delved to the very back of the shelves.

'Nothing,' he announced, swinging the doors shut. The scent of moth-balls gusted out, almost a pleasant perfume in contrast to the air I was so unhappily breathing.

Jesperson stood still for a moment, lightly slapping his leg with his cane as he looked all around, taking the measure of the room. Embarrassed by my own idleness, I went to the dressing-table and pulled open each of its drawers. Scissors, string, rolls of gauze, pots of ointment, various oddments, but no papyrus, and nothing else that looked suspicious.

I turned back just in time to see Jesperson crouching to look under the bed.

'There you are,' he said softly, and hauled the mummy out.

It had been covered with a bed-sheet, but there was no disguising the human form of the thing.

'No wonder he wouldn't have a housekeeper,' said Jesperson as he lifted the sheet to reveal the mummy in all its hideousness: the terrible lipless grin on a face with sunken eyelids, the shrunken concave chest with only one arm. The head and upper torso were unwrapped; the lower trunk and legs remained bandaged in strips of stiff and dirty cloth. I saw that one foot was missing.

'Hullo, what's this?' Jesperson exclaimed. Only when he picked it up did I see the square of heavy, cream-coloured paper that had been resting on the sunken chest. I moved closer to try to read the words inscribed there, but the line of hieroglyphs was completely indecipherable to me.

Jesperson continued to stare at it, his lips moving silently, as if he could translate it by sheer force of will, until, with a sigh, he tucked it away in a pocket. 'I don't recognise any words. We'll have to get it translated later. Can you help me—? No, never mind; you just keep that box safe. I'll carry this thing, if you go ahead of me to open the doors. It hardly matters if I bash it about a bit.'

'Where do you want to take it?'

'Into the back garden. There's sure to be a spot for burning the garden waste. Luckily, it hasn't been so dry of late that we'll have to worry about a few flying sparks.' He hoisted the filthy old thing in his arms. 'I hope that once we're rid of this thing, it will be enough to set poor Henderson free.'

Paraffin and the wherewithal to set it alight were easily acquired in the scullery on our way out. We were grateful for the enclosing wall around the garden that would hide us from view as we carried out our grisly task. In a far corner, behind a rose-bed, we found a shallow declivity, though hardly deep enough to be called a pit, which had evidently served for years to incinerate garden waste.

Jesperson laid the mummy down on the bed of ash, I gathered up as many dry twigs and dead leaves as I could find, Jesperson smashed up the humidor, and all this we scattered on top of the mummy.

'What about the hand?' I asked.

'We'll burn it with the rest. But not the ring.'

The idea of keeping anything connected to this old priest-magician made me profoundly uneasy. 'It might be dangerous to keep it,' I suggested, and somewhat to my surprise, Jesperson agreed.

'Yes, anything powerful is dangerous. But fire alone will not destroy it. Even if the flames burn hot enough to melt the silver, the stone would survive. In the end, we may have to pulverise it, but there is no need to rush into doing something we may regret. We might find it very useful to possess such an object of power.' As he spoke he had been tugging at the ring and twisting it, but he still could not get it to go over the knuckle. He paused, thinking, and for a moment I was afraid he would decide to keep the hand with it on.

Instead, he took out his pocket knife and after a bit of sawing,

251

the desiccated finger gave way. He caught the ring as it slipped off the severed end and dropped it into his pocket.

He placed the hand and severed finger on top of the mummy. 'The first thing is to get rid of this . . . this *spirit-anchor*, and release old Henderson. If that does not work, well, then I must concede to your idea that the man who kept this horrible thing beneath his bed was in thrall to nothing more than his own madness, in which case we'll try to have him locked away for the safety of all.'

After liberally dousing the thing with paraffin, he struck a match. We both stepped back before he dropped it into the little pile of kindling in the hollow of the chest.

Within moments the flicker became a spark, and then a flame that licked along the branching runnels of paraffin soaking into the dried-up flesh and ancient cloth until it became a smoky stream of brightness. With shocking suddenness, a blazing fire was born, roaring like an animal as it began to feast greedily upon the meal Jesperson had prepared for it. We backed further away from the increasing heat.

I am not sure how long we stood there until at last the fire subsided, but at some point during our vigil I heard the bells from St Michael's chiming the noon hour as sullen puffs of ashy smoke were carried away on the summer breeze.

Jesperson found a stout stick on the grass nearby and used it to smash the grinning skull to powder. Then he set about breaking up the rib-cage and the long bones of the thighs until they were no more than a collection of shards, like a heap of shattered china.

Panting slightly, he tossed aside the stick and reached for his pocket handkerchief to wipe his face – and when he pulled it from his pocket, the mummy's ring came, too.

I cried out a warning and he lunged to catch it, but too late: it struck the ground, bounced into the pyre and landed on top of the still-smouldering remnants of bone.

For a moment we both stared, unmoving. I wondered, horrified, if the ring had the power to restore life, imagining the pieces of bone re-fitting together like pieces of a puzzle. Or would it burst into flame, in sympathy with its former owner?

To my relief, nothing like that happened. Jesperson stepped closer to the smouldering pile and used his pocket knife to fish out the ring. 'Undamaged,' he said, waiting until it was cool enough to wrap in his handkerchief before restoring it to his pocket.

'Shall we go?'

'And leave all this?' I gestured at the still-smouldering mess on the ground.

'Surely this is the best place for it.' He grinned. 'I hope you weren't hoping to bring home a souvenir?'

Burning a mummy is thirsty work, it turned out. Passing a tea-shop on our way to the hansom cab rank in Highgate, we decided to stop for refreshment. Jesperson took the opportunity to examine the mummy's ring more closely and discovered an inscription on the back of the scarab. After peering at it he handed it to me. 'What do you make of it?'

I squinted at the hieroglyphics briefly and gave it back, unwilling to hold it a moment longer than necessary. 'It's all ancient Egyptian to me.'

'Very droll.' From another pocket he brought out the card that we had discovered lying on the mummy. 'Is this the same?' Frowning, he stared at the writing on the card and then peered again at the ring before declaring they were completely different.

'What would it mean if they were the same?'

He shrugged and put away the card. 'I thought Henderson might have copied what was on the ring – presumably under instruction from the ancient spirit. If so, I would guess it would have been intended to provide additional protection for the mummy, to keep it safe. The Egyptians always tried to protect their dead, adorning their tombs and coffins with multiple amulets and spells as additional layers of protection.'

'But since they are not the same?'

He replaced it in his pocket, saying, 'I can only surmise . . . and why do that when there is someone not so very far away who will be able to read it for us?'

We had finished our tea and set off for the British Museum, but neither Mr Budge nor Mr Sand were anywhere to be found. Eventually, we encountered an attendant who was able to tell us that the Keeper and his assistant had had a late night consulting with the police, and then been summoned in the early hours to take charge of the mystery mummy, so Mr Budge had decided, quite sensibly, to take some time off and had granted Mr Sand a two-day holiday as well. He knew that if either of them came in they would swiftly find themselves set upon by reporters.

We left feeling discouraged, but looking down from the top of the steps, Jesperson spotted someone in the courtyard and his mood immediately lifted.

'Why, what luck! Look, Miss Lane, it's Pagan Brown.'

The legendary figure was a very ordinary-looking man in early middle age, dressed in a rather shabby, rumpled suit. His thinning grey hair was grown long enough to straggle down untidily on either side of a long, thin, bespectacled face.

'I say, Brown! Cometh the hour, cometh the man – and you are the very man we need,' Jesperson called to him as he came up the steps.

He looked up, surprised, and his face creased in a shy smile. 'I say, Jesperson, you have a way of making a fellow welcome – you are joking, of course.'

'I am entirely serious. May I introduce you to my partner, Miss Lane? Miss Lane, meet Mr Brown.'

'An honour to meet you, Miss Lane,' he said with a slight bow. 'How do you do?'

'Very well, thank you. And you?'

'Enough of that, if you please,' Jesperson cut in impatiently. 'Save your social niceties for some other time. We are here on a mission, Brown, and we need your help to translate two bits of text. The first is an inscription on the back of a small stone scarab, set in a ring that I have just taken from a mummified hand.'

Mr Brown's eyes – they were the same colour as his name – widened. 'Naturally, I should be delighted to take a look, but surely Mr Budge—'

'Mr Budge has taken a holiday – but do not imagine that you are second-best, because I have a great respect for your scholarship and, considering the provenance of these items, you may be even more helpful to us than Mr Budge.'

'Come, come,' murmured Mr Brown shyly. He gave a little cough. 'Er, when would you like to show me this inscription?'

We had gradually moved together to one side of the portico and were standing beside a pillar, out of the way of other visitors coming and going from the main entrance.

'Now, if it is convenient. I have the ring here in my pocket.' He took out the bundled handkerchief. 'I hope there is enough light for you to see it properly.'

Mr Brown pushed his spectacles higher on his nose and craned his neck with obvious interest. 'Given its size, it cannot be a very long inscription; one would expect some sort of blessing or an invocation to a particular god, and perhaps the name of the owner.' He put out his hand and Jesperson gave him the ring.

Removing his spectacles, Mr Brown held the ring close to his eyes, examining the carved scarab before turning it to read what had been carved into the base. 'Hmm, yes, a woman's name with a common phrase invoking the protection of Ra – their supreme god, the sun god, you know. The scarab represented the sun, and the power of life, which makes this a doubly powerful charm – but look, more unusually, Thoth is also invoked.'

'Why?'

'Well, you see, Thoth was supposed to have invented the art of writing, so he was usually invoked on amulets worn or carried by scribes. It was quite a common thing, rather like people today might wear a religious medallion or carry a lucky charm.'

'And you expect only a scribe to invoke Thoth?' Jesperson asked, frowning slightly.

'Not necessarily, but I am surprised to find this on a *woman's* ring. Men, not women, were scribes, priests and magicians. In fact, if not for the name, I would guess this ring belonged to a magician.'

'Why?'

'Because of something else etched into the stone. Here, can you see these smaller glyphs, around the lower edge, below the name of the owner?' He held it out, and Jesperson leaned in so close to look that his nose nearly touched the other man's hand.

'Ye-es.' He drew back. 'What does it say?'

'Nothing. I mean, they are not words . . .'

Jesperson frowned. 'You cannot read them?'

'Oh, I can read them – in a sense. But they are untranslatable, sounds without meaning.'

'Are you sure? Why would anyone go to so much trouble? It is not like a child scrawling random letters using ink or paint on paper. Hieroglyphs are not that easy to carve. They must mean something.'

Mr Brown looked nettled by the implied criticism as he settled his spectacles back on his nose. 'Very well, you may wait to ask

Mr Budge. But I assure you he will give you the same answer. No one could translate these symbols into English – or even Egyptian words. It was no child and no ignorant fool who put them here to be read, but a magician: these are words of power, to be used to compel the gods and do impossible things.'

'Words of power,' said Jesperson. 'Forgive me. I meant no slur on your scholarship. I had no notion – were they always meaningless syllables like these?'

'One rather assumes their meaning was masked from mere mortals, that they would have been received as a gift from the gods, or stolen from some other race of powerful sorcerers. They may have been corruptions of foreign words or phrases, like the "abracadabra" recited by our own stage magicians. Over time, passed down from one generation to the next, the original meaning would be lost, but that was no matter. Words, like names, had power, and it was not necessary for the sorcerer to understand them for them to have the desired effect.'

'I see. And – if you were to venture a guess – why were these words etched into the stone of this ring?'

'As I said before, to protect the life of the woman named. Possibly even to bring her back to life, if she died.'

'The hand that wore this ring belonged to a man. You are quite certain that the name is that of a woman? Were there no names that could have been used by either sex?'

'The name is marked by a character indicating that the person was female. The fact that a man wore it, even unto his grave, suggests he was this woman's protector – and a great priest or magician. Even after death the soul faced danger, including that of another and more permanent death. Both body and soul of the deceased required continued protection, perhaps even more than when the person was alive.'

He took a breath, apparently quite prepared to continue explaining the Egyptian ideas of reincarnation, but Jesperson had another question.

'Can you tell us the woman's name?'

'Certainly.' He looked at the inscription again. 'The meaning is "She Who Loves Silence", or, as the ancients would have said' – he cleared his throat – "Meret-Seger".'

CHAPTER TWENTY

Planning and Preparations

Although it was no great revelation, to find Meretseger's name on the ring certainly felt like some sort of validation.

'Are you familiar with that name?' Jesperson asked Mr Brown. 'Have you encountered it anywhere else before today?'

Mr Brown gave it some thought and handed the ring back to Mr Jesperson. 'Not that I recall. Do you have reason to think she was a woman of importance?'

Jesperson smiled to himself as he put the ring back in his pocket. 'I had hoped you might be able to tell me. What about this?' As he spoke, he withdrew the card we had found resting on the mummy's chest. 'Can you translate this?'

Mr Brown ran his eyes over the line of hieroglyphs and gave a little laugh. 'But this was made very recently, and by someone without much knowledge . . . indeed, I should say, with *no* understanding of the signs at all.'

'But they are genuine hieroglyphs? I am sure I recognised some, at least.'

'Yes, of course. They are recognisable — serpent, mouth, reeds and so on. Someone copied them — not too badly — but as for meaning, there is none.' Then he reflected for a moment. 'Unless it is a coded message? But you will know more about that in your line of work.'

He held out the card, but Jesperson did not take it. 'Could they be words of power?'

With another look at the hieroglyphs, Mr Brown said, 'They may well have been *intended* as such. Were they written by a child? No? Well . . . I cannot say they are *not*.'

'But you do not think they are,' said Jesperson, taking the card from him. 'Why?'

Mr Brown gave his little self-deprecating laugh. 'Oh, call it intuition. When one has read as many old magical treatises and seen as many spells from a particular culture as I have, one comes to recognise the form. And this, or I should say *these*, if the spacing is meant to indicate they are three separate words — do not have the ring of authenticity. But who am I to say what some ancient magician might not have considered useful for commanding the spirits? I can only say that they do not convince me. They do not look right to me; that is all; they do not look properly *Egyptian*.'

'You are certainly well-qualified to judge,' said Jesperson. 'Thank you. And now, we had better not keep you any longer. Thank you so much for your help.'

'A pleasure,' said Pagan Brown, shaking Jesperson warmly by

the hand. 'Good day to you, Miss Lane. Please feel free to call upon me at any time. I believe you have my address?'

'I do. But I also know we are more likely to find you here. Thank you again, and good day.'

A letter from E.A. Wallis Budge awaited us at home.

He wrote in haste, he said, to give us his heart-felt, personal thanks for all our efforts on his behalf, and to let us know that the stolen mummy had been returned to the Museum. He had been angry with us at first, but had quickly realised that we, too, were victims of Henderson's duplicity. It might seem a minor crime to the police, but he had emphasised to them that Henderson was a cunning and duplicitous criminal who might be mad, but should not be allowed to remain free to commit more crimes. He hoped that the thief would be locked away for a very long time, perhaps in an asylum for the criminally insane.

At present, the mummy was back in his office, but he intended in due course to have a special glass case constructed to contain both the beautiful sarcophagus and its mysterious inhabitant for display in one of the Egyptian galleries. He had decided against attempting another public unwrapping.

Due to the unfortunate events of the previous evening, the curiosity of the press had been aroused, so he was taking his summer holiday a bit sooner than originally planned; he expected that by the time he returned to London, the jackals of the popular press would have found some new victims to harry, and the whole affair forgotten.

Jesperson smiled. 'I hope he will have a pleasant holiday. The fact that he is away will make it much easier for us to steal the mummy.'

'*Steal it?*'

He looked at me in surprise. 'But of course. We have dealt with one problem, but Miss Matilda will not be free from Meretseger's control until her mummy is destroyed as well.'

'But . . . what happens when Mr Budge hires us to find it again?'

'He will not, not if all goes according to my plan. Come, aren't you hungry? I know there's roast chicken left over from yesterday, and those lovely ripe tomatoes would just hit the spot. We can talk afterwards.'

How strange – how wrong it felt, to steal the very thing we had been hired to find! But Seshemetka believed Meretseger was a danger not only to Matilda, but to anyone she thought might stand in her way. The theft and destruction of one ancient mummy was a very little thing in comparison with what an ancient power-mad Egyptian princess might do if we did not stop her.

'We must destroy that mummy – destroy it absolutely. It is the only way to be certain.'

'But are we certain?'

My question brought him down to earth. He frowned thoughtfully as he said, 'You are right, of course. It was wrong of me to make such an assumption. We must see Henderson – speak with him – observe him – I wonder if he would agree to be hypnotised?'

'By you?' I rolled my eyes. 'I doubt he would be so trusting. He can't be very fond of us. I wonder if Violet could help? If Seshemetka's uneasy feelings could alert us—'

'What a good idea!' A happy smile spread across his face. 'Yes, that should do it. No need to tell him why; it should be easy enough to bring them together by some small subterfuge. Perhaps you could write to Miss Dawes and explain?'

Jesperson told me his plan, to leave another mummy in place of the one we were stealing, so the crime should go undetected.

'Where are we to find another mummy?' I asked.

'Oh, that will not be difficult. You might be surprised at how many there are in private ownership, scattered throughout the country. And sometimes they are for sale. I have already made enquiries.'

This was a surprise. 'You have? When?'

'A few days ago. I happened to see a small ad in one of the papers, and . . .' He flushed slightly, looking embarrassed. 'I don't know why, but I thought it might come in useful. I hope you will forgive me for not consulting you, but I acted on impulse. Almost as soon as I had posted my letter, I wished I had not. It was such an absurd thing to have done – what were *we* to do with a mummy? What would you think of me? What would Mother say? I really could not justify it, even to myself.'

'And now?'

'Now it turns out we have use for one, and there is a man in Hitchin willing to sell us a mummy. At least, I hope he still has it.' He leapt to his feet. 'I had better send a wire at once.'

'Wait— You haven't told me why we need another mummy,' I protested.

'It is vital to my plan. It is rather complicated, so either wait until I am back, or come along and I will explain as we go. If there is something I have got wrong or overlooked, I count on you to point it out.'

The next day we took the train to Hitchin, where resided the gentleman, one Mr Brosnan, who had advertised the mummy for sale. The address he had given turned out to be a modern bungalow-style house, a most unlikely home for an ancient Egyptian mummy. As it transpired, the mummy had been stashed in a garden shed for several weeks.

'My wife won't have it indoors,' Mr Brosnan explained as he led us around to the back of the house. 'She says it makes her skin creep, even if she can't see it, just knowing it's in the same house with us. Her mother never wanted it, neither, but she had to put up with it because her husband liked it – marriage was a different proposition in those days! I don't know why her Ma didn't get rid of it after he died – maybe she didn't dare; he was always a strong-willed man, my wife's Da – but she wouldn't have the thing glaring at her in the parlour any more. She hid it behind all the boxes of stuff her husband had brought back from his years serving abroad and probably forgot all about it. I came across it after she died, when I had to clear the house.

'My wife said I should have left it there, let the landlord decide what to do with it, or throw it on the bonfire, but that didn't sit right with me – it's not just rubbish, you know, and I thought surely someone would want it, a collector of antiquities, maybe a scientist or a scholar? People do buy all sorts. I made a few bob off some of the other things from the house, the furniture and the little painted figures, wooden masks and such, but this wasn't so easy. One fellow wanted the case – he reckoned he could fix that up to look nice as new – but he wouldn't take the mummy with it, and I figured it would be hard to get this poor old chap off my hands without it.' He scratched his head. 'And it's not doing it any good, staying out in this shed. So what do you think?'

The mummy was in better shape than its case, that was certain, but it was considerably grubbier and, I feared, smaller than Budge's mystery mummy.

'I suppose it's not too bad,' Jesperson said, sounding dubious. 'How much?'

The man named his price, Jesperson sucked in his breath and slowly shook his head.

'In that condition? You'll be lucky to get anything for it now.' He made a very much lower offer for mummy and case combined.

Mr Brosnan affected to be affronted, then they started haggling and I could see it was all for show, for the man was eager to be rid of it, while we had not let him know how urgently we needed just such a thing. In spite of my doubts about its appearance, it had the great attraction of being available to us here and now. The price was soon agreed and

Mr Brosnan was kind enough to convey it, and us, in his cart to the train station.

Back at home in Gower Street, we were able to examine our purchase at leisure, while arguing over its merits. Having lost it once before, I had noticed Mr Budge had paid much closer attention to Mummy X on its return, which made it more likely, I thought, that he would see the differences.

Jesperson did not agree. 'When he comes back, if he does perceive anything, he will think his own memory is to blame. Anyway, the state and colour of the wrappings can undoubtedly be improved – Mother will be able to help; she has a knack for cleaning and making repairs to all things. And her artistic sense is very fine – she will manage to do something about restoring the case – just wait and see.'

And, indeed, Edith Jesperson, with her store of household wisdom, knew of more than one method for cleaning cloth, and she was very happy to take charge of the task of making our rather mouldy specimen more closely resemble Mummy X.

It was when she saw the coffin case that her eyes lit up, and it was clear she relished the opportunity to indulge her artistic side. I did not see the point of expending much time or energy on the case, which was nothing more than a way of smuggling the *doppelgänger* mummy into Budge's office; but it occurred to me that Jesperson might have made the suggestion for his mother's sake, knowing how much she would enjoy the task.

'When do you need it?' she asked, examining the battered sarcophagus.

'The important thing is that it is ready to go – glue and paint all dried, the new work not looking obvious – by Wednesday afternoon.'

'I will make a start this evening, while the bandages are drying. I used to make lampshades and boxes from papier-mâché when I was a girl, you know, and this is not so very different. It's just the palette, which is a darker one than I ever used – so much black and red! I preferred softer hues, pinks and blues and yellows. But don't worry, I mean to match the style, not to express myself. The repairs will hardly be noticeable when I am done.'

The house on Gower Street was a pleasant, comfortable residence, large enough for the three of us; however, it had one drawback: there was no garden, just a small, stone-flagged area at the back where the bins were kept and washing was hung out to dry, which was shared with the news-agent next door and overlooked by neighbours on all sides. This made it impossible to work on the mummy out there. Tongues would wag and rumours spread; any chatter with an Egyptian flavour was likely to reach the ears of Mr Budge sooner or later.

By the following day, the kitchen, where the mummy lay with its bandages drying, smelled strongly of Borax, while our office, where Edith, humming happily to herself, worked diligently with pots of paint and strips of wet paper and cloth to repair the ancient cartonnage, had the odour and atmosphere of an artisan's workshop.

There was no room for us to work, and Edith had dismissed any offer of help – in fact, our presence was evidently *de trop* – so on this fine morning, we must go out.

I should have been happy enough to take a holiday and enjoy a good long walk in the summer air, but Jesperson, with still-unanswered questions buzzing in his brain, declared that we must go again to Highgate.

CHAPTER TWENTY-ONE

Return to Swains Lane

'We never found those two animal mummies, or the missing papyrus scroll,' he said as we left the house, as if I needed reminding. 'After the exhaustive search we made of Henderson's house, I simply cannot believe they are there. Therefore, we must search the house next door.'

'And how do you propose we do that?' Remembering the excuse he had given Mr Henderson, I said, 'I hope you won't say another poisonous snake is on the loose.'

'Why not? It could work.'

'Honestly, do you want to give poor Mrs Munro a heart attack? She might insist on calling the police.'

With a cheeky grin he said, 'Do you think "my mate's lost his ferret" would be better?'

'I do not.'

'I am teasing. There is no need to search the whole house. They must be in Matilda's own room, and somewhere they would be unlikely to be discovered by the maid.'

'Do you think Mr Henderson gave them to her?'

'It is beyond credible that a young lady could have walked in her night-dress from Highgate to Bloomsbury and then, after somehow breaking in to the British Museum, returned home with the stolen goods without attracting a great deal of attention, at the very least.'

'I wonder why she – you-know-who – wanted them.'

'Does it matter? The ancient Egyptians held a very different view of animals – the existence of so many mummified creatures attests to that. And only consider how the cobra's death affected Seshemetka.'

'Yes . . . that was strange. No matter how she revered the species, surely she is not so sensitive as to feel the death of *every* serpent? Although, if it was the reincarnation of a cobra from her own time . . . but is that likely? That even animals are born again?'

Jesperson's rapid pace slowed as he said thoughtfully, 'Hmm. Now there is a question . . . I find it hard to imagine that the soul of one snake should be very much different from that of another. Cats, of course, are different; they are notorious for their individuality. But that I cannot say the same for snakes is perhaps only a reflection of my own prejudice.'

He turned his head at the sound of an approaching omnibus. 'Here, if we catch this one, it will take us near enough,' he said.

When we were settled inside, he resumed the conversation. 'Your remarks have given me an idea. This is only speculation, but it might explain something about the snake's unnatural behaviour.'

'Unnatural?' I repeated, puzzled. 'Surely there is nothing unnatural about a cobra's strike?'

'It did not behave normally in the cemetery. A snake will strike when attacked, or when it feels threatened – as it may have done with Leary. But why should it attack you or me, unless it was compelled to do so? Is it possible that the ancients had more power over animals than we do today? And if one was able to transfer the spirit of a creature from that era into a living body . . . then one might be able to control their actions. This explains as nothing else could why those animal mummies were taken.'

'And the papyrus scroll?'

'For the contents, surely. We will know when we find it and have it translated.'

I was not quite sure where we were when we alighted from the omnibus. Jesperson looked surprised. 'Do you not see the church-spire? And over there, that's part of the cemetery wall. If we walk quickly, we'll be at Swains Lane in five minutes.'

I stopped him. 'You do not mean for us to go to Matilda's house directly? Without so much as a note?'

'Matilda invited you to call in whenever you wished, and did she not make a point of saying you were not to stand on ceremony?'

'Oh, yes of course. But Mrs Munro might prefer receiving notice.'

'Considering our plans, I had rather give no advance warning. Besides, we are nearly there.'

When we knocked at the door of 'The Laurels', the maid answered the door, took the card Jesperson gave her and, with an apologetic bob and murmur, shut the door. A very short time later it was opened again, this time by the beaming Matilda.

'Di! How lovely! Oh!' The smile froze on her face as she noticed my tall companion. She stared at him for a long moment, strangely bereft of words and looking rather dazed. 'Oh, and Mr Jesperson – how nice to see you, too.'

'Forgive me, Matilda,' I said quickly. 'We happened to be in the area, with a little time to spare, and I hoped you would not mind if we stopped by. But, of course, if it is not convenient—'

'Of course it is! Please, come in. You should be in already! I have told Trent that you are *never* to be left standing on the doorstep – silly girl! I suppose it was your giving her that card.'

'We did not wish to presume,' Mr Jesperson said in a colourless voice. 'Mrs Munro might have other plans—'

'But you are not calling on my grandmother – you are calling on *me*.'

'If Mrs Munro is not busy, we should like to see her, too, of course.'

'And so you shall.' She turned her smile in my direction, yet I had the oddest feeling that she was not actually looking at me. 'Grandmama is writing some letters – I am sure she must be finished by now, but she will be glad to stop if she isn't. It's so nice to have company, and the four of us will make quite the little party.' Matilda spoke in such a rush she was almost gabbling. I was uncomfortably aware of a strange, strained atmosphere between the two people beside me.

'Shall we go into the garden? I shall ask Trent to bring us something cool to drink. It is rather close today, do you not agree? But otherwise such a lovely day.'

'And such a lovely garden,' I agreed, my heart beating a little faster.

Mrs Munro made herself available and we were soon seated around the table on the smooth green lawn beneath the leafy chestnut tree. The maid had been despatched to make lemonade and after some desultory remarks about the weather and other inanities, Jesperson launched into a story that promised to be long and satisfyingly complicated.

This was my cue.

Leaning close to Matilda I murmured, 'If you will excuse me a moment . . . no, don't get up, I remember the way.'

As I had expected, she let me go without protest, caught in the tale-teller's snare.

With pounding heart I hurried upstairs. Matilda's bedroom was easy to find. It was a comfortable, cosy room, clean and tidy, the only evidence of disorder being the clutter of books, cards, ribbons and other trinkets on the dressing-table. I began my search there, checking one drawer after another, but found nothing of interest.

The only thing under the bed was a new pair of pink

slippers, so I turned my attention to the bookcase. Normally, I would have been interested in the titles, but now my one concern was for potential hiding places. Having ascertained that there was nothing hidden behind or on top, and that all the books had been pushed to rest flush with the back of the case, I stepped back and sighed, wondering if, instead of a scroll, I should be looking for pieces of papyrus flattened and folded – or even cut into pieces which could more easily be hidden within a book or an album (Mr Budge himself had once done this, he had told us, in order to smuggle a valuable collection of papyri out of the country) but that seemed unlikely.

My eyes swept the room as I searched for possible hiding places. Was there a loose board under the rug? And what about the space *beneath* the bookcase?

As I crouched down to look, my eyes came level with a fat volume, *The Works of Homer* printed in stark black letters on the spine.

The incongruity struck me. Tales for children, poetry and thrilling romances by contemporary authors filled the rest of the shelves. The Homer was bigger than the other books – it could have been a school prize, but Miss Verver had never gone to school. As soon as I had pulled it from the shelf I realised it was not a book at all, but a box designed to look like one.

A papyrus scroll was inside that box.

I had worn a skirt with a cleverly concealed inside pocket for this very possibility. With hands trembling with excitement, I quickly secreted the scroll and returned *The Works of Homer* to its place between *The Soul of Lilith* and *Treasure Island*.

How long had I been in Matilda's bedroom? I had no time to waste as I hurried across to check the wardrobe, the largest piece of furniture in the room. One half of it was for hanging clothes; the other had been fitted with shelves, each one filled with piles of delicate garments, gloves and scarves and lacy under-garments, all sorted by type and so carefully arranged that I hesitated, wondering if it were possible the ancient animal mummies had been disguised by being wrapped in something and stuffed beneath so neat a pile of clothes. Any search would be bound to cause some disarray, and no matter how careful I tried to be, it would be obvious to anyone – and, thinking of 'anyone,' I remembered the maid. It was surely she, not Matilda, who kept it all so tidy, who washed and ironed and neatly stacked the garments, and if there was anything so alien as the wrapped remains of a three-thousand-year-old cat inside the wardrobe, Trent would have been bound to have discovered it and reported the matter to Mrs Munro.

No, Matilda would not try to hide anything here. I closed the wardrobe doors and looked up to see four round hat-boxes lined up on top of it.

Standing on my tip-toes and stretching up as far as I could, I managed to brush the sides of the boxes with my finger-tips, but I was too short for the task of fetching one down. Matilda's grandmother and the maid were both near my own height, but she, who was so much taller, could probably reach her hats unaided. That made it a good hiding place.

I grabbed the little round stool tucked beneath the skirt of the dressing-table. I felt a qualm about standing on the cushioned pink velvet seat, but there was no time to unlace and remove my boots, so I quashed the feeling, placed the stool where I needed it, and stepped up.

I reached for the first box, pulled it close and lifted the lid to reveal a hat. My anxiety rising – I had been gone such a long time, I was certain – I returned the box to its place and performed the same ritual with the second, with the same result. When I lifted the lid of the third, I saw no hat, only a froth of pale tissue paper. This might hide a brand-new headpiece – or something else. Plunging my hand into the crinkly depths, I felt something solid, thick, with the texture of rough homespun cloth. My heart beat faster – but as my fingers closed around one end of the unseen thing, a low, whining growl close by stopped me cold.

Still clutching the hat-box, my fingers gripping the thing inside, I turned carefully to look behind me. There in the door-way was the big striped cat I had seen before, crouched low to the ground, yellow eyes narrowed, ears flattened and long tail lashing, unmistakably an animal readying for an attack. Equally unmistakable was the fact that the object of its attack was me.

I shifted my position and holding the box with both hands, I turned to keep my eyes on the creature, wondering if throw-ing the hat-box at it would scare it off. I dismissed the idea swiftly, for it was not very heavy, so unlikely to do any damage even if it struck – and if the cat then launched itself at me,

I should have nothing to defend myself but my bare hands. I could almost feel claws raking my arms and fangs sinking into my tender flesh . . .

Shuddering, trying to ignore the cat's low, moaning cry of warning, I told myself to stay calm and concentrated on working out a plan of action.

For nearly a year now I had been practising an ancient Oriental way of unarmed defensive combat, but all the movements I had learned were based on the assumption that my attacker would be a person – a human being with two arms and two legs, probably capable of reasoning, probably larger than myself – and not a cat. Evasion was always a better choice. In the words of Jasper Jesperson, who was, with the aid of his mother, my instructor: 'Whenever possible, run away.'

I practically threw the hat-box back on top of the wardrobe, jumped down and snatched up the stool. Brandishing it at the creature, I muttered fiercely, 'Shoo! Shoo!'

The cat rose, pulled back his head and gave me an affronted look. The change was instantaneous, from wild, threatening animal to a household pet unkindly abused. Emitting a series of tiny, pathetic mews, he hurried past me and leapt onto the bed. As I stared, taken aback by this sudden transformation, he settled into one of those peculiarly unpleasant positions so often resorted to by felines, especially in polite company, and commenced a vigorous licking of his nether regions.

I put the stool back where it belonged and left the room.

Tall glasses of lemonade were being served by Trent, the maid, when I returned to the garden, where Jesperson was winding up his fanciful improvised tale.

A silence fell. We sipped our drinks.

I turned to Matilda. 'I must apologise. I am afraid I opened the door to one of the bedrooms by mistake and before I could shut it again, a cat ran in and jumped up on the bed.'

Mrs Munro made a tutting sound. 'That must have been Matilda's room.'

'I do not mind,' Matilda said, and reached out to pat my hand. 'That's my Mewki.'

'Well, I mind it,' said Mrs Munro. 'You should not encourage that animal to sleep on your bed. His place is downstairs – and preferably, out of doors. Cook used to feed him scraps on the doorstep and somehow he came to make himself at home,' she explained to me. 'He slept in the kitchen when it was cold or wet outside, but I never thought he would become a house cat.'

'He likes me the best,' said Matilda.

'How long have you had him?'

'Three or four years, I think. Do you know, Grandmama?'

'It cannot be more than three years, for he turned up soon after the Hendersons took the house next door. I remember we thought it must be their cat and I told Cook not to encourage it or it would never go home.'

'That's right – but he wasn't theirs. He didn't have a home, and he didn't have a name until I gave him one.'

'And you must have been giving him something else, to make him follow you around the way he's been doing lately. I hope you haven't started keeping food in your room, young lady, because—'

'I haven't! I don't have to tempt Mewki with food, not the way Cook did. He likes to be with me because he loves me. And I love him,' she added defiantly.

'I know, dear. Only it is a rather inconvenient passion to develop just now. Everything was all arranged for our visit to Scotland and now we shall have to take a cat, too.'

'It's not so great an inconvenience as all that,' Matilda said, pouting. 'He'll stay in my room and I shall feed him and look after him. He will be no trouble to anyone. I know he couldn't bear it if I went away and left him for nearly two whole months.'

'Yes, yes, no need to argue it all again,' Mrs Munro murmured, shooting an apologetic, embarrassed look at Jesperson and me. 'It is settled now. Mewki will come with us. I was worried because my brother keeps dogs – but never mind. Let us speak of something more interesting.'

I would have been most interested to learn the precise date the passionate connection between Mewki and Matilda had become manifest, but I felt confident it had been after, not before, the theft of the animal mummies.

After a little more general conversation, imaginary business elsewhere was used as our excuse to depart. Matilda reminded me that she would be at home for a little more than another week and pressed me to call again – and to stay longer next time.

As soon as we were away from the house Jesperson murmured, 'Success?'

'With qualifications. I found the mummies, in hat-boxes on top of her wardrobe – but that wretched cat threatened to scratch my eyes out if I dared try to take them away. It may not be as deadly as a cobra, but a cat that size—'

'What about the papyrus?'

'That, I did get.' I patted my skirt.

'Well done!' He smiled at me warmly. 'I feel certain it must contain something of great importance. And those dead animals are less so – at least now the snake is dead.' He stopped by the gate to Mr Henderson's house.

I looked at him. 'Another unannounced social call?'

'As we are here, why not? I am eager to see if we can detect any obvious, evident difference in the man since the mummy was destroyed. Is he aware of a change?' He put his hand on the latch and opened the gate.

Even before we reached the front door, Jesperson said, 'The house is empty. No one has entered since we left.'

Not liking to reveal the deficiencies of my own powers of observation by asking how he knew, I said only, 'Perhaps he is still in custody, awaiting trial.'

'Most unlikely. Not impossible, but— There has been nothing in the papers about it. And there should have been.' He stood, chin in hand, considering the matter.

'Perhaps he simply went away for a while?'

'Without coming back here to pack a bag?'

'Maybe the police let him pack what he needed before they took him in?'

His sceptical glance told me what he thought of that, so I went on, stubbornly, 'Maybe he went in by the back door. He could be inside even now, despite appearances.'

'He is not — but go ahead and knock if you like.'

I did, and we waited, but there was no answer. He was right; no one was home.

'May we go to the police now?'

CHAPTER TWENTY-TWO

What Happened to Henderson

The constable on desk duty was the elder of the two we had met outside Henderson's house three nights before. He looked surprised as he recognised us in turn.

'Why, Mr Jesperson – Miss Lane – you have heard the news already?'

'News? You mean about Mr Henderson?' I asked.

'You're not here on some other matter?'

Jesperson answered slowly, 'No, no other matter. We have indeed come about Mr Henderson.'

'A sad case,' said the constable lugubriously. He shook his head. 'Very mysterious. He was quiet as anything until—'

'Dunstan.' A stern-looking man with luxuriant sideburns and a magnificent moustache emerged from another room. 'What is this about?'

'Sir. This gentleman is Mr Jesperson, with his partner, Miss Lane. They are the ones—'

'I know, the Henderson case. I shall take it from here,

Dunstan.' He turned to us and, his face only slightly less stern, said, 'Pleased to meet you. I am Sergeant Bottomley. I think you will be more comfortable in my office, if you'd like to follow me? Oh, and Dunstan, tell the boy we shall want tea.'

We followed Sergeant Bottomley into his small office and he closed the door.

'I have heard good things about the firm of Jesperson and Lane and had looked forward to meeting you and thanking you, only now . . . now I hardly know what to say, considering how it has turned out. I wish I had not given the orders; I wish I had never heard the name of Henderson.'

I had the suspicion he had only just stopped himself from saying, 'or Jesperson and Lane', and felt a nameless dread stir within me.

Jesperson said not a word, only waited while Sergeant Bottomley chewed his moustache, then smoothed it down and took a deep breath. 'I suppose you want to hear the whole story.'

'Please – and in every detail. Something that might have appeared insignificant to you may be of greater importance than you know.'

'I don't know about that – I am sure we did nothing wrong. Feel free to ask questions.' He cleared his throat. 'To begin with, Mr Henderson gave us no trouble. Of course he was not happy to be told he must spend the night in gaol, but he made no fuss; he understood that what he had done was a crime, and he was resigned to the consequences, or so we thought.

'I cannot tell you if he lay awake or had a good kip, but come morning, he ate his breakfast and spoke normally to the duty sergeant. He was annoyed at not being allowed to shave, but he understood when we explained why we don't give razors to prisoners, no matter how gentlemanly. He knew he would be brought before the magistrate later in the day – his case was on the docket for three o'clock – and he was . . . well, again the word I must use is "resigned". He did not say much, but everything indicated that he understood his situation. He spent most of Thursday morning very quietly. Perhaps he was reflecting on his sins, or praying – until, all of a sudden, and quite without warning, he began to scream.'

Jesperson sucked in his breath. 'When was this?'

'No cause that we could find. He could not or would not tell us what the matter was, only he kept crying out like a man in torment.'

'But *when?* What hour of the day was it?'

'The time?' His eyebrows rose dramatically. 'Does it matter? A bit before mid-day, I would guess, perhaps a quarter of an hour? He didn't stop his noise until half-past the hour, at least.'

Jesperson had turned sickly pale, and I, remembering the sound of church bells striking noon while the fire still blazed, felt as bad as he looked.

'What . . . what happened then?'

'It was not long before one when the doctor arrived. Mr Henderson was unconscious and not responding to our efforts to revive him, though the doctor found nothing obviously wrong. There were no wounds, no broken bones, not even bruising.

His pulse, heartbeat and temperature were normal. We had taken good care of him, and there had been nothing to make him scream – well, not unless you believe in invisible demons, jabbing at him with their red-hot pokers.'

'Maybe it was something like that.'

Sergeant Bottomley gave him a sour look. 'That is more or less what the doctor thought. He said it must be a case of what the alienists call "hysteria". He said a man could feel so ashamed and guilty that he would punish himself, feeling his own emotions as if it were a physical attack, even to the point of fainting from the pain. He told us to leave him be, but to keep an eye on him; he said that Mr Henderson might wake up in a better frame of mind, but if he took a turn for the worse, we should send for him at once.'

The door to the office opened and the boy came in carrying a large tray on which three cups rattled in their saucers. He put the tray gingerly down on the desk, avoiding the stacks of paper as best he could.

'And did Henderson take a turn for the worse?' Jesperson asked impatiently.

The sergeant waited until the boy had closed the door behind him before he replied. 'Sometime in the early evening – after seven o'clock, before you ask, and before seven-thirty, because we looked in on him every half-hour – he was heard to call out. The officer on duty tried speaking to him, but could get no sense out of him.'

'How do you mean?'

'He was speaking gibberish – utter gibberish. He could understand us, more or less, but we could not understand him. I was sent for, and so was the doctor.'

'You're certain it was gibberish and not a foreign language?'

'Not one anyone could recognise. The doctor speaks German and French besides Latin and Greek.'

'Mr Henderson spent a few years in Egypt,' I offered.

The sergeant's eyebrows went up. 'Thought they spoke French out there.'

'Arabic, mostly, nowadays,' Jesperson said.

'Never mind. It was all gibberish to us, but he must have thought he was making sense, because he got angrier and angrier when we did not understand. He kept looking for something in his bag, something he needed, and it wasn't there. He was mad about that, too – you didn't have to understand his words to see he was furious with whoever had packed his bag for leaving out something vitally important.'

I thought of the hand we had burnt, and the ring it had worn, and wondered if Jesperson still carried it in his pocket.

'What next?' Jesperson asked. 'He's not here now, I take it.'

A cloud passed over the sergeant's face and once again he began to chew his moustache, before becoming aware of it, shutting his mouth and reaching for a handkerchief which he used to delicately dab it dry. At last he said, 'Dr Marshall has a part-share in a private sanatorium in Kent, where Mr Henderson could be well cared for. We had not been able to make contact with any next of kin, and it was not practical to keep him here until we did. The order of committal came through yesterday, and Dr Marshall made the arrangements. Mr Henderson was transported in a closed carriage with an experienced nurse.'

He took a gulp of tea before he continued, 'Although no trouble was anticipated – indeed, Mr Henderson was quite happy to be leaving – the doctor gave him a sedative, not so strong as to render him unconscious, but it made him drowsy and docile.'

After a deep breath, he plunged ahead. 'Unfortunately, it appears to have worn off too soon. According to the report I have – and there will be a further enquiry, I do assure you, to ascertain all the facts – they had almost arrived at their destination when the driver of the carriage was required to stop at a railway crossing for an approaching train.

'Perhaps the steady movement of the carriage had soothed the prisoner – I mean, the patient – and when it stopped, he was jolted from his gentle dreams, or it may have been that the noise of the train alarmed him. All I can tell you is that Mr Henderson reacted very suddenly and unexpectedly when he bolted. How he got the door open – for I can tell you of my own certain knowledge that it was locked when they left here – well, that is one of the things for the Enquiry Board to establish. The nurse tried to stop him, of course, but Mr Henderson fought like the very devil, he said, and certainly the poor man was left with a broken arm and two black eyes. The driver had his horses to worry about, for they were spooked by the commotion, but he saw everything that happened and his statement corroborates that of the unhappy engine-driver.

'The madman ran onto the tracks; he ran directly towards the on-coming train. He was shouting, words the driver said he could not understand, although he heard them clearly enough. But the words were not in English, so it is anybody's guess what Mr Henderson thought he was doing. The engine-driver saw him and tried to stop, but given the speed at which the train was travelling, and the fact that Mr Henderson was racing full-on towards it, the collision was unavoidable. Mr Henderson was mown down – he must have died almost instantly. His body was so torn and mangled that if we had not known who he was, it— Oh, I do beg your pardon, Miss Lane. It was a terrible end – a terrible story, to be sure.'

I had covered my mouth, sickened by the images that rose unbidden in my mind. Glancing at my partner, I saw how his freckles, usually scarcely visible, stood out darkly on his pale face, and knew we had had the same thought: *we* were responsible for this.

All the way home we scarcely spoke, our thoughts, I am sure, running on parallel lines. With the best intentions, meaning only to set poor Mr Henderson free from an invasive spirit, we had brought about his death, an unnecessary and a horrible end at that. How had it gone so badly wrong? Had we completely misunderstood the situation? Had we, perhaps, been tricked? But how? Had it always been too late to save him from the ancient soul that had lodged within him?

We could not destroy Meretseger's mummy if there was any chance of the same thing happening to Matilda.

But Mr Henderson's may have been a special case, the result of what had happened to him years ago in Egypt, because the mummy had contained the Ka of an ancient, powerful magician. Matilda's was a different situation, or so I hoped.

'But why did he want to kill himself?' I asked, breaking the silence at last as we walked away from the tram-stop towards Gower Street. 'If he had given it more time, he must have realised he would be able to learn our language, make himself understood. He could have continued with his plans . . . why did he give up like that?'

'I do not believe he gave up,' Jesperson replied. 'Quite the contrary. I believe he had no intention of dying. It only looks like suicide to us because we know about trains. But consider how that snorting steam engine would have appeared to someone from ancient Egypt – especially to a priest-magician suddenly thrown into the nineteenth century, and especially if he was someone who believed in the existence of strange and powerful beings, and was confident of his own ability to command them with words of power.

'Imagine it,' he urged. 'This priest-magician, having lost contact with the mind and soul of Henderson, is utterly ignorant of modern technology. He has been praying to the gods with all his might for rescue, and perhaps he thinks his prayers have been answered when he hears the fierce, whistling shriek and sees plumes of smoke as an enormous, powerful creature comes rushing across the land. Its arrival forces the driver to pull up his horses and stop – why should the priest not believe this was a god or demon coming to destroy his captors and bear him away to victory?'

As he spoke, I could see it, too. It felt true to me; it made sense, there was even a sort of justice to it, in that he had been destroyed by his own mad beliefs. But although it was good to know that the wicked ancient Egyptian was finally and forever extinct, I knew, too, that it was we who had caused the death of Mr Henderson.

I stopped on the corner, overwhelmed by feelings of guilt and remorse. 'If only we had not burned it, he would still be alive,' I murmured, as helpless tears sprang to my eyes.

Mr Jesperson took hold of my arm and moved me out of the way of a young man, evidently a scholar, who was reading a book as he walked along, paying no attention to anything else. Having saved me from a collision, he then managed to keep me walking, pulling me in close to his side. The unexpected contact, the warmth of his tall, slender body and the novelty of feeling his every movement as he walked was more disturbing than comforting, but in my annoyance at his daring to take such a liberty, my tears dried and I tried to pull away, but Mr Jesperson's grip was too secure. He continued to hold me for a few more seconds, only letting me go once we reached our front door.

Inside, I made a dash for the staircase.

'Miss Lane, wait!'

Despite the urgency in his voice, I did not pause or look back as I mounted the stairs. It must mean – or so I hoped – that he wished to apologise, or at least explain that it was only his concern for me that had led him to take hold of me in that way. However, he must be made aware of my displeasure, and therefore, he would have to wait.

'Miss Lane, you still have it – have you forgotten? I *must* see that papyrus—'

I *had* forgotten. My cheeks were burning. I was desperate to splash some water on my face, to check my appearance in the glass, to have a moment to myself to settle my feelings. Without looking round I called, 'In a moment. Only give me a moment to get it for you.'

When I returned downstairs, papyrus scroll in hand, I reminded him that I had secreted it in a pocket concealed beneath my skirt.

'I do beg your pardon,' he said kindly. 'I tend to forget how dashed awkward women's clothing can be! I hope I did not embarrass you with my impatience – have a biscuit,' he went on, thrusting a plate at me. 'Sit down and rest – Mother is making tea – you've had a dreadful shock.'

I made my way to the most comfortable chair in the room, which was by the fireplace and distanced from our desk. I skirted the coffin case, now smelling of paste and wet paper from Edith's clever repairs, and gave it a baleful look. What a waste of time and money that plan had been. I wondered what we should do with it now.

Once I was settled, I looked across the room at Jesperson, who had taken his accustomed chair behind the desk and was now carefully unrolling the papyrus. 'You say that I have had a dreadful shock – but it must have been equally dreadful for you, too.'

He frowned as he weighted down the two ends of the papyrus with some Chinese bronzes that he used as paperweights. 'Of course – I never expected anything like that – how could we, how could anyone have expected such a thing? That a long-dead magician could have taken over – *inhabited* – a living man like that? It is still almost inconceivable. How did it happen? Was it truly that night in Egypt, in the tent, when *something* flew out of the mummy and Henderson fell unconscious? Or was that only the seed, needing time and care to grow as it did? I thought that destroying the mummy would cut the cord between their two souls – and it did – but with what a terrible result!

'We could not have left things as they were. Perhaps there was some other step we should have taken, a ritual to be performed, maybe? But if the accident had not happened, if greater care had been taken in transporting the prisoner, then that man would still be alive – but he would not be Henderson. Locked away in an asylum, the Egyptian priest would have learnt our language and our ways, learnt to pretend to be a harmless widower, sent mad by grief, but now restored to sanity, returned to a life in our world, and free to practice whatever mischief he had planned.'

'That mischief was connected to Matilda – now that he is gone, will she be all right?' I wondered aloud.

With a grim tightening of the lips Jesperson shook his head. He looked down at the papyrus spread out on the desk, staring at it as if by sheer force of will he could summon meaning from the rows of hieroglyphs.

'Why is that papyrus so important?' I asked.

'It was important enough to someone to have it stolen, however that was arranged. We must find out about its content before we can know why.' He stood up abruptly, just as the door opened and his mother came in with the tea-tray.

'Jasper, where are you going?' She looked at him in surprise as he headed for the door. 'I have just made the tea you wanted.'

'That is for Miss Lane, to settle her nerves.' He snatched a biscuit as he passed her. 'I have an urgent wire to send.'

Edith set down the tray on a small table, poured for us both, then took the seat beside me. Looking at me with her wise, gentle gaze, she said, 'Would you care to talk about it, Di?'

CHAPTER TWENTY-THREE

The Return of Pagan Brown

Jesperson was restless and unsettled for the remainder of the day. He had sent a wire to Pagan Brown asking him to come at once, but there was no reply, and no knock at our door, even after nightfall.

The wait was prolonged through Sunday morning, when Jesperson went to call on Mr Brown in his rooms, only to return with the news that his landlady knew only that he had gone to visit a friend in the country and she did not expect him back before Monday.

Jesperson groaned. 'And Budge away as well – ah, what shall we do?'

'Think of other things and wait until Tuesday,' I responded pragmatically. 'After all, what can be so urgent about translating a papyrus written more than three millennia ago that another day or two will make any difference?'

He sighed and made a brief, futile attempt to smooth down his hair. 'You are very logical, Miss Lane. Impatience has always been my besetting weakness. Urgent or not, I find it hard to think of anything else with this preying upon my mind. I shall have to take a stab at translating it myself – and hand my work over to Brown to laugh at when he finally turns up.'

With that, he sat down and began to study Mr Budge's primer, that same book he had found so interesting during his own sojourn in Egypt as a boy. I was rather surprised that he needed to refer to it at all, knowing his fantastically retentive memory. At least occasionally, perhaps, some things must be pushed out to make way for new and more useful knowledge. This was surely the first time in many years that Jesperson had felt the need to recall the meaning invested in those mysterious and beautiful ideograms.

He broke off his research long enough to dine with us, and while we ate, explained some of the peculiarities of this writing system he was struggling to master.

I knew from my own visits to the Egyptian galleries that before the Rosetta Stone, discovered nearly a hundred year ago, made decipherment possible, hieroglyphs were thought to be a system of ideograms, each one expressing a particular idea, which the Egyptians used for religious or magical purposes. The very meaning of 'hieroglyph' was 'sacred signs'. Most of the symbols did mean what they represented – owl, cat, viper, water, for example – but twenty of them also had a phonetic value, much like the twenty-four letters in our own alphabet.

Jesperson smiled approvingly and went on, 'Indeed, you are right, Miss Lane. So the sign that looks like an owl might be used to mean an owl, or by extension birds in general, but it also represents the sound of our letter M, and will more usually be used in that way. So far, so simple.

'But it gets more complicated. As with other languages from that part of the world, vowels tend to be omitted from the written texts, which means that many completely unrelated words are spelled the same way. In his book, Budge gives the example *nem* – spelled with the sign for water, n, and the sign for owl, m – which might mean "to sleep" or "to walk" or "again" or "tongue". It might be obvious in context which word was intended, and the Egyptians made it easier to know by having another class of symbols used solely as determinatives, to indicate the category of the word that either precedes or follows it.' He rolled his eyes heavenwards. 'Oh, yes, and I should say that one does not immediately know if a given text should be read from right to left or left to right or up or down. Anyway, the determinatives – if there is one indicating "a thing of the flesh" either before or after this *nem*, it must mean "tongue". And if the determinative is for an activity, then it must be one of the verbs – but which one? Budge is unclear on the question of how the reader is to know if the writing concerns walking or sleeping.'

'Or perhaps sleep-walking?'

He did not respond to my facetious question. 'That is only an example to indicate the difficulties. Oh, probably in a week or two I should master it. When I was a boy, it was only a game to me. Now it is deadly serious.' He gave a gloomy sigh. 'If only Brown or Budge were here; I cannot do this on my own.'

Although he sounded on the brink of giving up, after a brisk walk to stretch out the kinks in body and mind, Jesperson went back to the papyrus with new determination. Scarcely a minute passed before he gave a triumphant crow.

'What is it?'

'Osiris – I recognise the name! – the great god of death and resurrection. Oh, and there it is again . . . and here, too, at the end.' His pleasure was suddenly dampened. 'Three times.' He sighed. 'That has the ring of a prayer or a ritual invocation. Is that all it is? A prayer for the soul of the dead?' He shook his head. 'No. It *must* be more than that. Such things were formulaic, readily available in the Book of the Dead and elsewhere. Why take the risk of stealing something that could be found and copied, or easily memorised, considering how short it is.'

He brooded for a moment. Then, with a surge of hope, said, 'Unless . . . is there something special about this particular prayer, or the papyrus itself?'

He took out his magnifying glass and adjusted the angle of the lamp as he began to peruse the thing with a different purpose, no longer trying to work out the words, but looking for something else.

Curious, I went to stand by his shoulder just as he caught his breath and murmured, 'Hullo! What's this? A different hand! These symbols – they lack the artistry and skill of the scribe who wrote the name of Osiris and all these others. And I think – yes, the ink too is different – fresher. There is no doubt: this line was written at a different time and by a different scribe. Do you see these sixteen hieroglyphs?'

Now that he pointed it out to me, I did. I frowned down at the row, wondering at its significance. 'Were they written in an empty space, or has something else been painted over?'

'Good question.' He turned the papyrus over to inspect the other side, then turned it back again and examined it through his glass. 'It looks as if they were written, although at a different time, on the same bare surface as the others. For some reason – and without being able to read any more than the name of Osiris I cannot hazard even a guess as to why – the space was left blank.'

He leaned back in his chair and steepled his hands beneath his chin as he considered the matter. At length he sighed and sat up. 'Until we have an accurate translation, there is no sense in worrying about it. With Pagan Brown and Mr Budge both out of reach, I'll have to find another translator. Undoubtedly there will be another Egyptologist who will be willing to help – I'll make enquiries at the British Museum tomorrow.'

As it turned out, Jesperson had no need to go in search of a translator, for Pagan Brown himself turned up on our doorstep at eight o'clock the next morning.

Jesperson greeted him joyfully, pulling him almost bodily into the house.

'I am glad I have not come too early,' he said blinking in surprise and smiling uncertainly. 'I read your message when I got home last night, but it was then much too late to call—'

'How could it be too late?' Jesperson demanded. 'Did I not say that you were to come at once? I thought I had made myself clear that it was a matter of urgency.'

Mr Brown gave his hesitant laugh. 'Urgency? I must say, even the most dedicated of Egyptologists would be unlikely to use that word about something written thousands of years ago! Not that I disapprove – indeed, I sympathise, and find your excitement quite refreshing.'

Jesperson steered our visitor into our office and pushed him into his own chair at the big desk. Carefully, almost reverently, he placed the papyrus before him and asked, 'Will you be able to read it to us now? Or will you need some time to yourself, perhaps some reference books to aid you?'

Pagan Brown cast his eye over the page. 'It appears to be an invocation to Osiris – quite a short text, and possibly formulaic. I do not anticipate any great difficulties, and given the – heh-heh the urgency you feel in the matter, I am happy to attempt a rough translation immediately.' He rubbed his hands together as if about to embark on a physical chore. 'Do you mind if I hold it?'

'Just as you like.'

He picked it up, ran his eyes over it and began, somewhat haltingly, to read:

'"O wandering soul, hear me now. I conjure you in the name of Osiris, the eternal, the mighty, King of the Dead and Lord of eternity, to attend my words and be ruled by them. I know your name. You are lost, having strayed too far from your proper place——" er, hmm, perhaps that should be, "your true and lasting physical abode" – in any case, what is evidently meant here is the mummy, or the body of the wandering soul who is being addressed – you understand?'

'Yes, yes,' said Jesperson tensely. 'Do go on.'

'Aah, where was I? Yes, yes —' He cleared his throat. '"Now you must return and wander no more. Be glad to be confined. Your body has been prepared with all proper respect and ritual. Your living name is written upon it——"' Here Mr Brown stopped and peered more closely at the papyrus. He shook his head. 'No, no, this is no name. What is this?'

Frowning, he looked up at Jesperson. 'Has this been tampered with?'

'How do you mean?' Jesperson spoke in a careful, studiedly neutral manner.

Mr Brown sighed. 'It appears to be genuine. And the spell is a plausible one, and looks to have been written by a proper scribe – until we come to the name, which is not a name at all, despite the determinative sign that indicates it is the name of a man.' He held the papyrus up towards the window to catch the light and inspected it more closely. 'Someone else wrote these' – he paused to count – 'these fifteen – sixteen if you count the determinative – signs. Someone who was not a scribe, and probably not well acquainted with the language – perhaps with no knowledge of it at all. They chose a few – let me see; there are seven hieroglyphs – perhaps making the choice because they liked the shape? Or for some other odd reason.

Then they copied them out without understanding, pleased to imagine they were composing something in hieroglyphics, as an English child might write O D Z O O D I Z Z and so on until he ran out of space.'

'You think it was an Egyptian child who wrote that?'

Mr Brown's shaggy eyebrows shot up, making him appear comically alarmed. 'Oh, no, by no means! I see I have chosen a bad analogy. Whoever wrote this line of gibberish into the spell was *not* an ancient Egyptian. Heh-heh, no. This was written considerably more recently than the rest of the text – I am by no means an expert on ink, but I have handled and examined a great many documents from ancient Egypt and I can tell the difference between theirs and ours. That' – he waved at the top third of the papyrus – 'is authentic. That' – he stabbed a finger at the line Jesperson had drawn my attention to the day before – 'was written in the sort of ordinary India ink you might buy in any stationer's shop.'

'Yes, I had noticed the difference myself,' Jesperson said. 'I am glad to have you confirm my own observations. And they were written *before* the end of the prayer, in a space deliberately left blank . . . do you know why that space was left?'

'Ah, yes, I believe I do. You will understand when I read it properly. Now, I shall start it again but leave out the gibberish, indicating where the space would have been.'

After clearing his throat, he began, his voice ringing out more confidently this time, '"O wandering soul, hear me now. I conjure you in the name of Osiris, the eternal, the mighty, King

302

of the Dead and Lord of Eternity, to attend my words and be ruled by them. I know your name. You are lost, having strayed too far from your proper, true and physical home, and now you must return to it. Wander no more. Let yourself be confined within it, and gladly. This body has been prepared for you with all respect and ritual, and your living name is written upon it. Therefore I command you"' – Mr Brown gave us a meaningful look as he went on *sotto voce* – 'hmm, hmmm, hmm fill in name here' then his voice rose again to pronounce, '"in the name of the mighty Lord Osiris, who rules over all immortal souls, enter in to this body. I call your name thrice, and it is done."'

Jesperson let a moment of silence elapse before he asked his question. 'Was that a usual thing?'

'The spell, do you mean, or the practice of leaving an empty space for the name?'

'Either.'

'As to leaving a blank space for a personal name, consider our own book of standard prayers, or any ritual in which a particular individual is making a declaration, or calling upon God or the congregation for a blessing. As to this particular spell, or prayer, no, it is not common. At least, I have never encountered it before. Of course, many things remain to be discovered. Egypt had a long history: over the centuries traditions were embellished and became more elaborate, the protections and precautions and rituals surrounding the dead increasing the more people imagined what might go wrong during the soul's journey through the Underworld.

'A prayer like this makes sense, when you consider how much care the Egyptians took to preserve the body of the deceased, and to come up with useful advice to help his soul survive all the trials they believed awaited in the Underworld. In order for the spirit to have a chance at resurrection, after it journeyed through the afterlife, it must return to its original body here on earth. That was the reason for the mummification process; if it was not preserved, the disembodied soul would also perish. It would never have the chance to be reborn.

'The reason for the use of anthropoid coffins and sarcophagi, the reason for painting the coffins with the likeness of the person who had died, and for inscribing the name of the deceased in so many places, was not only to preserve the memory of the deceased and offer that particular form of immortality that comes from remaining in the minds of the living; it was also a way of ensuring that the soul would find its way back home again. Tomb-entrances must be sealed and hidden from grave-robbers, but what if the spirit was also deterred by these precautions? What if it needed more guidance to keep from going astray or getting lost, to find its way back to its own body? I do not know how much anyone worried about that, but if they did, they would certainly be willing to pay a priest to say a special spell for the soul. In such a prayer, invoking the aid of Osiris would be natural.'

'Might it be used in another way?' Jesperson asked when Pagan Brown finally paused for breath.

'I do not understand.'

'This name,' Jesperson began, tapping the papyrus.

'That is not a name, as I have told you.'

'Perhaps not. But whatever it may be, I think the writing is the same as that on the card left atop the mummy we found in Henderson's house.'

'Who is Henderson? What mummy?' He sounded bewildered.

'It is a long story,' Jesperson replied as he took out his pocket book. 'I shall tell you later. But you remember the ring I showed you – with an inscription which you kindly translated? – and this piece of card with the unintelligible hieroglyphs?' He put the card down on the desk beside the papyrus. 'They are the same, are they not? The ones on the card are bigger, and spaced out into what appears to be three words, and easier to make out – which is, I suppose, no surprise, as there was very little space on the papyrus, and only one chance to get it right. But, look – here are the same seven hieroglyphs in the same order. They make up three different words. The first is written serpent, mouth, serpent; the second: rope, reeds, water, mouth, reeds; the third: rope, reeds, water, hand, mouth, folded cloth, water. It is evidently the same name as on the papyrus.'

Pagan Brown stared at Jesperson, his gaze a mixture of wariness and exasperation. 'Why do you insist that it is a name? You admit you cannot read the writing, and I have told you it has no meaning. It is sheer gibberish.'

'Like the words of power on the ring, but different.'

'Different,' Mr Brown said, with an emphatic nod. 'And if *those* were meant to be words of power, why should they be written in the space left blank for a name?'

305

'Because it is a name,' Jesperson said softly, 'but not an Egyptian one. Correct me if I am wrong, but each of these particular symbols has its own distinct phonetic value – like the letters of our own alphabet.' He gave him an enquiring look, holding it until Pagan Brown agreed that was so.

'And you could pronounce them, could you not? Even though they have no meaning, you could sound out these nonsense words, yes?'

'Yes, I could, but why?'

'Humour me, please. I want to be certain that what I think I see is really there. If you could simply set aside your knowledge of Egyptian words and forget about any meaning, only concentrate on the sounds, it would be very helpful. You may remember, when I first showed you the writing on this card, you said that it might have a meaning, if someone – an English person – used it as a form of code.'

'A coded message?' The idea perked up Mr Brown. 'Is that your idea? Using the sound equivalent of each hieroglyphic to spell out a simple message in English?'

'Something like that. So the way to say serpent mouth serpent . . . ?'

'*Djrdj*,' Mr Brown said promptly. He coughed and shook his head sadly. 'Alas, quite as meaningless in English as in Egyptian – of course, I cannot be quite certain about my accent; it might be better pronounced as *djaaardj* or *djrrrrdj*,' he said, rolling the 'r' exaggeratedly.

'Very good! Thank you. And the rest? If you would be so

kind as to read the whole sequence, with breaks between the words where indicated.'

Smiling, not taking it seriously but willing to play along, Mr Brown looked at the card again, cleared his throat, and read out, '*Djrdj hyinree hyind-rrr-sn.*'

The hairs rose on the back of my neck. 'George Henry Henderson?'

Mr Brown frowned. 'Henderson again? Who——?'

'He was the man who came back from Egypt with a mummy he stored beneath his bed. The mummy was missing an arm. The hand was found elsewhere in the house, wearing the ring I showed you before. And the card with those hieroglyphs spelling out the name of George Henry Henderson was lying on the mummy. The papyrus that you have just translated for us, with the spell encouraging the soul of George Henry Henderson to enter into the mummy with his name on it, was not there, but . . .' He hesitated, then went on, 'It was found . . . somewhere else. This papyrus was stolen from the British Museum. Someone, most likely the thief, filled in the blank with what appears to be gibberish until it is sounded out phonetically.'

'Dear me!' He rose from his seat and stared at Jesperson, the card fluttering in his hand until Jesperson relieved him of it. 'I can see from your faces this was no joke. You mean to say that someone thought to force a living man's soul into the dead husk of an ancient mummy? But who could be so mad, and why would . . .' His eyes widened. 'You said it was urgent. Please tell me what you meant. Are we too late? Is the gentleman all right?'

'You had better sit down. You are looking quite pale. Would you like a glass of brandy?'

He sat down, but made a protesting gesture. 'No, no, it is far too early for spirits. And I am not ill, only rather . . . rather . . .'

'A glass of water?' I suggested. 'Or a cup of tea?'

'Tea?' He brightened. 'Tea would be lovely, thank you.'

'I'll see to it,' I said, and left Mr Jesperson to explain how Mr Henderson had become involved with an ancient Egyptian priest, and how we had come to the conclusion that their fateful first encounter had eventually culminated in an exchange of bodies that had proved fatal to them both – and how it all tied in with the ancient princess and the mystery mummy.

CHAPTER TWENTY-FOUR

The Silent Friend

By the time I returned with tea and plenty of hot buttered toast (for it had occurred to me that Mr Brown's feeling of weakness might be the result of having come to see us before breaking his fast), Jesperson had reached the end of Henderson's story and was explaining how his demise had affected our plans to banish the wicked princess by destroying her mummy.

'Your translation has given me new hope,' he was saying as I set the tray down.

'After hearing what happened to Henderson, we were afraid that poor Matilda would be doomed to a similar fate, but now that we have a better understanding of what happened to him, we may, with the help of this spell, be able to free the young lady and send that ancient Egyptian spirit back to her own mummified remains.'

Mr Brown murmured his thanks as I handed him his cup.

'What do you think?' Jesperson asked him.

He stirred in a second spoonful of sugar. 'I think it is a most astonishing and terrible story.'

'But what do you think of our chances?'

'Is the mummy in your possession?'

'Not yet. We hope to secure it on Wednesday evening.'

'That is good. And you know her name – both their names. That is most important. The name, to the ancients, was a vital part of the person, and the key element in magic. Names conferred power. To confer a name on an inanimate object could imbue it with life. To know the secret name of a god could give a magician god-like powers.' He paused and took a bite of toast.

'We don't know any secret names,' I reminded them.

'You probably don't need to worry about that,' he said. 'That, I think, was mainly an issue with gods and supernatural beings. Perhaps magicians, too, guarded a secret name that could protect them, and pharaohs all had special "throne names", different from those they were given at birth. But as for mere mortals – well, from the evidence, the public name of George Henry Henderson was quite sufficient to requirements.'

Jesperson had been listening intently. 'Do you think the same spell would work for someone else? If we inserted a different name?'

Mr Brown thought about this. The tea and toast had done the trick, for he was already looking much brighter, the natural colour back in his face. 'Well . . . if you were a magician, there would be no doubt about it.'

'It was a priest-magician who cast the spell previously,' I said.

'But the priest could only have worked through Henderson. Could he cast such a spell *on himself*?' Jesperson mused aloud.

'It must have been Matilda, channelling the spirit,' I said,

310

suddenly feeling certain. 'In my former employment, I have witnessed Violet Dawes taken over by the personality of Seshemetka when she entered the trance state at a séance.'

Mr Brown shrugged. 'If a woman was able to cast this spell, I see no reason why it should not work for you as well. I say, Miss Lane, is there any more tea in the pot? Ah, lovely, thank you so much.'

'I hope we may count on your help, Pagan,' said Jesperson.

'Me? Why, of course – if there is anything I can do, I am more than happy to put myself at your disposal.' He paused, a peculiar expression on his thin face. I suspected he had surprised himself with his ready agreement. This was confirmed by what he said next, once again speaking in his usual, more hesitant way. 'I had always thought our modern-day black magicians must be utterly deluded in the belief that they could summon the old Egyptian powers to use in today's world. The ancient gods must have died with the people who worshipped them; their occult powers and world-view as well. But if even one or two of those antique souls have managed to survive, with their beliefs and personalities intact—Well, that throws my own settled view of reality into turmoil. And portends something potentially more disastrous.'

With a shaky laugh, he found his pocket handkerchief and dabbed his mouth before going on, 'Never did I imagine that my studies into a dead civilisation could ever become of such vital importance to anyone else! But my duty is clear. I will help you in whatever way I can.'

'Thank you, Pagan. Your help has already been of inestimable value. Would you be so good as to call in here tomorrow? I should like to be tutored in the proper pronunciation so I may recite the spell myself inserting the name of the ancient one we must banish. I am a quick study; I will be able to commit it to memory. After that – but that will depend on the outcome of our plans for Wednesday.'

As soon as Mr Brown had left, Mr Jesperson went to pay a call on Mr Sand at the British Museum, to arrange a meeting with him in two days' time. 'Wednesday afternoon it must be,' he told me as he adjusted his hat, 'and as late in the afternoon as we can make it. It will be harder for him to refuse me face to face. I hope he won't kick against the timing, but if he does, I shall simply have to kick harder, because any other day would make it more difficult for us to carry the thing off.'

'Why does he leave work early on Wednesday?'

'That is when he meets with his tutor – he is improving his ancient Assyrian. He had to cancel the lesson last week to assist with the unwrapping, so I think he will be even more determined to get away on time this week. As soon as I've confirmed it with Sand, we'll let Mr Creevey know when to come.'

Mr Arthur Creevey was the owner of a small business that rejoiced in the name of Creevey's Careful Removals. He had been one of our early clients, and so deep was his gratitude to us for solving the sinister mystery that had blighted his life that he had sworn to provide his personal service to us at any time we required transport for anything, anywhere.

My partner soon returned, looking pleased with himself. Despite some reluctance, Mr Sand had agreed to an appointment at the Museum for the day after tomorrow, at four o'clock in the afternoon; it could not be any later, because he must leave at a quarter to five. Jesperson had promised that the meeting would take no more than five or ten minutes of his time at most: he had only to accept (in the absence of Mr Budge) an object that was being donated to the Museum. The unspecified object had belonged to the late husband of a friend of his, Jesperson had told him, and being an eccentric lady, she wished, while remaining anonymous, to see the item personally handed into Mr Budge's care – or, in his absence, Mr Sand's – before she departed for the Continent.

I was to play the part of this mysterious nameless lady, of course, standing silently by while Mr Jesperson (as usual) did all the talking. We could not risk the possibility that Mr Sand might recognise my voice, and it suited me to be the silent partner in this.

On Wednesday, I tried on my costume several times before I was confident of being able to take it off at speed. It had to go on over my own dress, which was awkward, but had the advantage of completely disguising my figure. With the hat covering my hair and the veil hiding my face, I stood before the looking-glass and did not even recognise myself. I saw what Mr Sand and anyone else we encountered would surely see: a small, shapeless, rather stocky widow, highly respectable and probably elderly. Even my customary stance and way of walking (not that I supposed for a moment that Mr Sand would have taken any notice) would be altered by the wide, cumbersome skirts and the weight of all these extra clothes.

At twenty minutes past four, the cart from Creevey's Careful Removals pulled up in front of the house and, heart pounding with excitement, I went upstairs to ready myself.

'Take your time,' Jesperson reminded me, and although I could not help but feel a trifle sorry for the anxiety our deliberate delay must be causing poor Mr Sand, I did just that. When at last I joined the two men in the hall, Mr Creevey took off his hat and bowed to me in silence. I guessed that our former client did not recognise me, seeing only a woman in deep mourning. Before I could dispel the illusion, Jesperson said, 'Excuse the lack of introductions, old chap, but our mission today is a sensitive one. It will be better for you to be uninformed, no more than a hired conveyance.'

'I pride myself on providing precisely the service required,' he replied, and bent to lift the crate we wanted him to deliver to the museum.

'May I give you a hand with that?'

'Oh, no, sir, thank you, but no. You had better attend to the lady. I am sure she must be in greater need of your strength.'

Taking the hint, I leaned more heavily on Mr Jesperson's arm, as if incapacitated by grief or age, or both as we left the house. When the crate had been loaded into the back of the van, I permitted tall, broad-shouldered Mr Creevey to effortlessly lift me onto the seat beside him.

'Stop in front of the main entrance, if you would,' Jesperson said as we approached the Museum.

'Deliveries are taken round the back,' Mr Creevey reminded us, but Jesperson was already explaining.

'I know, but I told Mr Sand to meet us at the front entrance, and as we are late already—'

'Late?' Mr Creevey looked unhappy.

'By design,' Jesperson assured him. 'Never fear, you are playing your part to perfection.'

We approached like ordinary visitors, for all we were an oddly assorted trio, through the front gates, across the open courtyard and up the long, wide flight of stone steps, although unlike most, we were moving at a funereal pace, entirely appropriate to one in deep mourning. The image we presented was enhanced, I thought, by the crate looking like a coffin, for all it was so lightly borne by the powerful man. In his dark suit and stove-pipe hat, Mr Creevey might even have been an undertaker.

Mr Sand's face was a study in conflicting emotions at the sight of us. 'I had about given you up,' he muttered sulkily to Jesperson, before his eyes widened as he noticed the man behind.

'But whatever is *that*? You said it was small!'

'In value, not in *size*,' Jesperson murmured. 'I was quoting Madame, who regrets she is unable to make some larger, more significant—'

'Yes, yes, very well,' Mr Sand said impatiently, 'but all such deliveries should be taken to the back.'

315

'Oh, certainly – if you wish—' Jesperson turned. 'I say, Creevey—'

'Not now, not now,' Mr Sand interrupted him, 'there's no time.'

For a moment I thought he would send us away, like a certain type of clerk who glances at the clock, shakes his head and seeing your anxious approach at one minute before the hour, smugly turns the sign to 'CLOSED'.

'I'm terribly sorry to be late, but it was impossible to get here any earlier because – well, if I may explain?'

Looking anguished, Mr Sand stopped him again. 'Never mind. You are here now, and we may as well go through. I say,' he called to Mr Creevey, 'you're all right with that by yourself, are you? Yes, I see you are. Follow me.'

Other visitors turned to stare as the large man passed them, carrying his burden so easily through the great marble halls as we trailed along behind. Mr Jesperson deliberately slowed his steps to a snail's pace as I leaned ever more heavily on his arm, giving the impression of severe debility.

Mr Sand and Mr Creevey were already in Mr Budge's office by the time we got there. We heard him giving instructions – 'Put it on the floor – just there – oh, anywhere, so long as it does not block the door. Anywhere, I said. Pray do not worry – really, it does not matter if – just set it down, will you? Mr Budge won't be back for another week; I'll move it if necessary, but I am sure it will be quite all right anywhere – yes, yes, there. All right. Good. That will do, thank you.'

As we reached the door, Mr Creevey was being ushered out by Mr Sand. Putting on a sudden burst of speed, Jesperson managed to get us both inside the office, ignoring Mr Sand's clear displeasure. However, the Assistant to the Keeper quickly masked his feelings and bent down to me. Speaking as if I had been a child, he said softly, 'Thank you so much for your kind and generous donation. I know that Mr Budge will want to write and thank you personally, Mrs . . . ?'

I shrank away, allowing Jesperson to place a protective arm around me as he said in a stern, quiet voice, 'Mr Sand, I thought you had understood me when I told you that the lady does not wish to be identified in any way, not even to be connected with this donation. She abhors publicity. If Mr Budge guesses her identity, he will understand her reasons; if not, that is even better. She is acting on instruction from her deceased . . . from a dear and recently deceased relation. She has come with me only to see that the gift safely delivered, and for no other purpose. Now, if you do not mind . . . ?'

Mr Sand blinked uncertainly, but he moved out of our way.

'There, you see, my dear?' Jesperson spoke to me in a soft, kindly voice. 'Your little gift is now safely delivered. This is Mr Budge's own office; he will be back in less than a fortnight to find it waiting, an unexpected gift to welcome him home. What's that you say?'

He bent down to me, although I had made not a sound, and in response I whispered something meaningless into his ear.

'Yes, yes, what a good idea,' he said, and straightened to his full height. To Mr Sand he said, 'She would like to visit the Egyptian galleries before we depart. But if you would like to inspect the donation first . . . ?' He gestured at the crate.

'No, not now, thank you very much.' Perhaps thinking that a rude response, he added quickly, 'I think it would be proper to allow Mr Budge to be the first to open it.'

Jesperson smiled. 'Of course. Has Creevey gone?'

'Your delivery man? I believe he is still in the corridor. Perhaps waiting to be paid?' Mr Sand was close on our heels as we made our agonisingly slow progress through the doorway. I heard his barely repressed sigh of relief when we finally left the office.

'Thank you, Creevey, that will be all for today,' said Jesperson. 'I will take Madame to look at the Egyptian galleries, then I'll see her home myself.'

Mr Sand locked the door and pocketed the key.

'I must apologise again for arriving so late – I hope we have not put you to any trouble,' said Jesperson.

'Not at all,' Mr Sand replied hastily. 'But if you will excuse me – I am in a bit of a hurry. Good evening!'

With that, he was off. I hoped he would not be too late.

Although we thought it unlikely that Mr Sand would waste any time before leaving, and even more unlikely that he would return for a forgotten umbrella or any other reason, we spent a good ten minutes loitering in the Egyptian galleries before making our slow way back to the Keeper's office, where Jesperson opened the door so easily, anyone watching would have thought he carried the key.

He locked it again from the inside, using the same small useful tool, as a precaution against interruption. After swiftly ascertaining that Mummy X was still in its sarcophagus, he pulled from a pocket a different tool with which to draw out the nails securing the crate. When they were out, I held the lid while Jesperson leaned in and pulled off Edith's painted cartonnage cover, revealing our own mummy.

My hands were trembling slightly as I fumbled with the various pins and combs keeping the hat and veil firmly attached to my head. Even though I had rehearsed the removal of this costume often enough that it should have been easy, my sudden attack of nerves turned it into a protracted struggle. In my determination to avoid damaging Edith's veil, I pulled out some of my own hair and felt the tears start to my eyes.

At last I was free of the accoutrements, although I feared I must look a fright, red-faced from the effort, with tangled, straggling hair. Fortunately, it was much easier to divest myself of the voluminous skirt and heavy jacket, and I was relieved to feel myself again, cooler in my own less restricting clothes.

Mummy X was waiting for us. Working together, just as we had practised at home, Jesperson and I dressed her. Our measurements had been accurate: the skirt brushed the floor, hiding the wearer's lack of shoes. We did not dare attempt to move the arms from the resting position into which they had been placed thousands of years ago, so I had used extra stuffing to pad out my jacket, which we now used to fill the empty sleeves. With needle and thread I put in a few swift stitches to secure the garments to the mummy's linens, to avoid any revealing gaps or slippage. We had already worked out the best way to achieve our desired impression, so we were able to labour easily together, as if at some regular daily task, with no need for words of instruction or correction.

At last, I stepped back to look at what we had made.

I saw a short, stout widow dressed in deep mourning, her hair hidden by an unfashionable hat and her face heavily veiled, standing next to Mr Jesperson, who was gently supporting her with one arm. Was that how I had looked? I remembered what I had seen in the looking-glass during our dress rehearsal yesterday through the gauzy haze of that same veil. He grinned at me now, the same grin I had seen then beside my reflection, and I experienced an uncanny sensation as I recalled the folk tradition of the *doppelgänger*, that to see one's own double is a forewarning of death.

I shivered and turned away.

He touched my arm, as if to remind me of what had to be done next. There was the open casket belonging to Mummy X, and there on the floor was another *doppelgänger,* the mummy we had bought a few days ago in Hitchin.

It was my job to deal with this one. I put aside the natural repugnance I felt at the idea of embracing a long-dead body and trying not to think about what I was doing, I bent and lifted the mummy. It was only a *thing,* I told myself, and light enough to lift by myself. The task was distasteful, but it was swiftly over.

There: it was done. The mummies had changed places. When

I looked at the one in the case, I could see no obvious difference. But Mr Budge had been fooled before; I wondered if that might make him more suspicious now?

I turned to Jesperson, who was studying it through narrowed eyes. Then he gave an abrupt nod, which I took to mean, *It will do.*

When I walked over to stand at his side, he moved the dressed mummy so that it was I who was supporting it, leaving him free to close the empty mummy case, return the lid to the crate, and then – after an alert pause for us to listen for any sounds that might indicate someone outside nearby – nailed it shut again with a few sharp taps of a small hammer.

Once he had unlocked the door, he took the veiled widow from my hands and after I had checked to ensure there was no one within sight, I hurried along the corridor and returned to the public galleries, my heart pounding hard. We had planned that I should leave the Museum first, and that our encounter in the street should appear to be by chance. Although it was not likely that anyone would notice us, and even more unlikely that anyone would have reason to be suspicious, we could not afford to be complacent.

After leaving the Museum I walked slowly, pausing to look in shop windows, trying to time my arrival at the corner of Bedford Square so that I should not appear to be waiting for anyone. When I saw my partner approaching, I was struck by the convincing realism of the illusion. There was nothing to lead anyone to suspect that the woman in mourning leaning on a young man's arm was not really walking beside him; women in long skirts can often give the impression of gliding, rather than moving their legs like a normal human being, and so it was in this case.

Jesperson and I exchanged our normal perfunctory greetings and I fell in beside him quite naturally, with the mummy between us. Whilst appearing to be relaxed, taking it in turns to smile and seem to converse amongst ourselves, we must remain alert and vigilant, aware of the potential dangers posed by every other person passing by, or approaching us on the pavement on this pleasant summer evening. I was wary in particular of encountering anyone we knew who might wish to stop us for a chat – and who would expect to be introduced to our silent friend.

The walk up Gower Street, moving at a suitably decorous pace rather than at Jesperson's normal long, loping stride, was endless, but we were almost home – when I saw Mrs Brewer bearing down upon us, skirts billowing like a ship in sail, her eyes bright and narrow with her usual hunger for gossip.

At that moment I wished with all my heart that we had not been so scrupulous about keeping Mr Creevey innocent and uninvolved with our crime. If we had been completely honest with him, we could have allowed him to decide for himself if he wanted to take the risk, and he might have agreed to drive the three of us safely and swiftly home.

Mrs Brewer and her husband Henry Brewer were the news-agents whose premises adjoined our house. That proximity, she reckoned, meant she could claim friendship with Edith Jesperson, although Edith treated her always with perfectly polite reserve. More annoying was the way Mrs Brewer always spoke to Mr Jesperson as if he was a child.

'Good evening, Miss Lane,' she said to me, with her usual dismissive nod. (She regarded me, I think, as nothing more than Mrs Jesperson's 'odd' lodger, a woman of no interest to her.) 'Jasper! How are you? How is your dear mother? And who is your friend? Will you not introduce me?'

'I am certain Miss Lane needs no introduction, Mrs Brewer,' he said, sounding surprised, and before she could respond to that, I'd moved forward and intercepted her. Taking her arm, I steered her aside, speaking in a low, urgent tone. 'Not just now, please, Mrs Brewer.'

'What do you mean, "not now"? Whatever is wrong?'

'We cannot stop to chat. I am very sorry,' I said, prepared to move away.

For most, that simple hint would have been enough, but Mrs Brewer strained to keep her eye on Mr Jesperson, who had walked on without me, slightly picking up his pace. Her movement suggested she intended to go after him – however, I had hold of her arm, and I did not let her go.

Frowning, she glared at me and said sharply, 'What is this, Miss Lane? Will you please let me go? I should like to have a word with young Jasper.'

'This is not a good time. The poor, unhappy widow . . . it is her first time out . . . I am sure you would be sympathetic, of course, but . . .' Realising I had all her attention, I let go of her arm. 'Anything, even the kindest of remarks, might upset her, in her situation.'

She stared after them, but I was relieved to see she made no further push to leave me. 'Of course, I would not wish to upset anyone. The poor old dear. But who is she? A relative, I suppose.'

I almost agreed, but neither the Jespersons nor I were exactly rich in kin – if I claimed her as an elderly aunt, Mrs Brewer would doubtless want more details, and just now I could think of nothing but mummies and ancient Egyptians. Even if I did manage to put her off now, she would be plaguing Edith with her questions for days.

So I relied on the truth, after a fashion. 'No. We came by her acquaintance as a matter of our business.'

She stared, her eyes narrowing, and her gaze sharpened still more. 'You mean your "detective" business? Well, well. Is she a client? Or a suspect? Was there a suspicious death? Was it' – she dropped her voice and moved her face closer to mine – '*murder?*'

I pursed my lips primly and lowered my eyes.

'Was it her husband? Just nod your head if it was.'

'Mrs Brewer, please. Professional standards prohibit me from discussing the details of any investigation. We owe our clients complete discretion and privacy.'

'But was it murder? Surely you can tell me that much.'

'No one thinks so, but . . . there is a mystery. We are determined to discover the truth.'

'It was,' she said gleefully. 'Bet you anything you like it was murder.'

What a bloodthirsty creature.

I said calmly, 'If it was, you may read all about it in the papers next week.'

'Really?' She actually licked her lips as she smiled, but when I bade her good evening, to my intense relief, she did not try to detain me longer, but let me walk away.

CHAPTER TWENTY-FIVE

Luggage

Edith had found a steamer trunk long enough to hold the mummy and deep enough to hold plenty of other things as well. She pointed out that the trunk would fit unobtrusively beneath the window in our office where it would be hardly noticeable, yet still close at hand.

Jesperson was puzzled. 'But – that is not our old trunk.'

'No, I knew ours would be too small. I measured it, to be certain. I asked around down at the market and one of the dealers turned this up for me. We agreed on a trade: two pieces of my old luggage for this one.'

Jesperson cast a more critical eye over the trunk and rubbed his chin. 'Dear Mother, you shouldn't have – your lovely matched cases for this battered old thing?'

'I don't need them, and you need this.'

'We do not need it,' he said abruptly before softening his tone. 'Sorry – I can see that it might be useful. But hardly necessary. A roll of canvas or an old carpet would do as well. We shall not be in possession of the old girl for long.' He cast an amused glance at the mummy, still disguised in widow's weeds, lying on the carpet beside our desk before going on, 'It was a kind thought, and I hope your dealer will be kind enough to take it back when you explain—'

'Jasper,' his mother cut him off, 'and Di, too, please do not think I mean to tell you how to go about your business, but from what I understand, that . . . *thing* . . . is connected in some occult manner to at least two deaths, and unless you dispose of it properly, more trouble will follow. Until that can be done, would it not be sensible to keep such a dangerous object securely hidden, locked inside a stout chest like this?'

I saw the look of chagrin on my partner's face. 'Sensible,' he muttered. 'Yes, I should have thought of it myself.' To me, he said, 'After all, there could be other, unknown parties waiting to serve the ancient princess – we can at least make it harder for anyone to steal the mummy.'

He sighed. 'That was an excellent thought, Mother. I am sorry you had to lose your nice matched cases, but I shall buy you new ones to make up for it.'

'No need, but thank you, my dear,' she said with a smile. Handing him the key to the trunk, she went out of the room, neatly side-stepping the recumbent mummy without sparing it another glance.

I crouched down beside the mummy to make a start on removing the clothes, no easy task, for I had put in a great many stitches to ensure no stray breeze or accident would reveal what lay beneath, but Jesperson stopped me, resting a hand on my shoulder.

'We may as well put it in the trunk like that,' he said. 'No one else would want to wear those garments if they knew where they had been.'

I shuddered at the thought and went to open the lid, leaving to him the task of lifting the body and placing it inside the deep trunk. After he'd locked the trunk, he put the key inside an enamelled tin box on the mantelpiece.

I sat down to write two letters. The first was to Matilda, inviting her to tea in Gower Street the following afternoon. Naturally, the invitation was extended to Mrs Munro – but I did hope her grandmother might be otherwise occupied, so that she and I might share a more intimate conversation. I was conscious that we were running out of time, as she would soon be leaving London. 'It will be our last chance to meet before September, remember – what a long time that seems!' I concluded, hoping she would be able to read between the lines.

I read that last aloud to my partner, worried that it might rouse her suspicions.

Jesperson looked up from his self-imposed task of copying the hieroglyphs that made up Meretseger's name. 'What suspicions? Anyway, there is no need to worry about getting the girl here on her own; Mother will take care of Mrs Munro.'

Absurdly, his words inspired a mental image of Edith Jesperson locking Mrs Munro into a cupboard, and I had to stifle a giggle. But I knew he was right, and Edith was easily capable of coming up with some ploy to keep Mrs Munro out of our way for half an hour, although we should not need that long; five minutes might be enough for our success – or failure, but I would not entertain that possibility.

Returning to my letter, I apologised for the short notice, that Friday afternoon would do just as well, but there was something I wished particularly to say to her before they left that I had rather not write in a letter.

There! The intimation of something secret she could only learn by coming here was bait I knew she would be unable to resist. Pleased with myself, I signed my name, blotted the ink, then sealed the envelope.

'She will come tomorrow,' I said with confidence. 'At least, she will if she gets my note in the morning. Now, another quick note to invite Miss Dawes for the same time – it could be helpful to have Seshemetka on our side. Then I will put them both in the post.'

The game is afoot, the game is afoot – the phrase pounded in time with my rapid footsteps as I made my way to the post-box. I felt certain Matilda would turn up tomorrow at four o'clock; her will would prevail over any other plans her grandmother might have. But tomorrow was so soon – *too soon* – Friday would have been better. It would give us more time – not to plan, but to prepare. It might be that Pagan Brown would come across some other old spell or ritual that would be useful . . .

As I turned towards home, another quotation from the Bard of Avon came to mind: 'If it were done when 'tis done, t'were well it were done quickly.'

She will come tomorrow, I told myself, *and we will be ready*.

But I was wrong.

When the telegram arrived the following morning, I was afraid it would be from Matilda, or even Mrs Munro, saying they could not come, and I was already cudgelling my brain for any possible excuse we could give for turning up at their house with a steamer trunk when Jesperson interrupted my thoughts with an exclamation.

'What's the matter?'

He handed me the telegram.

Another one gone. Need your help. Please come at once to premises on Heath Road. (signed) JP & M Conrad

I stared at it in astonishment. Leary was dead. Henderson was dead. Who could have stolen *this* cobra?

'When was the last time you saw it?' was Jesperson's first question when we were once more inside and enveloped again by the foul smells and pathetic cries of the captive beasts and birds surrounding us.

'Tuesday morning,' Matthew Conrad answered decisively. 'Early. I happened to look in on it as I was going to feed the tortoises.'

'And when did you know it was gone?'

'This morning, barely an hour before I sent you the wire. It must have been taken on Tuesday, because they were our only walk-in customers that day. We stayed locked up all yesterday, so busy we were with animals we needed to ship – but that is by-the-by. The important thing is that we have been very careful about keeping the place locked, and there has been no sign of a break-in. At least one of us has been on the premises constantly, and no one else set foot in here except those two pretended customers on Tuesday.'

'You cannot call them "pretended" customers when they paid for a pair of gerbils,' his brother pointed out.

The noise of the birds and animals had subsided so completely, I could almost fancy they were listening.

Mr Conrad cast an irritable look at his sibling. 'Criminal customers, then, is that better? Anyway, I reckon the only reason they bought the gerbils was by way of aiding and abetting or attempting to disguise their crime.'

'I beg your pardon,' said Jesperson, 'but what are gerbils?'

'A gerbil is a small, furry rodent from the Arabian desert. Ladies, even those who shriek at the sight of a mouse, often find them charming. This one did, or so she let on.'

Surprised, I asked, 'The thief was accompanied by a lady?'

Mr Conrad gave me a mournful look. 'The lady *was* the thief.

'If not the young lady, then the old one. They both carried a lidded basket. Our snake would have fitted inside very neatly. If she knew what she was doing, the transfer from serpentarium to basket could have been accomplished swiftly and without any fuss.'

His brother broke in to say, 'They were in on it together. A less likely-looking pair of thieves I've never seen, but there is no doubt now that is what they were. We have gone over it together, reviewing every single thing that happened on Tuesday, and there's no question but it was them. They came in together, and they did not stay together. The young one was all over the shop, looking at everything, and I tried to keep up with her, but the old woman kept tugging at my sleeve to ask about something else. The two of them were in cahoots, no doubt about it.'

'We never suspected it at the time because, although they were strangers to us, they looked like quality – they were well-dressed ladies, well-spoken, of course,' added Matthew Conrad, and I noticed a dazed expression coming into his eyes as he remembered.

'The young one was a stunner: tall and shapely, with masses of golden hair, full red lips, beautiful eyes . . . she was a right picture.' He sighed. 'How could a lovely girl like that steal anything except . . . a man's heart?'

'She probably charmed the snake the way she charmed you,' said his brother sourly.

'Don't you try and make out it was my fault,' said the other. 'You were here, too, the whole time. *You're* the one who let them in; *you* let them out.'

Turning his back on his brother, Mr Conrad Junior said, 'Well, you have heard a description of the young lady; I cannot wax so poetical about the old woman. She was a harmless-looking tiny grey thing with a bit of a Scotch lilt to her voice. She had a vague sort of look about her, as if she were half-asleep – but maybe that was put on. They paid for the gerbils right enough, and carried them away with them, so we do not have names or addresses to give you, I am sorry to say.'

'Never mind,' said Jesperson grimly. 'We know where to find them.'

Meretseger was more powerful than we had imagined if she was now controlling Matilda's actions in her waking life. Was Matilda's soul already imprisoned within the Egyptian's mummified corpse?

'I think that most unlikely,' Jesperson said when I expressed this fear as we made our way on foot from Heath Road to Swains Lane. 'When and how would she have the opportunity? Her situation is quite different from that of Henderson and the nameless priest.

'First, consider the location of the mummies. Henderson was in close – indeed, one might say *intimate* – contact with his for years. Something happened that bound them together at the time of their first encounter in Egypt. And since coming back to England, the mummy was kept beneath his bed, and I believe that proximity may have allowed the priest more influence over his dreams and gradually increasing power over his waking life well before the final soul-migration was sealed with the spell on the stolen papyrus – read, we assume, by Matilda, channelling – I need not mention the name. But who was there to perform that service for young Miss Verver?'

'The priest – through Mr Henderson, of course.'

'When? Remember, the papyrus containing the spell was stolen quite some considerable time *after* the mummy, and unlike Henderson, who kept the priest's mummy in his bedroom, Matilda could have had very little contact with the other one. By the time that papyrus was in her possession, the princess' mummy was locked in the cemetery vault. Yes, I know Henderson had the key to the vault – but Matilda could hardly have gone there with him, not when she was awake. And, of course, there is the fact that we found nothing with Matilda's name written on it in close contact with the mummy.'

I thought of something else. 'Who stole the papyrus and the other things that sent Mr Sand to us for help?'

'I suppose it must have been Matilda.'

I protested that he had already disparaged the idea that Matilda could have stolen anything from the museum.

Patiently he replied, 'She could not, as a somnambulist. But consider what we have learnt from this latest theft: it proves that she needed only the opportunity, with cover provided by her grandmother. We might ask Budge when we have the chance if they ever paid him a call. He has an eye for beauty – a visit from Matilda Verver will not have slipped his mind.'

'Matilda told me she doesn't care for museums.'

He snorted. 'I do not doubt it. But it is the sort of place her grandmother would not have objected to taking her. And consider what was stolen – not only the useful papyrus and the useful ancient cobra, but an unusual amulet, made of a material greatly valued by the people of the mummy's day – something she gave as a gift, a grave-good, to protect the body of her friend Emma Henderson – and a mummified cat. She liked the idea of having a pet cat, she told me. I suppose both the ancient and the modern souls were at one in that. The priest wanted the papyrus – he needed a copy of that spell – and it may be that the mummified cobra was his idea as well, but as I have just explained, it was Matilda who desired the amulet and the cat.'

'And how did she get away with all that?'

'The same way she carried off the living snake. She must have had a bag or a basket. Budge was pleased to give them a tour behind the scenes, and once she knew where the papyrus was, Matilda could have put the basket down and "forgotten it" for an excuse to go back into the storeroom. Or she managed it some other way – with a pocket under her skirt, like yours, or I am sure you could think of half a dozen possibilities. She worked quickly, with a minimum of fuss, and Budge saw nothing.'

Musing, he went on, 'I wonder, if Sand had reported the thefts to Budge immediately, would suspicion have fallen on the lovely young girl who visited the Museum with her doting grandmother?'

'Of course not,' I said at once, remembering a few light-fingered ladies I had encountered. If they came from respectable homes, if they were blessed with good looks, if they were endowed with certain graces, they could get away with almost anything. 'If it had been only the tyet or the papyrus, perhaps, but—'

'But which gently bred young lady ever picked up a mummified cat to admire and then accidentally, absentmindedly, hid it under her skirt?'

We both laughed, although it wasn't really funny, and I felt there might be a touch of hysteria in my own. We had nearly reached Swains Lane and I had no idea what on earth we would say to Matilda, or to Mrs Munro. Perhaps, after all, Mr Jesperson would once again claim he was searching for a friend's missing ferret?

The maid answered the door, surprised to see us, and Jesperson apologised for turning up unannounced once again. 'But I hope Miss Matilda will not be displeased . . .'

'Miss Matilda is not at home.' Her answer was automatic.

'No? Well, perhaps Mrs Munro?'

'Mrs Munro is not at home either. I am sorry, sir, but they've gone.'

'Gone to Gower Street?'

Giving him a perplexed look, she shook her head. 'Why should they—?'

'May we come in, please, Miss Trent?'

His manner was such that she gave way at once and let us in.

A steamer trunk, considerably smarter than the one in our own home, took up a great deal of the entrance hall. Jesperson bent down to inspect the tag tied to one handle.

'Where are they?' I asked the maid.

'In Scotland, Miss.'

336

I was taken aback. 'Already? But – they weren't to go until next week.'

'Yes, Miss, I know. That was the plan. But then they received an invitation to a house party, a small party, but very select, and Mrs Munro thought it would be impolite to miss it. She said it would be the perfect start to their summer, for Miss Matilda would have the opportunity to meet some of the best people in intimate surroundings. And then, oh, such a fuss – such rushing around! Miss Matilda insisted she must go out for something – I don't know what, but her grandmother never could deny that girl anything she had set her heart on, so off they went, first thing on Tuesday morning, leaving me to attend to everything else. Of course I would be doing the packing in any case, but without them to supervise – well, I just hope I haven't left out anything important. Of course, it's all about Miss Matilda – this is her chance to make sure she meets the right people, makes a good impression—'

'You say they left on Tuesday?' Jesperson spoke sharply, interrupting the veritable fountain of information flowing from the aggrieved maidservant.

'Yesterday.'

'You said Tuesday morning.'

She looked at him reproachfully. 'No, sir. I said that they were *out of the house* on Tuesday morning. They were shopping. They came back with several parcels – I don't know what, Miss Matilda did not tell me, and she packed her basket herself. They took the early train to Edinburgh yesterday.'

'Leaving their luggage behind?' I asked, a little surprised.

'Oh no, Miss. This is for Rookwood House. That is where we shall be for most of the summer. It is only the first week that we'll be at Blair Castle.'

I gave her a quick look, noting her 'we' as well as the address, and she responded with a wide smile. Her eyes bright with excitement, she said, 'Oh, yes, they couldn't go somewhere so grand without me; who would dress them both? I am booked on the early train tomorrow.' With a nod towards the trunk, she added, '*That* will be sent from Edinburgh to Rookwood House. My own things, and a few more things for my ladies, I will take with me to Blair Castle.'

'I suppose it would be too much to hope that the Duke of Atholl is amongst your circle of acquaintances?' Mr Jesperson asked me in the hansom cab returning us to Gower Street.

Simply because I happened to have made the acquaintance of a few titled ladies and gentlemen through my work with the Society for Psychical Research, Jesperson imagined I must know anyone listed in Debrett's Peerage. But dukes and duchesses were far out of my own sphere. I made a face. 'I don't – and in truth, I cannot imagine how Mrs Munro does.'

'Mrs Munro's mother was a Murray,' Jesperson pointed out, 'and Blair Castle is the ancestral home of Clan Murray. I imagine there is probably some family connection. That she has a beautiful granddaughter will have added to her appeal as a house-guest.'

I did not understand why he looked so grim. Hoping to cheer him, I said, 'It is hardly the end of the world. We'll have to go to Scotland, of course, but that will give us more time to plan. If I am invited to Rookwood House—'

'No, we are not going to Rookwood. We must go at once to Blair Castle – there is no time to waste. We can take the overnight train to Edinburgh and then – well, I shall have to consult Bradshaw's for the rest. I do hope Pagan Brown will be able to accompany us, even at such short notice.'

Even accustomed as I was to my partner's impatience, I thought such haste unwise and unnecessary. 'Will it not look very strange for us to go racing up to Scotland after them? They may already be finding our actions a little suspicious – if they decide they want nothing more to do with us, one could hardly blame them.'

'We'll concoct some story,' he said, waving away my concern. 'In our line of work, we might have to travel anywhere at short notice.'

'And if we cannot tell a story good enough to tempt Matilda away from the illustrious company at Blair Castle?'

He raised an eyebrow. 'After all this time, you doubt me still?'

I sighed. 'I do not doubt that if Matilda could not come to us, you would find a way to get yourself inside the castle – with the mummy, and Mr Brown, too. But why? It would be so much easier next week, when they will be settled at Rookwood House.'

'We cannot afford to wait.'

'Why not? What makes it so urgent?'

He gave me a hard look. 'Do you not know which other guests are expected shortly at Blair Castle?'

I almost laughed. 'How could I?'

'The same way I do – and as I keep telling you! – *read the newspapers.*'

'I do,' I said, feeling self-righteous, for I had stuck to my new regime of self-improvement. 'Not every one of the rags *you* peruse, true, but *The Times* every day, as well as one or two of the weekly journals you recommended. If there was anything about the forthcoming gathering at Blair Castle it must have been published somewhere more obscure.'

'It was in *The Times*, and had you studied the Court Circular closely enough, you too would be aware that the Prince of Wales is expected at Blair Castle on Saturday.'

'And what has that to do with—?'

'You know the Prince's reputation,' he snapped, sounding as if he were losing patience with me. 'Matilda is precisely the sort of young beauty to catch Bertie's eye. Does it not occur to you that the future King of England might be seen by that young lady as the surest route to the power she craves?'

'But he's already married,' I started, until Jesperson's short bark of a laugh brought me to a halt.

'You must surely be aware that his marital status has never stopped him before. And there have been plenty of mistresses of Royal Princes who have had more influence over the man than the official wife.'

My cheeks were hot, but I had to say it. 'The Prince already has a mistress.'

'She won't be there.'

'How do you know? I'm sure *that* was not in the Court Circular.'

'Blair is too close to Balmoral. She could never accompany him there. And his fondness for her has not stopped him from taking pleasure in other women, when the opportunity presents itself.' His look darkened as he brooded on it. 'We must get to her – we must save Matilda before it is too late.'

But would Matilda *want* to be saved? She longed for excitement. To find herself an object of interest to the heir to the throne was hardly a fate worse than death. By all accounts, the prince was an agreeable fellow, and if Matilda was unwilling, he would not force her. And even if she was flattered into yielding, there was Mrs Munro . . .

But Mrs Munro's physical presence had not inhibited her granddaughter; it had, in fact, facilitated her theft of the cobra, which suggested that Meretseger's control could extend to others. I still found it hard to imagine Matilda having the cool nerve to do such a thing, but the dead princess had used the girl as her puppet before and it was becoming clear that her powers were greater than we had imagined. The longer we let her continue, the more powerful her control would become, and if we did not act soon, that ancient Egyptian spirit would take over so thoroughly that there might be no 'Matilda' left to save. Somehow, we had to break the psychic link between their

341

two souls and destroy one while saving the other – which we had signally failed to do for poor Mr Henderson.

I had a mental image of the Egyptian priestess as a gigantic cobra, stretching her jaws wide to swallow a Matilda shrunk down like Alice after consuming the 'DRINK ME' potion. Once within the cobra, how long could Matilda herself survive?

At last I met Jesperson's brooding stare. 'We'll leave tonight.'

CHAPTER TWENTY-SIX

To Scotland!

We found Mr Pagan Brown awaiting us when we got back to Gower Street.

'I'm sorry, old man, but the bird has flown – to Scotland. No time to waste. Will you come with us? We leave tonight.'

However startled he must have been by the abrupt change of plan, Mr Brown responded with admirable aplomb. 'Of course. I'll just go home and pack a few things. What time is the train? The overnight? Will I meet you here, or on the platform?'

When Mr Brown had gone, Jesperson delved into his Baedeker and Bradshaw to plot our journey, then wired to the Atholl Arms for two rooms from tomorrow.

Even Jesperson had to admit that Blair Castle was hardly the sort of place one could simply 'drop by', so without a formal *entree,* we must induce Matilda to come to us. According to Baedeker, the castle was a short walk from the village. Given how unlikely it was that some completely unrelated business of ours should have drawn us to the very place in Scotland Matilda

343

was visiting, I thought it would be best for me to admit from the outset that I had gone there deliberately to find her.

Jesperson had been pacing the room in thought while I was at the desk, getting ready my pen, paper and ink. Now he stopped beside me and frowned. 'But we must not give her cause to suspect us.'

'Not *us*. I shall pretend to have fled to Scotland to get away from you.'

'From me!' He looked at me in astonishment. 'Why? Will you say you have caught me out in a fraud — some act of dishonesty — and realised I was not to be trusted?'

I supposed he must be thinking of the situation that had led to our first meeting, when I had fled from a supposedly haunted house in Scotland upon the discovery that the friend with whom I had been working was aiding a fraudulent medium.

I smiled up at him. 'I would not so blacken your name.'

'Oh, I am not worried about *that*,' he protested. 'You may say what you like about me! I am only curious as to what story you mean to spin.'

'I shall be discreet: I shall give no details, merely suggest that my circumstances are rather desperate, and that I stand in need of a friend. Your curiosity is as nothing to what *she* will feel when she reads my letter! But she must wait to hear the whole story; only when she meets me at the hotel will she discover what is amiss.'

He looked at me through narrowed eyes. 'But why should you go to Blair Atholl? Have you no closer — and older — friends, that you must seek out such a recent acquaintance, and one so far from home?'

'Perhaps I have relations in Aberdeen – Blair Atholl is on the route from Edinburgh to Aberdeen, a natural place to stop on the way. Knowing that my aunt is unlikely to be sympathetic, and feeling the need to tell someone my troubles, I decided to break my journey and see if I could not find Matilda, for I know her to be a ready listener.'

'Even so, to think you would turn for help to a girl you barely know – will she believe it?'

'She will believe because she *wants* to believe. Matilda really has no friends. She longs for intimacy as much as for excitement. My letter, holding out the promise of both, ought to be an irresistible lure.'

I turned away from him and picked up the pen. 'I must write it now – if it is not posted at once, my clever conceit will be of no use.'

The letter was sent, and soon after, Violet Dawes arrived, in response to my earlier invitation, visibly nervous but determined to let Seshemetka help us with the anticipated encounter with her ancient Egyptian enemy. Jesperson was at first inclined to say simply that our plans had changed, and send her away, but I felt she might still be able to help, so I told her everything.

When Miss Dawes departed, it was with the firm promise to meet us later at the railway station.

So there we were, a party of four with one large trunk and four small pieces of luggage. We had not anticipated that by purchasing our tickets so late in the day, all the sleeping cars would be taken, so we had perforce to travel in a second-class carriage. But we had the carriage to ourselves, so we decided to consider it instead a piece of good fortune, for it left us free to discuss our plans and gave us the opportunity to learn how to pronounce the words of power and to practise the ritual. As the night wore on, we could feel quite safe in 'catching forty winks', as Mr Brown so picturesquely termed it.

Mr Brown and Miss Dawes were a bit wary of one another at first. Violet, I knew, was accustomed to meeting with disbelief, amusement or even hostility to her claims that she could remember an earlier lifetime, and I supposed that Mr Brown would have the usual scholar's scepticism for anyone who claimed to have supernaturally inspired knowledge of his own specialism.

When Mr Brown expressed uncertainty about how certain ancient Egyptian words would have been spoken aloud, Violet volunteered to help, holding out her hand for the papyrus.

He gave it over reluctantly. 'I do beg your pardon, Miss Dawes if I have misunderstood, but I thought you had no – or very little – knowledge of hieroglyphics?'

'Thank you,' she said, with a quick flash of a smile. 'It is true I do not, myself, but Seshemetka served in a temple, so it was necessary for her to be able to read.'

With that, she turned her attention to the scroll, holding it open on her lap and studying it for several minutes before closing her eyes and murmuring, 'Seshemetka?' She waited a moment, then carried on, 'Seshemetka, I am calling on you to

help. Will you read out what is written on this papyrus? Leave
out the name, for we have no wish to cast a spell. But if you
could read the other words so my friends can hear, we will praise
your name and your enemy will be defeated.'

When Violet stopped speaking, the rumbling noise of the train
seemed to grow louder. We watched and waited as patiently as
we could, wondering what would happen, but it was only a few
seconds before her face underwent a change, subtle and hard
to describe, but noticeable, even in the dimly lit carriage, for it
was almost as if she had become a different woman. I was not
shocked by this, having witnessed transformations of this sort
in my previous career, with those spirit mediums who did not
insist upon total darkness for their work. And I had seen how
my own sister, when fully absorbed in the role of a character
on the stage, looked physically changed. I had concluded that
this must be something natural, a part of human nature, rather
than anything supernatural; just as anyone might, depending
upon the circumstances, do things that were considered out of
character, becoming unrecognisable even to the people who
thought they knew them best.

Thus did Violet become Seshemetka before our eyes.

Seshemetka's voice, lower, richer, fuller than Violet's lighter
pitch, spoke the words from the papyrus.

Violet's ability to read with her eyes closed was impressive,
and hard to explain, I had to admit.

Mr Brown stared, utterly transfixed, until she had finished.
When her eyes opened and she met his gaze, he exclaimed,

'That is wonderful! Truly wonderful – and accurate, of that I have no doubt. Thank you, Miss Dawes! But – dare I ask you to do it again? If I am to retain the proper pronunciation, I must hear the words more than once. It need not be immediately – I would not wish to tire you! But, if you could, whenever you are ready . . . ?'

Violet's lips curved in a faint smile and she dipped her head in an almost regal manner. Again, she looked down at the papyrus, then closed her eyes; once again came the change, like the passing of a shadow across her face, and, again, more slowly this time, her altered voice carefully pronounced each word.

This time Mr Brown was able to concentrate more fully on the words; his lips moved in silent imitation as he absorbed sound and meaning together.

Silence fell when Seshemetka had finished and we waited for Violet to come back to herself. With a deep sigh she opened her eyes and gently smiled at Mr Brown. 'Did you get it?'

'Yes – yes, thank you very much. Some of the words were as I had been saying them to myself, but others – and the emphasis – were different. And it occurs to me that rather than risk mistakes' – he looked at Jesperson, then me – 'it might be better, since Seshemetka was herself a priestess, that she should do the honours.'

'Oh, no,' Violet exclaimed, 'no, I cannot – *she* should not; indeed, she *must* not.'

We all looked at her, surprised at how emphatically she refused.

'Why?' I asked.

'Only a magician can use the words of power and expect to be successful, no matter what gods they invoke,' she said. 'Magicians and priests – in Egypt they were one and the same – and none were women.'

'But I – I am neither magician nor priest,' said Mr Brown. 'I am merely a scholar.'

She gave her gentle laugh. '"Merely", you say. How modest you are! How else could a man be a magician, except that he is first a scholar? He must study and learn, seek out the wisdom of the ancients, memorise spells and rituals, discover the words of power . . . you are already on that path, Mr Brown. The scholar of today would have been a magician in the past; of that you can be certain. I make no pretence to the understanding that is necessary, and nor does Seshemetka, for we are only women. But you – you can do it, Mr Brown, and you must.'

I found I could not sit by and listen to another woman denigrate the whole of our sex like that. 'Come now, Violet – there have been many fine female scholars through the ages, women who have persevered, even though the whole world has been against them. And as for priests – it is only the misogyny of the established Church that keeps the priesthood entirely male. There have been notable spiritual leaders born amongst women too – think of Madame Blavatsky, or Mrs Mary Baker Eddy. And you must have noticed in Spiritualist circles, talented women far outnumber the men.'

Violet looked at me, cringeing slightly. 'Oh, please do not be cross with me, Di! I did not mean it like that.'

349

'Then how did you mean it? I am not cross, only—'

'Only you must think that I am speaking of *today* – and I am not, I promise you,' she said earnestly. 'Oh, *I* make no claim of scholarship myself, but I know there are a great many gifted women – gifted in all manner of different fields. But remember, we are dealing with a spirit from another age. Mer— *that one* was a woman who thought she possessed divine powers, or at least, that she should, but that did not gain her any sympathy with other women. Far from it, for thinking herself exceptional, she measured herself only against men. She rather despised women. *She* might invoke the gods to work on her behalf – but if a mere temple maid like me, I mean, Seshemetka, if we dared to tell her what to do, if we thought we might command someone who had shared the Pharaoh's bed and throne?' She rolled her eyes. 'No, Di, she would not be ruled by me – or you. The words alone might not be enough to stop her, which is why they must be spoken by a man – and one who truly understands the words and their meaning.'

Although I did not like it, Violet was right: we might have just one chance to stop Meretseger and we could not afford to get it wrong. After a little more discussion, with Mr Brown attempting to talk Jesperson into playing the role of mighty magician (and I could see that my friend was sorely tempted), we all finally agreed that Pagan Brown was our priest-magician; he had to be the one to say the words that would – we devoutly hoped – send Meretseger's *Ka* out of Matilda's young and living body and back to where it belonged – within the ancient mummy.

And then?

But any decision about the mummy's fate must wait until we knew the results of our exorcism, most particularly, what effect it would have on Matilda.

Conversation drifted to other subjects, from the beliefs of the ancient Egyptians and the holdings of the British Museum, to how Miss Dawes had become aware that she had long ago lived as an Egyptian priestess named Seshemetka . . . Somehow, this turned from a general discussion into a *tête-à-tête*, and by the time Violet, still the object of Mr Brown's fascinated gaze, was well-launched on a story I had heard before, I gave up any pretence that I was part of it. Instead, leaning back in my seat, I observed my partner, who had been enveloped in a brooding silence for some time now. There was something in that silence which worried me; this was not his usual thoughtful reverie, but had something sulky about it. I wondered if he was secretly displeased that Pagan Brown had taken over the role he might have expected to play, that of the conquering hero, the one who saves the innocent young maiden from the forces of evil threatening to annihilate her.

Aware of my attention, he met my gaze and said quietly, 'I might marry her.'

There was no need to ask who he meant. I looked in vain for a twinkle in his eye or a faint tremor in his cheek that would let me know he was joking, but he was evidently entirely serious.

I stared, speechless, as he continued, 'I have been thinking about our options – what if she does not return to her former self? Indeed, what do we even mean by that? What was her former self? She was a child – and, if she was born the reincarnation of the Egyptian woman – as Miss Dawes has been – we can hardly presume the existence of an entirely separate former self, for even the infant Matilda was no *tabula rasa*, not if she already contained the memories and desires and character of an ambitious, ruthless woman. To cast off that particular internal spirit, not to mention the influences of a culture and religion very different from – one might say almost *antithetical* – to our own, will not be an easy task. Matilda will need help, perhaps even more afterwards than she does now.'

'That is not our problem,' I said, and I winced at how harsh I sounded.

Before I could soften my response, he spoke again. 'We have made it our problem.'

'Yes, but . . . but it was never our *fault*, and we are doing our best to make things better. No one could expect our responsibility extends to – to—' I could not bring myself to say the word 'marriage' and so I struggled on, 'to being required to take care of Matilda for the rest of her life! She is at a difficult age now, caught between child and woman, and that is a time when everyone grapples with change. After all, she is not alone in the world. She is in a comfortable situation, with her grandmother—'

'Her grandmother has no idea of what is at stake. In any case, she has lost the ability to control her granddaughter.'

'Nevertheless, Mrs Munro is Matilda's guardian. Do you imagine she would be quite happy to hand her beloved grand-daughter over to you?'

He looked a trifle hurt. 'I thought I made a good impression. I thought she quite liked me.'

'That does not mean she would see you as a suitable match for Matilda.'

He absorbed this, nodding slightly. 'Yes, I can see she probably thinks I am too young and reckless – or she might even imagine I am a fortune-hunter. But Mrs Munro is hardly a barrier. She'll come round to it, after.'

'What do you mean, *after*? Matilda is too young to marry without her guardian's consent.' I was suddenly feeling anxious.

'The law is different in Scotland,' he said calmly. 'We can get married in a day.'

I surreptitiously caught a bit of the flesh at my wrist between my fingernails and gave it a sharp nip; that brief spurt of pain told me this was no dream. But I still felt light-headed.

Then Violet spoke, and I realised our conversation had not been as private as we had thought.

Her tone was sharp, accusatory. 'Mr Jesperson, do you mean to say you and Miss Verver have planned to elope? Have you brought us along merely to provide cover for your plan?'

He stared at her indignantly. 'No – most certainly not! I would never dream of enlisting you or Pagan under false pre-tences. My plan – *our* plan – is no more and no less than what we have discussed.'

Violet still looked suspicious. 'So there is no secret engagement?'

His normally pale face was now quite flushed. 'No, of course not. Matilda has no idea. She thinks – if she knows anything about it – that Miss Lane is travelling to Scotland alone. She will not be expecting me.'

'And yet you speak of marrying her.'

He scowled. 'The idea just came to me. It would be a way of looking after her – of keeping her safe – if worse comes to worst and we do not fully succeed in our mission. I meant only to share my thoughts with Miss Lane.'

Violet drew herself up. 'I can assure you, Mr Jesperson, I am not in the habit of eavesdropping. You should have realised that we are all four travelling together in close proximity, and if you wish to share a secret with one and not the rest, you must take that into consideration.'

'I beg your pardon, Miss Dawes,' he replied stiffly. 'I did not mean to offend you, or to imply any blame. It was quite natural that my words should be overheard. But you may have invested my idle remarks with more gravity than they deserve.'

'Hmm.' She looked at me. 'Di looks like she is taking them seriously enough.'

Afraid of what she might already have read in my face, I turned my head away and said nothing.

She returned her gaze to Jesperson's still-flushed countenance. 'The idea of marrying that young lady came to you just now?'

'I often have ideas,' he said rather helplessly, as if confessing

354

to a tendency to catch cold. 'I was considering the problem of how we could know for certain that we had been successful, and how Matilda herself might be affected. I could not bear the thought of inflicting more suffering upon the poor girl, and then to abandon her to it . . .' His whole body was taut, his expression anguished. 'I thought by destroying the mummy we would be saving Henderson, but what really happened to him was hideous. I could not take such a risk again. I feel a responsibility for her future health and happiness.'

I knew Henderson's death had affected my friend strongly, but this was surely too extreme a reaction. Besides, we had learnt from our failure: we would be taking every precaution against the same thing happening to Matilda. I guessed he must be in love with her, or he would not be so willing to tie himself to her for life – yet how could he care for her so deeply when he did not know her one bit? He did not understand her even half as well as I did; all he knew was her outward appearance. With a spasm of pain, I remembered how he had gazed at Matilda, like a love-sick puppy. I had not wanted to admit it to myself then, but now it was out in the open. Even the certainty that it was only infatuation did not make me feel any better. How could my talented, intelligent friend be such a fool?

'I think you are over-estimating your own responsibility,' said Violet gently. 'Does she know how you feel? Has she given you any encouragement to believe that she has, or could have, tender feelings for you?'

'She hardly seems to notice me,' he admitted, 'and we have never been alone together.'

Violet tossed her head and tutted. 'There are ways — you need not be a detective to know when someone is interested in you and sense whether they return that interest, or rather, wish you would go away.'

'It is true she has shown more interest in Miss Lane,' he said, frowning in concentration, 'but I do not think she dislikes me . . . I believe she does like me, or would, if given the chance, but . . . whether she likes me enough . . .'

Had we been at home, I should have got up and left the room long before now, but we four were shut into a moving train, not even in a station, and there was no escaping this agonising conversation.

Then Mr Brown declared, 'You cannot do it, Jasper.'

'Do what?'

'Elope to Gretna Green.'

'I never said anything about Gretna Green,' he answered coldly.

'It was only a matter of speaking — everywhere in Scotland is under the same rule of law. And the old-fashioned elopement, whereby an English couple could dash across the border to be wed and return home the next day? That has not been possible since 1856.' He smiled. 'I know, because that was the year of my birth, and the year Scots law was changed. Luckily, it was the year *after* my parents eloped to wed against my grandparents' wishes. Otherwise, I should not be sitting here with you now.' His smile broadened.

Jesperson did not return his smile. 'Evidently you know more about Scottish law than I. How has it changed?'

'The legal age for both parties is still sixteen, with no need for parental permission. But nowadays at least one party to the marriage must have been a resident of Scotland for at least twenty-one days. Three weeks is not a very long time, but it is quite long enough for both parties to feel more certain of one another, and to know the marriage is truly desired by both.'

Speaking slowly, thoughtfully, Jesperson said, 'It should not require that long to see how Matilda has been affected. She may turn against us both, of course.' He turned to me. 'But if she wants a friend, it is more likely that you will be the one she wants by her side, Miss Lane. Perhaps you could stay on for a few days, if she asks?'

I agreed, of course, but I was taken aback by the speed with which he had dropped the idea of marriage. Was it possible he never had been serious about the suggestion?

Not long after that, Jesperson announced that he was going to sleep and, moving to one corner, leaned back, crossed his arms on his chest, stretched out his long legs so they rested under the seat opposite and, to all appearances, at least, was asleep in moments.

I did not possess my partner's enviable ability to regulate his conscious mind as easily as he might turn a gas-light up or down, and so could not go to sleep anywhere at whatever time I chose, but despite the gentle low murmur of conversation that continued for a time between our two travelling companions,

I too managed to doze off, and only came fully awake as we arrived in Edinburgh.

We breakfasted at a café inside Waverly Station before catching the fast train to Perth. On this second leg of our journey (which took a little over an hour) I noticed that any formality between our travelling companions had vanished with the night. They were now 'Violet' and 'Pagan' – and I also noted that they conferred and usually agreed on every issue.

At Perth we had to wait a little while to catch the train to Dunkeld, but when we got there, the last leg of our journey was a short one, and we finally arrived at Blair Atholl in the afternoon.

The hotel was conveniently placed beside the station. When we checked in, the manager offered to store our trunk in the luggage room, but Mr Jesperson said that as the ladies would require it, it should be taken upstairs. He had barely finished disposing of our possessions before he was enquiring if it would be possible to send a message to a visitor at the castle, for, he said, 'We should like to let our friend there know we have arrived.'

'Certainly, sir. No trouble at all. The boy will gladly run your message over just as soon as you wish.'

I had already written my brief note, addressed to Miss Matilda Verver, care of Blair Castle, and I gave it to the boy. 'Could you give it to Miss Verver herself?'

He looked doubtful. 'I'm sorry, Miss, but it's an awful big place, and they don't let just anyone in. If you like, I could say I've been told to wait for a reply.'

I wished I had thought of so sensible a solution myself. 'Yes, please. Thank you.' Luncheon was still being served in the dining room, but with no idea of when Matilda might arrive we could not risk settling down to eat. If she had received my letter, she would, I hoped, now be waiting impatiently and would waste no time in coming to the hotel. Despite the tempting meal on offer, we went directly up to our rooms.

CHAPTER TWENTY-SEVEN

Matilda and the Mummy

Violet and I had done little more than freshen up when we were startled by a knock on the door. I opened it cautiously and found a young boy standing there. 'If you please,' he said, his voice high and unbroken, 'there is a lady downstairs asking to see Miss Lane. Would you like her to come up?'

'No, I shall go down to meet her,' I said. I found a penny for him, enjoying the beaming smile as his fingers closed around such largesse.

I turned to Violet, who stared at me, wide-eyed. 'Already?'

'Tell the men and get ready.'

I left her knocking on the door of the next room and, taking a deep breath to steady myself, went downstairs. After the endless hours we had spent travelling, it all was happening too fast.

Matilda saw me as soon as I reached the lobby and rushed to seize me in a warm embrace. 'My friend! Oh, how wonderful to see you again! How *are* you?' She pushed away, held me at arm's length to inspect me, frowning slightly. 'You look well enough, although a bit strained – worried – almost frightened? But whatever has happened? What made you go rushing away from London – and to me! Oh, I hope I can be of help – you don't know how it made me feel, to think that you should turn to *me,* of all people! But you must tell me everything you – you explained precisely *nothing* in your letter, and I have been quite mad with curiosity these past two hours – I have already been to the train station, hoping to meet your train – but now I cannot stay long – I had to promise to be back inside the hour – how maddening it is, to have been bored all my life, and now all this excitement comes rushing in at once! I already have so much to tell you – you will be amazed by how much has happened – and my new friends – but first I must hear your news.' She looked around the room, so crowded and busy with people coming and going. 'But not here. Shall we go for a walk?'

Feeling like Judas, I gave her a kiss. 'No, we can be more comfortable and more private if you come up to my room.'

'Oh, yes, of course, that will be better – but I cannot stay for long, alas. I am nearly dying from curiosity, you know!' Bubbling with excitement, her colour high and eyes shining, she had never looked prettier.

'I won't keep you long. This way.' I beckoned her to follow me. When we got to the landing, I led her along the corridor and opened the door, then stepped back to let her go in ahead of me.

'What a nice— Oh!' she cried out in surprise when she noticed the three people standing in a row like an odd reception line, waiting for her. 'Why, Mr Jesperson! What are *you* doing here?' She looked round at me, her eyes wide. 'I thought – but you said . . . and you said you were alone!'

I closed the door and stood with my back against it. 'I never said so.'

'You did, you said—' She groped for words, trying to remember the actual brief, ambiguous, deliberately obscure lines of my letter. Then, with a gasp, her mood changed to one of excitement and she whispered, 'Is it an elopement? Are you to be married?'

But as she looked again at the other two, standing with their grim faces in silence beside Mr Jesperson it must have struck her how unlike a wedding party they looked. Did she also notice that the man was clutching a papyrus scroll?

Her demeanour changed again; backing away she muttered, 'Who are these people, Di? What does it mean? Why did you come here?'

'To help you, Matilda.' My voice cracked. 'We want to help you.'

'But I don't need help – I thought *you* did.'

As she spoke, Mr Brown and Violet moved to one side and Mr Jesperson to the other and the mummy was revealed, lying atop the trunk, still dressed in the clothes in which we had disguised it. It might have been taken for a veiled lady, just another of my travelling companions, if not for the sheet of paper inscribed with large black hieroglyphics lying upon that motionless bosom: a discordant note which at once proclaimed that this still figure was not a living person.

The stiff papyrus rustled as Mr Brown unscrolled it. He nervously cleared his throat.

I held my breath as I waited for him to begin his recitation, but Matilda spoke first.

'You!' she exclaimed, her eyes narrowed and fixed upon Violet Dawes. 'What are you doing here?'

Violet trembled, her eyes rolled up in her head and she swayed, rocking on her feet as if she would fall. Mr Brown forgot all about what he was supposed to do and went towards her, his arms reaching out to catch her.

But she did not fall. Instead of buckling, her legs abruptly stiffened as she sucked in a long, deep breath. Her eyes closed, she stretched out one arm to point a finger at Matilda, and began to speak – to chant – loudly, clearly enunciating the antique words we had first heard from her on the long train journey from London.

A second voice chimed in: Jesperson too had stretched out his right arm and was pointing his finger at Matilda – and on that finger, I saw the scarab ring that had once been used to protect Meretseger and would now, we hoped, help defeat her.

Their two voices rose and fell, mingling in an eerily perfect harmony. Mr Brown looked quite bewildered, clutching the papyrus, looking down at it and then up again. I realised he wanted to join in, but was afraid of inadvertently disrupting or interrupting the rhythm. But when they came to the end and drew breath for the second of the three iterations, he was ready and joined his voice to theirs as he read aloud from the text.

As for Matilda, she stood as if entranced, staring straight ahead, motionless and unresisting, at least so far as I could tell.

After the third repetition, the other two fell silent and Jesperson pronounced the words of power that were inscribed upon the ring, then described a sweeping arc with the finger that wore it, moving from pointing at Matilda to the mummy.

Matilda's legs gave way and she crumpled. Jesperson dashed forward and caught her in his arms before she quite touched the ground. He lifted her gently into an armchair.

Mr Brown and Violet stood watching the girl for any sign that might reveal if the spell had been successful or not, but Jesperson, although he left one hand resting on Matilda's arm, had turned away from her to look at the mummy.

I followed his gaze, but it lay as still and silent as ever, with nothing to indicate that anything had happened. And that was surely as it should be, I thought, whether the spell had done its job or not. Any change would be invisible, internal – it was only by talking with and observing Matilda, probably over some stretch of time, that we should know if she was freed from the clutches of that ancient, undying spirit. But Jesperson thought it necessary to observe the mummy, and Matilda had two other pairs of eyes fixed upon her, so I too continued to study the veiled figure, wondering how long would be long enough.

And then . . . *a rustling sound* . . .

It was slight, but I knew I had heard it, and that it came from the mummy.

I tensed, stared harder. The sound came again, but still I could not see what was causing it. Could there be a mouse, nesting in those ancient linens? Then I saw the piece of paper tremble and shift, then slip to the ground.

The mummy was moving.

The veiled head strained forward, and there was a cracking, creaking sound as the body rose up with some difficulty, almost reaching a sitting position before suddenly falling sideways, off the top of the trunk, and landing on the floor with a bump.

Violet gave a low cry of alarm.

Jesperson took a step towards the thing that was now twitching and shuddering spasmodically on the floor, evidently at once fascinated and wary. How could this dead thing be moving? I too was anxious – its movements, though sluggish and uncertain at present, might become stronger with time. I thought of demonstrations I had seen by performers who were mysteriously able to free themselves from the bondage of multiple knotted ropes or even chains; they, like this overdressed body on the floor, began slowly, apparently helpless, only to emerge triumphantly free within a matter of minutes.

What, I wondered, still hardly able to believe my eyes, would *this* thing do if it could cast off the bonds of ancient bandages and modern clothes and rise up free?

Then another noise came from it, louder than the rustling and sliding and creaking sounds of its struggle. Almost ordinary as it was, the low sound chilled me to the bone:

Heh . . . heh . . . heh . . . heh . . .

Was the dead thing *breathing?* It sounded enough like panting, the exhausted breathing of someone who pauses in a physical struggle, to make me wonder.

Heh . . . heh . . . heh . . .

Every hair on my body prickled with an ever-deepening dread as I wondered if it was not merely breathing, but trying to speak. Was someone trapped within that long-dead body crying out for help? And *who* was it?

Remembering the terrible fate of poor, unlucky Mr Henderson, I was afraid I might be sick. I looked away from the thing on the floor to the young woman lying slumped unconscious in the chair, just as she stirred, making a small sound, somewhere between a sigh and a groan.

Jesperson too heard or sensed the change in the girl and quickly moved in front of her, blocking her view. 'Put it in the trunk,' he snapped. It was not clear for whom this curt instruction was meant, but Mr Brown moved towards the twitching figure on the floor, while I hurried to open the lid. I caught sight of Violet, staring so blankly that I wondered who was looking through those pale grey eyes: she, or the temple maid Seshemetka.

Mr Brown seized hold of the animate mummy, lifted it and dropped it inside. As it fell to the bottom, the hat, with the veil attached, slipped to one side and a piece of the veil was caught as I let the lid fall.

'Latches,' said Jesperson, but I was already fastening one, the task made more difficult by my trembling hands, as Mr Brown pushed the other into place.

Backing away, I stared at the little bit of pale gauze veiling poking out, until Mr Brown said, 'Violet, what have you done with the key?'

I saw Violet was now kneeling on the floor beside the arm-chair, holding Matilda's hands and gazing into her now-open eyes.

I went to join them. 'Violet – the key?' I said softly and urgently.

Violet got up and I took her place. 'Matilda. How do you feel, my dear?'

Matilda gazed up at me, bewildered 'Di! Thank goodness. I am so glad to see you; I thought I was amongst strangers. But . . . but where am I? What happened?'

'You are in my room at the Atholl Arms. We met downstairs – do you remember?'

At her uncertain nod, I went on, 'We had just come upstairs and I was about to introduce you to my friends when you fainted. Please – do not think of getting up. Stay where you are. How do you feel?'

'Very well, thank you.' The response came automatically. She frowned, thinking about it, then relaxed. 'It is true; I do feel very well. I cannot imagine why I should have fainted. I can hardly blame the heat; it is so much cooler here than in London. Although I did almost gallop across the park to get here, when . . .'

She sat forward, her eyes widening. 'I remember now. You told me – you led me to believe you had come here alone! But then we came upstairs to your room, and there were all these other people waiting – even Mr Jesperson.' She looked at me suspiciously. 'Whatever is the meaning of all this?'

'I can explain,' I said slowly, desperately hoping that some explanation would come to mind – it always seemed to work for Jesperson, after all.

'Well? Then do, please.' She folded her arms across her chest.

My mind was blank, except for the things I knew I must not speak of – the mummy, undying spirits from ancient Egypt, the dead priest . . . 'It is a rather long story, I fear,' I started.

She smiled. 'I do not mind. The longer the better, I think. After all, I know so little about you, Di – not even your full name! I want you to tell me *everything*.'

'Perhaps not all in one day,' I said dryly.

'Very well, I shall let you off. But you must begin with your explanation – what was the meaning of that very mysterious little note you sent me – and why, *really*, are you in Scotland?'

Distracted by muffled sounds of thumping, I turned, my heart in my throat, to see Mr Jesperson sitting on top of the trunk and drumming his heels against it. He grinned impishly.

'Oh, don't mind me, ladies. I find that after sitting still for so long on all those trains, I am restless.'

Matilda glared. 'But I do mind.' She pressed her hand to the side of her head. 'And all of a sudden, I have the most frightful headache.'

I didn't need to look at Jesperson to know I should take her away from there. I could feel everyone's tension, and the worry that, even locked away out of sight, this mummy was still a grave threat.

I laid my hand gently on hers. 'Fresh air would do you good. Let me take you outside.'

With that calm, stubborn look I had seen before she answered, 'But you have not introduced me to your friends.'

Violet and Mr Brown had moved away, and were standing by the window, their backs to the room. As I hesitated, uneasy at the thought of saying their names aloud – was it irrational of me to think it could be dangerous? – Mr Jesperson spoke.

'Those two are new clients and nothing to do with you, Miss Verver.'

She frowned at me. 'Clients? Are you here together on *business?* Then why did you write to me as you did? Why did you make me believe that you two had – well, that you had run away from him?'

I was cross at myself for not preparing a better story, but I had been so concerned with the problem of getting Matilda here that I had not thought beyond that. Of course I should have realised I would need to explain my lies, and most likely by telling more lies. She was staring at me so steadily that I was sure she would recognise my fabrications for what they were the moment I began to speak.

Then my partner came to my rescue. 'I do not know what Miss Lane wrote to you, Miss Verver, but that she left alone was true. We had a foolish quarrel – it was my fault entirely. Although I thought she would surely return once she'd had time to reconsider, I could not take that risk – I knew I had to go after her at once, to make her understand how much I need her.'

Although Jesperson looked and sounded utterly serious, Matilda was evidently not convinced. 'Oh, how romantic – and you took your clients along to help plead your case?'

'Mr and— But no, they wrote to us in confidence, which I shall not betray. In fact, it was Miss Lane herself who decided to take on their case – it was one of the things we had been arguing about before her abrupt departure. They had written from Edinburgh, and Miss Lane took the decision to call upon them there and learn all the details before—' He made a show of stopping himself. 'But that is none of your concern.'

'Hmph.' With that sceptical note she turned to me. 'Is it true?' She peered at my face more closely and her dimples appeared. 'Oh, you are blushing! So it is! How romantic.'

Was I really blushing? I felt hot, but I resisted the temptation to touch my face and said, rather stiffly, 'There is nothing romantic about a disagreement – a misunderstanding – between . . . between business partners.'

'Is that all you are? Your blushes tell another story!' She laughed. 'Sometimes, you know, a disagreement can lead to a new . . . *agreement* . . . between two people. At least, that is how it happens in novels.'

Noises were coming from the trunk once more, and Jesperson's efforts to disguise their source was making Matilda wince again – or perhaps it was something emanating from the thing inside the trunk that was paining her?

I took her hand and held it firmly. 'Come, let us go now. You told me when you arrived that you could not stay long. I shall walk you back to the castle and you may question me to your heart's content.'

To my relief, she got up. 'What is the time? I had quite forgotten my promise . . . I must go. And you will come with me, Di? Lovely! For a change, I have things to tell you, as well. Goodbye, Mr Jesperson,' she said more coolly. 'I am sure you will not be sorry to see *me* leave – and I promise to send Miss Lane back to you very soon.'

Rising from his seat on the trunk, Mr Jesperson bowed gallantly and told her, '*Au revoir.*'

As we left the room, she murmured, 'Is it the fashion, or does he think it clever to speak French when saying goodbye?'

'Perhaps he meant it was not really goodbye, as he will see you again soon.'

She snorted. 'I cannot imagine any reason why he should.'

But we had scarcely reached the lobby when Jesperson appeared on the stairs behind us, wearing his hat and carrying his cane.

In the forecourt, where we found a coach and four standing in wait for a touring party, Matilda stopped and turned to glare at Jesperson. 'Are you following us, sir?'

With an ironic bow he said, 'I beg your pardon, Miss Verver. I am quite certain I shall soon be well ahead of you.'

'Where are you going?'

'To the castle, on urgent business.'

'So urgent that your clients have stayed behind?'

'They have other business to attend to,' Jesperson replied quietly, and I knew that meant Mr Brown would already have started another spell, one he had collected during his studies, this one designed to quiet a restless spirit. I checked my partner's hand, but it was unadorned by jewellery. I guessed Jesperson must have given Mr Brown the ring, hoping that the inscription and the words of power would ensure the success of this spell – and of course, he had Seshemetka there to help.

'Oh, indeed,' Matilda said scornfully. 'I suspect their "business" at the hotel is just as likely as yours at Blair Castle. Are they really your clients? No, do not bother to answer; I do not know if I can believe anything you say. You are two-faced.'

He shrugged, clearly indifferent to her opinion, and I was struck by how very different his manner was with her now, compared to those occasions when we had met her in London. 'You are entitled to your opinion. I hope nevertheless that you will believe what Miss Lane tells you, for she deserves your trust. I will leave her to tell you about my business at the castle – and the snake. Good day.'

With that, he broke into a long, loping stride and quickly moved away from us.

After staring at him for a moment, she turned to me. I saw the unease in her expression. 'What did he mean? And why . . . why did he look at me like that? As if he hated me!'

'He does not hate you.'

'But I thought he liked me – oh, he has changed towards me! It cannot be denied how he has changed. That is why I said he was two-faced. But you still like me, don't you, Di?'

'Of course I do – and I can assure you that we are both very concerned about you – concerned for your safety.'

She looked bewildered. 'My safety? Do you mean—? Am I in danger?' Gradually her annoyance and bewilderment was transformed into a more agreeable excitement. 'You think I am in danger? Is that why you have come here, to protect me? Out of friendship? Or – did someone hire you? But not those people in your room; I never saw them before, and they cannot know me. Who could it be? Oh, it is like a novel! But what is the danger?'

'Come, let us walk,' I said, taking her arm. People coming out of the hotel were looking at us curiously – Matilda's beauty always attracted attention – and I did not wish our conversation to be overheard.

'What did he mean about a snake? Not a real one?'

'Oh, yes, quite real. There is evidence that an Egyptian cobra has been smuggled here, to Blair Castle – most likely in your luggage.'

She stared at me, her eyes as wide as ever I had seen them. Her voice filled with horrified excitement. 'A snake – in *my* luggage? Someone – in London – meant to *kill* me?'

'No—'

'But who? No one has been near my things except Rose Trent.' She gave a shrill laugh. 'The idea! Poor Rose! I am sure she would not want to hurt me, not for any amount of money. And if someone did it at the train station – or *on* the train – well . . .' She squeezed my arm as we walked along. 'The large trunk was locked, of course, and they should have realised that a maid would open it to unpack it at the castle, not me. So it would be a very silly way to try to kill me.'

'No one is trying to kill you, Matilda – but now the serpent is in the castle, it will be a danger to everyone.'

She shook her head. 'I still don't understand. What makes you think there is a snake at the castle, or that it came there in my luggage?'

'We were informed that a deadly cobra was found to be missing from the premises of a menagerie near Hampstead Heath, following your visit.'

'*My* visit?' She stopped walking and gave me a disbelieving look. 'Who said so? When was this supposed to have happened?'

'You and your grandmother paid a visit to their premises shortly before you left London – do you not remember anything about it?'

'There is nothing to remember.' She forced a laugh. 'Whoever told you such a thing does not know me or my grandmother. She would never even step inside a shop selling live animals – she thinks they are filthy places. Even if I had wanted only to look at that one snake, safe behind glass, she would have tried to stop me – if she could! I knew I must be quick if—' She stopped in confusion.

'You have remembered something,' I said softly.

'Only a dream.' She began to walk, no longer arm in arm, but moving away from me with short, rapid footsteps.

I caught her up. 'Tell me about the dream.'

'Why? It is only a dream – dreams are not real.'

'You told me once that you did not have dreams – at least, none that you remembered.'

'Yes.' Her footsteps slowed. 'That is true. And I suppose that is why it seems so real – the memory of it. But it was only a dream.'

'Are you sure of that?'

'Of course! I would never go into a place like that – so smelly and noisy, with all the birds and animals shrieking and screeching – and if I ever did, why would I want to look at the snakes?' She laughed breathily. 'In the dream, I only *pretended* that I did, to tease my grandmother. The young man was looking at me – the way men do, you know? – and he would have followed me to the back of the shop, perhaps he imagined I wished him to! – but Grandmama kept him talking. And then—' She touched her head as if it was hurting. 'But it was only a dream. Because what I did then I would *never* do in all my life.'

'What did you do, in your dream?'

'I picked up a snake, and I was not frightened, not one bit. I knew it would not harm me – I knew that it loved me. Now is that not the silliest thing you ever heard? Surely you will not try to tell me that really happened.'

'The two men who were there on Tuesday morning have given a description of you and your grandmother.'

She caught her breath, then shook her head firmly. 'They must have seen two other ladies.'

'And yet you had the dream—'

'A dream is not real.'

'Memories do sometimes seem like dreams. You have walked in your sleep before, you know,' I reminded her, 'and done things you have not recalled upon awakening.'

'But never have I sleepwalked in the daytime, my eyes open, holding conversations, and in company with my grandmother!' She sounded positively indignant as she added, 'Besides, I am no thief. And – a snake! It makes me shudder just to think of it.'

'Matilda, dear, people are not responsible for things they do when they are asleep, or hypnotised, or otherwise out of their—'

'Do you think I have been hypnotised?'

I ignored this to ask if she had ever found things in her room that should not have been there.

'What sort of things?'

'Unusual, surprising things you would not want, perhaps never saw before, and you know they are not yours but cannot think where it came from. Something like . . . a papyrus scroll?'

'You mean the sorts of things Mr Henderson collected? He never gave me anything like that. Indeed, I once gave *him* a present – a little silver-coloured amulet. What did he call it? Oh, yes, I know, it was a "tie-it".'

My heart beat faster. 'You bought it for him?'

'I suppose I must have done.' She sounded uncertain. 'I do not remember exactly where . . . it was some weeks ago. I saw it, and thought he would like it, so . . . Grandmama does give me pocket-money, you know, which I may spend as I like.'

I changed the subject swiftly. 'Were there any gerbils in the shop in your dream?'

'Gerbils?'

'Small furry animals, a bit like mice.'

I recognised from the change in her breathing that she had remembered something. 'How strange,' she murmured, as if to herself.

'What is strange?'

'That you should mention them. I had quite forgotten their name, although the nicer of the two men told it to me and he let me hold one. He said that many young ladies kept them as pets and I said I would as well, and I bought two.' She gave a short laugh, surprising me.

'So there you are! I bought two gerbils – *not* a snake. And where are those dear little creatures now? I do not have them – they are not in my luggage, I can assure you. You may search my room and never find them, because they were only real in my dream, Di – it was only a dream.'

Of course there were no gerbils for us to find, for it was likely she had bought them not just as a cover but to feed to the snake. But it would have been cruel to tell her so.

'Your Mr Jesperson will want to go rifling and rooting through my things,' Matilda said, walking faster. 'Well I shan't let him. I hope the servants will turn him away at the door. He has no right to come and bother us with his wild story about a missing snake. Surely you can't believe I would ever do such a thing? He is a horrid fellow, Di, you must leave him. *Really* leave him this time.'

When I did not reply, she said shortly, 'Unless, of course, you agree with him. And if you have such a low opinion of me, we cannot be friends.'

CHAPTER TWENTY-EIGHT

At Blair Castle

At the castle, we were met by a very superior-looking butler who greeted Matilda with unexpected warmth. 'Ah, Miss Verver, your return is most fortuitous. There is a gentleman here who wishes to see Mrs Munro on what he says is a matter of some urgency.'

The gentleman in question was, of course, Jasper Jesperson. I had caught sight of him as soon as we entered the lofty, Baronial-style entrance hall. He took no notice of us, his attention held by the display, high on a dark wood panelled wall, of a collection of weaponry used at the Battle of Culloden.

'I do not know what business that impudent young man can possibly have with my grandmother, but surely it is up to her to decide if she will see him,' Matilda replied. 'Have you sent someone to find her?'

'Yes, Miss. But no one knows where Mrs Munro might be found – except you, Miss.'

'Me? How should I—?'

'You told Mrs Lockhart that your grandmother was on no account to be disturbed, did you not?'

Matilda interrupted him. 'That was this morning. I only meant Grandmama needed her sleep; if she did not come down for breakfast, she would not appreciate being wakened.'

'Yes, Miss. But before luncheon, Mrs Lockhart tells me, you gave her to understand that your grandmother had requested no one should enter her bedroom, whether she was there or no, until her maid arrived.'

'That is nonsense! I never said—And in any case, that is not like Grandmama at all. I do not know what the housekeeper was thinking . . .' Matilda stared at the butler's imperturbable face, lost for words.

'I beg your pardon, Miss Verver. There must have been some misunderstanding. When neither you nor Mrs Munro sat down to luncheon, it was generally assumed that the two of you had gone out somewhere together.'

'Nothing of the kind,' Matilda exclaimed. 'After such a sub-stantial breakfast, I could not face another meal so soon, so I went for a stroll by myself. And then I went looking for—' She gestured vaguely in my direction. 'But where is my grand-mother?' Abruptly breaking away, she headed towards the far end of the hall.

With a murmur of apology to the butler, I hastened to follow, hurrying past Jesperson through a beautifully carved archway to a wide staircase. When I caught up with Matilda, she gave me an accusatory look. 'This is mad – nearly as mad as your story about a snake. But the housekeeper . . . why would she say such a thing?'

'Did you speak to your grandmother this morning?' I asked as we mounted the stairs.

'I thought it best to leave her sleeping. She was tired after our long journey. I wrote her a note before I went out, so she would not be worried.'

'You share a room?'

'No, but they are adjoining, with a dressing-room in between. I left the note on the dressing-table.'

I could hear Jesperson coming after us, although he was keeping his distance.

Corridors branched off in three directions from the landing; Matilda had to stop and think a moment to make sure of which to take. There was no difficulty in recognising the room, for each door was distinguished by a small painted picture of a different flower or bouquet.

'Violets — this is Grandmama's,' she said, and rapped on it with her knuckles.

Getting no response from her repeated knocks, she took hold of the doorknob, but it did not open.

She was surprised. 'Why would she lock it before going out?'

'Perhaps she locked it when she went to bed?' Jesperson's voice behind us made Matilda start.

Annoyed, she asked, 'What are you doing here?'

Instead of answering, he bent down to put his eye to the keyhole. 'The key is in the lock. Is there another way in?'

'Through Matilda's room,' I told him.

She had already marched off to the next door, which was decorated with a single daisy, and we followed her into a pleasant, tidy room, then into a smaller dressing-room. The second door opened into a dim, shadowed chamber. The curtains were still drawn against the bright afternoon light and there was an unpleasant, sickly smell in the close air. I could make out tumbled bedclothes, and the shape of someone beneath them in the big four-poster bed.

'Grandmama? What's the matter, dear?' Matilda spoke in a high, worried voice. 'Why are you still in bed? Are you unwell? *Grandmama?*'

As Matilda went towards the bed, Jesperson, already at the window, was parting the long, heavy brocade curtains to let in the light. Now we could all see the still figure of Mrs Munro in the bed. Her eyes were open, staring, but without sight. Her throat was swollen, dark purple, the wound on it making it obvious what had caused her death.

With a shocked cry, Matilda reeled away from the bed. Then she started whimpering. 'Oh, no, oh no, oh no . . . Grandmama! What happened? What is it? What is wrong? I must find a doctor! Wait, oh, please wait, my dear, wait until I get help—'

'She is beyond help now,' I said gently, but Matilda did not heed – perhaps did not hear – my words. She ran to the door and seized the handle, only when it did not open remembering it had been locked. She turned the key, flung open the door and ran out into the corridor, calling in a high, wavering voice for help.

'Where's the snake?' I asked, low-voiced, casting nervous glances about the room.

'Probably in the dressing-room.'

'The connecting door was closed,' I said, surprised by his conclusion, and then realised how absurd my objection was from the look he gave me. Of course . . . it could have been left open all night and closed this morning by Matilda. 'Where?'

'Surely you noticed the basket? The very type of wicker basket with a lid that Mr Conrad said the two ladies were carrying.'

I shook my head, abashed.

'Keep practising,' he said encouragingly. 'It was on the floor, in the corner. I went ahead of you, so it may be you couldn't see it past my legs. Look, there.' He stopped short of the doorway and gestured.

Following his hand, I saw the basket, scarcely visible in the shadow beneath the dressing-table. The hairs rose on the back of my neck. 'You really think—?'

'Easy enough to find out,' he said. 'Stay back.'

I was more than happy to obey his instruction, watching from a safe distance as he used his walking stick to gently lift the lid. We had a brief glimpse of the coiled black body before he gently lowered the lid. On top of the table there was a tray with hair-pins, combs and ribbons laid out; Jesperson took one of the longest ribbons, then crouched down, pulled the basket out and quickly wove it through the lid, sides and handle. 'There,' he said as he tied a knot, 'that will hold until we find something more secure.'

Hearing the sound of the door opening, we straightened up and turned back into the bedroom in time to encounter a middle-aged gentleman in full Scottish array – or at least as it has been re-imagined by the romantic gentry. His kilt was the dark blue and green plaid of the Murrays.

He looked at us in surprise. 'Hullo. And you are——? I don't believe I've had the honour.'

Jesperson bowed. 'Jasper Jesperson, at your service, my Lord, and may I introduce my companion, Miss Lane?'

I dropped a curtsey.

'Delighted, charmed, how'd'ye'do?' He spoke automatically. 'Friends of Mrs Munro, I suppose? How *is* the poor dear?'

He turned, and, catching sight of the lady's face, was shocked into instant understanding. 'Oh, my word. I had not – the poor little missy was right after all. I had thought she was having a fit of hysterics, and it might all be . . . But oh, my. The poor wee woman. The doctor has been sent for, but I see . . . I see he will not be of much use.'

'He will at least be able to certify and attest to the cause of death.'

'The cause?' He blinked up at Jesperson in surprise. 'Her heart, I suppose. Or a stroke? I must say, she was in fine fettle last night, but she must be – must have been – well, she was twenty-five years older than I am.'

'She did not die naturally. Look at her closely, my Lord.'

'Oh no, I say – that sort of thing is for the quack, not me.' Despite his mild protest, the Duke of Atholl moved nearer the bed and looked at the dead woman properly for the first time. 'Good heavens – the wound on her neck – I have seen that sort of thing before. If we were in India, I should say – but it cannot be.' He turned to Jesperson. 'What d'ye make of it?'

'I should say she was killed by the bite of one of the more deadly African cobras.'

From the look on the Duke's face, this confirmed his own view, but he exclaimed, 'In Scotland?'

'Indeed. A few days ago, a cobra was stolen in London. We were engaged to track it down and recover it. The trail of evidence is what has brought us here, to Blair Castle.'

'How very odd . . . What are you? Experts in poisonous serpents?'

'No, my Lord, Miss Lane and I are private investigators. Here is our card. The stolen cobra is not the only matter – I fear it is tied into a larger, more complicated affair.'

The Duke glanced uneasily about the room. 'What has become of the snake? Have you searched the room?'

'Have no fear. We know exactly where it is.'

'Good, good. And what of the villain who brought it here? Surely not one of my guests?'

'No, my Lord, not one of your *invited* guests. And we can assure you that none of your household, servants or staff were involved.'

He sighed with relief. Then he frowned. 'But then, do I take it you know the thief's identity?'

'Yes.'

'And has he been arrested?'

'The villain has been apprehended and will soon be properly dealt with,' Jesperson said firmly. 'On that matter, you can set your mind at rest.'

The Duke shook his head slowly. 'But why was the snake brought to Blair Castle? What was the intention? I cannot imagine any reason for it— I assume by the way you are carefully avoiding any mention of the villain's name that you are not at liberty to discuss the case?'

'You are correct, my Lord – at least, not at present. We are grateful for your understanding.'

'Understanding! I have none; none at all. It is incomprehensible to me that such a thing could happen in my own home, and to my own relation! Poor Minnie! She was a cousin of my late mother's, and one of her dearest friends. Such a horrid death for a sweet, harmless, utterly inoffensive little lady. And what a bizarre accident – her in her bed, and the snake . . . how did it get in here?'

'I imagine that it escaped,' Jesperson said quickly, before the Duke should stumble on to another more sinister thought. 'If the window was open, and the snake was looking for somewhere warm and dark, it might have found the bed an attractive hiding place, and when she lay down . . .'

The Duke winced unhappily. 'I am surprised she did not

call for help. Of course, there *is* no help; the bite of a cobra is invariably fatal. But how dreadful, to be suffering such agony all alone as she waited for the inevitable end.'

'Perhaps it was quicker than that,' Jesperson said. 'It might be that the very sight of the snake – and her realisation of what had happened – was enough to cause heart failure before the poison could take hold.'

'May she rest in peace,' murmured the Duke, bowing his head, and we followed suit, standing in silence for some minutes. He was the first to break it, saying sadly, 'I had better go down and break the news – and when the doctor arrives, perhaps he can give young Matilda something to settle her nerves. Poor little girl! What a shock for her to find her grandmother like that . . .' He looked worried. 'Does she know—? Did she see . . . ?'

'She saw, but what she made of it, I do not know.'

He took a deep breath. 'I should prefer to keep the details of how Mrs Munro met her untimely demise quiet, at least for the time being. Do you agree?'

Jesperson nodded, and the Duke went on, 'Bad enough that I must tell everyone of her death. When the doctor arrives – I say, would you mind terribly just waiting here until he does? You might have a word with him, concerning the circumstances – the criminal you have pursued here from London . . . ?'

'Certainly – anything we can do to help.'

'I am much obliged to you, Mr Jesperson. I shall tell Blasket to send the doctor up immediately he arrives. He will see Miss

Verver, and me, afterwards. I'll be downstairs but do let me – or Blasket – know if you have any requirements – anything at all.'

The first thing Jesperson did when the Duke had gone was to open a window, 'to let the bad air out,' he said

'Why did she do it?' I asked. He stood staring out the window and made no reply.

I said, without believing it, 'Perhaps it was an accident?'

'You know better than that. If Mrs Munro got into bed and unwittingly put her head down on it – which I would think highly unlikely, especially as no one heard her scream – it could only be because the snake had been placed there beneath her pillow. And if, as I suspect, the lady was asleep at the time . . . well, it is only the king cobra which will strike without provocation. All other cobras – indeed, nearly all venomous snakes – bite only to kill their prey, or because they feel threatened. I am certain that this attack was somehow *directed*.'

I shuddered. 'But why? Mrs Munro was a harmless old lady – and her own grandmother!'

'It was not Matilda who did this. She was just as much under the control of another as that snake. From everything we know or may surmise, the princess was a cold-blooded killer who never hesitated to remove anyone she considered an obstruction – or even a bit of a nuisance. I wonder if the difficulty of acquiring the second cobra was the final straw? Henderson and Leary were both dead, and for all she had managed to gain more control over Matilda, a girl of her class and in her situation did not have the freedom to go anywhere and do everything that our mummy required. It might have been a struggle to keep Mrs Munro acquiescent and at the same time in the dark – I wonder how she did it? Hypnotism, magic, even a drug?' He sighed. 'We may never know. But evidently it was not easy, or not as easy as she wished, and it must have tried her powers greatly when she must control Matilda and the old lady and keep the Conrad brothers occupied and unaware all at the same time.'

He looked at me, but I was facing the light from the window and could not make out his expression. 'There is no need for you to wait here with me – I'll speak to the doctor when he comes. I will meet you downstairs.'

Not wishing to seem squeamish or cowardly, I protested that of course I would stay with him.

'But think of Matilda. She has had a very great shock, and now – alone amongst strangers – she might benefit from your presence, your understanding. You are at least a friendly face.'

As I was about to leave I thought of something else. 'The animal mummies must be in Matilda's room. I saw the hat-box as we came through.'

We returned to what I suppose must be called the daisy room and I pointed out the hat-box, innocently resting on a shelf. 'It might be difficult to walk off with someone's hat-box without some awkward questions – do you have anything to put them in?' I asked.

Of course he did. The square cloth he took from one of his pockets looked like nothing more than a napkin, but when unfolded, it was in fact a sack more than large enough to hold a mummified cat and the ovoid shape of a long-dead snake. Pulling the drawstring tight, he promised, 'Don't worry: if that blessed cat comes back and tries to interfere, I have my sword-cane to see it off.'

Downstairs, I was pleased to encounter the superior butler as soon as I reached the entrance hall. I asked if his name was Blasket, just to be sure, and his lips quirked into the merest hint of a smile.

'Yes, Miss Lane. How may I be of service?'

'I should like to speak to Miss Verver, if you know where she is.'

'I will take you to her now, if you would care to follow me?' As we started off, I asked if he knew what had become of Matilda's cat.

'The young lady asked if one of the stable boys would look after it. She did not like to keep it locked up and had an idea it would enjoy the opportunity to hunt mice.'

Blasket took me through a series of vast, chilly, unoccupied chambers before opening the door upon a smaller room, comfortably furnished and warmed by a cheerful fire in the hearth. Matilda was sitting upon a Chesterfield beside an attractive, well-dressed young lady who was holding her hand. In a chair nearby was an older lady in a becoming lavender gown, and standing to one side, leaning against the marble fireplace, his eyes fixed with evident fascination upon Matilda, was a sturdy man sporting a violently coloured yellow and green check jacket.

Matilda looked up at my approach. Of course not even the redness of her eyes or pale, tear-stained cheeks could detract from her beauty. 'Has the doctor arrived?' she asked.

'Not yet, but he is on his way.'

She wiped her eyes. 'It is too late, isn't it?'

I bit my lip. 'I am afraid so.'

The older lady said to Matilda, 'There is nothing you could have done, my dear. It is hard, but it was her time and now she is in a better place. Remember your grandmother as she was last night, happy in company and enjoying a game of cards.'

'She was happy,' Matilda agreed listlessly, 'but how can she be gone, just like that? She looked so well last night. When Emma died – that was my dear friend, Emma Henderson, who passed away last month,' she explained to the other women, 'with Emma, we all knew what was coming. She had been unwell for years, and in her final weeks she gradually faded away, so we were all very sad, but not shocked. But Grandmama was not ill. We never thought she would not live to see me married.' Tears welled up in her eyes again, and as I witnessed her unfeigned grief, I knew I would not mention the snake we had discovered in her basket in the dressing-room; I wished I had never told her about the stolen cobra, or forced her to recall fragments of what I hoped she still believed had been a dream.

'Eugene, will you please fetch a chair for this lady?' the lady in lavender asked the young man in the violently coloured jacket.

He gave a start, like one who is awakened from a dream, and hurried off to do her bidding.

'Allow me to introduce myself,' she said to me. 'I am Mrs Potter. And you, I know, are Matilda's friend from London . . . ?'

'Miss Lane. I am pleased to meet you, Mrs Potter, albeit in such sad circumstances.'

The younger lady sitting next to Matilda was introduced to me as Lady Evelyn, one of the Duke's daughters. The young man who returned with a chair for me turned out to be a visiting American from the state of Ohio by the name of Mr Eugene Cyrus Lloyd.

For the next few minutes we spoke in generalities, the conversation understandably inhibited by Matilda's stunned grieving, kept going largely by Mrs Potter and Lady Evelyn. Mr Lloyd said little, content to gaze almost worshipfully at Matilda.

'I am so glad that Miss Verver will have the support of at least one old friend at this difficult time,' said Lady Evelyn with an encouraging smile for me. 'Although she has won our hearts already, and we care about her very much, still, new friends cannot take the place of old. Will you be staying in Scotland for very long?'

'Not for very long,' I said uncomfortably, 'and only another day or two in Blair Atholl – I am only passing through, and thought to see Matilda on my way—'

Matilda spoke up suddenly, fixing her gaze upon me. 'On your way to Aberdeen? Or so you said.'

This was not the moment to try to justify myself to Matilda, and I did not feel like telling any more stories, so I said nothing, and luckily was rescued by the reappearance of Blasket with the news that light refreshments were being served in the Small Drawing Room, where other members of the party had gathered. Unless we should prefer a separate tea-tray brought in to us?

Lady Evelyn asked Matilda for her preference. 'Oh, we may as well join the others,' the girl replied in a dull voice.

'Thank you, Blasket,' said Lady Evelyn, and turned to me. 'Will you join us?'

I looked at Matilda, who was staring down at the carpet, and felt my stomach twist with sympathy. I had opened my mouth to accept when the memory of the mummy, yet to be disposed of, stopped me. 'You are very kind,' I said, 'but I really cannot stay. Matilda, may I call on you tomorrow?'

She regarded me for a long moment before she replied, 'Yes, if you like. If it is no trouble.'

'Of course it is no trouble. Matilda, I am so sorry.'

Her lip trembled. She moved towards me and embraced me, just the briefest of hugs, before she stepped back, saying softly, 'We'll speak more tomorrow.'

Then she took Mr Eugene Lloyd's waiting arm and they followed the others out the door.

CHAPTER TWENTY-NINE

The End of the Mummies

The hotel room was oppressively warm, for in our absence, Mr Brown and Violet had elected to light a fire, which was now blazing fiercely in the grate.

'We thought the sooner we could get rid of the foul thing, the better,' Mr Brown explained.

I cast a doubtful glance at the fireplace, trying to imagine how we'd manage to fit the whole thing in. And what if it began to wriggle or thrash about . . . ?

'We'd have to chop it up, first, of course,' Mr Brown went on, as if reading my mind, 'but didn't you say you brought an axe with you?'

'I am not sure this is really the place,' Jesperson murmured.

'Ah – yes, I suppose it might make rather a mess.' Mr Brown looked disappointed.

'But we could at least get rid of the animals,' said Jesperson.

'What animals?' Violet asked sharply, for the first time noticing the lidded basket and sack he had put down on one of the small tables in the room. 'What have you got in there?'

'Never mind that for now – it is this that I meant.' He reached into the bag and pulled out the two mummies. He took the smaller one, which we believed held the mummified remains of a cobra and was presumably home to the spirit with which Meretseger had controlled two living serpents, and tossed it into the heart of the flames.

Apart from a slight shifting of the coals, nothing happened at first – then, slowly, faintly, the thing began to emit light grey tendrils of smoke, which thickened, became darker and more furious. Instead of going up the chimney like the smoke from the coal, it gushed, thick and stinking, into the room.

I quickly covered my nose and mouth with a handkerchief, but the rancid odour stung my nose and I felt the acrid tang at the back of my throat. Violet and Pagan Brown were both coughing into their own handkerchiefs as Jesperson hurried to open the window.

There came a frenzied knocking from the trunk, which startled and distracted us all, as well as covering the noise of something else in the room. I glimpsed a flash of movement from the corner of my eye – and turned to see the basket had fallen and somehow, the lid was open.

Now the snake emerged in a rapid rippling motion, like a dark, oily stream flowing across the carpet.

Violet screamed as Mr Brown gave a startled yell, but Jesperson, standing nearest to the fireplace, grabbed the poker.

Both men moved at the same time towards the rapidly moving serpent, but Brown somehow managed to collide with Jesperson and that brief delay was enough to allow the snake – moving far faster than I could ever have imagined possible – to reach the open window and slip out of the room.

'Keep your eyes on it – watch where it goes – tell me,' Jesperson said urgently as he darted across to the wash-stand, lifted the ewer, emptied the water into the bowl and, still in possession of the poker, strode rapidly out of the door.

I ran to the window. The smoke was beginning to clear, but the disgusting smell still lingered. I leaned out the window and breathed in deeply as I looked cautiously about, wondering if the snake could survive a fall from a first-storey window.

But it had not fallen all the way to the ground, I realised. Our room was just above the front entrance, which was set within a portico. The roof was no more than two feet below our window, which was flush into the stone wall. It took me a few moments, staring at the flat roof below, to make out the cobra against the dark surface, but I spotted it as soon as it moved. The short drop had evidently done it no harm. I watched it wind its way across to the raised edge at the front. This miniature wall (as it must have seemed to the creature) stopped its progress. It rose up, hood expanding as the head lifted, and then swayed from side to side, tongue flickering out to test the air. Higher and higher it rose until it could see over the edge. Whatever it saw, or sensed, made it decide to sink down again and withdraw. It slithered along the edge to the corner, where green leaves swayed in the breeze, evidence of the climbing plant that must be covering the wall to the right side of the portico.

The snake rose again and moved as if to the music of a snake-charmer for a few moments before poking its head over the edge, and then sliding over the side to slowly vanish from view. The last inch of its tail had just gone when I saw Jesperson emerge from the building. He looked up at me. 'Where did it go?'

'It's just gone into the creeper on that wall,' I called, pointing the direction.

With the jug in one hand and the poker in the other, he ran off, quickly disappearing from view.

Mr Brown suggested we might see better from the next room, so Violet and I left him to keep an eye on the fire to ensure the mummified snake was thoroughly destroyed.

I opened the window and we both leaned out to see Jesperson below, standing in the deceptively relaxed posture I understood to mean he was on the alert against danger from any quarter. A trembling in the leaves was the only indication of the snake's presence. Perhaps it would decide to stay there? I hoped we should not have to wait long for it to emerge.

Suddenly the rustling increased; the vines shivered and the cobra slipped out onto the ground.

Keeping his gaze fixed upon the snake, Jesperson bent and carefully placed the big water jug so it was resting on its side. He began to whistle as he twisted and turned, moving his body in a slow, rhythmic way that might almost have been a dance, but that he scarcely moved his feet. I thought of what I had read about snake-charmers and I wondered if he could really make this deadly creature do his bidding.

The cobra raised its head, the hood extending, and even from up above I could see the quick, flickering movement of its forked tongue as it began to sway back and forth, mirroring the movements made by the man in front of him. As it drew nearer, Jesperson shifted his position incrementally. He stretched out the poker, holding the iron rod lightly, as if it were a willow wand, and gently touched it to the cobra's head. With utmost gentleness, he pushed until the snake responded by collapsing its hood and lowering its head. Then he led it with gentle, steady pressure to the open mouth of the ewer. Later he would tell me that although it had looked so easy, it had required the utmost concentration and care to keep the tip of the heavy poker only just in contact so it would not be sensed as a potential danger, to be resisted. The cobra had to feel that it was moving freely, while in fact he was making it go where he wanted.

The moment the snake was near enough to the jug, Jesperson lifted the poker away. Released from that slight pressure, confronted by just the sort of cool, dark, enclosed space that was its natural refuge, the cobra shot forward.

Jesperson grabbed the handle and instantly set it upright, pulled a cloth from his pocket and draped it over the top. Only then did I recognise the bag he had used to bring the two animal mummies from the castle. I had never even noticed him pocket it again.

He wrapped a piece of string around the bag and the throat of the ewer, securing it firmly with a tight knot. Then he looked up at me and Violet, smiled, and made a bow to the audience. I resisted the urge to applaud.

Mr Brown had put more coal upon the fire and all that was left of the mummified snake was a slight oily residue and a lingering acrid smell.

'Now for the cat,' said Jesperson, placing it on the bed of hot coals.

I reflected that the living animal should be better off as a normal, modern-day household pet, rather than the servant of a murderous ancient sorceress.

I clapped my handkerchief to my nose and mouth and hastily moved to the window as a jet of gritty smoke shot out from the fireplace, but Violet was not so fast and was seized by a fit of coughing. Alarmed, Mr Brown took her arm and steered her towards the door. 'Miss Lane, you had best come too. We can go next door.'

Jesperson agreed, shouting at us to leave him to it. With one hand clasping his own handkerchief over his face, he was using the poker in his other to break up the noxious thing in the fire.

Although I thought it unfair that he alone should be exposed to all the risks, there was no point protesting, as my presence was clearly unnecessary. To my relief, Jesperson soon joined us.

'I smashed it up pretty well,' he said, 'but I don't think we can possibly burn the other one indoors. It's not just the size, but her powers of self-protection – we cannot risk the possibility that she might try to take us with her by burning the place down. I had better look in on the cat again, to guard against the risks of flying sparks.'

While Jesperson dealt with the last of the cat mummy, we returned to our discussion about how to dispose of Meretseger's mortal remains. We settled on transporting the trunk containing the mummy to some remote location and there burning it on a funeral pyre. I thought it should be easy enough to hire a conveyance that we could drive ourselves; the only problem was to find some sufficiently solitary place where we would not be overlooked or disturbed before we had finished our business. But in addition to our trusty Baedecker's Guide, which assured us this northern region was rich in secluded forests and long-deserted glens that might be suitable, Jesperson had managed to find a map of the local area. It was nearly fifty years old, but the wilder regions of the country had seen little change in that time. Comparing Baedecker's descriptions of viewpoints and interesting drives to our map, we were soon able to mark a likely spot with an X.

Before we could take care of that, however, I insisted we do what we could to clean the other room before some poor serving girl was forced to confront the inexplicable and disgusting ashen film that had settled everywhere.

'How did one small dead cat manage to contaminate the entire room?' I wondered as I started wiping away the greasy residue from the mantelpiece.

Violet, who had been shaking the hearth rug out of the

window, began to cough again. She dropped the rug to the floor and bent over, her hands cupped over her mouth as she made a harsh gagging sound.

'Violet, my dear, are you ill?' Mr Brown sounded deeply concerned, but I got to her first and supported her as she heaved, coughed and coughed again. At last, she straightened – and pulling her cupped hands away from her mouth, she stared down into them.

Curious, I leaned in to look too, and saw what anyone who has ever lived with a cat would recognise.

It was a hairball.

Her lip curling with disgust, she threw it out the window, then, her colour still high, turned to look anxiously at me. 'Do you suppose . . . ?'

I hugged her closer and with all the certainty I could muster, said, 'It is out of your system now.'

After a while, Jesperson left us to wire the Conrads for advice about the cobra, while Mr Brown was dispatched to hire a suitable conveyance. When we finally met in the hotel's restaurant, we were all ravenous. It might have been a little too early for the other guests, but we had not eaten since the train and felt much in need of sustenance; fortunately the staff were willing to accommodate us.

This far north, darkness would not prevail until nearly eleven, so no one would think it strange for a party of visitors to go out for a drive, for all it was well past six o'clock. I worried that someone might think it odd that we had such a large bundle of travelling rugs (they were to hide the mummy; I thought taking the trunk away might have looked like we were flitting), but probably the only suspicion we aroused was of us being two courting couples in search of a suitably romantic glade to spend a few pleasant hours.

We found our spot within the hour: an open space bordered by forest, bisected by a fast-flowing burn, as they called such streams in Scotland, with a roofless stone cottage beside it. We decided this was where we should build our bonfire. The tumble-down walls would help to contain it and prevent it spreading to the surrounding moorland.

Beneath the rugs that held the mummy there was also a sack of coal, a small axe, a hammer, and a bottle of paraffin. We three scurried about gathering twigs, branches and anything else we could use as fuel while Jesperson split some larger logs and bigger branches into shorter lengths. Working silently, with grim purpose, we built our bonfire, a pyramid with a good scattering of dry kindling, then the coal we'd brought and finally, the largest pieces of wood.

The men rolled the mummy out of the last of the rugs and set it on top of the waiting pyre, then Jesperson uncorked the paraffin and liberally doused the mummy with it before lighting a match. He tossed it with perfect accuracy onto the mummy's chest.

The match went out. Mr Brown had meanwhile managed to kindle a small flame below the mummy's feet. Jesperson tossed another lit match at the mummy before he bent to light more of the kindling.

The match hit the mummy's chest. This time it did not go out – but nor did it stay there long enough to set the mummy on fire. The mummy shifted, and the movement sent the little flame flying, then falling down deeper into the piled wood.

We should, of course, have been alert to the possibility of the mummy's revival after what we had earlier seen and heard, but we had been lulled into a false sense of security since then, believing in the power of Mr Brown's invocations.

But it had clearly been biding its time.

The mummy rolled off the pyre, landed on its feet and lurched towards Jesperson before anyone had realised the danger.

It was fortunate the mummy chose Jesperson, not another member of our party, for his reflexes were so quick; he never appeared in the least bit surprised by an attack from any quarter – indeed, one might have imagined he had been waiting for this very moment. Now, wielding one of the longer branches protruding from the bonfire like a lance, he thrust it into one of the creature's armpits, lifted it and knocked it back into the fire that had just begun to take hold.

But it had by no means finished with us, for it rose up, now with a ripple of flame running across its shoulders, and staggered again towards Jesperson, and once more, he used his makeshift lance, catching the mummy off-balance and pushing it back once more.

I turned to Violet just in time to see her eyes roll back in her head as the sonorous voice of Seshemetka emerged from her mouth, chanting what I guessed must be another ancient spell. Mr Brown must have recognised it, for he joined in immediately, adding his own determined voice to hers.

What could I do? I had my own supply of safety matches, and there were still a few dead branches lying about. I grabbed the biggest I could wield, tied my handkerchief around one end, then snatched up the discarded paraffin bottle, relieved to find it not completely empty. With the last few drops inside, I anointed the handkerchief, struck a match and lit my torch.

The mummy, now emitting puffs of pale, ill-smelling smoke, got to its feet again, but this time, rather than charging at Jesperson, it went for Mr Brown. To my horror, I saw his eyes were shut as he concentrated on the words he was reciting.

I rushed forward and thrust the flaming tip of my homemade torch at a bandage flapping loose about the mummy's neck. Jesperson arrived beside me a moment later and now holding his own stick like a cricket-bat, he swung it hard at the mummy's head. There was a loud thump and a cracking sound as the creature's head came off. It flew through the air to land in the bonfire, where the flames at once began to lick and then to feast upon it.

The loss of its head, however, appeared to be in no way an impediment to the mummy, which continued, implacably, towards Mr Brown, the ragged arms stretched out to seize his throat.

Our cries of warning alerted Mr Brown just in time: his eyes opened and he jumped out of the way before the fumbling dead hands could touch him. He took up a fierce, protective stance in front of the entranced Violet, his own hands curling into fists and rising in the defensive posture of a pugilist.

In unspoken accord, Jesperson and I attacked the headless mummy in tandem, one on either side, thrusting at it with our sticks. Moving in concert, we caught it beneath its out-stretched arms and lifted it with ease – it was surprisingly light, I found to my surprise. It began to twist and flail, but it was too slow and clumsy to succeed against our determined effort, and together we pitched it back into the now-blazing fire.

At the same moment, Pagan Brown and Violet Dawes – Seshemetka – roared out the words of power.

Whether it was those words, the more elemental power of fire or perhaps a combination of the two that finally defeated the ancient animating force within the mummy, we will never know, but the mummy did not walk again, unless the rising of its ashes within clouds of smoke might be construed as its final movements. As the fire burned hotter and more fiercely, the headless once-human figure crumbled in upon itself and was lost to the consuming flames.

We stood in silence, bearing witness, and waited for the fire to die down. When at last it did, Jesperson searched for anything even remotely recognisable as a bone fragment and gathered up every bit. The four of us, using the back end of the axe, the hammer and some goodly sized chunks of rock, smashed each tiny piece to powder, which we then dispersed widely, mixed with the wood-ash and earth, until there was not a trace left of the body that had once belonged to Meretseger. Without a body to return to, we could expect her soul to perish also, and there would be nothing left but our few memories of her existence.

'What about the ring?' Mr Brown asked. 'It is inscribed with her name – and you know the power the Egyptians invested in a name.'

Jesperson pushed a lock of hair away from his eyes, leaving a sooty streak on his forehead. 'Let us do what the ancients would have done and obliterate the name. Have you a pocket-knife? The name was carved into the stone so it can be excised – it should be easier to score a few lines than it would have been to carve the characters.'

Mr Brown agreed to this plan at once. 'I shall do it. And after that – I suppose you will want the ring back?'

'I?' Jesperson's eyebrows shot up. 'Why should I want it? It was never mine. No, no – you should keep it, since you are one who can read and use the word of power.'

Mr Brown smiled, looking very pleased, but before he could say a word, Violet exclaimed, 'No! You must not – oh, I beg your pardon, dear Pagan, but even when her wretched name is erased, that ring will carry such a freight of memory that it frightens me to imagine. As long as *anyone* remembers her name – even if it is only the four of us – there is danger. And after we have worked so hard to destroy her,' she rushed on breathlessly, 'I do not mean to say that the ring should be destroyed, only that the thought of it in your possession, continuing to be in such close proximity to your own person disturbs me—'

Pagan Brown gently caught her hands in his. 'My dear Violet, there is no need to explain. Your wish is my command.'

They gazed at one another in rapt silence until Jesperson cleared his throat and claimed their attention. 'Shall we donate it to the British Museum? Damaged, with the name excised, it may not be considered attractive enough to have on public display, and will probably be stored out of sight . . . and out of any chance of causing harm.'

We all agreed to this very sensible compromise.

CHAPTER THIRTY

Farewell to Scotland

I called upon Matilda next morning. The reality of her grandmother's death had impressed itself upon her, and although she was subdued, no longer the lively, careless girl I had first met, she was endeavouring to come to terms with her changed situation.

The death of Mrs Munro had naturally cast a pall over the entire party and all planned festivities had been cancelled. The Prince of Wales would defer his visit to Blair Atholl until later in the summer. Most of the Duke's other guests were preparing to leave, if they had not already departed.

'Everyone has been so very kind to me,' she said. 'The Duke and Duchess have said I am welcome to stay for as long as I like, and I have had invitations for later in the summer, although, as I shall be in mourning, I do not know if it would be quite proper . . . in any case, it is better for me to go to my great-uncle's house, as planned. He is my closest living relative, for the Duke, generous and kind to me as he has been, is only a *very* distant cousin.' She sighed. 'I suppose . . . I suppose my home will be in Scotland now, and something must be done about the house in Highgate. It is mine now, you know. But – oh, I simply cannot imagine it without Grandmama.'

'You must let me know if there is anything I can do for you.'

She gave me a sharp look. 'There is something.'

I waited, feeling a little anxious.

'I have a question for you. My grandmother had a wound on her neck. I asked the doctor what it was, but he said something in Latin and I knew it was meant to put me off. But you saw it, too. You must tell me. Why did she die?'

'What did the doctor say?'

'Never mind what the doctor said, I am asking you. You told me yesterday – you admitted that Mr Jesperson came here to look for a poisonous snake. Is that what killed Grandmama?'

I saw no point in denying it.

She nodded. 'I was angry with you at first because you told me so many stories, things that were not true, and because you were blaming me—'

'I do not blame you,' I said quickly, earnestly. 'Truly, I never did.'

'You surely never thought I would steal a snake! So why did you speak to me the way you did?'

'I thought you might know something about it.'

'But why? Why should I? You do not imagine that I wished to kill my grandmother?'

'No, I am quite sure you loved her very much, as she loved you.'

'And no one else could have any reason to kill her. There is simply no reason for murder, so it must have been an accident.'

'Of course.'

'But not a *normal* accident,' she added darkly. 'We are not in Egypt, and my grandmother was not poking around in some old ruins in the desert. There was no reason to expect to encounter a snake in a Scottish castle. It must have been brought here – but why? And how? Someone . . . perhaps they *did* put it into our luggage on the train. Maybe it was the only way they could get it into the castle? It must have been some villain, but was he known to the police? Whoever it was, they could not let themselves be connected with the snake and the death it would be dealing. It was meant to bite someone else. But who?' She was watching me like a hawk, waiting for confirmation.

I gave a helpless shrug.

'You know who. *He* was your client, I am certain of it. But that's all right, Di. You don't have to make up any more stories. I understand that you are bound to secrecy – but I have figured it out.'

'You have?'

She looked at me with a small, secretive, triumphant smile and whispered, 'H-R-H.'

When I did not respond, she expanded her reply. 'The Prince of Wales. The heir to the throne.'

I held my tongue.

'Anarchists, foreign agitators – oh, do not pretend you do not know who might have wanted him dead!' She patted my hand. 'Never mind. I understand you are not allowed to speak of it. But – have you caught him?'

'We caught the snake, so you have no reason to fear.'

'Where was it?'

I thought it best to tell her. 'We took it away in your basket – that was where it had gone to hide.'

'My basket?'

'The one with a lid – in the dressing-room.'

'But I never brought such a thing with me.'

'Perhaps it was your grandmother's,' I said, remembering that the Conrads had said the ladies had each carried one.

She said slowly, 'Her knitting basket! Oh! How dreadful. She probably opened it to get her wool, and—' She winced. 'Oh, the poor dear!'

Wanting to steer her mind from such unhappy thoughts, I asked about her cat. For a moment she simply stared blankly, as if she had no idea what I meant, but then, with a sigh, 'I fear I may no longer call him "my" cat. His interest in me has entirely vanished. It seems he far prefers the company of the stable boys – and perhaps the chance to hunt mice and birds – to the comfort of my bed.'

'I am sorry,' I said, thinking it must be hard for her to have lost her grandmother and her pet at the same time.

But she shrugged it off. 'It is just as well, for I expect my great-uncle's dogs would want to tear him to shreds if they had the chance.'

★

411

On the train to Perth, we discussed Matilda and her situation. I described how downcast she was by the loss of her nearest and dearest relation, but that she did not appear to be in any way affected by the destruction of Meretseger's mummified remains.

'I knew there should be no problem with that,' Violet said emphatically. 'That one's *Ka* was exorcised, cast out of the girl and back into the mummy, just as we planned. I made sure of that when the girl opened her eyes and I looked into them – I should perhaps rather say, *Seshemetka* looked into them, through me, and she perceived only the soul of the innocent young girl, just as it should be.'

'Yes, her mind and personality appear completely unaffected, thank goodness,' I said. 'I am sure that within a month or two she will be just as she always was, albeit a little sadder and wiser.'

'Herself again, but not as she always was,' said Jesperson, giving me a strange look. 'Did you not perceive the great difference in her, after the *Ka* was expelled? No? I see that you did not. That is amazing. To me, it was immediately obvious, even in the hotel room. I could see—' He stopped, as if to more carefully consider his words. 'But "see" is perhaps the wrong word; some other, different, sense was involved. There was something about her . . . a kind of glow, but invisible to the eye; a force, then, yes, a physical force as strong and inexplicable as gravity, or magnetism. Like a magnetic force, it pulled one—' He stopped again, this time to eye me speculatively. 'But evidently it did not affect *everyone*. An attractive force, but perhaps it worked only on some people. Did you really not feel it, Miss Lane? Were you utterly immune?'

I shifted in my seat, feeling uncomfortable. 'I could see that she was very beautiful.'

He waved his hand dismissively. 'That is not what I meant. You did feel drawn to be her friend, to look after her, to help her – and so you became her friend. Is that not so?'

I thought of the mixed emotions the girl aroused in me: as much annoyance – or perhaps even more – than any attraction. And yet I could not deny that I had responded to her demands, even felt obligated in some way to try to help, when it should have been just as easy to refuse, even to rebuff her overtures entirely with a few chilling words.

'It is difficult to explain,' I said slowly, 'but I certainly never felt any great desire for her company. On the contrary, I had rather stayed away. She was a bit of a nuisance. Yet I did feel sorry for her, and reluctant to hurt one so young, and an orphan . . . I suppose I felt an obligation to be kind, as one does when appealed to for something that one could supply easily enough. It would have felt mean to refuse her, but that made her more a burden than a friend. Friendship, to be worthy of the name, involves a sort of moral equality, with giving and taking on both sides.'

He gazed at me in evident fascination. 'Interesting,' he murmured. 'So very different from my own response . . . I had not realised . . . Hmmm. This suggests – do you agree? – that the power of attraction was to some extent within her conscious control? I do not mean Matilda, of course, but Mer—' Catching Violet's tense look, he stopped short of saying the name, and said instead, 'I mean that controlling spirit within. And if it required the use of the will, or what we might think of as some sort of mental muscle, presumably she could turn it off and on, and direct it where she wished. But there must also have been limits; some people must have a stronger resistance to the force, or it could be that she could only effectively direct it at one person at a time. The necessity, when she went to J.P. Conrad & Sons to acquire a snake, to keep Matilda under her control, her grandmother pliable and at the same time dazzle both the Conrad brothers was almost too much.'

'It probably only worked on men,' Violet interjected.

'What about her grandmother?' I asked.

'The old lady was already blinded by a deep and unquestioning love for her granddaughter. But when it comes to casting a spell on total strangers . . .' She sniffed. 'Women could see through her. Men are fools for a pretty face.'

Jesperson was annoyed. 'Your argument is illogical, Miss Dawes, as well as an improper generalisation. Not all men are the same. Matilda is no less beautiful now than she was two weeks ago, and while I can still appreciate her physical charms, I no longer feel that force of attraction. I think it more reasonable to presume that she *chose* her victims – and with a purpose in mind. She used her power on me because she sensed I posed a threat . . . and because she failed to enthral Miss Lane, she had no alternative but to allow Matilda to try, in her clumsy, childish way, to "make friends".'

Violet sniffed again. 'Well, it may come as a shock to the girl that life is no longer so easy; although it is entirely possible that without her grandmother's steadying presence, she may yet have quite a career as a heart-breaker!'

I remembered the way that Mr Eugene Lloyd had gazed at her in awe-struck silence . . . but I did not wish to contribute to any further gossip or speculation about that unhappy young lady, so I said nothing.

It was very late in the day by the time we reached Edinburgh, so we decided to break our journey there. We engaged two rooms at the Balmoral Hotel, situated conveniently close to the station on Princes Street, and after ensuring the serpent was still secure in the stout wicker basket, now firmly wired shut – I would be so relieved when Jesperson had handed it back into the care of the Conrads – we booked a table to dine.

Two bottles of champagne appeared as if by magic on our table, and we were all surprised – although not for the same reason, for Mr Brown and Jesperson had each, independently, ordered a bottle.

When the first bottle had been opened and our glasses filled, Mr Brown gave a shy cough and explained, 'I should like us all to celebrate this very special day. Violet has done me the great honour of agreeing to make me the happiest man in the world. In short, we are to be married.'

Grinning hugely, Jesperson slapped him on the back, nearly making him spill his glass. 'Congratulations, old man! May you know every happiness together.'

Wishing her the same, I gave Violet a hug and asked, 'When is it to be?'

'Late September or early in October. We should like to honeymoon in Egypt, and before October, you know, the heat would be too much.'

Jesperson raised his glass and proposed a toast to the happy couple.

After we had clinked glasses, cheered and sipped the fine, bubbly wine, Violet asked, 'And yours, Mr Jesperson? What is it you wish to celebrate?'

'My dear, the answer is surely obvious,' said Mr Brown. 'It is to celebrate our success, and the defeat of—'

'No,' said Jesperson gravely. 'Of course I am glad to be able to draw a line under this investigation and know that evil has been averted – with the invaluable help of you all – but the death of Mrs Munro was sobering, and makes such a celebration inappropriate.'

A little cloud of gloom fell over our happy gathering, but only for a moment.

'Still,' said Violet, 'you must have had something in mind that you wished to celebrate or you would not have ordered champagne. Why keep us in suspense?'

'Today is an important day for us,' he said, looking at me with a smile that sent a jolt of obscure emotion through me.

Violet's own smile widened, as did her eyes, and she looked a question at me.

Jesperson, too, watched me, as if waiting for me to speak, but I did not know what to say.

'I did not think you would forget,' he said, with a faint note of reproach. 'Today is the anniversary of our first meeting, and the first anniversary of our partnership.'

Pagan Brown raised his glass. 'A toast! To Jesperson and Lane – long may their partnership continue happy and successful.'

Several more toasts followed, to each other, to our futures and our health and happiness, until Violet protested that we really must have something to eat – after all, there was still that second bottle of champagne to get through.

'Did you really forget?' Jesperson asked me in a low voice as we all became absorbed in scrutinising the extensive menu.

'No, how could I?' But my protest sounded weak to my own ears and I thought how silly it was to lie, especially to him. 'You must remember, we were speaking of it only a few weeks ago, just before this whole affair began. But these last few days . . . after so much rushing around, well, I scarcely know what day it is.'

He smiled, satisfied, and reached into his pocket and withdrew a small pasteboard box tied with a white ribbon.

I was so far from expecting anything like this that I scarcely knew what to say. 'Oh, but you shouldn't have! I didn't—'

'Oh, it's only a small thing – a memento, if you like.'

I pulled the ribbon loose and lifted the lid. Nestled inside on a bit of cotton wool was a silver ring bearing the Eye of Horus.

'If it does not fit, the jeweller said he could make it a bit bigger or smaller.' He sounded a trifle anxious. 'But I think I have correctly judged your size, if you wear it on your index finger. That is the finger used for casting spells, you know.'

I gave an involuntary shudder as I remembered Meretseger's ring on the mummified hand. Jesperson noticed but misunderstood. 'If you don't like to wear a ring — how foolish of me; I should have asked — you could put it on a ribbon, or let me buy you a silver chain for it. That is the wadjet eye, you know, the most protective of all the amulets. Of course, that is only superstition.'

'It is beautiful.' I slipped it onto the first finger of my left hand. 'And a perfect fit.' I gazed into his blue, blue eyes. 'Thank you. I think it is the nicest gift I've ever been given.'

Epilogue

When we were back at home in Gower Street I wrote a proper letter of condolence to Matilda. I encouraged her to stay in touch.

She wrote back within the week, mentioning her many new friends, and how kind everyone was being. From her tone, I guessed she was not having such a bad time and, apart from her natural grief at the loss of her grandmother, was reasonably happy, leading a far more varied and interesting life than had been available to her in Highgate.

I answered promptly (although I had little enough to say to her), but as the days and then the weeks went by without a reply, I guessed she now had too many friends to find me very interesting, which I had to admit was a relief, and a satisfactory ending to our acquaintance. I gave her scarcely another thought until the day in early September when I recognised her hand-writing on a letter postmarked from Southampton.

Dear Di

You will be surprised, I am sure, to hear that I am now a married woman. I hope you will wish me happiness.

Do you think it precipitous? I can only say that the past two months have been like a whole life-time to me.

You may think (like my aged relatives) that I am too young to wed, but fortunately, the laws of Scotland allowed it, and the fact that I will not come into my own inheritance until I am twenty-one does not matter a jot to my darling Eugene. He comes from a wealthy family, who will now be my own. Eugene intends (with his father's blessing and support) to run for a political office . . . I do not yet understand the system of American government, so I cannot say much more than that he is confident of being appointed, or elected, or however they manage these things, and that he sees it as but the first step on a journey that he hopes will eventually bring him to the highest office in the land. In other words, that he has the expectation of someday becoming the President of the United States – and I, beside him, as First Lady of all the Land. Is that not exciting?

I will send you our address once we are settled.

Until then, I remain,

Your friend,

Mrs Eugene C. Lloyd (Matilda)

ACKNOWLEDGEMENTS

E.A. Wallis Budge (1857-1934) was a real person. E. Nesbit's *The Story of the Amulet,* one of my favourite books ever since I first read it aged nine, was dedicated to him 'as a small token of gratitude for his unfailing kindness and help in the making of it'. Among other things, he made her a gift of the titular amulet – a tyet. Budge makes a brief cameo appearance in Nesbit's classic fantasy, but plays a much bigger role in mine: I hope he would not have been offended by my imaginary re-invention.

The Seventh Duke of Atholl (1840-1917) was also a real person, but is here in fictional guise.

A big, big thank you to my editor, that legend in her own lifetime, the magnificent Jo Fletcher, whose encouragement, support and friendship have meant so much to me over the years, not least for her invaluable help with this book.

Thanks are also due to my wonderful, long-suffering agent, Howard Morhaim, who, in spite of provocations, has not given up on me.

And always, for everything, to Colin.

Finally, here are some books I found particularly useful:

Baedeker's Guide: Great Britain 1890 (Old House Books)

The Nile: Notes for Travellers in Egypt by E. A. Wallis Budge, (Thos. Cook & Son, 1895; reprinted 1984)

The Mummy's Curse by Roger Luckhurst (Oxford University Press, 2012)

Symbol & Magic in Egyptian Art by Richard H. Wilkinson (Thames & Hudson, 1994)

Signs and Wonders Upon Pharaoh: A History of American Egyptology by John A. Wilson (University of Chicago Press, 1964)